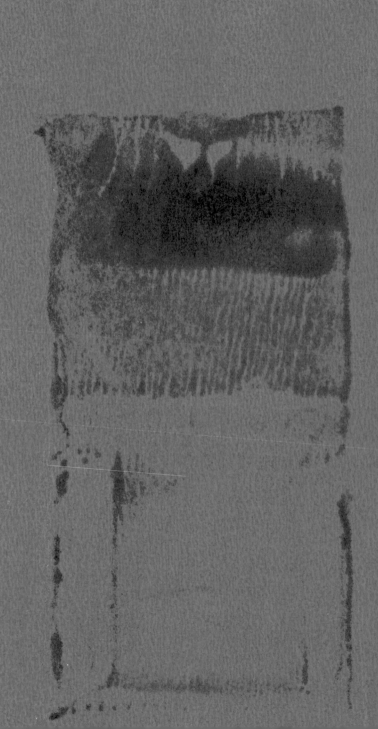

Other Books by
Joyce Carol Oates

Joyce Carol Oates

The Goddess

and Other Women

The Vanguard Press, Inc., New York

Library of Congress Catalogue Card Number: 74-81808
ISBN-0-8149-0745-8
Manufactured in the United States of America

Designer: Ernst Reichl

To Blanche Gregory

Things naturall to the Species
are not always so for the individuall.

       —John Donne

ACKNOWLEDGMENTS   These stories have appeared previously in the following magazines, often with different titles and in slightly different forms: *Atlantic Monthly, Southern Review, Epoch, Transatlantic Review, Shenandoah, Quarterly Review of Literature, Family Circle, Ohio Review, Antioch Review, Mademoiselle, Remington Review, Viva, The Falcon, Fiction International, Cosmopolitan, McCall's, Antaeus, Journal of Existential Psychology and Psychiatry, Confrontation.* A special limited edition of "The Girl" was published by Pomegranate Press, Cambridge, Mass. The six lines from "The Rock" by Wallace Stevens quoted in "Magna Mater" are copyright 1954 by Wallace Stevens from *The Collected Poems.* Reprinted by permission of Alfred A. Knopf, Inc.

Contents

Contents

The Goddess

AND OTHER WOMEN

The Girl

I Background Material

Came by with a truck, The Director and Roybay and a boy I didn't know. Roybay leaned out the window, very friendly. I got in and we drove around for a while. The Director telling us about his movie-vision, all speeded-up because his friend, his contact, had lent him the equipment from an educational film company in town, and it had to be back Sunday P.M. The Director said: "It's all a matter of art and compromise." He was very excited. I knew him from before, a few days before; his name was DePinto or DeLino, something strange, but he was called The Director. He was in the third person most of the time.

Roybay, two hundred fifty pounds, very cheerful and easy and my closest friend of all of them, was The Motorcyclist. They used his motorcycle for an authentic detail. It didn't work; it was broken down. But they propped it up in the sand and it looked very real.

A boy with a scruffy face, like an explorer's face, was The Cop. I was The Girl.

The Director said: "Oh Jesus honey your tan, your tanned legs, your feet, my God even your feet your toes, are tan, tanned, you're so lovely. . . ." And he stared at me, he stared. When we met before, he had not stared like this. His voice was hoarse, his eyebrows ragged. It was all music with him, his voice and his way of moving, the life inside him. "I mean, look at her! Isn't she—? Isn't it?"

"Perfect," Roybay said.

The boy with the scruffy face, wedged in between Roybay the driver and The Director, with me on The Director's lap and my legs sort of on his lap, stared at me and turned out to be a kid my age. I caught a look of his but rejected it. I never found out his name.

Later they said to me: "What were their names? Don't you know? Can't you remember? Can't you—?"

They were angry. They said: "Describe them."

But.

The Director. The Motorcyclist. The Cop. The Girl.

I thought there were more, more than that. If you eliminate The Girl. If you try to remember. More? More than two? Oh, I believe a dozen or two, fifty, any large reasonable number tramping down the sand. There was the motorcycle, broken. They hauled it out in the back of the truck with the film equipment and other stuff. I could describe the Santa Monica Freeway if I wanted to. But not them. I think there were more than three but I don't know. Where did they come from? Who were they? The reason I could describe the Freeway is that I knew it already, not memorized but in pieces, the way you know your environment.

I was The Girl. No need to describe. Anyone studying me, face to face, would be in my presence and would not need a description.

I looked different. The costume didn't matter, the bright red and green shapes—cats and kittens—wouldn't show anyway. The film was black-and-white. It was a short-skirted dress, a top that tied in back, looped around and tied in back like a halter, the material just cotton or anything, bright shapes of red and green distortions in the material. It came from a Miss Chelsea shop in Van Nuys. I wasn't wearing anything else, anything underneath.

Someone real said to me later, a real policeman: ". . . need your cooperation. . . ."

The Director explained that he needed everyone's cooperation. He had assisted someone making a film once, or he had watched it happen, he said how crucial it is to cooperate; he wouldn't have the footage for re-takes and all the equipment had to be returned in eighteen hours. Had a sharkish skinny glamourish face, a wide-brimmed hat perched on his head. Wore sunglasses. We all did. The beach was very bright at three in the afternoon. I had yellow-lensed glasses with white plastic wrap-around frames, like goggles. It wasn't very warm. The wind came in from the ocean, chilly.

The way up, I got hypnotized by the expressway signs and all the names of the towns and beaches and the arrows pointing up off to the right, always up off to the right and off the highway and off the map.

"Which stretch of beach? Where? How far up the coast? Can't you identify it, can't you remember? We need your cooperation, can't you cooperate?"

On film, any stretch of beach resembles any stretch of beach. They called it The Beach.

II The Rehearsal

The Director moved us around, walked with us; put his hands on me and turned me, stepped on my bare feet, scratched his head up beneath the straw-colored hat, made noises with his mouth, very excited, saying to himself little words: "Here—yeah—like this—this —this way—" The Motorcyclist, who was Roybay, straddled the motorcycle to wait. Had a sunny broad face with red-blond-brown hair frizzy all around it. Even his beard was frizzy. It wasn't hot but he looked hot. Was six foot three or four, taller than my father, who is or was six foot exactly. That is my way of telling if a man is tall: taller than my father, then he's *tall*; shorter than my father, *not tall*. The world could be divided that way.

No, I haven't seen my father for a while. But the world is still there.

The Director complained about the setting. The beach was beautiful but empty. "Got to imagine people crowding in, people in the place of boulders and rocks and scrubby damn flowers and sand dunes and eucalyptus and all this crap, it's hobbling to the eye," he said. He had wanted a city movie. He had wanted the movie to take place in the real world. "Really wanted Venice Beach on a Sunday, packed, but room for the motorcycle, and the whole world crowded in . . . a miscellaneous flood of people, souls, to represent the entire world . . . and the coming-together of the world in my story. In The Girl. Oh look at her," he said dreamily, looking at me, "couldn't the world come together in her? It could. But this place is so empty . . . it's wild here, a wild innocent natural setting, it's too beautiful, it could be a travelogue. . . ."

The Cop asked about splicing things together. Couldn't you—?

The Director waved him away. It was hard to concentrate.

The Cop giggled and whispered to me: "Jeeze, these guys are something, huh? How'd you meet them? I met them this morning. Where do you go to school? You go to school? Around here?"

I snubbed him, eye-to-eye.

He blushed. He was about sixteen, behind his bushy hair and sunglasses and policeman's hat. It had a tin badge on it. The Director had bought it at a costume store. The Cop had only a hat. The rest of him was a T-shirt and jeans. A club two feet long and maybe an inch and a half in diameter, but no gun. The Director had found the club in a garbage can, he said, months ago. He carried it everywhere with him. It had generated his need for a film, he said; he kept taking it from The Cop and using it to make lines in the sand.

The Director's mind was always going. It was white-hot. His body never stopped, his knees jerked as if keeping time to something. I felt the energy in him, even when he wasn't touching me. Only when he held the camera in his hands, between his hands, was he calmed down.

After a while, Roybay said, sounding nervous: "What do we do? What do I do? Somebody might come along here, huh?—we better hurry it up, huh?"

"This can't be hurried," The Director said.

The Motorcyclist was the only one of them I knew. His name was *Roybay*. Or *Robbie*. Or maybe it was *Roy Bean* (?) . . . sometimes just *Roy* or *Ray*. Said he came over from Trinidad, Colorado —I think. Or someone else his size said that, some other day. Had a big worried forehead tanned pink-red. You don't tan dark, with a complexion like that. He wore a crash helmet and goggles and a leather jacket, the sleeves a little short for his arms. The night I met him, he was explaining the fact that vegetables are not meek and passive, as people think, but exert great pressure in forcing themselves up through the soil . . . and think about vines, twisting tendrils, feelers that could choke large animals to death or pull them down into quicksand. . . . He was a vegetarian, but he scorned meekness. Believed in strength. Up at 7 A.M. for two hours of weight-lifting, very slow, Yoga-slow, and a careful diet of vegetables and vegetable juices. Said fruit was too acid, too sharp. Explained that an ox's muscles were extremely powerful and that the carnivores of the world could learn from the ox.

Or his name could have been something like *Roy baby, Roy, baby* if someone called out and slurred the words together.

The Director placed rocks on the sand. Kicked dents in the sand. He cleared debris out of the way, tossing things hand over hand, then he found a child's toy—a fire truck—and stood with it, spinning the little wheels, thinking, then he moved one of the rocks

a few inches and said to me: "You walk to this point. Try it."
They watched.

The Director said that I was a sweet girl. He said that now I
should practice running, from the rock out to the water. He followed alongside me. He told me when to stop. He kissed my forehead and said I was very sweet, this was part of the tragedy. He
tossed the toy firetruck off to the side. Rubbed his hands together,
excited. I could smell it on him, the excitement.

"I'm an orphan," he said suddenly. "I'm from a Methodist
orphanage up in Seattle."

The Motorcyclist laughed. The Cop grinned stupidly; he was
still standing where The Director had placed him.

"You don't get many chances in life," The Director said, "so I
would hate to mess this up. It would make me very angry if something went wrong . . . if one of you went wrong. . . . But you're not
going to, huh, are you? Not even you?" he said, looking at me. As
if I was special. He had a sharkish look caused by one tooth, I think
—a side tooth that was a little longer than the rest of his teeth. If
you glanced at him you wouldn't notice that tooth, not really; but
somehow you would start to think of a shark a few seconds later.

In a magical presence. I knew. I knew but I was outside, not on
film. The Director walked with me along the beach, his feet in
ankle-high boots and mine bare, talking to me, stroking my arm,
saying . . . saying. . . . *What did he say? Don't remember?* No, the
noise was too much. The waves. Gulls. Birds. Words come this way
and that, I don't catch them all, try to ease with the feeling, the
music behind them. I took music lessons once. Piano lessons with
Miss Dorsey, three blocks from my grandmother's house; from ten
until thirteen. Could memorize. Could count out a beat one two
three, *one* two three, one *two* three, a habit to retain throughout
life. When The Director told me what to do I listened to the beat
of his voice. I knew I was in a magical presence, he was not an
ordinary man, but I was outside him, outside waiting. I was not yet
The Girl. I was The Girl later.

It was a movie, a movie-making! I screamed. When I woke for the half-dozenth time, snatching at someone's wrist. I clawed, had to make contact. I didn't want to sink back again. I said: *It was real, it was a movie, there was film in the camera!*

You mean someone filmed it? Filmed that? Someone had a camera?

The Director carried it in his hands. Had to adjust it, squinted down into it, made noises with his mouth; he took a long time. The Cop, licking his lips, said to me: "Hey, I thought the movie cameras were real big. Pushed around on wheels. With some moving parts, like a crane or something . . . ? Where are you from?"

"You couldn't push wheels in the sand," I told him.

The Director looked over at us. "What are you two talking about? Be quiet. You," he said to The Cop, "you, you're not in the script yet, you're off-camera, go stand on the other side of that hill. Don't clutter my mind."

He walked out to the surf, stood there, was very agitated. I looked at Roybay, who was looking at me. Our eyes didn't come together; he was looking at me like on film. The Girl. Over there, straddling the broken-down rusty-handle-barred motorcycle, was The Motorcyclist. He was not from Trinidad, Colorado, or from anywhere. I saw The Cop's cap disappear over a hill behind some spiky weeds and ridges of sand.

The Director came back. He said to The Motorcyclist, "What this is, maybe, it's a poem centered in the head of The Cop, but I had it off-center; I was imagining it in The Girl. But . . . but . . . it wasn't working. It's a test of The Cop. I don't know him. Do you? I don't know who the hell he is. It will be an experiment. He rushes in to the rescue . . . and sees the scene and . . . the test is upon him. The audience will see it too. I've been dreaming this for so long, this tiny eight-minute poem," he said, putting his arm around my shoulder now, excited, "I can't miss my chance. It's not just that it's crowding my head, but people are going to be very interested in this; I know certain people who are going to pay a lot to see it.

Look, it's a poem, honey. The parts must cooperate. Nothing un-
ripe or resisting. All parts in a poem . . . in a work of art. . . . Please,
do you understand, do you?"

So sensitive. It was a sensitive moment. Staring eye-to-eye with
me, dark green lenses and yellow lenses, shatter-proof.

I told him yes. I had to say yes. And it was almost true; some of
his words caught in me, snagged, like the rough edge of a fingernail
in your clothing.

The Director said softly: "What it is . . . is . . . it's a vision, it
can't be resisted. Why resist? Resist? Resist anything? If a vision
comes up from the inside of the earth, it must be sacred, or down
out of the sky—even, equal—because the way up is the same as the
way down, the sky is a mirror and vice versa. Right? I wanted The
Girl to resist The Motorcyclist and I wanted The Cop to use the
club like a Zen master's stick but now I see it differently, with the
scene all set. It goes the way it must. You can't control a vision.
It's like going down a stairway and you're cautious and frightened
and then the stairway breaks, the last step gives way, and you fall
and yet you're not afraid, you're not afraid after all, you're saved.
You don't understand me, I know, but you'll feel it, you'll understand in a while. Don't resist," he said to me. "If you deny the way
things must operate, you turn yourself and everyone else into a
phantom. We'll all be here together. One thing. We'll be sacred.
Don't doubt. Now I'll talk to The Cop, the Savior . . . he's the
Savior. . . . I wonder can he bear the weight of the testing?"

III *The Performance*

Space around me. Hair blowing, back toward shore an arrow out
of sight. The air is cold. Nervous, but doing O.K.

The Director says in a whisper-shout: "Okay. Okay. No, slow
down . . . slow . . . slow down. . . . Look over here. . . . The other
way. . . ." It is very easy now that the camera is working. It is very
easy. I am The Girl watching the film of The Girl walking on a
beach watching the water. Now The Girl watching The Girl turn-

ing The Girl in black-and-white approached by a shape, a dark thing, out of the corner of the eye. The eye must be the camera. The dark thing must be a shape with legs, with arms, with a white-helmeted head.

Now the film speeds up.

A surprise, how light you become on film! You are very graceful. It's a suspension of gravity. The Director calls to me, yells to me: *Run. Run.* But I can't. I am too light, and then too heavy; the hand on my shoulder weighs me down. I think I am giggling. *Hurry up! Hurry up!*

The marker is a real rock.

Scream! cries The Director.

But I can't, I can't get breath. They are at me. I scramble up onto my feet. But. But I have lost hold. I can't see. The Director is very close to us, right beside us. *Turn her around, make her scream—hurry up—do it like this, like this, do it fast like this—come on—*

The film is speeded up. Too fast. I have lost hold of it, can't see. I am being driven backwards, downwards, burrowed-into, like a hammer being hammered being hammered against all at once. Do I see noseholes, eyeholes, mouthholes?

Something being pounded into flesh like meat.

IV *A Sequel*

I was babbling, hanging onto someone's wrist. Not the doctor, who was in a hurry on his rounds, but a nurse. I said: "Did they find them? The police? Did it get in the newspapers? Was the movie shown? Was it—?"

What? What? At the important instant I lost sight of her, one adult face like another. Then it contracted into someone's regular-sized face. The ceiling above him seemed to open behind his face and to glow, fluorescent lighting as if for a stage, a studio. Why, this must be someone who knows me! He is looking at me without disgust. I don't know him. But I pretend. I ask him if they were caught, if—He says not to think about it right now. He says not

to think about it. He says: "The police, they won't find them anyway . . . they don't give a damn about you . . . don't torture yourself."

But, but.

Raw reddened meat, scraped raw, hair yanked out in handfuls. A
scalp bleeding and sandy. Sandy grit in my mouth. It was a jelly, a
transformation. But I wanted to know. Wanted. I reached for his
wrist but couldn't get it.

You can be real, but you can be stronger than real; speeded-up,
lighted-up. It does take a camera. The Director helped them drag
me back saying *Oh it was beautiful . . . it was beautiful . . .* and
there were tears in the creases around his mouth. I strained to get
free, to break the shape out of my head and into his. Strained,
twisted. But there was too much noise. The back of my head was
hurt and emptied out. Too much battered into me, I couldn't tell
them apart, there were two of them but maybe two hundred or two
thousand, I couldn't know.

But I couldn't talk right. The man tried to listen politely but
here is what I said: ". . . rockhand, two of them, birdburrow, truck,
toy, wheel, the arrow, the exit, the way out. . . ." Another man, also
in the room, tried to interrupt. Kept asking "Who were they? How
many? Five, six, a dozen? Twenty? Where did it happen? Where
did you meet them? Who are you?" but I kept on talking, babbling,
now I was saying saints' names that got into my head somehow . . .
the names of saints like beads on a rosary, but I didn't know them,
the saints had terrible names to twist my head out of shape: ". . .
Saint Camarillo, Saint Oxnard, Saint . . . Saint Ventura . . . Saint
Ynez . . . Saint Goleta . . . Saint Gaviota . . . Saint Jalama . . . Saint
Casmalia . . . Saint Saint Saint. . . ."

V   The Vision

A rainy wintry day, and I crossed Carpenter Street and my eye
drifted right onto someone. The Director. I stared at him and
started to run after him. He turned around, staring. Didn't recog-

nize me. Didn't know. Behind him a laundromat, some kids playing in the doorway, yelling. Too much confusion. The Director
walked sideways, sideways staring at me, trying to remember. He
hadn't any sunglasses now. His skin was sour-looking.

I ran up to him. I said: "Don't you remember? Don't you—?"

I laughed.

I forgave him, he looked so sick. He was about twenty-eight,
thirty years old. Edgy, cautious. Creases down both sides of his
mouth.

He stared at me.

Except for the rain and a bad cold, my eyes reddened, I was
pretty again and recovered. I laughed but started to remember
something out of the corner of my eye. Didn't want to remember.
So I smiled, grinned at him, and he tried to match the way I looked.

"I'm new here, I just came here . . . I'm from. . . . I'm from up
the coast, from Seattle. . . . I don't know you. . . ."

A kind of shutter clicked in his head. Showing in his eyes. He
was walking sideways and I reached out for his wrist, a bony wrist,
and he shook me loose. His lips were thin and chalk-colored, chalky
cheesy sour-colored. One of his nostrils was bigger than the other
and looked sore. That single shark tooth was greenish. He said:
". . . just in for a day, overnight, down from Seattle and . . . uh . . .
I don't know you. . . . Don't remember. I'm confused. I'm not well,
my feet are wet, I'm from out of town."

"What happened to the movie?" I asked.

He watched me. A long time passed. Someone walked by him on
the pavement, in the rain, the way passersby walk in a movie, be--
hind the main actors. They are not in focus and that person was
not in focus either.

"Was it a real movie? Did it have film, the camera?" I asked.
Beginning to be afraid. Beginning. But I kept it back, the taste in
my mouth. Kept smiling to show him no harm. "Oh hey look," I
said, "look, it had film, didn't it? I mean it had film? I mean you
made a real movie, didn't you? I mean—"

Finally he began to see me. The creases around his mouth turned into a smile. It was like a crucial scene now; he put his hand on my shoulder and kissed my forehead, in the rain. He said: "Honey oh yeah. Yeah. Don't you ever doubt that. I mean, did you doubt that? All these months? You should never have doubted that. I mean, that's the whole thing. That's it. That's the purpose, the center, the reason behind it, all of it, the focus, the. . . . You know what I mean? The Vision?"

I knew what he meant.

So I was saved.

Concerning the Case of Bobby T.

June 28, 1952

Bobby T. struggled with Frances Berardi and yanked her to the side, as if trying to knock her over. But she twisted her small body to keep from falling. She was screaming. They were near the boarded-up cabin in Reardon Park—a refreshment stand not open this summer, though painted a tart black-green that still smelled fresh—and three friends of Frances, girls her own age, were on the wide dirt path nearby, watching, and other people in the park turned to watch, hearing the noise. Bobby T. noticed nothing. He shook Frances so her head swung forward and back and her long black hair flicked into his face, stinging his eyes.

This seemed to drive him into a frenzy, her hair stinging his eyes.

She fell to her knees. Bobby T. was gripping her by the upper arm, and he yanked her back up onto her feet again and gave her a final shove, back at her friends. She collided with one of the girls. The girls were so surprised by all this that they hadn't had time to cry for help until it was all over and Bobby T. was running. By then people were coming—a man who had been sitting on a blanket nearby, with his wife and baby and a portable radio, and some Negro men who were fishing at the river, and some boys on bicycles, attracted by all the yelling. But by then Bobby T. had run crashing through the bushes and was gone.

That was around seven-thirty on a very hot evening in Seneca, New York.

August 9, 1971

Frances Berardi, thirty-one years old, separated now for nearly two months from her husband, stood behind the counter in her father's music store and thought about Bobby T. Cheatum.

In spite of the airless heat of the store, she was shivering. She stared, fascinated and contemptuous, at the prickly flesh on her bare arms.

She was helping out at Berardi's Music Store, in its "new location"—since 1969—on Drummond Avenue. Her father was giving an organ lesson to a widow named Florence Daley, in the soundproof room at the rear of the store. Twelve free lessons came with each purchase of an organ; Mrs. Daley's son and his wife had bought her an organ for her birthday. From time to time Frances could hear the muffled breathless shrieks of the organ, though maybe she was imagining it. The room was supposed to be soundproof. She inclined her head, listening. Yes, she did hear the shrieks. She heard something.

If Bobby T. walked through the door she would say to him, *I'm not Frances Berardi any longer. I'm Frances Laseck.*

Her father's store was small, only half the size of the shoe store on one side of it and perhaps one-third the size of the drugstore at the corner. He had crowded it with merchandise—pianos and organs lining the walls and out in the middle of the floor. It was hard to walk around in here. There were several counters of smaller musical instruments—accordions and guitars and drums—and racks of sheet music and records, though Frances's father made no effort to compete with the discount department stores that sold popular records so cheaply. He wouldn't compete with them, he said angrily; there, records were stocked "by the foot" according to what sold fast, and nobody cared what kind of music was being sold. He didn't want to compete on that level, he said. But Berardi's Music Store kept going, year after year. Frances liked helping her father because the store was so familiar, so contained, like a box seen from the inside. There were no surprises here. She loved the smell of the clean polished wood, the pianos and organs that looked so perfect, handsome and mute and oiled, with their white and black keys.

If she had to wait for Bobby T., she was safer here than at home.

Her eyes felt bright and glittery, her neck strangely long and thin. She had not slept well for several nights. She knew that her collar bones showed in this dress, and that she looked wispy and shrill in it, like a bird, but she had worn it anyway. If Bobby T. did come to look her up, after so many years, he might take pity on her when he saw how thin she was. After the baby she had never gained weight. After the trouble with her husband she had never gained weight.

Frances checked her watch: four-thirty. A very long, hot, quiet afternoon. She looked at the clock on the wall behind her: four-thirty. Outside, people strolled by on the sidewalk and did not come in, sometimes didn't even glance into the window. Now someone was slowing down, lingering—a middle-aged woman in a housedress, who stared at the small $898 organ for sale there, and at the music books displayed on a velvet cloth, "Gershwin's Finest Hours," "Two on the Aisle," "Songs from South Pacific." The woman's name was Mrs. Fuhr; Frances knew her daughter Maude from high school. She hoped that Mrs. Fuhr wouldn't come in the store.

Only an hour and a half, Frances thought. Then they could close the store.

July 2, 1952

Again and again they asked Frances what had happened. Her face was hot and stiff from crying. If she cried hard enough they might let her alone. Why wouldn't they let her alone? Her mother sat broad and creaking in a cane-backed chair, ashamed, silent. Her father was unable to stay in one place, kept jumping up from his seat and pacing around, making everyone nervous. "Just tell them, Frannie. Tell them again. Speak up nice and tell them, please," he said.

They were in the downtown police station, in one of the back rooms. The police station! Frances knew that Bobby T. was locked up somewhere nearby.

"Repeat, please, what you told us. Then what? Then, after he knocked you down, then what?" a man was asking her.

Frances went through it all again.

Her upper arm was bruised, ugly orange and yellow and purple bruises—look at that, her father said, turning Frances's arm for the man to see. Yes, he saw it. Her knees were scratched bad. The policeman tried not to look at Frances's knees. Anyway the scratches were covered with bandages and adhesive tape her mother changed several times a day.

"She could get infection—bad infection—" her father muttered.

"Yes," said the policeman. He was a sizable man with a gleaming bald head, her father's age. He did not wear a uniform like the other policemen who were listening. As he talked, Frances stared at the grim creases around his mouth. From time to time he rubbed a handkerchief into these sweaty creases because it was so hot, even with the fan going. It had been hot now, up in the nineties, for over a week. Everyone in Seneca was sick of the weather.

"Bobby T. Cheatum was always a wise guy, smart-assing around," the policeman said, "but I never thought he'd go crazy like this."

"You just keep him locked up," Frances's father said loudly. "If he breaks out—"

"He isn't going to break out."

"No? Who says so, a jail like this? I know this town. I know how my kids and my neighbors' kids get chased around—boys or girls, it don't matter—Look, you see this goes to a trial—in a courtroom, with a judge and all that," he stammered, "because there are some things this town should learn—"

"Yes, Mr. Berardi, that's right. I happen to agree with you," the policeman said, wiping his face.

Frances had no more tears left. She wondered if they had come to the end of the questioning. For four days now she had been kept in the house, her father had closed up the store and stayed home, sometimes weeping angrily in the bedroom, sometimes storming out of the house, bypassing Frances, not even looking at her. As if he hated her. Frances had cried until she was worn out. She thought in a flash of anger that Bobby T. was a stupid goddam nigger, though he thought he was smarter than the other niggers, and the next time she saw him she would tell him so.

November 19, 1956

"My name is Herbert Ryder from Legal Aid. I came out here the other time with your sister Bonnie. Do you remember me, Bobby?"

Bobby T. Cheatum sat with his arms listless on his big knees, knees parted and tilting to either side of his body. His face was oily with a peculiar sweatless perspiration, especially the wings of his broad nose. His eyes were yellowed. Sometimes his lips were pursed, sometimes slack. He did not glance at Herbert Ryder.

"Bobby, I want to ask you a few questions. Are you listening, Bobby?"

They were in a visitors' room, an alcove off the veranda used for

arts and crafts instructions on certain days of the week. This was a
Wednesday evening, the only time Ryder could come to the hospital. The alcove was quite cold. There was no one around except
a nurse at the reception desk in the foyer; she was typing in brief,
hacking spasms, and listening to music on a small transistor radio.

"As soon as you can be examined again and released from here
we'll get you on the court docket. I'm confident the charges will be
dismissed. Bobby, are you listening?"

Bobby did not reply.

"Why aren't you listening? Don't you trust me? Your sister Bonnie came to me for help—don't you remember, she introduced me
to you? You know who I am. You want to get out of here, don't
you?"

Bobby shrugged his shoulders. "Hell," he mumbled.

"What?"

"Hell with it," he said hoarsely.

"What do you mean? Don't you want to get out of here?"

Bobby stared at the floor. His hair was oily and very woolly. The
tight, tiny curls gave his face a look of tension that was misleading.
Really he was very relaxed, slack, almost unconscious. He sat sunk
into himself, his beefy bare arms heavy on his thighs, his big hands
loose on his knees. Though it was drafty in the alcove he appeared
warm; the large pores of his nose glowed.

"Everything will be cleared up . . . I'm confident the charges will
be dismissed. But you have to get well. I mean you have to be
declared well. If you would only make an effort. . . ."

Suddenly Bobby appeared to be listening.

"When you're scheduled to be examined, if you would only try
to be . . . try to. . . . If you would only make an effort to act normal. . . ."

The nurse in the foyer began typing again, interrupting the
music. Bobby T. flinched: it had been the music he was listening
to, not Ryder.

"Do you want to rot in here?" Ryder asked impatiently.

Bobby T. did not bother to reply.

July 6, 1952

Bounding on and off the prison cot at the downtown Seneca jail, shouting. On and off the bars, throwing himself against the bars, which he couldn't believe in. They had dragged him here and locked him in! Bobby T. Cheatum himself!

When he got out—

He mashed his sweating face against the iron bars. His eyeballs itched with the heat and this way he could scratch them. Roll them hard against the bars, then harder, and then he knocked his forehead against them—it maddened him to think of how he was locked up while everyone else was loose. Probably laughing at him. Shaking their heads over him. His mother had predicted all this, with her used-up sour laugh. *Bobby T., your troubles and mine are set to begin soon, with that lip of yours.* She wouldn't come visit him. But she sent him a message through his sister: *I give you my undivided love and attention. God bless you always.*

He kept hearing Frances Berardi's scream. Why had that little bitch made so much noise? And when he looked around, sure enough Roosevelt had run, and the girls started to scream for help —Where had those girls come from, anyway? Dawdling on the path, holding back and then walking forward, fast, right up out of the awful waves of heat, heat like air easing out of an oven, and no place to hide from it. He had worked all day at Allied Storage, loading and unloading vans, and what he looked forward to was the evening—strolling down to Reardon Park to see who was around.

He could shut his eyes and see everyone there, hanging around the concrete abutment, telling jokes about how Bobby T. had gotten dragged off to jail.

He banged his head against the bars to see what would happen. Suddenly he liked the hard-soft feel of the iron, its cool flatness, the way it pushed back at his hot face. There was something to respect in those bars.

. . . He remembered the little brash-faced Italian girls from when he'd been in school, how they joked with him and didn't even mind sitting next to him on the Uptown bus. He had gotten along with all of them. Everyone liked him. The kids from Lowertown all stuck together, riding the bus three or four miles up to Lawrence Belknap School. Frances Berardi hadn't been on that bus—she was younger than Bobby T. and his friends—he wasn't sure what age she was, but she was young. The little white bitch, with that yell of hers. . . .

His mouth had been cut on the inside and he'd spat out blood, but no doctor would come to see him.

He pressed his face, his cheek, his jaw against the bars. An idea came to him slowly. He could see it, beginning as a pinprick in his head, then swelling. He watched it swell until it was too large to stay inside his head.

"You let me out!" he yelled.

The noise of his voice astonished him. It was the noise he'd heard in the fight with Frances—not really his own voice, but another, that pushed its way out of him. Now that it was free it yelled again: "You're listenin'! You guys're listenin'! You let me out—you—"

He paused, panting. His heart was pounding now as if it had gotten away from him, jubilant and wild. *Yes, yes, Bobby T.,* he thought to himself, a thought that was like a shout, and something seemed to burst in his head. He picked the mattress off his cot and, grunting, threw it against the wall. Then he wheeled around and saw the frame and seized it—it wasn't heavy, it was disappointing, but anyway it was something to grab, a real opponent. Not like little Frances Berardi who turned out to weigh almost nothing, for all her smart-aleck taunts—he could have snapped her neck in a second—

That face of hers froze in his head. He remembered the sudden springing madness he'd felt, Frances's face, how she'd turned against him and slapped him, right for everybody to see— He began slamming the cot against the wall. Again. And again. Beating the cot against the wall and the bars and yelling for them to let him out, until he couldn't stop, didn't want to stop—

"Let me out 'n' I'll kill you—the goddam bunch of you—"

July 9, 1952

Nine-thirty in the morning. He knew that from seeing a clock. All night long Bobby T.'s eyes were rolling like crazy in his head, wanting to get loose. Leather belts kept him in bed. To spite the nurse he wet the bed on purpose—let her clean it up. Sponge it up. She was a claw-handed white bitch, afraid of him, wouldn't come near him if she could help it. He tried to throw up on her but it caught somewhere inside him—wouldn't come up. So he had to taste it, seeping back down his throat. That drove him wild.

A shot in the left buttock and then he was up and into somebody's clothes, not clothes he recognized. Now his head was very heavy, though he knew it was only nine-thirty in the morning and he had a long day ahead. They walked him out to an ambulance and helped him up and closed the door on him, with more leather straps to keep his arms against his sides and an attendant sitting by the door to guard him. A white punk of maybe twenty, staring at Bobby T. as if he expected Bobby T. to leap at him.

So they really thought he was crazy!

He had to laugh, that was such a joke. The white boy by the back door, sitting on a little stool, stared at him and said nothing.

So he was mentally unfit to stand trial—so they said—so he had fooled them, all of them—

Mentally unfit to stand trial! He was fooling them all.

June 28, 1952

Frances Berardi and some friends of hers, girls her own age, were cutting through Reardon Park, it was after supper and everyone was out. They talked for a while with some boys they knew, and Frances took a few puffs of a cigarette from one of them—a small, dark, ferret-faced boy named Joe Palisano. She smoked with a squinting, adult detachment, as if assessing the taste of the smoke carefully and finding it not bad. She and Joe were not older than the others but they acted older; but then he started to tease her about certain things, about something that had been written about her on a viaduct nearby, and she told him to go to hell.

She led her friends away, walking stiffly and angrily. "I don't like guys who talk dirty," she said. "I don't have to put up with that crap from anybody's mouth."

She spoke with a tart philosophical air. She and her friends wandered down to the river, where people were fishing—most of them Negroes, boys and older men, even a few heavy black women, sitting on upended boxes and sighing with the heat. There was no one here that Frances was interested in. She and her friends walked along the abutment, kicking Mallow Cup wrappers and popsicle wrappers into the water. It was a very hot, airless evening.

Frances was wearing jeans cut off high on her thighs and a jersey blouse that pulled tight over her head, pink and white stripes and a white stretch collar; she had bought it just the Saturday before, at an Uptown store. She knew she looked good in it. She was twelve years old but mature for her age, her black hair glossy and loose, her bangs falling thick over her forehead so that they brushed the tops of her thick eyebrows. She was short, trim, athletic, with quick eyes and a brief upper lip, a little loud in her laughter and joking. You could always hear Frannie from a distance, one of her sisters complained—at school or hanging around the grocery store or here in the park, always Frannie Berardi with her big mouth, fooling around. Her friends stood around her, envious and uneasy.

There was nothing to do by the river so they headed back up toward Market Street. Joe Palisano and his friends were gone. Frances regretted walking away like that, but she had thought maybe he would follow her. Right now she might be riding on the crossbar of his bicycle, hot-faced and excited. . . . "The hell with him," she muttered. She and her friends walked slowly, scuffing their feet. They all wore moccasins made of imitation leather, a bright tan, and decorated with small colored beads, bought at the same store Uptown. It was a thing they did, scuff their feet, especially when they walked on the pavement. They scuffed their feet now in the dirt. They all had the same dark-bright faces, dark eyes moving restlessly. Their minds were tipped in one direction by someone honking a horn up ahead—but it was nobody they knew—and then another way by a blast of music from someone's radio—but it was just a married couple with their baby, lying on a blanket nearby, a cousin of Frances's and her husband—and then in another direction by two Negro boys up ahead. Frances knew one of them, Bobby T., a big boy wearing jeans and a buckled belt and a white T-shirt tucked into the belt.

"Look who's hanging around," Frances called out to him in a drawl.

He turned to her with a surprised grin. "I see a cute little fox," he said, raising his hand to sight her through his fingers, a circle made by his thumb and forefinger.

Frances laughed. "That's all you got to do, huh, hang around here? I thought you had a car. How come you're hanging around here?"

"Taking in the sights," Bobby T. said.

Frances looked Bobby T. straight in the eye. He was nineteen and had been in the same class with her brother Salvatore. But he acted younger and was always lots of fun. He was a good-looking black boy.

"Out for any special sight?" Frances said. She was hot-faced and bold. Her friends giggled at the way Frances walked right up to him with her hands on her hips, like someone in a movie.

"Could be we might take a drive Uptown. Want to come along?" Bobby T. said.

"Not tonight." Frances saw that he was barefoot and that his feet were powdery with the dust. She giggled at the size of his feet.

"Anyway, I heard your car broke down. That's what I heard."

"How come not tonight? You got some special business?"

Frances shrugged her shoulders. She was very excited, almost giddy. It was as if someone were pushing her from behind, pushing her toward Bobby T. *Come on, don't be afraid! Stand right up to him!*

"Hell, my father would kill me," Frances said.

"Who's gonna tell him?"

"I heard your car broke down and anyway I got better things to do."

"Your father ain't gonna know about it—he never knew about it the other time, did he?"

Frances hoped her friends hadn't heard that. A kind of flame passed over her face and she poked Bobby T. with her forefinger, right in the center of his chest.

"Somebody's got a big mouth," she drawled.

Bobby T. just grinned.

That made Frances mad. Something was beating furiously in her. She had to stand back on her heels, with her head tilted, in order to look up straight into Bobby T.'s face. She wasn't going to back down from him.

"I got better things to do than ram around with you," she said.

"How come you so fussy? That's never what I heard about Frannie Berardi."

She almost laughed. Then, lit by a sudden giddy excitement, a daring she had rehearsed in her imagination many times—slapping Joe Palisano's face in front of everyone—Frances reared back and struck Bobby T. on the side of the face, with the flat of her hand, slapping her palm hard against his cheek—

April 23, 1960

"So I slapped his face. I was just kidding around. And he grabbed my wrist and started shaking me . . . and I tried to kick him . . . and. . . ."

Frances hesitated, staring at Father Luciano as if she expected him to nod, to remember. But he couldn't remember. He couldn't see that summer evening, the park and the wide dirt path and the boarded-up refreshment stand and Bobby T. and her. . . .

"Didn't this all happen a long time ago, Frances? Years ago?" he asked.

"Yes, before we all moved Uptown, a whole lot of us moved," Frances said slowly. "It was like the kids themselves decided to move—you know—kids who were friends with one another—now it's mostly all Negro down there. By the river. Eddie drives me by there sometimes and I look at our old house and it's all colored, a big family. . . . Lowertown used to be all Italian and colored, now it's just colored. . . . It's funny how that changed."

Father Luciano smiled a pursed little smile. His expression looked out of focus, not quite right. Wasn't he listening? Frances sat forward. She had to make him understand. There was something urgent she had to explain, she must ask his forgiveness and his absolution, she must confess it and get it all straightened out so that she could forget about it and get married and pass beyond that part of her life.

"It was a long time ago, yes," she stammered, "and I was such a brat, it makes me sick to remember myself! I was such a show-off. . . . We'd go roller-skating on Saturdays, and kid around with the Uptown boys, and ride our bicycles all over. . . . It makes me so ashamed to remember myself," she said. She took a tissue out of her purse and wiped her forehead. "And Bobby T.—Bobby T. Cheatum—he was a neighborhood kid a little older than we were. He went to school with my brother but dropped out. Everybody played together, you know, white and colored, in the park and at school and all over, and Bobby T. was always a nice kid—kind of daring, the way he would climb across the railroad bridge when a train might come at any time, and you know how that thing wobbles—"

Why was she saying all this? Father Luciano didn't know what she was talking about. Probably he had never even driven down to Lowertown. He was new to the city of Seneca itself and his parish was nowhere near the hill. He was from Buffalo, forty miles away. Frances was confused. She wanted to make him understand, she wanted to make him remember—those years in the cinder playgrounds, in the park, at Lawrence Belknap school, she wanted to make him remember again the kids in the neighborhood, who were all grown up now, a lot of them married, some still in the Navy or the Army, a few of them gone on to college, or disappeared, two of them killed in car accidents, and a few of them with crazy bad luck —like Bobby T., locked up in the state hospital all these years.

"Would you like to begin your confession now?" Father Luciano asked.

"No, not yet, no, wait. . . . I want to explain something. . . ." she said slowly, confused. Out in the anteroom Eddie was waiting and she could imagine him smoking a cigarette, frowning. This was taking too long. She knew what was coming: a little lecture on birth control, the paper she would have to sign swearing that she would not use any artificial methods of birth control and that her children would be brought up Catholic. Yes. She was ready for that. But first she had to explain something about those years of her childhood, her young girlhood, when she was twelve years old and had bought that pink and white blouse she liked so much, when she had walked up to Bobby T. Cheatum that night in the park. . . .

"You said that the boy is in the hospital," Father Luciano said, when Frances did not speak for a while. "Don't you think he's in good hands there? He's out of danger and he can't cause danger to others. . . . I'm sure they have an excellent staff there to help him. If he were out on his own he'd just be a threat to himself and to others."

"But I was such a brat, I was always shooting my mouth off. . . ."

"And the court showed the proper wisdom, I believe. I'm sure of it. Does anyone else ever talk about this incident, Frances? Does anyone else even remember except you?"

"Oh, no. No," Frances said at once. "Not in my family. We

stopped talking about it right away. And Eddie used to live outside Seneca, he's from the country where his parents have a farm. . . . The kids are all sort of scattered now, except for some girls I see around, you know, shopping. We all moved Uptown. And Bobby T.'s people, well, I didn't know them. . . . his father died a few years ago, I heard . . . but probably people don't remember. . . ."

Father Luciano shifted his weight in his chair. Over his shoulder Frances could see the lawn out front and the grilled iron gates decorated with golden crosses, cross after cross stretching along the sidewalk. She looked down at her hands, at the frayed damp tissue. She couldn't remember having taken it out of her purse.

"If he were out on his own," Father Luciano said gently, "he'd just be a threat to himself and to others. Isn't that so?"

"I thought if I could visit him . . . maybe I could explain it to him. . . . But that would drive my father wild, I couldn't even bring it up. Once some lawyer came to see me, he was from Legal Aid. I think that's what it was called. He was trying to get Bobby T. set for a trial or something. He asked me questions but my father was right there with me, so I had to keep saying the old answers. . . . And. . . . Oh, I don't know. That was a long time ago too, three or four years ago. I suppose people don't remember now."

"I'm sure they don't," Father Luciano said.

August 9, 1971

Frances answered the phone on the first ring.

"Frannie? How is it there?"

"What do you mean, how is it?" she said irritably. "The four o'clock lesson came and went—the lady with the organ lessons—and it's dead as hell in here, and hot. Why he wants to stay open till six is beyond me."

"You sure nobody came in?"

"If you mean Bobby T., he's nowhere in sight and what's more no Negro is in sight or has even looked in the window all day. So. How's everything at home?"

"Frannie, I just happened to mention that this colored boy was

being released today, you know, I just happened to mention it to
Edith Columbo, and she said maybe we better notify the police. I
don't mean to be asking for trouble, Frannie—but just be sensible—
to give warning—"

"No."

"You should let Eddie know, anyway. He would want to know.
He would be worrying about you right now."

Frances made a despairing droll face that her mother should be
so stupid! That her mother should think Eddie gave a damn about
her!

"How's Sue Ann?" Frances asked flatly.

"Outside playing with the kid next door. . . . You sure nobody's
hanging around there? Out on the sidewalk?"

Frances's father came out of the back room, looking at her. She
mouthed the word "Mama" to him and he nodded, his face closing
up. He walked to the front of the store and gazed out at the street.
Traffic passed slowly. After a few minutes Frances said, "Mama, I
got to hang up, a customer is coming in—"

She stared at her father's back, his damp white shirt, and
wondered what he was thinking. Not of Bobby T. No. He wouldn't
spend five minutes in all these years thinking of him: that black
bastard, that maniac, beating his daughter up the way he did, and
then running so wild it took three policemen to drag him away. . . .
Frances took out her compact and checked her face. It was always
a surprise, that she should look so cute. *Cute.* That's all you could
say for her face but it was enough—with her short upper lip and her
long thin nose and her dark, darting eyes, and the way her hair
didn't turn kinky even in this hot weather. Yes, she was cute. Short
and cute. What had someone said to her once?—Bobby T. himself?
—*The best things come in small packages.*

Once she had been under the awning at the Rexall Drugs on
Main Street, waiting for rain to stop, and cruising along the curb in
his rattletrap jalopy was Bobby T. and that friend of his with the
funny name—she couldn't remember it now—and Bobby asked her

how'd she like a ride home? Because they lived near each other. Frances hesitated only a second, then said Okay. Great. And she had jumped in the back seat. She had always had a lot of nerve. They drove right down the big hill to Lowertown, Bobby T. showing off a little bit, thumping on the steering wheel as if it were a drum, but putting himself out to be nice to her. Yet he let you know, that Bobby T., that he was always thinking around the edges of what he shouldn't be thinking. That was the day he had said, teasing her, *the best things come in small packages.*

Bobby T.'s friend—his name was Roosevelt—couldn't keep up with her and Bobby T., the way they kidded each other. What a nerve she had! She knew her father would kill her if he saw her in a car with any boys, let alone colored boys. But she had jumped in the car anyway.

Then, as they approached her own neighborhood, she began to wonder if this had been a good idea. Someone on the street might see her and tell her father. So she poked Bobby T. on the shoulder and said, "Hey, maybe you better let me out here."

"In the rain, honey? You'll spoil that high-class outfit of yours!"

She snorted at this—she was wearing shorts and a soiled blouse.

But Bobby T. let her out anyway, near a grocery store so that she could wait for the rain to stop. Nobody had seen her, evidently. Nobody told her father. And yet now, today, so many years later, she wanted to tell her father about that ride. How they had all giggled together....

"I've been thinking about Bobby T. all day ..." she said softly.

Her father stood with his back to her, blunt and perspiring. He had grown heavy and bald: once a good-looking man, even when his hair had thinned unevenly, now he sagged with worry and irritability. Frances was a little afraid of him. She feared his peevish scowl, that scowl that had been directed at her over the years— because she was no good at the piano, because her marriage had been bad from the start, most of all because she had a pert, impatient, unserious scowl herself.

"What did you say?" her father said, turning suddenly.

His face warned her: *Better shut up, Fran. Shut your cute little mouth.*

"Nothing," she said.

"It better be nothing," her father said.

August 9, 1971

They had located Bobby T.'s older sister, Bonnie, who was married and living now in Buffalo. At first she had said no, no, she couldn't take him in, she was afraid of him, and her husband was in and out of trouble himself.... What would Bobby T. do around the house? Wouldn't he be dangerous?

A woman social worker told her: "Bobby has ten years' experience working in the hospital laundry. He'll be able to get a good job in a laundry. He only needs to adjust himself to society again. He needs a friendly home for a while, to get him started again."

"How long's that gonna take, to get him started again?" Bonnie asked suspiciously.

She was a grave-faced, thick woman in her mid-forties, with a habit of shaking her head negatively as she thought, as if nothing seemed right to her. But in the end she agreed to take Bobby T. in.

So they brought Bobby T. to her one Monday afternoon. He turned out to be a tall, thin black man with a slight stoop, shy and apologetic. He was carrying a small suitcase. He had five dollars release money.

"Well, Bobby T.," she said awkwardly. "Such a long time...."

They shook hands like people in a movie. Bonnie didn't know what to do: she remembered her brother as taller and heavier, and maybe this man was someone else.

"Hello," he said.

A voice like a whisper, so hoarse! She didn't recognize that either.

She cleared off a place for him to sit on the sofa and he set the suitcase primly at his feet. So this was her crazy put-away brother Bobby Templar, the one nobody in the family liked to talk about.

. . . He had a curious way of ducking his head. He would not meet her gaze, not directly. A tall thin scrawny bird, birdlike in his nervousness, with a glaze to his dark skin that was like permanent sweat, and a smell in his clothes of panic. Bonnie stared at him, her heart sinking. This was a mistake and she couldn't get out of it.

"Been a lot of time since we seen each other," she said slowly. "They treated you okay there, huh?"

"Yes," Bobby said.

"The big trouble—you know—the courtroom and all—I mean the trial—that got all cleared up, huh?"

"The charges were dismissed," Bobby T. said softly.

"Charges were dismissed, oh yes," his sister said seriously, nodding. That was an important fact. That was good news.

She couldn't think what to do—start supper with him sitting here?—so after a while she suggested that they go down to the corner to get some things she needed. "Just a five-minute walk," she said.

Bobby got to his feet self-consciously and followed her out of the building—she had an apartment on the first floor, a good location—and she noticed out of the corner of her eye that he walked in a kind of crouch, leading with his forehead. He didn't look crazy, not the way some people on the street looked, but he didn't look quite right either, with that stiff walk of his, like an old man's walk and not a man of—what was he now?—thirty-eight? He kept staring out at the street, at the buses and trucks.

At the intersection he froze and didn't seem able to move. "It's just across the street, that's the grocery right over there," Bonnie said, panicked herself. *Oh Jesus*, she thought, *they brought him to me still crazy and they drove away again!* "Look, Bobby T., it ain't nothing to get across this street—nobody's going to hurt you—"

What was wrong with him? He stood on the curb, sweating, and wouldn't step off onto the street. He was staring ahead, his eyes wide. He stood in that crouched-over, crazy way, his shoulders hunched as if for battle. Bonnie broke out into a sweat, standing beside him. She didn't know if she should touch his arm, or what. He looked paralyzed. And all around them people were passing, some of them staring at him—didn't he have any shame, to act like this on the street?

"Bobby T., there just *ain't* no trouble getting over there. . . ."

He didn't look at her but he seemed to be listening. After a long wait he took one step forward, off the curb and into the gutter. Bonnie drew in her breath slowly, cautiously.

"See, how there ain't any trouble? It's real easy," she said.

He took another step, slow as hell; at this rate it would take them an hour to cross the street, but anyway it was a start.

She took hold of his arm and led him. "Okay, Bobby T., you see how easy it is, huh . . . ? See how easy . . . ?" He was slow as hell and she was burning hot with the shame of it, but he was her brother, after all. Her baby brother. Anyway, today was a start.

Blindfold

I A Drive Outward

The blindfold was in the glove compartment. He opened it to take something out, a map of the northern part of the county, and she saw it in there—a pale pink blindfold. It looked like a dusting rag. Her mother had rags just like it, torn from sheets that were too old to use on the beds. Those rags had a fresh smell to them because they were laundered all the time, just like the regular laundry. The blindfold smelled different: it smelled of the car and the glove compartment.

They were driving out. She had charge of the map. "You're the navigator; you're giving the orders," he said. The car had a strange wide sweep in back and seemed narrow in front; it seemed to bend slyly against the wind of the highway. It was a new car. The windshield's glass was tinted green. And so everything was a lightly bitter green, especially the grass—the sky was a deep green-blue. She squinted at the map and saw how the lines ran squiggling together, separating and coming together again, lines of black and red. The big double line was the road they were on. It cut through the county, cutting it in half, and as it went back down into the city it cut the city neatly in half. She saw suddenly that someone had planned all this, grown-up men had planned it. They had sat down at drawing boards and charted everything, all these lines of red and black, dividing the county and the state and the nation into certain parts that made sense.

"Do I continue straight? Straight ahead?"

"Yes."

"How far?"

"A long ways."

"How long will it take us?"

"I don't know."

"Try to guess! How long did it take us last time?"

"Last time. . . ."

"Last time we went to the lake. Don't you remember?"

She tried to think. She felt his sunny, green-tinted smile and knew that she was expected to be smart, to show off, for her uncle often asked her questions like this when they were out somewhere, in a restaurant or in a park, overheard by strangers. He wanted her to show off because she was his favorite; he liked her brothers well enough but never expected anything from them, and she was conscious of the need to please him. Maybe they were practicing now for questions he would ask her later.

"One hour . . . ?"

"One hour! Excellent! That's exactly right!"

She held the map up before her. Its folds were new and not worn, like those in her father's map. Her father's map lay in the back seat of his car, by the back window, or stuffed into the glove compartment, not folded right. Her father's car did not sound like this one and it wobbled when it was driven fast. Every year her uncle bought a new car, each year a different color, and sometimes the windshields curved and reflected the sunshine with a peculiar power, as if knowing something she did not know, and sometimes the heavy body of the car, being stationary most of the time, the heaviness of chrome and metal and glass, made her understand that the car knew nothing, even its intelligent vibrations meant nothing, no thinking, no knowledge.

"I'm thinking about lunch."

"Can I have ice cream?"

"I'm thinking about a hot dog and potato chips and mustard and relish. Whose favorite lunch is that?"

"Mine!"

"Should we stop at Howard Johnson's and have a hot dog? And an ice cream cone afterward?"

"Yes."

She thought about the flavors of ice cream. She moved her tongue in her mouth, mutely, as if trying to stir up thoughts of ice cream, but for some reason she could not think of anything, not even the restaurant, which was her favorite. Her eyes were dazzled. The map promised an adventure, but its abrupt edges told her that they could not drive very far—the men who had planned the map had wisely cut it short, put the county in a paper rectangle. Again she realized, suddenly, that adult men had planned this for their own secret reasons, taking time, sitting at drawing-boards the way her own father sat at a drawing-board, drawing lines. These thoughts came to her with a slight wave of queasiness, as if the green-tinted sunshine were making her sick.

"Is anything special on tonight?"

He meant on television. She loved television.

"Captain Sweeney's on. The Circus is on."

"Do you like Captain Sweeney?"

"Oh yes."

"Why do you like him?"

She could not think. "I don't know...."

She would have hid behind the map, but it was too big to bring around between her uncle and herself. Anyway, he would pull it aside, peeking at her.

"He's funny . . . he talks real loud and gets mad at the kids, but then he . . . he sees how he was wrong. . . . I don't know, I just like him."

Her uncle smiled at her. After a moment he said, "But big men like that shouldn't get mad at children."

She nodded.

"When your mother gets mad at you it's different. She's very tired, your mother, she has a hard life . . . if she makes you cry it's because she has so much work to do. . . . Boys like your brothers are lots of work. She doesn't mean to get mad and scold you."

That morning her mother had slapped her. She said nothing to her uncle.

"Your mother...."

A few days ago she had overheard her mother and her father talking in the kitchen. Her father had laughed about something; then he said, "Well, he's your brother. He's your problem." Her mother had said sharply, "Why do you push everything off on me?" And her father said, "Just keep him out of here when I'm home."

But her uncle had not heard that. Now he was like a captain steering a boat; she was the navigator in charge of the map. When she looked at the side of his face she did not feel that sensation of dazzling light; it was only when he smiled at her. He said, "Your mother is a wonderful woman. Someday you'll understand."

But she was stubborn and silent. In a minute her uncle would try to make her say the names of people she loved, beginning with the ones she loved most. She was stubborn, looking at the map. She would not talk.

Yes, now he was saying: "First of all you love your mother, Betsy...?"

Her mouth went dry. Her tongue was larger, dry. She moved it as if to get ready for the ice cream.

Finally he gave up. "Should I put on the radio?" he said.

"Yes!"

He turned a shiny silver dial. A man's voice rose out of the depths of the car. She pretended to listen to it because everything that was on in her presence—a radio, a television set—was something that should be listened to while she thought her own thoughts. Sometimes she sat watching Captain Sweeney himself, and while her eyes were on the picture her mind was off speeding in a car, her own car. It soared right off the edge of the map. The danger was that someone might ask her what was happening and she wouldn't know. Her uncle, dropping by sometimes when her father was out, would squat next to her and ask, "Oh, what's happening? What did I miss?" and she would stare at the television screen, trying to think what to say. Her mother never asked what was happening. Her father, walking through one room to another, sometimes called out, "What's up, kid? You're pretty quiet!" but it was not a question to be answered.

"How old is Mrs. Pack?"

Mrs. Pack was an old woman who lived across the street from them.

"I don't know."

"Take a guess! How old is Mrs. Pack?"

She began to giggle. Mrs. Pack was a joke in the house. "I don't know."

"Mrs. Pack said to me the other day, 'I'd like a little girl just like Betsy!' "

"She did not!"

"She did too!"

She shook her head from side to side, it was so silly. The map slipped from her hands but it was too large to fall onto the floor.

Her uncle kept on talking. His voice was mixed up with the voice

of the man on the radio. Ahead of them was the zoo, or the lake
that had swans on it; ahead was a hot dog in a real restaurant,
where she would sit in a real booth, not at the counter, and her
uncle would give their orders to a waitress, as if they were both
grown-ups; they would both get ice cream cones on the way out.
She would bite into the ice cream, eating it fast, and her uncle
would give her his when she finished her own, because he liked to
watch her eat. Now she was beginning to remember. She swallowed
hungrily.

"How far do we have to go now?"

She looked at the map.

"A hundred miles. . . ."

"What, a hundred miles!"

"A thousand miles!"

She began to giggle. The map slipped out of her hands.

"You're a silly little girl, aren't you?"

"No."

"What would happen if a ship's navigator read the map like
that? What would happen?"

"They'd go down."

"Would they sink?"

"They'd all sink!"

She thought of this car, with her uncle and herself and the radio
announcer's voice in it, going down. They would sink slowly and
nothing could save them. Today they would drive out to a lake but
park on the edge of the lake, or maybe they were going to the zoo
or to the movies . . . she couldn't remember. One of the lakes had
swans and geese and ducks on it. Another lake only had ducks. She
and her uncle fed all the birds, they even bought boxes of crackers
at a refreshment stand, crackers just for the birds. If they went to
the zoo they ate in the outdoor restaurant; they ate ice cream
sundaes with red plastic spoons. Everywhere at the zoo children
were running around. Children were shouting, crying, giggling,
pushing. She couldn't stop giggling herself.

"Aren't you silly? Aren't you silly for a six-year-old girl?"

"I'm seven!"

"Five years old and so silly, such a big girl, what makes you so silly . . . ?"

He smiled at her with his dazzling smile. She looked away from his face and mouth and to his hands on the steering wheel, which were easier to look at. There was something about his knuckles that interested her. The knobs of knuckles under the skin . . . they moved under the skin like something moving by themselves, having their own thoughts. Sometimes she felt those knuckles moving when she could not see them. Her father's hands were big, with dark hairs on them. His knuckles moved in a different way. Everything he did was in a rush. Her uncle was never in a rush, he would slow down for her . . . she thought of a television show the other night where a man in a helicopter swooped down to rescue some people on an iceberg. He was like that.

At school she would go for her lunch bag and press into the coats, pushing against the back wall. She was not crying. She pushed against the wall and stood there with her eyes closed until someone found her. She did not giggle too much at school. Her teacher thought that was silly, her teacher did not smile when she said it was silly. So she did not giggle. Now she felt the giggles inside her, like bubbles in soda pop.

"Can I have some pop too?"

"What kind?"

"Grape."

"Maybe and maybe not."

Her mouth watered. Now she was able to think clearly of the lake and the rowboats, of the refreshment stand, the cold bottles of pop, the peanuts, the crackers for the ducks, and afterward the restaurant and the waitress and the ice cream and when they went home her mother asking her, "What did you and Uncle Dick do today?"

"No, I want orange pop."

"Maybe. If they have any."

"Sure they have orange pop!" she laughed.

"Sometimes they don't on Saturdays."

Today was a Saturday.

"Then I want root beer."

"We'll see."

"No, I want cherry pop!"

"Maybe."

"I want strawberry pop!"

The map slid down onto the floor. She kicked it off her legs. She kicked it down onto the floor.

"Don't rip our map. . . ."

She kicked it again.

"Betsy, fold it up and put it away. You mustn't rip it. How will we get home?"

She thought of a lake, a park, a field in the country; she thought of the car parked; she thought of the game of blindfold, her uncle tying the blindfold tight around her head. It made a strange pressure on her eyes. With it on, she could feel her eyes in her head, two round thick things; the rest of the time she could not feel them. They walked together in a field, in weeds, and she could feel the sunshine on her legs mixed in with the prickly weeds; she walked carefully because she was "it," she was blind, and her uncle held her hand to keep her from falling off the edge. . . . She could not take off the blindfold. She thought of how tight it was around her head, and then she thought of the restaurant. Howard Johnson's had a special place mat that was really a map of the United States. On it were all the Howard Johnson's restaurants. She liked to make a line with her fingernail from one orange dot to another, linking them, figuring them out. The place mat was a rectangle, like most maps. She thought of that. She thought of the blindfold finally being taken from her head, very gently by her uncle, the knot slipping up the back of her head, mussing her hair. Then her uncle would comb her hair for her.

Last Christmas her uncle had given her a doll house. The roof came away; you could see into every room. It was as big as a real house, almost. She dreamed of getting small and crawling into it, hiding, up in the baby's room. She dreamed of that. Her uncle had given her a tricycle a long time ago and then a regular bicycle. He gave her dolls and clothes for them. When they ate their ice cream cones in the car, he would say, "The big secret is the blindfold game. Nobody can know about that but us." She thought of her three brothers. They would want to play the game, they would push her aside. They always pushed her aside. "Nobody can know about that but us," her uncle said. His skin was fair, a little pink, and under it thoughts seemed to move, rippling, never coming to a stop. Her father's face was different. Sometimes she saw him asleep and his face was asleep; her uncle's face was never asleep. She saw the thoughts slide under his skin and something sharp rose in her, made her want to giggle, or cry out, like a sharp thought of her own coming at night. . . .

"That's our secret. Nobody can know about *that*," he said.

She nodded.

"If anybody tries to ask, if anybody wants to know anything—"

She nodded before he had time to finish his sentence. She would take bites of ice cream though it made her teeth ache violently.

II A Drive Home

Noise in the grass and a sudden shout, close by. Someone shouted, "Hey!" It was so close she thought at first it was someone she knew, maybe her father, his husky "Hey!" that always terrified her.

She stood without moving. Everything was dark to her. She heard her uncle's voice getting very fast, getting mixed up—"Why, what do you want?—what are you— what—"

She tore the blindfold off her head.

A man and a woman had come up to them, and now the man was shouting something. He was a small angry man in a yellow shirt. The woman was pulling at his arm; she had gray hair and a

gray puckered face, like Mrs. Pack. Her uncle stepped back. He held
his raincoat wrapped around him oddly. He began to cry.

The man in the yellow shirt stared over at her.

The woman said, pulling at his arm, "Come on, please, please
don't. . . . Come on."

Her uncle was crying. One hand held his raincoat closed and the
other tried to hide his face. He was trying to explain something but
it did not make sense. He shook his head. It was a very sunny day
in June. She was nine years old. She backed away from her uncle
and the two strangers and stared up curiously at the sun, wondering
if it would stop in the sky and everything would come to a stop,
fixing them all right where they were. She had yanked the blindfold
off by herself. She had never been allowed to do that before.

"Come on! Please, Tony, don't get mixed up—come on—"

After a while the man turned and walked away. The woman
hurried after him. Her uncle followed them for a few steps, still
explaining something in his shrill voice. At the edge of the field he
stopped. The man and woman went away, down toward the cars.
Her uncle stopped and stood there alone, calling after them. She
checked the sun to see if it had moved—nothing had moved. What
if they would always be like this, herself in a field of weeds and tiny
yellow flowers and the hum of friendly bees, her uncle on the edge
of the field, crying?

A few minutes passed. Finally her uncle came back to her. He
took the blindfold from her and untied the knot; his fingers were
trembling. It turned into a rag again. He pressed it against his face.
He stood there for a while, shuddering, with the rag pressed to his
face.

"I didn't mean—I'm sorry—"

But he was not talking to her. She thought he might be talking
to that man, but the man was gone.

Her uncle took her by the hand and they went back to the car.
Two other cars were parked there. Around a big barrel heaped with
trash, butterflies and flies and bees buzzed.

"How come he was mad?" she asked.

Her uncle said nothing.

"Why was he yelling?"

She felt her uncle's trembling. She pulled her hand out of his. She looked around for the man, as if that stranger were more important now than her uncle, as if she might run over to him and get into his car. . . . Why was her uncle crying? She was embarrassed. His fair, slippery face was hateful to her, wet with tears, his mouth distorted. *I hate you*, she thought in triumph. She sat in the car and stared out at him, while he stood alone, leaning against the fender, crying, entirely alone. So she thought, *I love you*. . . . But still she looked around for that man. Her uncle wept and his shoulders shook with weeping. His fair, graying blond hair had come loose in two parts, showing how the skin of his head shone beneath. His necktie, which was very pretty, had come loose.

When he got in the car he wiped his face, hard, with the rag, and she saw that his eyes had been rubbed too hard. The lashes looked broken. She closed her own eyes at once. She thought of the restaurant they would go to, of the dark, cool booth and the paper map on the table. . . .

Her uncle started the car. Still she did not open her eyes. She thought of the restaurant and her uncle giving the waitress their order, pronouncing every word carefully. The car was moving now. Her uncle drove slowly, jerkily, bouncing along a rutted lane. A family was picnicking nearby. She stared out at them, wondering who they were and what they were having to eat.

"How come he was so mad . . . ?" she asked again.

She was afraid to look at her uncle, but finally she did look. His face was very pink. It looked as if rivulets had been worked into the pouchy flesh beneath his eyes just by those few minutes of crying.

She was frightened.

On the highway he began to drive fast. The car sped beneath them. She whispered, "How come we're going this way . . . ? Are we going right home?" This frightened her too. Her uncle said nothing.

He was breathing hard, in gasps. He was driving like someone on television. That meant someone was following him, maybe the police. But she could see no one behind them.

Her uncle was still crying. It had something to do with the field, with the man and the woman, with the blindfold. She had snatched it off herself. She had never done that before. Now her uncle was crying and his breath came in rough gasps. She squinted toward him sideways, not wanting to see anything she shouldn't see. His face was very red. The muscles in it moved as if by themselves.

"Did I do something bad?" she said. She wondered if she should cry. "Aren't we going to Howard Johnson's?"

A gagging noise came from her uncle. She looked sideways at him, narrowing her eyes as if narrowing them against sunlight. Something bubbled out of his mouth. He gagged and retched and vomited onto the steering wheel, onto his own lap. His face was red and slippery. The car began to accelerate as if shamed by him, this man vomiting on himself like a baby.

She leaned away from him. The car leaped forward into the highway. Her uncle's fingers, slippery on the steering wheel, worked crazily to keep the car on the road. Now they were passing a big truck. Now they were ahead of the truck! Now, swerving a little, they were gaining on a convertible with its top down. Now they were heading too close to the car's bumper, she gave a little scream, and now her uncle wrenched the wheel around and they flew off to the left and passed the car in a second! Something began deep in her uncle's chest. She could hear it, a strange dark shudder working its way to the surface. She could feel it in the vibrations of the car. Ahead was an intersection and the light was changing from yellow to red, but her uncle's car leaped forward anyway into that dizzying space between roads, and someone began to honk his car horn angrily . . . but her uncle fled onward, shuddering, now bent over the steering wheel as if holding himself up by it, his hands and lower arms and elbows pressed tight against it. She saw behind them two cars nearly collide, yanked together by the tug of air from her uncle's flying car. "Stop it!" she cried. "I won't tell about the blindfold!" But her uncle did not hear her, he had begun to moan above the shuddering of his chest and stomach, and still the car accelerated into the light of the highway, a car brand new only that month, and washed only that morning for this Saturday drive, and she saw a line of signs rushing toward them, white signs with black lettering she had no time to read, and the car jumped up onto the green of the middle of the highway, then swerved back onto the road again, jerking and bouncing angrily, and now it was another big truck that seemed stubbornly in their way, itself carrying brand-new cars on its back. "I won't tell! I won't tell about the man!" she screamed. But her uncle clawed at his chest, clawing at the front of his shirt. He began to gag again. His face was bright red. The front bumper of his car touched the back of the truck, the car swerved, and then was drawn back mysteriously by the truck, as if anxious to plow through it. The truck also swerved. It moved at once over to the left to clear a lane for her uncle. But there were more cars ahead! They would never get home! She heard her uncle whimper in terror, as if he too realized they would never get home, and he headed into the far right lane and braked the car and skidded off onto the shoulder of the highway, skidding, lurching, bouncing. She screamed. She was thrown against the windshield. The drive came to an end.

Her uncle lay collapsed over the steering wheel. His face was a strange face, twisted and red and very wet.

Her mother led her out of the hospital and to the parking lot. There were five small white bandages on her arms and legs. Some man had given her a strawberry lollipop but she threw it away when they got to the car.

Her mother opened the door for her. It had to be yanked open; it made a small shrieking noise.

"And I don't know where your father is . . . why didn't he say where he was going. . . . I don't know what to do. . . ."

She stared at Betsy. In the hospital she had been asking a nurse, "What do I do? How do you arrange for a funeral? What do I do?" and Betsy had been embarrassed. Her mother's face was savage and red; there were lines of surprise that ran from her nose to the edges of her mouth.

"What if you had been killed. . . ?"

She tried to embrace Betsy, weeping over her. But Betsy pushed away. "Is he dead?" she shouted.

Her mother stared.

"Is he dead? Is he?"

"Your uncle . . . ?"

Her mother's face looked out of focus. Betsy could smell about her the odor of fear. For a minute they stared at each other, then Betsy crawled into the car. Her mother pushed the door shut.

"I'm glad he's dead," Betsy said out the open window.

Her mother stared at her.

"I'm glad he's dead, he did things to me! He made me close my eyes, he put the blindfold on me, he wouldn't let me take it off! A man was going to arrest him! The police were chasing him! I'm glad he's dead, I don't want to see him again, I hate him!"

Her mother turned away. She opened her purse and took out a pack of cigarettes and lit one. Betsy was breathing hard. She watched her mother, because she could tell things by watching her mother. They were in the parking lot; other people were around. Betsy's mother lit a cigarette and walked slowly in one direction. She stumbled a little. She stopped at the edge of the parking lot. Betsy waited.

Finally she came back and got in the car. She began the drive home, slowly. They hugged the right lane. "Yes, I'm glad he's dead," Betsy said shrilly. She hiccuped. Her mother sat stiff, not looking at her. To get her attention Betsy picked at a bandage on her knee.

"Betsy," her mother said at once.

She pressed the bandage back into place.

Her mother wore a dark blue dress with a white collar that was a little soiled. Her eyes were strange—they looked glassy. Betsy stared at the side of her face and suddenly she saw her uncle's face there, the side of his face, and she shut her eyes hard to get rid of it . . . when she opened them she saw only her mother again.

"He died in awful pain . . ." her mother said wonderingly.

They were on a street near home.

"You're not glad he's dead," her mother said. She cleared her throat. "How can you say anything so awful? You . . . you won't see him again and he was so good to you. . . . There weren't any police chasing him."

"Yes, a police car with a siren!"

"There weren't any police! Nobody said anything about any police!"

"A police car. . . ."

Betsy's mother said angrily, "Don't you make up any lies about the police, or anything like what you said, the crazy things you said, you hadn't better ever say them again! You hadn't better!"

Betsy felt a tickling inside her that meant she would have a fit of giggling, and, if she did, her mother might slap her; her mother did not like giggling. She did not tease her about it the way her uncle did. Her mother did not like her to cry either, when she sometimes cried and could not stop. So she forced the tickling to go away.

"All those lies. . . . You better not say them again. . . ."

She parked the car in the driveway. She came around to open the door for Betsy, who was feeling too light to walk, as if the tickling had gotten loose in her blood. Her mother gathered her up into her arms as if Betsy were a little girl. She said, frightened, "You made up such lies, what are things like that doing in your mind. . . ?"

Betsy stared at her mother. Something was ragged about her mother's eyes, the edges of her eyes, the lashes. They looked bent.

Her mother took hold of her by the shoulders and gave her a small, panicked shake.

"You're sorry he's dead!" her mother said.

Her mother was breathing hard. Around her was the smell of panic and sweat. Betsy hoped her mother would not vomit, would not die, collapsing red-faced into her arms.

"You're sorry, aren't you sorry? Nothing else but sorry?"

Her fingers dug in, panicked. "Please, please," her mother said, staring at her. At last Betsy nodded until the terror in her mother's body had passed away.

*T*he Daughter

One day in August a woman and her daughter were traveling by Greyhound bus from the city of Derby to the Rapids, a section of dairy country to the west. It was late afternoon and they had been on the bus since six, with only two rest stops so far. The mother, Anna, lay back sleepily in her seat beside the green-tinted window, gazing out without much interest at the muted streaks of land. She was a handsome woman of about thirty, with short, streaked blond hair, a tanned face that looked rather cunning in repose. Yet she was thinking of nothing: the unfinished bar of chocolate in her purse, perhaps. But she could not eat it because her aunt would have supper ready for them when they arrived and she did not want to spoil her appetite. So she sighed and looked back out at the infrequent houses and stretches of low dipping land dotted with cows.

51

The country came to her like slabs of the past. This gazing pasture —little hills frantically sloping in and around, twisting back upon themselves to avoid shallow streams—with its cows and occasional horses and its attendant houses and barns, all streaming fluidly by her window as if offering themselves to her judgment: the land of her childhood, of her past, kept absolutely unchanged for her return. Yet she felt almost nothing. On her lap her rather stubby fingers were locked together lazily, colorless nails filed down short and neat, at rest, in a kind of stupor that seemed to overtake her often. She thought suddenly that she could ride on this bus forever. She loved everything she had known—her daughter and her apartment in the city and the man she was going to marry and her husband, though she had not seen him for some time, and the food her aunt would prepare for her and the new shoes she was wearing, impractical though they were for the bus (spike-heeled white shoes with little golden buckles): and yet she could surrender them, forget them, and go on riding. She would be too lazy to get off the bus. She was too lazy to keep her eyes open, and her thick pale lashes lowered to confuse the land outside the tinted glass, so that it blurred into what memory should be, something powerless and inconsequential.

Thalia, her daughter, was pretending to read. On her lap was an old library book with its pages stained and dog-eared. Nervously she bent a corner of the page back and forth until it came loose in her fingers—then she did not know what to do with it. She slid it in between the pages at the back of the book. She forced herself to read:

'What new phase of this character is this?' exclaimed Mrs. Linton, in amazement. 'I've treated you infernally—and you'll take revenge! How will you take it, ungrateful brute? How have I treated you infernally?'

'I seek no revenge on you,' replied Heathcliff less vehemently. . . .

A child began to cry in one of the seats ahead and Thalia looked up.

She had a thin, narrow face, rather large eyes that seemed to attach themselves anxiously to objects, as if she could not see well. Her hair was brown, cut short like her mother's, but straight while Anna's was wavy, so that she sometimes looked years younger than fourteen. When she thought of her age, or of herself, she thought also of her stepfather, as if they were collaborators in something, and now the realization that they were going to see him rushed upon her again, unbelievable and frightening. Her mother called him Jake. When she wanted to, she spoke of him as if he were off in the next room and not miles away, years away. Thalia could not call him Jake and had no other name to call him, nothing at all, so she could never speak of him first but had to wait for her mother to mention him. Sometimes when weeks passed without Anna speaking of him, Thalia would begin to think that Anna had forgotten him. But no, he was always there, he might have been locked in a closet, safely kept, the man Thalia remembered sitting by himself on the front porch of that old house in the country, waiting for supper, waiting for Anna, sitting and doing nothing but thinking, silent and unhappy, a tall dark-haired man who had seemed to her then very big, with hands she stared at, they were so rough and stained with work, and streaks of perspiration on his back like twin wings when he got up finally to go inside. Thalia stared at the back of the seat before her—part of the plastic seatcover had been ripped and was starting to unravel. Her hand jerked out to fix it, press the edges together. Then she let it go. She tried to read:

'What new phase of his character is this?' exclaimed Mrs. Linton, in amazement. . . .

"Oh, what the hell time is it?" Anna said, shaking her head. "I fell asleep, my neck hurts." She picked her purse up off the floor and took out her package of cigarettes. "Will you ask that man across the way what time it is, honey," Anna said. "God, I hate these buses. I used to ride in them when I wanted to go anywhere, living out in the sticks like this. I should have let Lewis drive us up, I suppose. But it's better for us to come alone, at first, then I can tell them about him and our plans, not that I give a damn what they think. . . . Thalia, ask that man what time it is. Over there."

"I don't want to," Thalia whispered, embarrassed. "It's about five o'clock or five-thirty—"

"I said ask him, go ahead. Why are you always so shy?"

Across the aisle a middle-aged man sat reading a newspaper. His head was tilted back slightly and he wore a tweedish suit that was too warm for August. Thalia peered at him timidly and was going to say, "Excuse me, please," when her mother leaned around impatiently and said, "Say, mister, what time is it?" The man blinked at her and at his watch. "Five-thirty," he said. "Thanks a lot," said Anna, sitting back. Thalia toyed with the other corner of the page. "Yes, I used to ride these buses all the time," Anna said. She had lit a cigarette and Thalia could see smudges of lipstick on it as she held it between her fingers. "Up and down the line. My girl friend lived four miles away, after she got married. I was married then too, that was your father I was married to then, and she and I had our babies right the same summer—I was fifteen then—God, fifteen, think of that! What a long time ago—" Thalia's face began to burn as if she had heard something forbidden. She stared at the print down before her but could read nothing. In that instant she hated her mother, of course she hated her mother. At school no one could pronounce "Thalia" and thought she was a foreigner: just because her mother had seen the name in a magazine and thought it "sounded nice." The only time Anna had ever been hurt by Thalia was the time Thalia had said she hated her name, but of course she was sorry and did not hate it, not really, just as she did not really hate her mother. . . . She would have liked to ask her about her stepfather now, since they would be seeing him so soon, but she did not know what to say. Anna sat smiling, lost in a recollection of something that pleased her; perhaps she was thinking of seeing Jake again. Thalia felt suddenly shy before her.

*

The bus driver announced, "Rapids Center, half-hour stop," in a flat, bored voice, as if he thought little of the Rapids. Thalia was leaning forward in her seat, looking out at the narrow street ahead, at the old-fashioned stores with their fraudulent third-story fronts, all curved and decorated with knobs and juttings. Thalia had not remembered that the town was so old. In the city, buildings were higher, newer. Cars were not parked as they were here, with their bumpers slanted up to the sidewalk so that the street had hardly more than two lanes for traffic. Downtown, people did not cross anywhere in the street, as they did here—Thalia saw a woman and two children and a black dog hurry in front of the bus and disappear onto the sidewalk, safe, without even glancing around. And everyone looked slightly different: just as Anna had always looked different from the women in the city, a slow complacent tawny cat, indolent with health, easily pleased, while the other women had meticulous porcelain faces and enameled nails and nervous mannerisms. "Hey, they fixed the bus station up," Anna said. The old building had been painted a thin white and had obviously been a gas station at one time—Thalia saw that now, but she had never realized it before. "And there they are, Aunt Ruth and Ernest—you remember them?" The bus had stopped. Anna urged Thalia out into the aisle; she was always anxious to be the first off a bus, the first in line, the first to be served. Thalia struggled to pull her suitcase down and Anna reached up to help her. "Here, honey," she said. "Now go up to the front. Get ahead of them in that seat there—go on."

Anna and the aunt greeted each other loudly. The aunt spoke with the Hungarian accent Thalia remembered and could detect in her mother's speech now and then; she hoped desperately that it was not somehow hidden in her own. Anna's cousin, Ernest, a plump man of about forty in a straw hat, picked up the suitcases, grunting. Anna kept tugging at Thalia's arm and saying, "Look who I've got here! Look the size she's got!" The aunt's wrinkled, rather cross face turned upon Thalia possessively; Thalia held her breath and allowed herself to be hugged. "Taller than you, Anna," she said. "Is this all? No other surprise, eh?" Anna and Ernest laughed at this; the aunt nodded wisely, making a face; Thalia did not understand. Following them to the car, Thalia listened to their voices and thought that what was happening was as she had supposed would happen: she did not fit in with them, the whole visit would be like this.

Now they were laughing at something—Anna was tapping Ernest's stomach—and Thalia lagged behind, she could not join them, she could not surrender to the rhythms of their speech. There was no one's language she could surrender to, really. Like her stepfather—she thought of him suddenly—at some picnic, a firemen's picnic years ago, when some friends of his had asked him to join a softball game and he had refused: he just could not do it, could not fit in with hilarity, did not have the grace that Anna possessed so richly. "Looking good, Anna, real good," the aunt said as they backed out into the street. She narrowed her old eyes to stare at Anna, rather rudely. Anna pretended to hide her face, laughing. "And now this about Jake," the old woman said slyly, "you know, he was over to see us when he got your letter, wanted to know if we got one too. I said where else should she stay except with us? That man hates us, don't he, Ernie? My boy here don't run into Jake much any more, Jake keeps to himself. But he got raised up at the job—got a better job there, where he waits around in the front and handles orders, answers telephone calls—" "Still at the sawmill?" Anna said. "Yes, still there, but now up front, where they have the office," the aunt said. "But still at the sawmill," Anna said, making a face, "and all that dust in his hair and skin—" "No, it's better now, he don't run the wood in the saws," the aunt said.

Everyone spoke loudly; Thalia winced. She looked away at the street, which was turning into a gravel road as they left town. Now she heard the name "Jake" from them, but it meant nothing. It was impersonal. They might have been groping for him, trying to prod him, hurt him, while their voices grew louder and occasionally a remark of Ernest's made them all laugh. "No, no, no woman that I ever heard of," the aunt said, shaking her head energetically, "no woman for him—I tell you no, not one, never heard of it. No." Anna expressed disbelief; she seemed quite excited. "No, no," the aunt insisted. They talked on. A recital of marriages and babies: Anna exclaimed at the mention of each. A short list of the dead. "And I should go out to George's grave," Anna said, but vaguely, "and put some flowers there. . . . How is his grave?" "Don't know, never remember to look," the aunt said. Thalia stared at the back of her head—an untidy knot of iron-gray hair—and thought that she hated this old woman too. George was her father. Thalia herself could not remember him, for he had died when she was six or seven and Anna had already left him for Jake. When she tried to remember him the only person she thought of was an old man who had lived down the road—and Anna had always laughed, as if Thalia's trying to recall this insignificant, dead, lost man was inexplicable.

"So I wrote him that five years of this was enough and I take all the blame myself," Anna said, leaning forward to talk with them better, "and we got to break it up once and for all—that's what was in his letter. He wrote me some letters a while back but I forgot to answer them. I'm not mad at him—what the hell was that going around here, that he broke my jaw or something? Who started that rumor? He never touched me, I never touched him. Nothing like that. He's the best man around here—you try to find a better one. I know. But wife and husband living in two places is wrong and so I want to end it." The aunt peered at Anna. "So you want to get the divorce, then?" "Yes, I want a divorce," Anna said. The word seemed to alarm them, it was so alien and legal; for a moment no one spoke. "How do you do that, get it done by a judge?" the aunt said. "I have a lawyer," Anna said. "He's coming up tomorrow. I want to talk to Jake by myself first, then all of us can talk together. Get everything straightened out." "How much does that cost?" said the aunt suspiciously. "You have a lawyer coming up here for

yourself? How coming, on a bus? How did you find out about how
to do it?" "A friend of mine is coming too," Anna said, smiling
slowly, "he's paying for it, he knows everything. Don't worry."
"Ah, a friend," said the aunt. After a while she said, "You want me
to cook for him too? How long staying?" Anna brushed her hair out
of her face angrily. "No, I don't want you to cook for him," she
said. She sat back, breathing heavily, and Thalia saw the skirt of
her dress twist into a new pattern of wrinkles as she crossed her leg.
They were nearly at the old farmhouse before the aunt ventured
to take up the conversation again.

Anna felt comfortable and welcome in her aunt's house, just as
she had felt as a child when her own parents had sent her to spend
the summer here, working in the dairy; Anna's parents had had
eleven children and Anna had been the youngest. But really no
memories distracted her from the meal—a rich goulash, exactly the
dish she had hoped her aunt would make, with homemade bread
and cherry pie afterward. Except that Thalia seemed to have little
appetite; but then, Anna had never been able to understand her
daughter and was inclined to dismiss her impatiently. At that age,
she thought, she had been a woman; she had had no real childhood
but had always been an adult, disguised as a child for years but
really an adult. She had worked like an adult, had listened quietly
to the conversations of adults, and had accepted everything. Never
had a corner of her mind resisted the illumination of knowledge,
any kind of knowledge: nothing had ever seemed to her too sordid
to be true. Gradually all things—her father's drunkenness, her first
husband's cowlike weakness, the cancer that had killed her mother,
the drought that plagued everyone in late summer, the bitterness of
winter, ants in sugar bowls, toothaches, the long lethargy of having
a baby, the finality of the grave that overtook everyone in time—all
—blurred as if they were no more than water in water, everything
blended to the same texture, so that Anna never condemned anything that was "the way life is." She had learned that as a child, but

Thalia had learned nothing. During supper Thalia had sat outlining the figure of a flower in the oilcloth that covered the table, not looking up, as if she thought herself too good for these people. No lights were on in the kitchen, and through the back window came long lazy rays of sunlight to touch the walls—woodwork from the rail down, gray striped wallpaper from the rail up to the ceiling—and to illuminate faces, making them subtle and tender, even Ernest's plump sweating face, and Thalia's face queerly strained and pretty, the face of someone Anna loved but did not really know.

After supper she was brushing her hair in the room she and Thalia were going to share while they were in the Rapids. "Is he coming over now?" Thalia said. "Where are you going?" "I'll make him take me to Sonny's—I always liked that place," Anna said. She noticed Thalia's face in the mirror, then, and was startled—Thalia was staring at the wall, at nothing, with her mouth twisted into an ugly smile. For a moment Anna thought that this smile was directed at something she had said. "What's wrong with you?" Anna said, turning. She pointed at her daughter with the hairbrush. "Why such a face?" Thalia was holding a book on her lap and now she raised it before her chest, as if frightened. "I was—I was thinking of him," she said. "So? What about him?" said Anna. "Just that I can't remember what he looks like," Thalia whispered. "I don't want to see him. I'm not going out." Anna shrugged her shoulders and turned away. "After five years, not even say hello to him? I thought you liked him better than that. What's wrong with you today?" Thalia was turning the pages of the book slowly. "You said you'd tell me why you left here," Thalia said. "When I got old enough. You left me with *him* for five months, I was ten then and I marked the calendar, and then you came back and said we were both going and you'd tell me why later on. You never told me." Anna hardly listened. She was pleased with her hair, which glowed in the musty light of this room—the shadowy background of mysterious cupboards and high ceiling seemed to push Anna forward into the mirror, the pores of her fine healthy skin illuminated, the firm line of her jaw emphasized, her eyes—Jake had said they were like cat's eyes—made complex by a pale tangle of lashes. "You said you'd tell me," Thalia said childishly. Anna stood. She picked up her purse. Had she heard a car outside in the driveway? She started to leave, but Thalia jumped up. "Mother," she said. The word was awkward between them, not a word Thalia ever used. "You said you'd tell me why you left him." Anna waved her back impatiently, dismissing her. "I'll tell you why when I leave the next one," she said. "Read your book."

Thalia lay on the bed. A single light was on, a little lamp on the chest of drawers that Anna said her aunt had won at a church bingo game years ago. The main part of the lamp was a tree, painted a vivid brown, against which two child-lovers sat, their cheeks a bright pink. The lampshade was a deep rich orange, scalloped at the bottom. Thalia stared at the little lamp and tried to concentrate her hatred upon it. When tears bothered her she rubbed her eyes viciously. She kept thinking of herself in this room when her mother went out, hurrying, her footsteps going right out to the side door and so out to Jake. Thalia had wanted to go with her, had been about to run after her, but had done no more than stand at the door, frozen, listening to the car drive off. Had he really been out there, was that really the man they had lived with at one time? Thalia felt dizzy, overcome by the riddle of life, by the mystery of love and relationships so abruptly lost, discarded. . . . Mr. Harber, who was going to marry Anna, was nothing at all like Jake. The other men Anna had brought to the apartment had been nothing at all like Jake. Thalia took her image of him from the house and the land that had surrounded their life at that time—the old house Anna had hated, with its mice and termites and rain barrels and the cistern in the damp cellar that would go dry in late summer, and the attic heaped with junk, stifling hot from June to September, and the abandoned barns and barnyard, and the sorrowing sunburned land, no longer farmed, that stretched back to a small woods Thalia had played in—and he seemed to her a figure not lost in this confusion, overcome not by the vastness of land he had inherited and could not sell or by the job he had had at the sawmill, back-breaking labor that paid little, but instead by the relentless gravitation of those he loved away from him: Anna mainly, for he had always loved her, he had loved her when there was no longer any reason for loving her. That was the part of Anna she hated, Thalia thought, that shadowy side that kept betraying her and others, smiling in that slow charming way with her eyes calm, her shoulders and arms at rest, her whole body at rest, nothing nervous, nothing anxious, a blond feline body that wished no one harm or pain and therefore never accepted the responsibility for the harm and pain people around her did suffer.

She woke suddenly. It was dark and Anna was in the room. "Thalia, honey," she said, "are you asleep? Get up, come on. He wants to take us down for some ice cream. A frozen custard stand, we passed it coming home, a nice new one, are you awake? Come on, you like ice cream." Thalia did not want to go, her heart had begun throbbing painfully, but Anna would not listen. "Your hair's all right, who's going to look at you?" she laughed. She pushed Thalia out ahead of her. Anna's happiness meant that Jake would be unhappy, Thalia thought; it had always been that way.

He was sitting with the car door open, waiting. "Hi, Thalia," he said. Anna was prodding her from behind. "Hi," said Thalia shyly. Anna's aunt had turned the outside light on, so that Thalia could see his face. He had dark, short hair, a firm chin something like Anna's and, like Anna, a face that told nothing about itself—except that with Jake it was restraint while with Anna it was simplicity. "Isn't she big? Taller than me," Anna said proudly. Thalia's face burned. She got into the car and sat between Jake and her mother. Her heart was pounding. Anna talked on while Jake backed the car out onto the road. Thalia stared at his hands on the steering wheel, such angular, hard, brutal hands, with tufts of dark hair faint on the back of each finger, and she had the idea that Jake was not listening to Anna either. Sometimes, in the old days, Anna had talked excitedly to him at meals, as if she had no reason to be silent before him, and he had not answered. When he had drunk too much he had not talked wildly, like other men, but seemed to withdraw into his silence as if it were a physical barrier that protected him. It was for his silence that Thalia loved him. Yet she felt guilt in his presence, guilt and shame for her mother's betrayal of him, and for her own part in it. For hadn't she wanted to go with her mother? When Anna had come back that day, the weeks of hating her had vanished at once and Ann's magical words and caresses had charmed Thalia completely; of course she had wanted to go. Through the pauses in her mother's conversation Thalia listened to her stepfather's silence, a silence like a vast shadowy hole into which all her strength was sucked. I love him better than her, Thalia thought. I know that now. I love him better than anybody, I want to make him happy, I want to make up for what she did to him. . . . "Lewis —you know—doesn't want me to work now but I won't give it up," Anna was saying. "I like to be my own boss, not just sit around home all the time. Thalia, what's wrong with you? Eh?" Thalia hid her face and began sobbing suddenly. She was overcome by shame. Anna put her arm around her, murmuring, "Now, now, all right, you're just tired from that bus. . . ." Thalia rubbed her eyes with her fists to make herself stop crying; she was desperate to think that her stepfather was impatient with her. After a while Jake said, clearing his throat as if he were not accustomed to speaking, "She's turning into a pretty girl, Anna." "Oh, yes, what did I tell you?" Anna said. She was stroking Thalia's hair. "But so young yet, so weak." In the silence that followed they thought of that: of weakness, of the ignobility of being weak, delicate, vulnerable to betrayal, loving rather than everlastingly beloved.

That night Thalia sat up slowly, listening to her mother's breathing. They were sharing the big double bed with its musty feather pillows. The room was faint with moonlight, and Thalia felt its cool sinister tranquillity calm her: for hours her mind had been racing helplessly, her heart had throbbed as if some crisis were about to be met. She got out of bed quietly. At first she had no idea what she was going to do and as she dressed her mind was empty—anything filled it: the shadowy clutter of the room or the sound of insects outside or Anna's peaceful breathing. Then, as she opened the door very carefully, her eyes narrowed, her body taut with listening, she knew where she was going.

Later she was to remember her leaving the house and running through the wet grass to the road as if it were a scene in a novel or in a movie, something that had happened to another person. Once on the road she had been beset by fears, by a clamor of voices, by a strange hysterical conviction that she had lost her way. A car approached; she hid, terrified, in the ditch. Nothing. She ran along the road until her chest rose and fell painfully, and then she walked, stumbling on small rocks that had seemed to her no more than shadows. The sky was riddled with clouds, high and milky, shot with moonlight on one side and on the other eaten with shadow, lost in the blackness of the sky. It took her no more than ten minutes to get to Jake's house and, as she approached the veranda, she realized that she had never seen it like this before: she had lived in it for years, had taken it for granted, but had never seen it as Anna must have seen it so often, blackened and desolate as the old farm buildings out back.

Jake let her in only a minute or so after she had knocked; he must not have been asleep. He stared at her and then behind her, leaning around in the doorway, while she began, at once, "I'm not going with her. I'm not going with them, I hate them both, I'm going to stay here. I want to stay here." Jake stared at her as if he did not quite recognize her. "What are you doing here?" he said. Thalia said wildly, "I'm not, I'm not going with them! I'm staying here. I'm not going." Jake closed the door slowly. He had turned on a dingy overhead light and now, as if moving clumsily in his sleep, he urged her somewhere—to the sofa. "Here, sit down," he said faintly.

"She doesn't know you're here, does she?" It was a statement, not a question, but Thalia answered it in a shrill angry voice, "She's asleep, she's always asleep. She takes naps every afternoon—nothing wakes her up. *I* can't sleep at night. Nothing bothers her." Jake went back to the door and peered outside. "What are you looking for?" Thalia said. "I'm alone, I came alone. I left her there sleeping—" He did not turn to her; Thalia stared at him as if trying to guess his expression, his thoughts; what was wrong? He wore a soiled pair of overalls and no shirt; he was barefoot. "How did you get here?" he said. Finally he looked at her, over his shoulder. His face told her absolutely nothing. "I'm not afraid," Thalia said. "I can walk anywhere by myself. I can do anything." "And why did you come here?" said Jake. "I can live here like before," said Thalia. "It can all be the same except for her—" "Why do you want to stay here?" said Jake. "He's got a lot of money, doesn't he?" "I hate him and her both, I wish they were both dead," Thalia said viciously. "I wish their car would crash when they go out driving—" She felt her mouth twist into something ugly, so that Jake himself lowered his eyes. He had begun to walk nervously around in front of her and now he paused, patting his pockets. He went into the other room and came back with a pack of cigarettes. Thalia was saying breathlessly, "This is such a big house, it needs somebody to clean it out and cook and fix up the yard—I could go to school in town, like I was. They don't want me anyway, if they go on that long trip—I don't have anywhere else to go but here—" Jake had lit a cigarette. He sat wearily on the arm of the sofa. Now Thalia saw how cluttered the parlor was: the rug was discolored with dust, the curtains limp, junk lay in the fireplace, on the old dining-room table newspapers lay scattered about. A few had fallen onto the floor. There was a faded rectangle on the wall near the door where a picture had hung for years—Thalia remembered it, it had been an aged photograph of Jake's grandparents on their wedding day. "Why don't you say something, what's wrong?" Thalia whispered. Something was going to happen to her, she thought, she was going to be sick, going to lose control of herself. She would run back to where her mother lay sleeping and seize her by the throat. . . . "I hate them, I wish they were both dead and myself too," she said bitterly. "I don't have anywhere to go. When she leaves him, what if she leaves me too? What if I have to stay with him?" "She never left you behind," Jake said sharply. "Once she did, you know she did!" Thalia cried. "She left me here with you and then came back! And the next one of them, after *him*, might not want me, what am I to do then?" "What's this about the next one?" Jake said. He was smiling contemptuously. "Does she have one in mind already?" "I don't want to be with them," Thalia said, "if I was just older now—eighteen—then I could come here and live somewhere so that I could see you. I could do that then. You couldn't stop me. I'd do that and come to see you and clean up here and cook things and we could be together." But it sounded wrong: she heard herself in astonishment. Jake flicked ashes onto the floor. "I could come here and be with you," Thalia whispered. "I love you." But, as she said this, suddenly she was not sure of what she meant or to whom she was speaking. "In what way do you love me?" Jake said coldly. Thalia stared up at him. "I'm not your father," he said. "I don't have anything to do with you." "But I love you," Thalia said. "What the hell," Jake said impatiently, "what's that? What does that mean?" "I said I want to stay here," Thalia cried bitterly, "you can't stop me, you're my stepfather—you have to take me if I want to come! If I keep coming and sleep out on the porch, you have to take me!" "Like hell I have to take you," Jake said.

Thalia stood. She went to the table and pushed the newspapers off, senselessly. "I said you have to take me! If you don't, I'll run away from her anyway and come back here, I'll hitchhike for rides, neither one of you can stop me! I don't care what happens! I hate them both and hate everybody, the kids at school and people in stores, her aunt and her cousin—and myself, most of all myself—The only person I love is you, I've been waiting for years to see you again and thinking about you, and now you don't say anything—I want to stay here again like before and I'm going to, I'm going to cook for you and clean up in here, I used to help her dust these things, and nothing would bother me—if the water runs low I wouldn't care—and she wouldn't be here for us to wait for at night— That used to make me sick, how you would wait for her, sitting in the kitchen—I knew it all, I saw it! I wished she was dead then!" "I wished she was dead too," Jake said.

Thalia felt suddenly exhausted. She stared at him; he did not meet her gaze, and she was terrified suddenly by the idea that she did not really know him—she knew someone, loved someone, but perhaps it was not quite this man. "She wouldn't let you stay here," Jake said slowly. "What?" said Thalia. He was rubbing his face wearily. His eyes were bewildered, suspicious; as always they asked why this had happened to him, why he was alone, what was wrong with him?—as if there were some joke about him that everyone else could see. "Then I can stay?" said Thalia. "I don't care what you do," he said. Thalia stared at him. She felt the table hard behind her, she was pressing back against it as if for strength. "Then I can stay?" she whispered. Jake shrugged his shoulders. "Stay," he said. He met her look and seemed to flinch slightly. Sitting on the arm of the sofa, he had let his shoulders slump so that his chest looked narrow and slightly hollow. He looked older than thirty-five. He looked vaguely like the man Thalia always thought of when she tried to remember her real father. . . . "Come here, sit down," he said. "You're tired or sick or something. You better rest. There might be something wrong with you." "No, nothing wrong, nothing wrong," Thalia said faintly.

She had fallen asleep on the sofa while Jake sat there, smoking. Anna came a few hours later. "Is this where she is? Is she in there?" Anna was crying, before Jake had even opened the door. "There—there," Anna said, pushing past him. She pointed at Thalia, who was lying on the sofa but with her eyes open now, blinking stupidly. "Look at this! Shame, shame! Snuck out of bed and come after him, I didn't know anything! Ernie and me, out in the car, we kept looking for somebody dead by the road all the way over here! Now you get out there, you! Get out there in the car!" She wore the yellow dress buttoned carelessly about her; in flat shoes she looked muscular and alert, as if she were ready to fly at one of them. She went to Thalia and would have yanked her up, except Thalia drew away with a queer contemptuous smile and said, "It's all changed now. I don't need to go with you." "What, all changed now? What's changed?" Anna said. She looked from Thalia to Jake. "What happened here?" "He said I could stay with him now," Thalia said. "Did you say that, you?" Anna cried. She tapped at Jake's chest with her fist. "That's what you told her, eh? Is it?" "Sure, why not?" said Jake. Anna was breathing heavily. She stood between them, glaring, biting her bottom lip with her teeth. After a moment she said, more quietly, "Thalia, you go outside to sit with Ernie. We must talk about this." "I don't need to," Thalia said, wiping her nose with the back of her hand. "I live here now. That's what he said." Anna was struck by the girl's face: she looked pale and terrified, the face of a victim seen photographed for newspapers or magazines, some anonymous creature half a world away. "But what is this, I can't understand," Anna murmured. "Thalia, please, go outside so we can talk. Your stepfather and me, we need to talk." "I'm not leaving," Thalia whispered. "If you make me leave, then I can't come back." "No, no," Anna said, "we just want to talk. We must straighten this out." "I don't need to go, do I?" Thalia said to Jake. "I don't give a damn about it," he said. "Look, please, tell her to go out there and wait," Anna said. "Why should I?" said Jake. "Please, you know better. You tell her, she wants to hear it from you." "All right, go out there," Jake said. Thalia sat up slowly. "Will you come out and tell me when to come back in?" she said. "Sure," said Jake. "Will you promise?" said Thalia. "Sure," he said.

She went out. They heard the car door slam. "Now, what's this business you're trying?" Anna said. "She came here by herself, I had nothing to do with it," Jake said. "Don't ask me." "But what's this

business you told her she could stay. What's this?" said Anna. "She
says she has nowhere to go. And she hates you. So what's wrong
with it?" said Jake. "Hates me?" said Anna. "No, my daughter, that
I don't believe—No, not that—Not my daughter—" she was pacing around, staring everywhere as if looking for help, strength. What
had happened? How had she lost control? She had been frightened
for the first time in her life by Thalia's tight, pale face, that grimace
that was the look of a dying stranger. She had been thinking of
Thalia as dead, and now she could not quite think of her as alive.
"What are you trying?" she said. "I'm not letting her go—I have
custody of her. You're not her father! What the hell, you telling her
she could stay! How would that look? My God, what a mess, I
never thought—When we had ice cream she was so quiet, all her
life she was so quiet, never did I—But anyway she can't stay here,
are you crazy? You have no right to tell her that!"

"When she gets old enough to leave you, then she'll come back,"
Jake said. "She promised me that."

"Promised you? Come back here, why? If anybody comes back
here, I'll come back," Anna said viciously. "Little bitch! Did you
make love to her? Eh, is that it? Dirty bastard—look at you, without
a shirt! Your feet are dirty! Isn't that dirt? So she promised you
that, did she? Coming back to do what for you? I never knew, never
knew—she doesn't talk to me about anything—So she's in love
with you."

"She has to be in love with someone."

"Yes, yes," Anna said nodding, "so right. . . . That's how we all
are, even me. Even you. Maybe I'll come back to you, what then?
You're better than him, I make no secret of it, but this goddam
town and that sawdust all over you, in your ears, and you were born
here same as me—I wouldn't find one like you again, but six years
we were together and that was that, the hell with it. And now her,
look at that! My God! You think you can get her from me! She
loves you, she fell in love with you somehow, she doesn't know it
herself maybe but I know it—Anyway you think you can get her!

You think I wouldn't know how to fight you! And what do you feel about her?"

"I don't know," said Jake.

"Do you remember her, even?" Anna's heart was pounding violently. Her face and body were damp with perspiration. "You, I could kill you," she muttered. She went to the side window and looked out: just before dawn, a hazy colorless sky, birds perched motionless in trees.

"She said she didn't have anywhere else to go," Jake said. "I know what that could be like. And this house here is so big, if there was someone here with me, someone to talk to—"

"So find another woman! Go out and get one, they all liked you!" Anna wanted to rush at him and claw at his face. She felt her fingers twitching. "Any woman would be glad for you, why have you wasted all these years? Five years, is it? Waiting for me? Goddam you for staying here and waiting! But if you're alone that's not my fault and not her fault, she's not going to ruin her life for you!"

"You can't stop her from it," said Jake. "One way or another—"

"Go to hell!" Anna screamed. They were staring at each other. Anna wiped her face against the shoulder of her dress, panting. "What a bastard you are after all," she said. "And this house, always so hot, this dirty country always so hot," she said, pulling at the collar of her dress, shaking her hair angrily out of her face. "Just like I remember. Everything." As if losing her patience, she jerked at the collar of the dress so that the first button came undone. "You bastard with your dirty feet," she whispered. "Just like that you came to me that time, where was I? Out by the mailbox. Come up in your car, thought you were smart, and the look you had then was dirty like dirt—how you looked at me! Then I would come back home and go to bed where he was sleeping, all those nights, and smelling of you right then—I told you that if I did that with you, then after I was married to you I would do it with other men. When it came true, why were you surprised?—What a hot old house, that attic hot all summer," Anna said. She had begun to smile at him. Jake, watching her, did not return the smile. She kicked her shoes off so that they struck the wall, one and then the other. "Smell the dust in here, what a nice dirty place," Anna said. "Nice dirty sofa there. What is your bed like, all sweaty and dirty?" She came up to him. In her bare feet she had to tilt back her head to look at him. She tapped at his chest with her fist. "You're not going out there, not going to see her again," she whispered. She brushed his hair back off his damp forehead. He drew away a little and she slapped his face, hard. Jake stared down at her. He resisted her smile. "Why are you waiting?" she said. "What the hell is wrong with you? Come to me, come, you know how nice I am, come to me, you want to let that little girl alone, you come to me instead! I want you here, you must know that, you can tell it—" She smiled at him angrily and unbuttoned the front of her dress. "All right, sure," Jake said. He touched her shoulder and she shook her hair back again impatiently. "Come to me, you know how you want to," she said, and as she spoke she began to lose control of her words, of her voice, so that she hardly knew what she was saying, did not have to think about it at all. She was confused, enchanted, and by his look she saw suddenly that everything was safe; she could not tell whether she lived in this house or had only come for some reason or was married to someone else, some man twenty years older than she; nothing mattered, she remembered nothing.

Thalia lay in the back seat of the car. She was waiting, for minutes and minutes she was waiting, then suddenly she quit; she seemed to have broken loose from something, become free, helpless, chilled. Ernest, in his straw hat despite the time of day, waited for a while in the front seat, whistling through his teeth. Then he got out of the car and strolled along the road, kicking at stones. Thalia lay and stared at the dirty back of the front seat. Some kind of woven seat cover, ripped and soiled. . . .

When she heard someone approaching the car she sat up at once.

But it was Anna. She walked through the high grass of the front yard to the car. She was barefoot, she carried her shoes in one hand; Thalia could see the firm muscles in her legs tense and disappear as she walked, assert themselves and vanish smoothly into the sleek line of her legs. Through the open window mother and daughter looked at each other for a moment, then Anna opened the door and got in. She sat in front, she might have thought herself alone. She took no notice of Thalia, did not glance over at Ernest, who was jumping a ditch to return to the car. She moved her arms experimentally as if she expected them to ache. She drew her hand across her forehead, hard, and lifted her hair from her neck: Thalia sucked in her breath to see the skin there raw and scraped, as if clawed, slashed by teeth. There was no blood, but little white flecks of skin protruded out from the smooth surface of her skin, and from them long reddened marks careened like sluggish worms burrowing to the surface. Ernest started the car. "So hot already," Anna said dreamily. She lay back against the seat, let her hair fall back against her neck. She might have been speaking to herself. "They're coming later today, then, that's good, I have plenty of time. . . . Then we can leave. How I hate this country, always so hot. . . ." Thalia did not look around at the house as they drove away. She did not look outside at anything. She watched the back of her mother's head, that jagged, streaked blond hair, and could see just beneath it the reddened marks that made so mysterious and beautiful a wound.

In the Warehouse

"Why does your mother do that to her hair? Does she think it looks nice or something?"

"Do what to her hair?"

"Frizz it up or whatever that is—she's such an ugly old bag! If I looked like that I'd stick my head in the oven!"

The two girls are standing out on the sidewalk before a house, at twilight. The taller one makes vast good-humored gestures in the air as she talks, and the other stands silently, her lips pursed. She has a small, dark, patient face; her brown hair falls in thick puffy bangs across her forehead. The taller girl has hair that is in no style at all —just messy, not very clean, pulled back from her big face and, fixed with black bobby pins, which are the wrong color for her dark blond hair. She has a lot to talk about. She is talking now about

Nancy, who lives a few houses away. Nancy is eighteen and works uptown in a store; she thinks she's too good for everyone—"I could show her a thing or two, just give me a match and let me at that dyed hair of hers"—and her mother is grumpy and ugly, like everyone's mother, "just an old bitch that might as well be dead."

It is autumn. Down the street kids are playing after supper, running along between houses or all the way down to the open area that is blocked off because of an expressway nearby. "You don't want to go in already, do you?" the taller girl whines. "Why d'ya always want to go in, you think your house is so hot? Your goddam mother is so hot? We could walk down by the warehouse, see if anybody's around. Just for something to do."

"I better go in."

"Your mother isn't calling you, is she? What's so hot about going in that dump of a house?"

I am the short, dark girl, and my friend Ronnie is laughing into my face as she always does. Ronnie lives two houses away. Her mother has five children and no husband—he died or ran away—and Ronnie is the middle child, thirteen years old. She is big for her age. I am twelve, skinny and meek and incredulous as she jumps to another subject: how Nancy's boy friend slapped her around and burned her with his cigar just the other night. "Don't you believe me? You think I'm lying?" she challenges me.

"I never heard about that."

"So what? Nobody'd tell you anything. You'd tell the cops or something."

"No I wouldn't."

"Some cop comes to see your father, don't he?"

"He's just somebody—some old friend. I don't know who he is," I tell her, but it's too late. My whining voice gives Ronnie what she needs. It's like an opening for a wedge or the toe of her worn-out old "Indian" moccasins. She pinches my arm and I say feebly, "Don't. That hurts."

"Oh, does it hurt?"

She pinches me again.

"I said don't—"

She laughs and forgets about it. She's a big strong girl. Her legs are thick. Her face is round and her teeth are a little crooked, so that she looks as if she is always smiling. In school she sits at the back and makes trouble, hiding her yellowish teeth behind her hand when she laughs. One day she said to our teacher—our teacher is Mrs. Gunderson—"There was a man out by the front door who did something bad. He opened up his pants and everything." Mrs. Gunderson was always nervous. She told Ronnie to come out into the hall with her, and everyone tried to listen, and in a minute she called me out too. Ronnie said to me, "Wasn't that Mr. Whalen out by the front door? Wasn't it, Sarah?" "When?" I said. "You know when, you were right there," Ronnie said. She was very excited and her face had a pleasant, high color. "You know what he did." "I didn't see anything," I said. Mrs. Gunderson wore ugly black shoes and her stockings were so thick you couldn't see her skin through them. Ronnie wore her moccasin loafers and no socks and her legs were pale and lumpy, covered with fine blond hairs. "Mr. Whalen stood *right out there* and Sarah saw him but she's too afraid to say. She's just a damn dirty coward," Ronnie said. Mr. Whalen was the fifth-grade teacher. Nobody liked him, but I had to say, "There wasn't any man out there." So Mrs. Gunderson let us go. Ronnie whispered, "You dirty goddam teacher's pet!"

That day at noon hour she rubbed my face in the dirt by the swings, and when I began crying she let me up. "Oh, don't cry, you big baby," she said. She rubbed my head playfully. She always did this to her little brother, her favorite brother. "I didn't mean to hurt you, but you had it coming. Right? You got to do what I say. If we're friends you got to obey me, don't you?"

"Yes."

Now she talks faster and faster. I know her mother isn't home and that's why she doesn't want to go in yet—her mother is always out somewhere. No one dares to ask Ronnie about her mother. In our house my mother is waiting somewhere, or maybe not waiting at all but upstairs doing something, listening to the radio. The supper dishes are put away. My father is working the night shift. When he comes home he will sleep downstairs on the sofa and when I come down for school in the morning there he'll be, stretched out and snoring. When my father and mother are together there are two currents of air, like invisible clouds, that move with them and will not overlap. These clouds keep them separate even when they are together; they seem to be calling across a deep ditch.

"Okay, let's walk down by the warehouse."

"Why do you want to go down there?" .

"Just for the hell of it."

"I got a lot of homework to do—"

"Are you trying to make me mad?"

The first day I met Ronnie was the first day they had moved into their house, about two months ago. Ronnie strolled up and down the street, looking around, and she saw me right away sitting up on our veranda, reading. She was wearing soiled white shorts that came down to her knees and a baggy pullover shirt that was her brother's. Her hands were shoved in her pockets as she walked. She said to me on that first day: "Hey, what are you doing? Are you busy or can I come up?"

Now she is my best friend and I do everything she says, almost everything. She keeps talking. She likes to touch people when she talks, tap them on the arm or nudge them. "Come on. You don't have nothing to do inside," she says, whining, wheedling, and I give in. We stroll down the block. Nobody sits outside any more at night, because it is too cold now. I am wearing a jacket and blue jeans, and Ronnie is wearing the same coat she wears to school: it used to be her mother's coat. It is made of shiny material, with black and fluorescent green splotches and tiny white umbrellas because it is a raincoat. As we walk down the street she points out houses we pass, telling me who the people are. "In there lives a fat old bastard, he goes to the bathroom in the sink," she says, her voice loud and helpful like a teacher's voice. "His name is Chanock or Chanick or some crappy name like that."

"How do you know about him?"

"I know lots of things, stupid. You think I'm lying?"

"No."

We walk on idly. We cross the street over toward Don's Drugstore. A few boys are standing around outside, leaning on their bicycles. When they see us coming they say, "Here comes that fat old cow Lay-zer," and they all laugh. Ronnie sticks out her tongue and says what she always says: a short loud nasty word that makes them laugh louder. When she does this I feel like laughing or running away, I feel as if something had opened in the ground before me—a great gaping crack in the sidewalk. The boys don't bother with me but keep on teasing Ronnie until we're past.

This street is darker. The houses are older, set back from the sidewalk with little plots of grass that are like mounds of graves in front of them. There are "boarders" in these houses. "Dirty old perverts," Ronnie calls them if we ever see them. One of the houses is vacant and kids come from all over to break windows and fool around, even though the police have chased them away. "In this next house is a man who does nasty things with a dog. I saw him out in the alley once," Ronnie says, snickering.

I have to take big steps to keep up with her. We're headed out toward the warehouse, which is boarded up, but everyone goes in there to play. I am afraid of the warehouse at night, because bums sometimes sleep there, but if I tell Ronnie, she'll snort with laughter and pinch me. Walking along fast, she says, "I sure don't want to miss that show on Saturday. You and me can go early," and then, whistling through her teeth, "One of these days that big dumpy warehouse is going to burn down. Wait and see."

Ronnie once lit a little fire in someone's garage, but it must have gone out because nothing happened. She wanted to get back at the people because she didn't like the girl who lived there, a girl ahead of us in school. At noon hour Ronnie and I sat alone to eat our lunches. If she was angry about something she could stare me down with her cold blue eyes that were like plastic caps; but other times she has to wipe at her eyes, saying, "This bastard who came home with her last night, he—He—" Or she talks bitterly of the other girls and how they all hate her because they're afraid of her. She has dirty hair, a dirty neck, and her dresses are just . . . just old baggy things passed down from someone else. At noon she often whispers to me about kids in the cafeteria, naming them one by one, telling me what she'll do to them when she gets around to it: certain acts with shears, razors, ice picks, butcher knives, acts described so vividly and with such passion that I feel sick.

Even when I'm not with Ronnie I feel a little sick, but not just in my stomach. It's all through my body. Ma always says, "Why do you run out when that big cow calls you? What do you see in her?" and I answer miserably, frightened, "I like her all right." But I have never thought about liking Ronnie. I have no choice. She has never given me the privilege of liking or disliking her, and if she knew I was thinking such a thought she would yank my hair out of my head.

Light from the street lamp falls onto the front and part of the side of the old warehouse. There is a basement entrance I am afraid of because of spiders and rats. Junk is stored in the warehouse, things we don't recognize and never bother to wonder about, parts from machines, rails, strange wheels that are solid metal and must weigh hundreds of pounds. "Let's climb in the window," I say to Ronnie. "The cellar way's faster," she says. "Please, let's go in the window," I beg. I have begun to tremble and don't know why. It seems to me that something terrible is waiting inside the warehouse.

Ronnie looks at me contemptuously. She is grave and large in the moonlight, her mother's shiny coat wrinkled tight across her broad shoulders. The way her eyes are in shadow makes me think suddenly of a person falling backwards, falling down—onto something hard and sharp. That could happen. Inside the warehouse there are all kinds of strange, sharp things half hidden in the junk, rusty edges and broken glass from the windows that have been smashed. "Please, Ron, let's climb in the window," I beg.

She laughs and we go around to the window. There is an important board pulled out that makes a place for your foot. Then you jump up and put one knee on the window ledge, then you slide inside. The boards crisscrossing the window have been torn down a long time ago. Ronnie goes first and then helps me up. She says, "What if I let you go right now? You'd fall down and split your dumb head open!"

But she helps me crawl inside. Why do we like the warehouse so much? During the day I like to explore in it; we never get tired of all the junk and the places to hide and the view from the upstairs windows. Machines—nails and nuts and bolts underfoot—big crates torn apart and left behind, with mysterious black markings on their sides. The moonlight is strong enough for us to see things dimly. I am nervous, even though I know where everything is. I know this place. In my bed at night I can climb up into the warehouse and envision everything, remember it clearly, every part of it—it is our secret place, no grownups come here—I can remember the big sliver of glass that is like a quarter-moon, a beautiful shape, lying at the foot of the steps, and the thing we call the "tractor," and a great long dusty machine that is beside the stairs. When you touch it you feel first dust, then oil; beneath the dust there is a coating of oil. Three prongs rise out of one end like dull knives.

Ronnie bumps into something and says, "Oh Christ!" She is always bumping into things. One time when she hurt herself— fooling around with some bricks—she got angry at me for no reason and slapped me. She was always poking or pinching or slapping. . . . It occurs to me that I should kill her. She is like a big hulking dead body tied to me, the mouth fixed up for a grin and always ready to laugh, and we are sinking together into the water, and I will have to slash out at her to get free—I want to get free. So I say, beginning to shiver, "Should we go upstairs?"

"What's upstairs but pigeon crap?"

"We can look out the window."

"You and your goddam windows—"

She laughs because I like to look out of the windows; she likes to grub around instead in corners, prying things loose, looking under things for "treasure." She told me once that she'd found a silver dollar in the warehouse. But now I go ahead of her to the stairs, a strange keen sensation in my bowels, and she grumbles but comes along behind me. These old steps are filthy with dust and some of the boards sag. I know exactly where to step. Behind me, Ronnie is like a horse. The stairs are shaking. I wait for her at the top and in that second I can see out a window and over to the street light— but past that nothing, there is nothing to see at night! The street light has a cloudy halo about it, something that isn't real but seems real to my eye. Ronnie bounds up the stairs and I wait for her, sick with being so afraid, my heart pounding in a jerky, bouncy way as if it wanted to burst—but suddenly my heart is like another person inside me, nudging me and saying, "Do it! Do it!" When Ronnie is about two steps from the top I reach down and push her.

She falls at once. She falls over the side, her voice a screech that is yanked out into the air above her, and then her body hits the edge of that machine hard. She is screaming. I stand at the top, listening to her. Everything is dry and clear and pounding. She falls again, from the edge of the machine onto the floor, and now her scream is muffled as if someone had put his hand over her mouth.

I come down the stairs slowly. The air is hard and dry, like acid that burns my mouth, and I can't look anywhere except at Ronnie's twisting body. I wait for it to stop twisting. What if she doesn't die? At the base of the stairs I make a wide circle around her, brushing up against something and getting grease onto my jeans.

There is this big girl half in the moonlight from the shattered window and half in the dark. Dust rolls in startled balls about her, aroused by her moans. She is bleeding. A dark stain explodes out from her and pushes the dust along before it, everything speeded up by her violent squirming, and I feel as if I must walk on tiptoe to keep from being seen by her. . . . Blood, all that blood!—it is like an animal crawling out from under her, like the shadows we drag around with, broken loose now and given its own life, twisting out from under her and grabbing her, big as she is. She cries out, "Sarah! Ma!" but I don't hear her. I am at the window already. "Ma!" she says. "Ma!" It does not seem that I am moving or hearing anything, but still my feet take me to the window and those words come to me from a distance, "Ma, help me!" and I think to myself that I will have to get to where those words won't reach.

At home our house is warm and my head aches because I am sleepy. I fall asleep on my bed without undressing, and the next day we all hear about Ronnie. "Fooling around in that old dump, I knew it was going to happen to somebody," my mother says grimly. "You stay the hell out of that place from now on. You hear?"

I tell her yes, yes. I will never go there again.

There is a great shadowy space about me, filled with waiting: waiting to cry, to feel sorry. I myself am waiting, my body is waiting the way it waited that night at the top of the steps. But nothing happens. Do you know that twenty years have gone by? I am still dark but not so skinny, I have grown into a body that is approved of by people who glance at me in the street, I have grown out of the skinny little body that knocked that clumsy body down—and I have never felt sorry. Never felt any guilt. I live in what is called a "colonial" house, on a lane of colonial houses called Meadowbrook Lane. Ours is the sixth house on the right. Our mailboxes are down at the intersection with a larger road. . . . I am married and have children and I am still waiting to feel guilty, to feel some of Ronnie's pain, to feel the shock of that impact again as I felt it when she struck the prongs of the machine—but nothing happens. In my quiet, pleasant life, when my two boys are at school, I write stories I hope may be put on television someday—why not, why couldn't that miracle happen?

My stories are more real than my childhood; my childhood is just another story, but one written by someone else.

Ruth

The Wreszins' mailbox was like most of the mailboxes along the road—bought at the Sears store in town, once a bright silver, now dull and rusty, its flag permanently down; people in the area sent out few letters. They paid their bills in person, in cash. The name Wreszin was spelled out in black letters on the box. Across the road a field sloped abruptly to a great mile-long swamp; it was overlaid with scum and gray, cobweb-like moss that hung dispiritedly from trees that were dying or already dead. At one time there had been a woods there, mainly oaks and elms, but construction of a new highway to the north had somehow blocked off its drainage—a process so utterly mysterious that it could not be explained to people in the area—and out of nowhere a rich, thick scum had risen, slowly, and for some inexplicable reason the trees had begun to die, dying from the inside, choked. A few were still living; most were trunks from which bark had fallen, as if peeled by hand. At night a vapor hung over the swamp and thousands of insects and frogs sang—in a way, it did seem alive. During the day it appeared sullen, ugly, dead, as if its secret life had retreated beneath the gray scum and could wait.

The Wreszin farm was nearby, on a fairly high hill. It was not exactly a farm now—like many farms in the area it was no longer a working farm, and yet not an abandoned one. They still used the garden and the corn field and the fruit orchards, but the rest of the land had gone wild. It paid no money—why the hell bother with it? Mr. Wreszin said, disgusted. The same was true with the cherries and pears and apples; they picked most of the fruit, some of it for canning, and they had a fruit-stand out on the highway where they tried to sell quarts and occasional bushel baskets of fruit to passersby or people from the city out for a Sunday drive, but that really did not pay either. It was more trouble than it was worth. Every week-day Wreszin drove to work in the town fifteen miles away, in the "machine shop" of a big factory. Alongside him in this unskilled section of the factory were other men like himself—farmers dispossessed by obscure economic changes—and their sons, who joked and punched one another and didn't seem yet to be aware of their condition.

When Wreszin forced the car up that steep drive every afternoon at five-thirty, he could feel waves of anger ready to break upon him. It was not because of the factory, which after all paid him money for mindless work, and not even because of the monotonous ride home, but rather because of the old farm itself: it had been his grandfather's and his father's and had worked out all right for them, and now what had happened? Wreszin had the uncertain, angry idea that he was out of place. He and his son had painted the farmhouse a couple of years ago, but it gave him no pleasure; he did not like to look at it. He would stop the car in the driveway and sit breathing hard, his arms slumped over the steering wheel as if he had at last attained something, but did not know what. Before he got out of the car he allowed himself an exquisite sadness—a luxury of an emotion, since he was not an emotional man—and even the threat of tears.

Wreszin was a big, hard-looking man, now beginning to go to fat but careful to hide it; with all his height and muscles, it was more difficult for him than for most men to keep weight down. He liked to eat and drink. He liked to sleep after supper, stretched out with his shoes off in the front parlor; he liked to sleep after Sunday dinner, in the same place, with the shades drawn down by his wife and the children sent out of the house—his wife, like Wreszin, was from this area and faithfully observed the customs of their parents. Men napped after they ate. Men had hard lives so they took whatever small luxuries they could and no one criticized them; women, however, never napped during the day.

When he came home after work he liked to go right in and find supper ready, and he was never disappointed. But one day in early June he knew that something was wrong, because the children were looking at him so intently. They were sitting at the table, in the kitchen, eating; and he noticed them watching him. Usually Wreszin read the newspaper at supper, but tonight he could not concentrate.

"What the hell's wrong?" he said finally.

"Ma's got some news," his daughter Betty said at once, as if she had been waiting for him to ask.

Wreszin's eyes shifted to his wife without any change; he might have been looking at a wall.

"Just some family trouble," she said.

She was a tall lean woman with a worried, unsurprised face. Wreszin caught the vicious glance she shot at Betty.

"You might as well tell me now," Wreszin said. Her family was always in trouble; her father probably wanted money again. While his parents had had enough sense to wear out and die, hers were still alive and doing nobody any good. "What happened?"

"It isn't Ma and Pa, like you always think," his wife said slowly.

He could not remember her as a girl and so he did not know whether she'd always been so slow and worried. Her face had the gaunt earnestness of a skull. She examined her long thin fingers and said, "My cousin Junie, that had all that trouble I told you about—"

"The one that ran away with a bartender," Betty said.

"Not a bartender, he wasn't a bartender," Wreszin's wife said patiently. Betty, at fourteen, was plumper and taller than her mother. She had a cat face and she smiled often and drew out her mother's anger in a slow, sly way that was worse than violent anger. "Well, she had a new baby a few months ago, and she then had the girl Ruthie and the boy, what was his name—And she found a place for the two of them and was going to keep Ruthie, but now she can't keep Ruthie either because she has to have a whole lot of operations—it's awful, a real awful thing for Junie—And he never gave her no money either, or what he did went for doctors' bills. She said—"

"What about the girl?" Wreszin said. He had to talk with his wife at these times by picking at incidental facts as she spoke. Like many of the women he had known, in his own family and elsewhere, her life was so empty that real news dazzled her and she did not know how to talk about it.

"The girl, Ruthie, the little girl, yes," Mrs. Wreszin said. She paused, staring at one of her fingers. "I told her it'd be the only thing to do, to take her in for the summer."

"Told her? When?"

"I told my aunt and she told her."

"We're going to take the girl in?"

"Just the little girl, Ruthie. Take her in for the summer."

Betty and the two other children looked at their father, their eyes bright and innocent. They saw so little of him these days that he had for them an air of novelty, like a performing animal that might be prodded into anger.

"No, we can't do it," he said, letting his breath out slowly.

"I told her it'd be hard, and you'd say something—"

"I said something, yes."

"But she's got nowhere else to go—she's just a kid, fifteen or so—"

"At fifteen she can go out and work. What the hell is this?" Wreszin said, looking from his wife to his children, as if he suspected them all.

"She's not too strong. She had a little trouble herself, was sick for a while . . ." Mrs. Wreszin said slowly. Then she paused. When she spoke again it was in another tone. "She's a real sweet little girl, I met her once. Junie took us out and bought us a soda in the dime store that time—couple of years ago—when I met her and she was in real bad trouble. So it isn't like I never saw the kid."

"We don't have any room here," Wreszin said.

"Billy's gone and won't be back from the Navy for a long time," Mrs. Wreszin said humbly. "She could help me with the canning, I thought. Betty here don't care to soil her hands."

"I do too," Betty said, hurt. "I helped you today."

"This girl would be real sweet to have around, I know it," Mrs. Wreszin said, her mouth twisting around the word "sweet." "They ask us to do things for Junie because we can afford it. I don't like them to think different."

Wreszin finished his supper in silence. The children relaxed, a little disappointed. Mrs. Wreszin ate humbly, her shoulders slumped with the passivity of the victorious; in a minute Wreszin would walk heavily out of the house and sit on the porch, brooding, but in the end he would come around.

After he left she said, "Your father's got a real good heart." She spoke sideways to Betty, her voice harder and faster now. "You kids remember that. When you got to think anything of us, remember how we helped other people."

Their children, already overburdened with other memories, would remember no such thing. Betty was thinking they were fools and she did not want another girl her age in the house; the two youngest children, a boy and a girl, felt vaguely alarmed at the coming of a stranger. They had been brought up to think of their lives as taking place in a kind of puddle that was always getting smaller. Nobody ever told them this, in fact Wreszin tried hard to make them think everything was good, but they knew somehow that the puddle was shrinking and they might someday drown in air they weren't ready for. In the presence of adults they were solemn and quiet like miniature grownups, as if understanding that grownups were to blame for everything.

"Well, she's not getting my room," Betty said.

"People should do good for other people," Mrs. Wreszin said. She stood and began to clear the table. Her daughter watched her sullenly, knowing that every minute her mother worked and she didn't would just cause trouble; but still she sat. The "good" Mrs. Wreszin did was always a weapon threatening her own family and she seemed to know she could control them with it.

"She's not getting my room," Betty said.

"Yes, you can move into Billy's room," Mrs. Wreszin said. "She's just going to be here for the summer and I want her to think well of us."

"Billy's room?"

"Yes, Billy's room, just for the summer," Mrs. Wreszin said quietly. She had an air of stooping under an invisible burden far greater than any she inflicted upon anyone else. She must have known Betty was staring at her in disbelief, so she did not look at her.

Later that evening Wreszin said to his wife, "If she's got nowhere else to go, all right."

Mrs. Wreszin smiled her slight, weary smile. "Then she can have Betty's room. I don't want them to talk about what a mess it is here. It'll be a lot of work for me, but I don't mind. One more kid don't matter when you can afford it."

"What about when Billy comes back on leave?"

"He ain't coming back for a long time."

Betty, who imagined she hated her mother, and was afraid of her father, argued only about trifles. The more trivial something was, the more passionately she argued, but about important matters she was shy—she was defeated by her mother's quiet, preoccupied stubbornness. So she gave in about the room, as she would give in about all important matters. Her brother, Billy, who at eighteen had given up looking for a job—he had looked everywhere for a year, as far as twenty miles from home—and had joined the Navy, had always given in too; but each time he had grown more violent toward other people, so it was time he left. The younger children—they were eight and eleven and looked alike, both small for their ages—hadn't any of the nerve of the older, as if they had given up at once. And Betty could sense her father gradually giving in to something— maybe not her mother, but something else that was just like her mother.

Wreszin might have sensed a kinship with his older daughter, had he bothered with her; but he never thought of it. His children were burdens to be protected but he did not think of them in themselves. In his world there had always been too many children—brothers and sisters, cousins, babies, neighbors' children. They were part of the landscape. You took care of them and worried about them, but you did not pay much attention to them until they did something wrong. Wreszin thought of the girl who was coming to stay with him as just another child. Anything outside his home usually was unpleasant to him, but Ruth would be just another child. He stood out by the front porch, looking across the weedy yard (the front door and the front walk were never used) to the sluggish swamp with its nighttime mist, and felt some satisfaction with it. It smelled and it was ugly, but it hadn't changed in years.

After work one day Wreszin turned left instead of right at the parking-lot exit and drove downtown to the bus station. People were standing around outside. Wreszin looked at them suspiciously and out of their midst appeared a young girl—there she was, he thought, that's her. She had a shy, dreamy look, nothing like the other women in his wife's family. Her hair was black and soft but cut too severely, so that it made her face look thin. Wreszin leaned out the window and tried to smile. The girl stared at him. "You're Ruth, right?" he said. "Come on and get in." He might have helped her with the suitcase, but for some reason he didn't; his knees seemed tired. With women he tended to be brusque and avoided looking them in the eyes.

She carried a big suitcase that scraped against the ground every few feet. It was strapped together—a queer thing made of cheap imitation leather, bruised and streaked on its sides. It must have been a man's suitcase originally.

Driving home he thought of things to say to her, but decided against them. His wife could do the talking. The girl made him nervous, just sitting there. Her hands were in her lap and her face was still. She seemed unhappy. Out in the country a strange thought crossed his mind: if he were to stop the car and make her get out, and then drive away, who would know? If she were to die somehow, out here in the country, who would know about it? He glanced at her as if afraid she knew what he was thinking—and she was the way she'd been at first, her pale face empty, her dark eyes quiet, secret, her hands limply in her lap. She wore a yellow cotton dress. He could never have guessed her age. She was like those strange, frightened, arrogant girls he saw sometimes walking along the highway, going nowhere and coming from nowhere: you could never guess how old they were. Who were they? It was better not to ask.

When they were almost home the girl began to cry softly. She turned away from Wreszin and did not bring her hands to her face. She cried as if she were accustomed to it.

"You'll be all right here," Wreszin said, startled and annoyed. "She's going to take care of you real well."

The girl continued to cry.

"You thinking about your mother?" Wreszin said.

The girl looked out at the swamp. Wreszin, his senses alerted by her, could smell its odor for the first time, really, in years; he had grown not to notice it.

"My baby, it was my baby that died," she said.

Wreszin felt something pull in his jaw, a muscle or a nerve. He glanced over at the girl and saw her in another way: she was leaning forward, tense and delicate but turned away from something she didn't want to see.

There was a moment when he might have said something, but he let the moment pass. Better not to have heard. Before talkative women—the usual kind—men like Wreszin became silent and bored; before women like Ruth, who said so little, they lost all standards for behavior and did not know how to act. He was amazed at her words, but he felt no need to acknowledge them. She was innocent, and this made him innocent too.

"We're going to take care of you all right," he said in the same voice he had used earlier. It was as if the girl had said nothing unusual.

Ruth made the house different. Everyone felt it but no one could have explained it—of the whole family, only Betty was the kind to "think" about things and figure them out, and no one listened to her. The girl was always quiet. This seemed to them a refinement, but it might have been only stupidity. They were not used to quiet people. Ruth, with her queer pale face and her big eyes with the circles under them that sometimes looked smudged, her habit of gazing down at the floor, moved silently and sweetly among them and did a great deal of work—Mrs. Wreszin apologetically found things for the girl to do toward earning her keep; "earning her keep" was a new expression of Mrs. Wreszin's.

Betty worked part time at a big fruit-stand some miles away, so many afternoons Mrs. Wreszin and Ruth were alone in the house. The children played outside and did not bother them; they were shy of Ruth. Mrs. Wreszin would invite Ruth to quit working and

sit down, and they would eat something together for a "snack"—
another new expression of Mrs. Wreszin's that she offered with a
bright, familiar casualness, as if it had always been part of her
vocabulary. They ate together; that was the important thing. Then
Mrs. Wreszin felt she could ask the girl about many things: about
the girl's mother, and about men her mother had known, and about
relatives. While they ate she would watch Ruth's serious face. "Yes,
life catches up with us all," she always concluded sadly after Ruth
revealed something, and both would pause as if trying to hear life
catching up with them. "But your mother's a real strong healthy
girl and's real sweet and she'll bounce back like new, you wait and
see. It's just hospitals I hate." "I hate them too," the girl said,
looking up in surprise. "And he's gone, huh? Just went off and left
her?" Mrs. Wreszin said, her spoon before her mouth. "They always
do," Ruth said humbly.

Mrs. Wreszin liked her because she was so quiet and submissive.
Betty always gave in, but not the way Mrs. Wreszin wanted her to
—you could tell by Betty's plump sour face what she really thought.
Ruth, however, did not think anything. She worked until perspiration was beaded on her face and her hair was damp, but she did not
think about anything. "Here, honey," Mrs. Wreszin said, "here's a
ribbon to pull your hair back. It's lots cooler that way." Mrs.
Wreszin liked the girl's hair and inside of two weeks she was
brushing it out for her, something she hadn't done for Betty since
Betty was six. This was in the early morning, when it wasn't hot yet,
and the two of them were in the bedroom where Mrs. Wreszin and
her husband slept, Ruth seated in front of the "dressing table"—
two orange crates on end with a board on top of them, covered with
five-and-dime flowered cloth and a ridge of ruffles, and presided
over by a round, gaudily framed mirror—and Mrs. Wreszin standing behind her, watching the girl's face in the mirror. "I used to
have real nice long hair myself," Mrs. Wreszin said. "If you think
Betty looks like me, you're wrong. Betty doesn't look like anybody
around here."

Sometimes Mrs. Wreszin and the girl shredded dried-up corn for the chickens to eat, moving their fists hard around the ears of corn. Mrs. Wreszin's hands were calloused and she could chatter as she worked without noticing anything; Ruth's hands were soft and sometimes bled.

"You run in and put them under cold water," Mrs. Wreszin ordered. Whenever any of her children were hurt she was always brusque, as if confused and embarrassed by someone else's pain. "You don't want no infection."

"I don't mind it," Ruth said. "It doesn't hurt."

Both women were sitting on the running board of one of Wreszin's old cars, parked forever in the back yard. They were shredding the corn into a bushel basket. A few chickens picked in the dirt around them and were washing themselves in the dust; one of the cats was sunning itself, rolling over to show them its stomach.

Ruth looked around and her gaze came finally to Mrs. Wreszin, who was staring at her. "It's bleeding, don't it hurt?" Mrs. Wreszin said, moved reluctantly to being sympathetic.

"I don't mind blood," Ruth said. She held a half-shredded ear of shriveled corn in her hands, dotted a little with blood. She looked around slowly at the back yard. Her eyes took in everything. Mrs. Wreszin, who felt at times uneasy and strangely excited in the girl's presence, looked around too and tried to see what the girl saw. She seemed to see the old place differently—what was there about it? It was bathed in sunshine, and even the dullest, emptiest spot of ground had a queer, beautiful look to it; the chickens scratching in the dirt were a little scrawny, but there was something nice about them. They were mainly reddish-brown chickens. The children had put rings on their legs, red and yellow and green plastic rings the man at the feed store gave them, and these made the chickens look as if they were imitating human beings.

"You all have got a garden here. A real nice garden," Ruth said.

"Yeah, we sure do," Mrs. Wreszin said at once, sarcastically. But she did not mean her sarcasm. She sat back against the warm door of the car and looked around. When you glanced out the back window and saw the sheds and the old shanty where the pigs used to be, everything ready to fall down and rain-rotted and choked with weeds, it looked like one thing. But here, with everything quiet and just spread around you, as if this were a dream, tilted buildings and the patches of blue-flowered weeds and even the fuzzy, frothy tips of dandelion flowers gone to seed looked like something else. Everything was quiet here; there was nothing to argue about. Mrs. Wreszin frowned, and the lines on her forehead creased as if with the pain of thought; but no thought actually came to her.

"Yeah, we sure do. A real garden," she grumbled.

But she had felt something pleasant and strange—she who felt so little—and after this her daughter Betty did not bother her so much. The girl's mouthings and snippy eyes didn't mean much; Mrs. Wreszin didn't have to pay much attention to her. She found herself watching Ruth, who was so pretty, and pretty in a way people around here were too stupid even to know about—not big and loud with lipstick all over like most of the country girls, Mrs. Wreszin thought severely—but pretty in a way that was all her own.

"If Betty looked halfway life that," she would whisper to herself, and sigh.

When she had nothing else to do she thought about Ruth's future: that pretty face would get her someone nice. The men with education and money wanted quiet, refined girls. Mrs. Wreszin tried to recall herself as a girl, before her marriage, but could not. That was a gray, twilit area made obscure by her ignorance; in those days she hadn't thought enough to remember anything. She hadn't known how fast the years would go. But she liked to imagine she had been like Ruth.

Wreszin began to take walks after supper instead of napping. If he was doing what his father and grandfather had done—for no reason, only "walking" out in the fields like someone from the city, he did not think of it in that way. He liked the looks of things, that was enough. If he saw the fields and saw them fallow, he would have had to be angry, but he simply saw them for what they were. His father would have been shocked at these abandoned fields—given over to weeds with thistles and yellow flowers and blue flowers and small wild trees pushing up thinly and stubbornly—and the slanting outbuildings that seemed now as if no one had ever bothered with them. But Wreszin was looking at them now without thinking of what they used to mean. His eye took them in as shapes and colors, and something in him could respond feebly to their beauty.

That was because, perhaps, of Ruth. She usually walked along with him and he caught from her a certain naïveté without ever knowing what it was. The two children and the old collie ran along with them, playing, but really it was just Wreszin and the girl. He liked her because she never complained about anything, nor was there a hint of discontent in her. At supper, everyone's eyes bothered him, as they had for years, except Ruth's. They were all thinking about something and they were all his responsibility, except Ruth. Ruth always sat with her back arched and her delicate shoulders straight, eating everything as if it were wonderful, a gift set down before her. None of his children had been good like her, he thought. What she had told him in the car, that first day, must have been a mistake; anyway, he never thought of it. She was a good child, he could tell by her face. She was innocent. Sometimes he stared at her while they ate and felt that all this had happened before: her face across from him, those downcast, submissive eyes, that delicate mouth. Betty's face was coarse and loomed next to Ruth's like a cartoon face. After Ruth had been living with them a month or so, Betty began to act strangely—she was childish and shrill and rolled her eyes much too often. Wreszin could not figure it out.

"Why don't you act nice and quiet like Ruth?" Mrs. Wreszin was always saying to her daughter. Ruth, present or not present, was like a rag doll dragged out and shaken in Betty's face. Wreszin did not bother with the children because Mrs. Wreszin never let them get annoying enough to upset him, but he disliked his daughter's antics. "You'd think she'd learn from Ruth," Mrs. Wreszin complained to him. "Ruth's from the city and has better manners. You'd think Betty would learn, wouldn't you?"

After the first week, Betty had her old job back of helping her mother with the supper dishes. Ruth, who had worked all day long, could go out walking—"walking"—and Mrs. Wreszin was pleased with the idea, as if it were a remnant of refined city life she knew enough to supply for her cousin's daughter. She knew very well that her cousin and Ruth, one of her several illegitimate children, had lived in an ugly tenement house where garbage was thrown out of windows, but she did not let this interfere with the idea of city life with which she hounded Betty. "Girls are polite there," she would say wistfully. "They wouldn't ever hitch rides like them Kramer girls, and if your father ever catches you at that. . . . They're prettier, too. You could tell Ruth is from the city just by looking at her."

"I wish Ruth would drop dead," Betty would say, making a violent face at the plates she was washing.

But these days she could say nothing to annoy her mother. Betty felt something like desperation—what could she do? Her mother thought only of Ruth. Her mother didn't pay enough attention to Betty now even to become disgusted. In Billy's old room up in the attic, she lay heavily on the bed under the slanting roof and cried. With her, crying was a kind of brutality; her sobs punished her. She was getting strange little lines on her forehead from worrying. Why did she worry? All her life she had worried and only now did the object of her worry make sense. She was afraid of Ruth.

"I'm afraid of her," she wanted to whisper to her mother, but who could talk to Mrs. Wreszin? "I'm afraid," she wanted to say to her father, but she never did. No one talked to him.

And he talked to no one, really, except a few men he knew who often met at a tavern a few miles away. Those men and Ruth.

After supper every night, if it didn't rain, he went out walking, as if the house were unbearable to him. He hated his job in the factory because it confined him, and lately he was beginning to hate anything that confined him. "That kitchen's too cooped up, it smells from canning all day long," he complained to Ruth. He would even have liked to sleep outside; if he woke suddenly he could look directly up at the sky and not at the ceiling.

Ruth walked along beside him, pleased with everything. But her pleasure was restrained and silent. She liked flowers but never picked them, liked the looks of the pears but would never eat them. "Oh, no, that's for picking. That's for later," she would say, surprised and coloring slightly when Wreszin urged her to pick a pear that was almost ripe.

They often climbed one of the hills behind the house and looked over at the swamp. At the horizon the swamp dissolved into a thick mist that always stayed where it was; even the sunlight could not penetrate it.

"It's sort of pretty," Ruth said.

Wreszin nodded.

"It looks like ghosts are there," she said softly.

"There aren't any ghosts," Wreszin said.

He walked with his hands in his pockets, sometimes chewing part of a cigar in imitation of his father, though he wasn't conscious of this. He took hard, heavy steps, feeling his feet sink into the ground. He had to wear thick shoes that pulled at his feet; in the factory he'd already dropped a tool on his foot and smashed the little toe. He made himself take great, dizzying breaths of the sweet air; sometimes he stood in a field and sucked in air as if he wanted to drown in it. On his face would be a look of rapt, almost terrified concern; he could have shown this with no one else except Ruth. After she had lived with them about two months he even began to talk to her. It was August now, and the sun set every evening with a brazen, golden glow, making the ugliest of the buildings something burnished and surprising, and the monotonous fields bizarre, like fields painted for a picture.

"With your ma how she is, you'd understand," he said. "The way things don't stay still but are always jolting you. It's like that here. My wife don't know it, nor my kids either, but I do. It's my burden. Things never stay still, it's like one of them trick rides at the fair— the floor starts tilting under you and you almost fall down. With your ma always in trouble and you being kicked out of places, you know what I mean."

She knew what he meant, of course. He felt she understood him completely. As soon as they were far from the house, they would walk along quietly, in no hurry to get anywhere. Owls made their wispy, forlorn cries back in the woods and some distance behind, the collie was barking. Wreszin never felt embarrassed with the girl. He talked to her about the farm, the way prices had gone down, people had moved out, about the factory and the other men, and his son Billy . . . things he'd argued about with his wife, who always had answers. Sometimes he spoke bitterly and angrily. He believed there was some "trick" being played on him and people like him, but he did not know what it was.

"We're just stupid bastards, people like us," he said. "We never know what hits us, even afterwards. That's how it is."

He went over and over with her the curious problem of his unhappiness. No one he had ever known had wondered about being unhappy—this was something no one thought of doing. He could not have said when he first began thinking about it, about the state of being unhappy, as if there were other possible states. "The job in town pays more than the farm did," he would say slowly, "but still . . . something ain't right. It ain't the same thing as the farm."

She had the sweet docile silence of a favorite animal—a cat not fully grown, perhaps. If Wreszin made a gesture of anger, slashing weed tops, she glanced around at him in alarm. She was not stupid, not mindless. Wreszin knew this. What he liked was the solemn way her throat seemed to hold itself still for his gaze, and the way she sometimes turned to see where a bird was hiding—her legs not moving, but only the upper part of her body moving, her waist suddenly becoming very thin, her ribs delicate above it as the dress was pulled tight, and her arms held in a childish frozen way as she listened to the bird's song.

It was in August that her mother died.

Wreszin was anxious—should he feel pity or not? Their walks after this were a little more self-conscious; that was his fault. Mrs. Wreszin had sent them out to walk; she had driven both Ruth and Betty to town to buy clothes. Both Wreszin and his wife were alarmed at death and were inspired to harshness by it; it was "trouble." They would hate their own deaths in time and expected each to hate the other's, so they saw no reason why they shouldn't hate the death of others—death was vexatious and tedious and expensive.

But Wreszin felt differently about Ruth. When she and Mrs. Wreszin came back from the funeral, he was almost shy before her. He spoke to her awkwardly, as if he were speaking to an animal, trying by chance to hit upon its language.

"Nobody should feel sorry for dead people," he had said. Ruth had looked at him as if she believed him. Wreszin had been grateful.

One evening, around sunset, he was inspired by something to talk in a wild, distracted way. He had been talking quietly enough at first, but then something had happened and his hands had come out of his pockets as if preparing to attack.

"Well, she was a bitch, but so what? You loved her probably. She was rotting inside, that's what killed her. There was a time I'd of hated her and you too, but not now. I don't hate anybody now." He looked at her as they walked. "We're all the same. Your mother and me, and my wife, and Billy, and my father that's dead—all the same. He worked like hell for us kids and we grew up big and strong and got left all his troubles, the same goddam things he worried about all his life. I see it now. And my kids, that I wanted to keep safe, they're getting those things from me. Those things are always passed on—worrying and being sick and seeing things run down and dying in the end. We have kids for these things to be passed on to. New bodies for us to pass into."

The girl raised her hands to her face as if she could not bear to look upon what he had said.

"Well, it's true! It's true!" he said in dismay. "That's why I can't hate anybody any longer—we're all the same!" He heard this new note in his voice, this childish, perplexed dismay, and wondered if he were going to cry. He had not cried since childhood.

Ruth seemed to recoil from his suffering. She moved back, her eyes half closed, and groped behind her with one hand as if she expected the earth to rise magically to her. "I wish everything didn't die," she whispered. "I wish it didn't have to die. . . ."

She lay down in the field. The grass was limp in spots and dried out in others, but everywhere around Ruth it looked weak and insubstantial and unreal, in contrast with the girl's vivid face and vivid black hair. Wreszin's heart pounded so hard that the air seemed to shiver before him. He stared at Ruth. She opened her eyes slowly as if coming back to life. "I wish it didn't die, I'm sorry for you," she said in her cool, sweet, small voice, raising her arms to him.

Wreszin made love to her, and in her arms a tumult of memories came to him: his wife as a girl, himself as a young man, a whirling kaleidoscope of suns and moons and trees. His blood was wild as it had not been for years before, and he could think of nothing but images that shot to his drowning mind from the past—things he once saw and touched and smelled. He wept upon the girl. His tears fell on her bare skin and he rubbed his face against them, whimpering and moaning.

"I love you," he said. These words, which he had not spoken for so long, made him dizzy. They echoed with the same words that had been said years ago and the echo jangled in his brain. "Are you happy?" he said desperately. "Is this right?"

"I'm happy," she said. Her eyes were vague and frightened, as if they had no idea of what her words meant.

After this he was tender to her, always. At mealtimes, around the house—conspicuously tender. Mrs. Wreszin, her narrowed eyes suspicious and excited, could not understand why she fussed more than ever with Ruth's hair, or why she had once wept, holding the girl's hand. She was not unhappy but she wept. She was not unhappy, but she thought of herself strangely as a ghost trailing Ruth around —the girl had long competent hands, now protected by calluses, and a way of sitting out back, singing to the cats, that made Mrs. Wreszin stare. The hands were hers, yes; but the voice was a stranger's voice, a stranger with a face that should have belonged to one of Mrs. Wreszin's own children.

One night Mrs. Wreszin got out an old candy box filled with photographs, to show to everyone. Even Wreszin was interested. He laughed at some of his pictures, pointing with a tobacco-stained finger. "Pretty handsome in those days, huh?" he would say, grinning at his wife. Ruth looked through the photographs with great interest. She and Betty were sitting on the couch, and Betty shrieked from time to time with laughter or with anger, snatching a photograph out of Ruth's fingers to hide it, but Ruth did not seem to notice her nervous behavior. They watched Ruth's face as she looked through the photographs, as if they were waiting for her to tell them something.

"Oh, who is this? She looks like you," she said, holding a photograph up for Mrs. Wreszin to see.

"My grandmother. That's a real old picture," Mrs. Wreszin said apologetically, for some reason hiding her hands in her lap. "She's dead now. . . ."

Ruth stared at the picture for a moment and then put it carefully down. She handled each of the photographs delicately, as if the lost, doomed, dead people might still be sensitive to pain.

After a while she closed the box and sat back against the couch, closing her eyes. She said nothing. They stared at her—even the children, even Betty—and Wreszin knew that he loved her and could do nothing about it. "It makes me feel sad," she said slowly.

Wreszin lit a cigarette with trembling fingers and picked up the newspaper again.

"You women with your pictures—!" he said.

"It wasn't my idea, they're not my pictures!" Betty said. She brought both feet down hard upon the floor, as if she had jumped from a height, in an exasperation she herself did not understand. No one paid attention.

"If you're tired, Ruth, why don't you go to bed? You can go to bed and I'll keep the kids quiet," Mrs. Wreszin said anxiously. She seemed to be waiting for Wreszin to glance up, as if to reprove him tenderly—but really she was not conscious of this, nor did he dare to look up.

Wreszin lived in a world that throbbed with his infatuation for the girl, but did not judge it. Sometimes they were alone in the house—his wife and the children went to bring eggs to their special customers—but they never made love anywhere except outside, in the fields or the woods. With her he sometimes glanced shakily back to his house and could see it with a terrible clarity: not just the house but his family and him in it, his life like something in an old-fashioned photograph of a vanished, buried tribe. Ruth was motherly with him, gentle and sweet, and her very submissiveness excited him so that even when he knew he was hurting her he could not stop. Her inexplicable tears seemed to clean them both. "I wish, I wish," she would whisper sometimes, but she did not know what she wished for. Wreszin wished for nothing.

With his wife and children he was a sleepwalker, kinder to them now because his eyes never really focused on them, but with Ruth he came alive—he was a young man—he was young as his son Billy. With her, nothing of his life remained except the bare, hard inside

of him—what was really him—and everything accidental and ugly
fell away, like soiled clothing cast down in disgust. He was no particular age. He had no particular job. He had married no particular
woman. He lived nowhere in particular, in no time or place, had
had no particular parents, thought nothing, expected nothing, but
belonged, like Ruth, to the world of birds and animals with pulsating throats that hid in the fields, and to the constant movement
of the sun and the moon, belonging to everyone and no one.

. He wanted to ask her if she loved him; he knew that she loved
something. Alone, around the house, they would stare at the things
Wreszin had inherited and he could feel her confused love for them
—wasn't that love for him?

"It's like a garden here," she said happily. Things grew in wild
profusion right around the house: lilac trees, elderberry bushes,
shrubs, snowball bushes, even a scattering of willow trees. Farther
out there were oaks, elms, trees without names, and then the big
garden itself—mainly Mrs. Wreszin's garden—where plants had
puffed out luxuriously now that their fruits had been picked, and
beautiful ferns had begun as if they had all the time in the world
before the frost. And, back of the house in the old orchards, there
were pear trees and quince trees and apple trees and cherry trees—
and even the most aged trees, with their bark soft and rotted, were
beautiful. Wreszin saw everything like a drunken man and hid his
face against Ruth, overcome with gratitude.

"Everything's beautiful here, like a garden," she said. "It's like
something I used to just see in pictures. And you people own it all."

It was sometime in early September that she told him she was
going to have a baby. This did not surprise Wreszin. He must have
wanted it or expected it, for he knew right away what they would
do: they would leave. They would drive away together. "Don't
worry," he said over and over. "I know what to do, don't worry.
We'll live someplace better than this and the hell with them all."

"I'm not worried," Ruth said.

Mrs. Wreszin seemed strange to him now. They moved together

in the same house and the same room, and when their eyes caught hold it was with the slightly embarrassed, half-friendly look of acquaintances that would get to know each other better if they had time. At night she slept heavily, as if her soul had sunk somewhere deep, and Wreszin lay awake and was able to think of his wife only through Ruth, remembering how he had thought of her while in Ruth's arms. He lay awake for hours, his head aching, thinking of the failure of his life—the failure his children were inheriting and the failure they would give to their children—and the love he felt for Ruth, who made this failure unimportant. If he could bury himself deeply enough in her he would forget everything, just as she seemed to forget everything. If they could run away far enough, he would begin life again—a young man again, maybe, with a young man's strength—and none of the failures of his life would be real.

He planned their escape carefully. It made him nervous: it was going to be like a wedding. On a Sunday he would think of driving down to get some beer, and on his way out he would ask Ruth to come along for the ride. The only bad thing was that they couldn't take anything with them. "I'd need some things," she said slowly, "but I s'pose if we can't do it, then we can't. . . ."

"We can buy new things. Everything new," he said.

The night before they were to leave, he could not sleep. His mind raced. He tried to think only of Ruth, of making love to Ruth—this was now the center of his life. But threatening this center were other things, images of violence and darkness, things on the edge of his mind that he could not drag into the light. He dreamed of the house burning down and his family burned to death, even Billy, and he woke sweating and shivering. He didn't want that, no. He didn't want that. He wanted only to be free of them and to drive as far as he could with Ruth, down the road and to the highway and to other highways, on and on into the distance in which they would be lost and no one would ever find them. . . .

Next day, supposedly on his way to the crossroads tavern, he paused in the kitchen where the three women were working.

"Maybe Ruth would like to go with me, for the ride . . ." he said abruptly.

This was something new, because he never let any of the children go there with him. But his wife and Betty did not seem surprised. "Sure, honey, you go with him," Mrs. Wreszin said. She did not even let Ruth finish the dish she was drying, but took it away from her—Wreszin saw that. Mrs. Wreszin stared at Ruth and reached up to take the ribbon away that held her hair back.

"It looks better without this," she said. "Don't it? She might find her a boy friend down at the crossroads. I wouldn't want her to look like anything except the best."

Betty, who was barefoot, watched woodenly.

"A nice girl like her, she'll find a nice boy friend someday," Mrs. Wreszin said. Her voice was harsh and hopeless.

Out in the car with her, Wreszin could hardly breathe. He had to lean over the steering wheel and catch his breath, like an old man.

"You're not afraid, are you?" he said.

"I'm not afraid."

He backed the car jerkily down the drive. It seemed to him that everyone must be watching, so he did not look at the house. Only when he was safe down on the road did he look up—he could see only the edge of the roof. "They won't know what happened to us," he said.

"I wish . . ." said Ruth, "I wish we didn't have to hurt them."

"To hell with them," Wreszin said. He began to drive fast now, as if released. His foot wanted to press down hard on the gas pedal. His hands on the steering wheel were hot and damp. The swamp moved by on their left like a picture fast unwinding.

He drove quickly along, saying nothing. He hadn't been with Ruth in the car since the day she had come, and her presence excited him; he wanted to touch her to make sure everything was all right. Her body was a mystery to him, like the land he had begun to see as something new—strange and lovely if one did not expect anything of it. It was wild with its own beauty, and her body was wild too, knowing no names for anything and ashamed of nothing, and deep inside it was his baby, hardly more than a seed, a fantastic seed that would grow and force her body out of shape—a tribute to his youth and strength, and he loved it and her, and himself in them. Before this, it had never occurred to him to love himself.

Suddenly Wreszin was afraid. He had left something behind but could not remember it.

"Don't drive so fast," Ruth whispered.

He pressed down harder on the pedal. He hadn't heard her. Panic spread in his brain like mud in clear water, for he knew that if he let himself remember, he would never be able to escape.

For a while he took the turns without thinking, his hands moving automatically, his body tensed, now leaning forward, now back, to the side, expertly, gracefully. This was his road, his world; he knew it perfectly. It was like himself—his own being, extended out before him so that he could see it. But gradually it turned into another road. It seemed to shift, to transform itself even as he was conquering it. . . . Why did Ruth paw at him, why was she protesting? She must have seen something ahead that he could not see. Wreszin, drugged and hard-jawed, found himself staring at the swerving line of trees but really saw nothing. He knew they were oaks, but his brain could not focus on them, on what they might mean. The car smashed into a wire fence—carried it along—headed for the trees—all of it happening so fast that Wreszin could not determine what the noises were about him—

"He's dead, I know he's dead—he's dead," Ruth said when they helped her, lifting her from the ground. She had been thrown into a shallow drainage ditch; she must have been thrown clear of the wreck. Her face was bleeding from a cut on her forehead, a single cut, and something had happened to one of her legs, though she seemed to feel no pain. In fact, she seemed to be angry. "Why do they die?—why do they die? It isn't my fault—" The girl was furi-

ous: it was her anger that frightened them more than the sight of
her and the sight of Wreszin in the car, jammed against the steering
wheel. He must have been dead: it looked as if his chest had been
crushed.

They left him there, not knowing what else to do—they were
country people, neighbors of the Wreszins'—and drove back to their
farm to telephone the state police. In the back seat of their car the
girl would not keep still. She terrified them, she was so furious.

"Why—why— It isn't my fault—"

*T*he Maniac

I

She saw a man at the railing.

Her gaze focused on him, on his back. He was leaning forward against the railing, so that his shirt strained against his back muscles and the muscles of his shoulders. At first she did not even notice the color of his shirt; then she saw, or half saw, that it was a light green, with stripes of some fair, vague color, beige or pale yellow. It was probably cotton. His trousers were made of some inexpensive material, khaki-colored, the kind her younger brother had worn in high school. She stopped looking at his clothes and stared at the back of his head. His hair was light brown and not very long—not exactly in the style of the day—though a few curls fell over his shirt collar unevenly. His hair was disordered from the wind but it was not

long enough or thick enough for strands to be blowing in the wind,
the way her hair was, and she wondered if he had to narrow his eyes
somewhat against the stinging sensation of the wind, as she did. She
felt how her eye muscles tensed, and she had the idea that his too
were tensing, as if he were suddenly afraid. She herself was not
afraid. But yes, in a way she was afraid, she had to admit that she
was afraid. Yes. Fear hovered about her but the intensity of her
gaze kept it away; she stared at the back of the man's head and
waited.

They were about twenty yards apart. He was leaning on the railing that overlooked a busy part of the city's harbor, and she was
standing quietly on the pavement. It was noon: many other people
were around them, walking past her, legs and children's quick eager
bodies and the arms of mothers, and shoes, walking, hurrying to the
water's edge and out of Yvette's vision, but she did not really notice
them. She did not notice the shrill cry of the gulls or the several
blasts of a tugboat's whistle, though her facial expression altered,
startled, and then composed itself again—how far away it was from
her, on the very surface of her skin! She knew it was a day of wind
and clouds, splotches of sunshine, huge boulder-shaped masses of
clouds, and then patches of wind-cleaned blue sky, but she no longer
really noticed this.

She approached him slowly. As she drew near him she felt an
odd precision to her body, to each movement of her body, and in
her mind's eye she had a flash of something like a dream: a vision of
herself as a skeleton, but made of nerves and nerve tendrils, not of
bone. It gave her the peculiar, pleased sense of a dream, the kind
one experiences just before going to sleep, a half-dream, then a sur-
facing to consciousness again, and then a sinking into sleep. *O my
love*. She felt a kind of music rise in her, the quivering of this nerve-
skeleton, a trembling, swaying, an utterly delicate structure of tendrils, and her heartbeat quickened, the pulse that led from the left
side of her jaw down thickly into her chest felt warm, certain. *Love,
my love*, she heard herself singing to herself silently, yet in her own

girlish voice, a voice she had discovered years ago—when she was twelve—and that she had never denied.

A woman with two children walked between Yvette and the man at the rail. One child on each side of the woman, a girl and a boy, a perfect balance, though the boy was tugging at his mother's hand and wanted to break free. Exclamations in a language Yvette did not know—probably Italian. She waited. The woman with her children went to the railing on the left side of the man and drew out of Yvette's vision, so that there was nothing between them again. Now she was perhaps four yards behind him. The wind snatched at her hair and made her eyes water, but she did not want to wipe her face for fear he might glance back at her just at that moment, and not see the entirety of her face. It was skin, a surface of skin that could be measured in square inches, but she realized it was very important to him.

The man shifted his weight. He brought his right foot up on the lowest bar of the railing and leaned forward again. His shoes were made of some canvas material. He was resting on his elbows. She could see that he grasped his hands together in front of him. Now, very slowly, almost cautiously, he was turning his head to one side . . . he moved too slowly to be attracted by the movements of a barge approaching from that direction; Yvette glanced at the barge, saw that it was an ordinary Rogers Sons Coal Co. boat, and forgot about it, all in the same half second. She smiled. In a sudden exaltation that seemed to course through her, illuminating her entire body, she drew in a deep breath as the wind moved onto her, and very slowly raised her hands before her—a gesture she reined in, made normal and even ordinary, by bringing her hands to her hair as if to protect it from the wind. Then, smoothing her hair down, she drew her hands slowly onto her neck, her fingertips on either side of her neck, moving slowly downward, and then onto her shoulders so that her fingertips rested at the very edge of her shoulders, lightly, so lightly that she could not have said what she was wearing, what kind of material her fingertips were actually touching. She knew she was wearing a summer dress without sleeves, because it was a very warm day in mid-September, but she had no real consciousness of it.

The man moved uneasily. She could see his profile now. He was a stranger, a stranger to her, yet she had already known that. The side of his face showed he was still very tanned from summer, and about the age she had imagined him to be—in his late twenties or early thirties—though this was not important. She smiled, not at him or at the two of them, but into him, and into the feathery image of herself as that nerve-skeleton, which could not be seen by anyone at all—not even the man—but which existed, secretly and permanently. She felt how the nerve fibers stimulated her muscles, how small darting pinpricks of excitement were beginning, in the area around her heart and stomach and the lower part of her body, but most precisely just around her eyes. It seemed almost that there were tiny stitches of nerves surrounding her eyes, or fibers thin and fastidious as lines made in ink, with very small pen points. Yvette let her hands fall slowly from her shoulders and in that instant the man turned, suddenly, and looked at her.

II

That summer Yvette was haunted by voices. They were high-pitched and thin and seemed to descend from the sky. After Emilio left for work in the morning at 7:30 she turned off the radio, sometimes in the middle of a news announcement or the weather prediction for the day, so she could hear better. As she did housework or walked through the three-and-a-half rooms of their apartment, on the top floor of a large brick house that had been converted into apartments years ago, she often paused to listen to these voices and to wonder whom they belonged to . . . whose wives . . . whose children. . . .

On windy sun-splashed mornings the voices sounded unreal, but they were real enough. Occasionally the children's voices lifted in shouts, blown across the dried-out expanse of lawn from a playground two blocks away. Then the voices were separate, isolated. But most of the time they were one wave-like harmonious sound, an almost inaudible music. Yvette and her husband lived in one of the few old houses left in this part of town, at the intersection of Waterman Boulevard and a narrow residential street called Post Street; across the way was a vast multi-acre complex of high-rise apartment buildings ("Parkville Estates") set at odd angles to one another, like dominoes upended playfully. There were six of these buildings and each was made of the same indefinable smooth gray material, and each was eleven stories high. On the far side of the Boulevard was a playground where young mothers took their children every day, if the weather was good; beyond the playground was a city park with a few acres of trimmed grass, a scraggy duck pond, and a rose garden in which roses were clustered together in thick untended bunches according to their colors—all the white roses together, all the yellow roses, all the red and pink and orange-red roses in big plots. Beyond this ordinary park was a stretch of open fields and woods that came to an abrupt end about four miles to the north, where the new interstate highway was being dug.

Waterman Boulevard led downtown, falling sharply in a series of hills to the small city where Emilio worked. He was a draftsman for a precision tool company that sold its products to one of the large automotive companies a hundred and fifty miles to the south, in Detroit; Singer's Precision Tools Ltd. was not a division of a larger company, but had to compete with other small tool-supplying companies, so its financial condition was always shaky. Yvette's husband did not discuss the future with her, except to warn her that they couldn't buy a house for a while, couldn't have a baby for a while, and Yvette did not argue.

Alone in the apartment, walking slowly from room to room before she got dressed for the day, Yvette thought of how safe everyone was, living in a set of geometrical shapes like these rooms or like the shape of the small city itself, which formed a half-moon on the river, or like the defiant shapes of the high-rise apartment buildings.

Yet these three-dimensional shapes were not so permanent as those formed by state lines, city limits, streets, boulevards, and highways. The old, shabby, dirt-soured house in which they rented a few rooms was scheduled to be torn down sometime after the first of the year. Their lease ran out on December 29, a date Yvette kept thinking about; they would have to move then, in fact, a few days before that date, and she hoped they would be able to move across the street into the Parkville Estates. This was the first apartment of their marriage and sometimes Yvette dreaded the thought of moving and having to watch the house razed; sometimes she was excited by the prospect of a change.

One Tuesday morning in late August she left the house, about 10:30. For an hour or more she had been hearing voices from the playground, laughter and cries and a mixture of sounds that were airy and musical. But when she came to the playground she saw only a few women there—no one she knew—and only a few children playing noisily on the swings. A small blond girl was standing on one of the swings, jerking frantically from side to side, screaming. Whose child? Who was her mother? Four young women stood together not far away, smoking cigarettes, and as Yvette approached they all glanced at her curiously, as if hoping she were someone they might know. They ignored the little girl's cries. Their faces were blunt and shining, without makeup; there was something sisterly about each of them, but they did not know Yvette and their expressions did not alter, did not soften, so that Yvette decided not to bother with them. *No. She didn't want them, not them.*

She walked around the playground, skirting the outside, avoiding the noisy cluster of children. One of the young mothers was watching her—a red-haired, barefooted woman Yvette's age, a stranger. *No. Not you,* Yvette thought. It was possible that they could become friends, but no, not today. Yvette felt a surge of excitement for some reason. She was not that woman, and she was not a woman known to the four young women in the playground; she was not the mother of the screaming little girl; she was a dark-haired young woman walking away quickly. So much energy in the children's bodies, so much noise!—but it had nothing to do with her. She walked past them self-consciously.

A very old woman was tossing bits of bread out at the white ducks on the pond; the ducks were not very hungry. The woman was wearing a coat that looked heavy, perhaps a winter coat. Yvette did not quite look at her, but walked along the edge of the pond, aware of herself, wondering what she was going to do. She had been drawn out by the voices from the playground, but they had disappointed her and had nothing to do with her, so that morning was open, uncompleted. Sunshine made the pond's surface gleam, in spite of the layer of seeds and scum and other debris. . . . Yvette narrowed her eyes and seemed to see another, deeper layer that was untouched. The surface film was uneven, oily, dotted with imperfections, the other layer was clear and invisible and yet very powerful. . . . Yvette tried to make out this deeper layer but was distracted by the old woman's voice. "Here, come here! You stupid things! Stupid things!" She was scolding the ducks but Yvette guessed the words were really for Yvette to hear. So she edged away.

At the far end of the pond a Canadian goose paddled, alone. Yvette watched the nervous but regal motions of the goose's wings, which seemed almost to be loosening, coming undone, then drawn back shrewdly to the bird's rounded, compact body. Its body was actually quite large. Its neck was snake-like, cautious, its eyes rimmed with black as if eyesight had to begin in such private, cunning darkness. The ducks' cries at the other side of the pond were harsh and exclamatory, over and over, an endless repetition of noise. Yvette had been hearing these noises all summer without quite realizing what they were. At a distance there was something human in their anger, and also in the oddly mechanical, repetitious form of that anger. *No. No. Yes.* They shouted their fleeting thoughts, they reversed their emotions, they made claims and then forgot them a half-second later. *Yes. No. No, I want.* . . .

Yvette wanted something herself. She did not know what it was.

In a way she knew it was not something she might possess and not
something that had happened to her before. If it had happened
once, it was completed; to make it happen again was to force a repetition. Her lips drew downward, as if tugged cruelly by gravity, slyly,
as she thought of the many things that had "happened" to her,
many times. But now she was a married woman and when she
thought *I want . . . I want to . . .* it was a woman's voice she heard
in her mind, not a young girl's.

She skipped the rose garden, which she disliked, and walked out
of the park. A wide, partly eroded path led up into the woods. There
were abrupt gullies a foot or more deep, in which someone might
turn an ankle, but she walked quickly, eagerly, as if expecting to
discover something just ahead. A wire-mesh trash can had been
overturned and a few beer cans and napkins and crumpled papers
had fallen out, but no one was around. This part of the park was
so wild it looked a little frightening, like something in a movie, a
scene into which one of the actors is about to walk. Yvette looked
around cautiously. A few birds hopped through the tall, browning
grass, crow-sized birds with gray and white patches on their wings
and slender, slightly curved bills. When she approached, they flew
away noisily.

She could not hear the ducks now, or the children. She imagined
she could still hear the low rumble of traffic from Waterman Boulevard: a steady fading roar, like breathing at the point of sleep. You
dropped from it, knowing how it would sustain you.

No one was around. She was alone. Yet her eagerness did not
fade; her heartbeat began to quicken, as if her body were aware of
something she herself did not yet know about. At the edge of the
path was a ditch or gully into which a few newspapers had been
blown, dried and transformed thinly into another kind of material,
skinlike, yet not human. Alertly her gaze leaped about the scene,
waiting to see something. *She stood where the path turned wild.
She was in her mid-twenties, long-legged; her hands at her sides but
each finger poised and expectant.* She saw that she was alone, yet

she could not help glancing over her shoulder again, quickly— *She glanced over her shoulder. But she saw no one.* When she turned back she noticed a few birds in the grass and perched in bushes nearby, black birds she couldn't name—she didn't know the names of most things that were not human—with short blunt tails. She stood in the grass and felt how there was a network of attractions here that somehow excluded her. Every motion of her body violated it. Her thoughts violated it.

To think of Emilio: no. Or even of her husband, *a husband*: that was a violation. To think of any man, or even the body of any man ... to think even of her own body ... that was a violation, a mistake in this place. She waited a while, and a small questioning smile seemed to shape her mouth from the outside. She felt her lips stretching into this smile. Helplessly, she would have to think herself back into nothing: a droplet of fluid, a single tear-sized drop in which a universe swam. Yet even that was a disturbance here. She wanted something else, she wanted to be free of such thoughts. In this network of dense, soft, fragrant connections, her own moving mind was a mistake.

She glanced behind her once more, self-consciously, and then went to sit in the grass. Her legs were bare, the dried weeds irritated them, a small swarm of dotlike insects blundered against her face. She waved them away. The weeds beneath her were dry, broken, silent. She waited a while, very still, and saw how the field defined itself into a multitude of separate things, shapes she had not noticed before. The intense sunlight had an autumnal slant to it and gave a sharp-edged brilliance to everything, but this seemed to distract from the unnamed, half-seen things populating the place.

Dreamily she heard the hum of insects. The skin of her left cheek flinched suddenly, shivered, as a fly brushed against it—the shock of that sensation, which she hated!—but she resisted drawing away. She remained sitting. She sat. After a while that part of her face relaxed again. *Now I want. . . . I want. . . .* But her mind went empty, dreamy. She seemed to be looking at a field of ordinary grass,

weeds that flowered in thistles and small yellow flowers, a number
of scrubby bushes. . . . Some of the bushes were partly denuded,
their leaves eaten by insects; filmy cloudlike cocoons hung on some
of the branches, motionless. There may have been life inside those
clouds but Yvette could not see it. The sun pounded on the back
of her head and she felt that something was good, something was
in its place. *She sat quietly, her shoulders drawn forward as if she
were awaiting something.*

Some minutes later she heard voices behind her and turned to see
two girls walking along the path. They were about twelve or thirteen, and wore jeans and loose boyish blouses. They were talking
loudly and didn't notice Yvette, who cringed a little. They walked
by. She noticed how the field about her had been disturbed by this
intrusion. It took some time before it returned to what it had been;
a queer dullness, a flatness, seemed to have slipped over it, as if a
thumb-smeared lens had been raised to Yvette's eye. After a while
the connections returned, a throbbing web of forces seemed to rise
to her vision like an infinitely detailed, almost invisible network of
nerves. . . . she half-closed her eyes and felt how the network eased
into her, into the skeleton of her own nerves. . . .

After a while she felt uncomfortable; she had been leaning on
one palm. She brushed bits of straw and dirt off it, noticing how the
skin was crisscrossed with lines, a jumbled confused pattern. Her
skin itched. She scratched it with one fingernail, slowly, pausing
to see how there was a pattern of lines and shapes impressed upon
her skin, which she had never seen before. It seemed to her suddenly very important. She drew in her breath, startled. She had
never seen this before, it was new to her, and what if she had not
understood it . . . ? Nothing was repeatable. Nothing came again.
She could not invent anything and so she could not reinvent it or
reimagine it, it could come only once . . . suddenly there was a terrible pressure in her brain to memorize this, to understand it.

No, help, oh no, help, help me. . . .

Almost, a kind of panic rose in her. Her jaws went rigid with the expectation of something, as if she were being observed and would now be laughed at. Like love, it was something like love . . . that same urgency, that half-questioning half-resisting acquiescence, that fear. . . . It was wrong, this way. It was a mistake.

Her mind propelled her backward, helplessly. She seemed to be inside the bedroom of their apartment—looking down at the bed-clothes, drawing one of the sheets up, going through the mechanical motions of making the bed. And she was inside, boxed-up, boxed-in. She felt and then saw the face of Emilio as he stared at her. He had been jealous for so many months, and even now he was watchful, contemplative . . . she felt boxed-in by his stare, his assessment, his perpetual intimate knowledge of her. She tried to get away from the memory of him. Her mind leaped onto the two girls who had just walked by on the path, and she summoned back their conversation, a fragment she'd overheard without thinking: "Oh yeah?— when? Well listen you can tell Holly how I—" The words seemed to her utterly empty, like the ducks' cries. Not even human. Not sane. She thought of herself as a girl of that age, cutting across someone's vacant lot on her way home from school, walking with another girl and talking in that same singing half-mocking way, as if this were a kind of music everyone knew, everyone embodied at a certain age.

O my love, love. . . . She heard her own voice say these words, as if she were outside herself. She could almost see her own face, her eyes, the shape of her mouth as she pronounced those words in wonder. Now a man was embracing her, now a man was entering her body, now she said those words aloud and experienced them for both herself and the man; then the words faded and she realized that she was sitting in a field, alone. The sun was beating on her. Somehow it was measuring her, using itself up as it caressed the back of her head in that pulsating warmth, in a rhythmic heat. . . . It was coursing through her and using her up, at the same time that it was using itself up, an unrepeatable process. She had to keep pace with it.

In a flood the field seemed to rush in upon her, pushing her aside. In relief she felt how her mind was snatched from her, torn away. Everything was blurred, sun-shot, blazing. Now she wanted nothing that she could name. She sat in a kind of peace, in perfection, inside a rhythm of grass stalks and leaves, contained inside a larger rhythm. She was not thinking anything. Only vaguely was she aware of some disturbance, some sound—it was an effort for her to turn her head, and to see someone walking by on the path again. This time it was a man in a yellow shirt, but he didn't seem to see her. He walked at a normal pace, not hesitating, not so fast as the girls. A man's shape, a man's presence, his footsteps: reluctantly, almost painfully, she thought of her husband and wondered if he might be following her?—but in the same instant she realized that this man was not Emilio. She had never seen him before and now he was out of sight. He was gone.

Something seemed to be happening to her that drew her sharpest attention and flooded her veins with a peculiar exulting certainty: that her personality was only now emerging, that another self, her truest self, was only now rising in her. Where was it, what did it mean? What would happen? She felt that she might be translated into something else. Slower and slower her breath, her heartbeat, and more vibrant the field about her: sounds of insects, of birds, wind fluttering leaves somewhere out of sight. The earth smelled warm. She could smell earth. Everything was calm, measured by a rhythm that was too large for her to assess, inside which she sat in suspension. A pendulum seemed to have swung far to one side and was now pausing before swinging back: in that heartbeat of an instant an entire world might spring into creation. She must hold it there. She must prepare for it.

A rhythm inside a rhythm, held somehow in suspension. She felt the sway of the earth carrying her with it. The pendulum did not swing back; she felt how it held itself suspended, like a breath. And in that instant she felt her body go transparent, utterly weightless, a substance like air that had somehow been given a density through thought, as if someone or something were watching her, buoying her up. She was a structure with enough dimensions to be seen, enough weight to keep her from slipping off into space. She felt a sun-warmed lushness that had something to do with the dimensions of her own body, its secrets, its memories and harmless adventures, unique and unrepeatable, and she realized why she had been loved, often, and why she was loved now, by a particular man who existed somewhere behind her in the city, who existed in order to love her and to stand in the place of someone, anyone, who might love her instead of him. . . . Yet it did not interest her, really, the thought of this kind of love. It fell away from her. It was only a thought.

Somewhere there was a sound, a rustling of grass. She heard it, yet did not hear it. *No. Keep away.* She opened her eyes and saw nothing. A few feet away, in the grass, was the body of a bird, partly decayed. She had not noticed it before. Now she found herself staring at it. It had once been alive . . . out of its warm flesh so many feathers had grown, black glossed with purple and green, sprinkled with tiny light spots, an entire universe of colors. . . . Something swayed in her, a thought close to panic, yet calm, rhythmic, beyond all emotion. She looked from the bird to her own hand and saw how the back of her hand was crisscrossed with infinitely small lines and wrinkles. There were slightly raised veins there . . . delicate knucklebones . . . fingernails evenly shaped, filed carefully. Why had she doubted anything? Why had she ever yearned for anything or anyone? She needed nothing; in herself she was complete.

"What's wrong? Is something wrong?"

She looked around. The man in the yellow shirt was approaching her, staring. His smile was strained. Yvette woke to that smile and saw how awful it was, how long-prepared for her. She felt a wave of darkness pass over her mind, like a seeping of dark blood inside her brain; for an instant she could not think at all.

Then she got up. "Nothing's wrong. Go away," she said.

He was in his forties, perhaps. No, older. She could not guess his age. She staggered a little, one of her legs was numb, weak, suddenly sickened. A sickness seemed to flash up her body, up her side and into her throat, a congestion in her throat. She did not think she would be able to scream. The man was staring at her, into her, with that peculiar hazy smile, a red haze over his features, everything blurred and throbbing and uncertain. Yvette took one step backward and then stopped. It would be a mistake to back away. It would be a mistake to run. She was able to think clearly enough: she would not run.

"I thought, uh, maybe you lost something—? I saw you there and was watching you and I thought—did you lose something? You want some help looking for it, maybe?"

Beneath that idiotic smile she felt his yearning for her. The sun expanded so that it seemed to contain him. And almost, in that moment, Yvette acquiesced to it, to him: why not press herself into his embrace, was it important enough to struggle?—why, if he wanted her, if he wanted to slash and tear at her, should she hold herself from him? It was so hypnotic, so blinding! She saw a human shape in him, saw how his arms might reach for her, it was a rhythmic entwining, a part-struggle, a coming to completion. At the back of her mind were words: *a man, a stranger, a man in a yellow shirt, a man in his forties or fifties, smiling, grinning, very nervous, he walked up to me in the park, in a field, he came up to me, he said, he wanted, he didn't say, he, he came toward me and. . . .*

"No, get away! Leave me alone!" Yvette said.

He paused. He stared at her. She could see how he measured the distance between them, and how he measured what had been said so far, which words, and what showed on his face. To stop now, or—? To keep going? Ah, how she knew him! She knew him from the inside!

He was a stranger with a balding head, a very warm, flushed face, a husky labored breath. There was a mole or a birthmark of some kind high on his forehead.

"Go away," Yvette said more calmly. "I don't need you. I'm all right. Go away."

"I just thought if—"

"No."

"If you needed some help or—"

"I said no."

"If you were waiting for somebody, or got lost—or if you were all alone and, uh, lonely—I thought—I thought—"

"No," Yvette said.

Then a boy on a bicycle appeared, and it was over. The boy was no more than eight or nine and he was riding a fairly large bicycle, panting with the effort of pedaling. Yvette broke out of her trance and ran onto the path after the boy. The man in the yellow shirt backed away; he looked stunned, idiotic. Yvette walked quickly away. She did not look back. Ahead of her the boy was pedaling, standing on the pedals, a child with white-blond hair and a grimy white pullover shirt, an incredibly thin, lithe body. It was over. Yvette walked back to the main path, she began to hear the ducks again and the children's cries, she began to hear a hoarse choked breathing that was her own. *No, don't, oh please, a mistake . . . a mistake. . . .*

When she returned to the apartment she was soaked with sweat. She felt the stinging stars of sweat at every pore. In a kind of dumbness, in a trance, she let herself into the apartment and stood there and only after a long moment did she realize she had better close and lock the door.

III

They had quarreled again.

He walked out at five minutes to ten, and by eleven-thirty she knew he might not come back. So she went into the bathroom and washed her face calmly, and dabbed some makeup on, and outlined her lips with a deep pink lipstick. *You bastard, why are you so jealous? Why, of what? What do you know?* she would ask him. But no, that was cruel, he'd slap her across the face if she ever said that; he had already slapped her once. Her mouth had bled. Her upper lip cut against her teeth: an effortless near-painless bleeding.

Then he had wept in his fury and jealousy and had had to love her, to make love to her. She didn't want him to strike her again. Or maybe she did want it, maybe when she caught up with him she would invite it after all. She couldn't be sure.

She picked up her white orlon sweater from the chair she'd thrown it on and went out and down the stairs. Downstairs, on the veranda, the landlady, Mrs. Chenault, was sitting with nothing to do except observe Yvette on her way out, obviously in a hurry. She had observed Yvette's husband a while earlier, no doubt. And now she would say *Isn't it late to be going out?*

"Kind of late and dark to be going out, isn't it?" she called after Yvette.

"Go to hell," Yvette murmured.

It was a block to the Drop Inn, but Yvette knew he wouldn't be there. She looked inside and didn't see him. *Bastard. Oh you bastard*, she thought. He wasn't there so she went all the way down to Howie's, walking fast and keeping her eyes averted when kids in cars sped past, because it was late, and the Boulevard down here was getting rough. The city was becoming dangerous, like a big city; like a real city. Emilio had yelled at her for leaving the door unlocked when he came home from work; he had walked in, had thrust the door open, had accused her of not caring, not caring what happened. Didn't she know there was a maniac loose out here? —hanging around the apartment buildings, scaring women in the laundry rooms, slashing a woman in the underground garage with a jackknife, didn't Yvette give a damn, hadn't she been warned often enough? Yvette had been defrosting some chicken parts, thighs and breasts, running water on them at the kitchen sink, and she hadn't even heard Emilio come in until he began shouting at her. That was at twenty minutes to six, hours ago. He had rushed into the kitchen and grabbed her and said, "You left the door unlocked again! Didn't I tell you about that? Goddam it, didn't I tell you?"

Yvette had stared at him in astonishment.

"Anybody could walk in here—" Emilio had said angrily.

"But—"

"But, but! Are you trying to drive me crazy?"

After a while he had calmed down, but during supper he'd been sullen and nervous, and shortly after nine o'clock he started at her again, accusing her, picking at her, the old jealousies, the old curious obscene wondering: how many other men? He knew there had been other men, he knew, he wanted her to know that he *knew*. But how many?

Yvette had laughed.

He wanted to know, How many?

She laughed and asked him how he could be so certain, how he could know?—There had been no one, no one at all.

"You're lying," he had said. But he stared at her hungrily, wanting her to lie. She felt the stab of his desire for her, impersonal and furious. It was urgent, intense, the same sensation of desire she'd felt in him at their first meeting, over a year ago now; yet it was not purely his own, it did not belong to him alone. She had felt it, in differing degrees, in many other men and in herself. "You're lying. I know it, aren't you lying?—aren't you? Why else would you leave the door unlocked?"

But this was a senseless remark and she had no need to answer it. Emilio hesitated, knowing he had made an error in this argument. Then he said bitterly: "At least you could be careful of yourself. You know about that maniac around here—it said in the newspaper for women to be careful and keep their doors locked and not answer the door if they're alone—"

"He wouldn't come after me," Yvette said.

"What kind of a remark is that? He wouldn't come after you!"

"He wouldn't. He wouldn't. He'd leave me alone," she said stubbornly.

So they had quarreled, off and on for an hour, and then Emilio had walked out. And now she followed him, down to Howie's at the corner of Waterman and Sears, where she had to push her way through the front door because a gang of kids was hanging out there, making remarks and yelling at passing cars. They gave way for her, she was in such a hurry and so angry.

"Hey, sweetheart, if you don't find him—"

"Hey, honey—"

She found him at the bar, she saw him at once, standing with his back to her. He was talking with another man. Or no: not talking, just standing there while the other man talked. Yvette didn't know the other man. She hesitated, her heart pounding. She had walked so fast, five long blocks, and now the blood rushed in anger into her face, her veins swelled, she felt herself flushed and exalted with the power of possession, of knowing what she wanted and how to get it. A number of men stood at the bar but her gaze only swept over them and dismissed them, and focused on Emilio's back. He wore a blue workshirt and his dark trousers, the trousers he'd had to have altered because he was so uncommonly long in the thighs, and his very black, very curly hair drew her gaze to it, seemed to concentrate light in its waves, its infinite beautiful waves. . . . She had no other lover but Emilio now. She would have liked another lover—a lover who was not a man, who had not a man's anguished thrusting hardness, his stab of desire, of pleasure—she would have given herself to this lover, this shape in the air, but she could not locate him, she did not know what she wanted, she thought herself half mad and then thought, in the next instant, that this man was enough for her, Emilio was enough, enough of a man for her, as good a lover as any.

Trembling, very excited, she stared at the back of his head and waited. Each movement of his body seemed to her beautiful, and the way he drew his hand carelessly and impatiently across the back of his neck—maybe bored with the other man's conversation?— showed her how much himself he was, always himself, *Emilio*, an unrepeatable body, unimagined until she had met him. She had to love him, she could not help it. She felt a kind of music rise in her, a thickening of her pulses, the central pulse of her body, all blood-thick, hot, dense, opaque, unshouted words, half-suffocated cries, repeating *Yes. Yes. No. I want—*

The man who stood beside him glanced at her, and his gaze took hold of hers. In that instant Emilio would know, from his friend's rapt, strange look. In the next instant he would turn to face her and it would be over: another quarrel, another night.

If she must love a man, she would love Emilio.

He jerked around to face her, his eyes strangely dark, as if the iris were expanded, enlarged, already staring into her before he could have known she was there. She felt the force of his stare like a blow. But she did not draw back, she only smiled a smile she knew would madden him. And so he grinned at her, angrily. He had not yet spoken. He was still angry; she felt the beating of his heart, his frenzied brain; she did not fear it but gave herself up to it. She would love him, then: since she had to love a man, she would love this particular man. It was over.

Free

I

She was from a good family, "from a good family," and it was a handicap like any other: like prominent teeth in high school, like a dancer's sudden loss of nerve. She was a tall, stern, smooth-faced girl with a rapid intense voice that put everyone who slurred the truth to shame at once. Lea herself told the truth and her telling it was an act of violence.

"They forced me to do stupid things, they forced me unconsciously," she complained to her friends, once she had left home. "On Saturday mornings I would go out and my mind was made up that I'd steal something, anything. I wanted to get caught, to humiliate my parents. But instead of stealing from a big store I always wound up around little grocery stores, you know, these sad little

125

places run by old men and women . . . and I'd steal something from them, something that was out in the open . . . a candy bar or something. . . ." It was disgusting, how she had stolen from the poor and not from the rich. It had been a mistake. But though she had grown out of her childhood and would never steal again, was contemptuous of stealing, still the shame remained with her.

The thefts took place when she was twelve years old. After that she entered the excitement of high school life, in which she did well. She had the long-haired, clean, blond look of a cheerleader, she was pretty, she knew how to smile and her smile could be dazzling. She lived in the best part of town. She threw off her younger, sullen, stubborn self and stepped into a new life; it was intoxicating to her, and this too became a kind of handicap a few years later—when her friends found out about her "normality," they were fondly scornful.

"So you were a real teen-ager, like in the comics?" they said.

Yes, she had been a real teen-ager years ago, and none of her present friends had been teen-agers at any time. They had the soiled, soft, aggressive gentle manners of perpetual children. They had never been teen-agers: had never been consumers. They scorned consumers, so they said. They scorned the American products beloved by consumers. They scorned Americans, America, but the very quality of their scorn was mocking, as if they realized that the object of their scorn was insignificant.

"And you really lived on a street called Lincolnshire Lane?" they said.

The house was enormous, in a suburb of a large Midwestern city: a white colonial with immense black shutters, built in 1870 and since then remodeled at great expense and outfitted with authentic antique furniture. Lea's mother was interested in authentic furnishings, down to doorknobs and converted kerosene lamps. She was a sweet, uncomplicated, rather domineering woman of the fortyish suburban type. Lea's father was a doctor, Dr. Gregg. He was an internist and a serious, successful man; he had won the tennis trophy at his club two years in a row. The house on Lincolnshire Lane was a model of authenticity. It needed nothing to complete it; it was perfect. When Lea stole things from little stores, she was not stealing in order to fulfill anything or complete anything in her life, but to tear a rent in it. Her life needed a sudden breaking-down, never a building-up.

"But you can't blame your life on your parents, not really," her friends wisely pointed out. "It wasn't their fault. What did they know?"

That was true, her parents were victims. In a sense they were children, but their power was so great that they were frightening. Like gigantic children, a god and goddess of Lea's countryside, they marched through their world and dragged Lea one way, and then turned around and dragged her the other way; they had her vaccinated and inoculated, they had her teeth outfitted with braces, her skin treated for blemishes when she was eleven, her hair was cut by Rocky of the Electra Beauty Salon, she was enrolled in swimming classes and in tennis classes at the country club, in riding classes at the Hunt Club, in ballet classes at a private dance school, in the eleven o'clock children's Sunday School. . . .

"But your father, now, your father must have been interesting," someone said to her once. This was at a party. She had come alone, feeling both arrogant and shy, and this young man sat down beside her. In ten minutes they had traded their life stories, already made brief by countless tellings. His life story (a mother widowed early, fatherless children, lack of male guidance, etc.) seemed to Lea a little familiar, but she showed interest. Her life story might have seemed to him a little familiar, but he too showed interest. He asked about her father: "I mean, now, a man that's a doctor, well, a man like that . . . he, well, he's *got* to come into contact with experience. Real experience. You know . . . life and death, suffering and all that . . . and happiness too, sometimes. . . ."

"No, that isn't true," she said with passion. She always cut through attempts at making conversation. This man wanted to be

---

pleasant, but he was patronizing her and she resented it. "No, not at all. Doctors don't know. They don't understand anything. To them people are just bodies; what is of most concern to them is their golf game or the squash tournament the next day. Or the dinner party on the weekend. They use the bodies of their patients to climb up from dinner party to dinner party. No, don't interrupt, please—I know. I know all about it."

"Look, I've known a few doctors myself. They're not all like that."

"The successful ones are like that. You probably only know failures," Lea said.

She felt his dislike for her at once. They stared at each other, locked in a peculiar warm affection, enemies who have sized each other up and are not displeased.

That man was Anthony, whom she met by accident at another party the following night, and with whom she fell in love briefly. He was a writer and he had had one story published so far, in a small, smudged magazine called *Godot*. Lying on his bed one day, Lea read this story, "The Many Transformations of Zeus," which seemed to be about violent acts perpetrated upon helpless victims, some of them animals. "Who in Christ's name are you imitating here?" Lea said, pretending amusement. She was really shocked. "You wouldn't know," Anthony had said. "No, please, tell me. Who is it?" she insisted. "Paul Bowles," he said. "Of course I know Paul Bowles! I've read Paul Bowles," she said, offended.

It was their habit to be truthful with each other. And they always did tell the truth. When she asked him, teasing, whether anything would come of their love, he told her, quite seriously, that he would perhaps put her in a short story. If only she could change her name! Lea Gregg was an ugly name and he put great emphasis upon names. "No, really," he said in his customary nervous, gulping, enthusiastic voice, "really that's so. Beyond names is nothing. Beyond words is nothing. Beyond 'Anthony Palarchio' there is truly nothing, but the name itself is a beautiful name—it happens to be attached to me. My soul has been named Anthony Palarchio and is therefore unique. Your soul, however, is Lea Gregg and that name is ugly, I'm sorry."

At first she had not liked to talk about her family, the peculiar love and hate of her life "back home" that was so singular to her. She was ashamed to talk so openly. But as time went on, as she moved from one loose group of people to another, finding and losing friends, breaking away from her job finally, she found that she had prepared a number of family anecdotes and that she could tell them quite easily. She never lied, of course.

"But essentially I agree with your mother. That's the perverse thing, actually," a friend of hers once said. This friend's name was Alice and she was an off-again, on-again fashion illustrator. The rooms of her small apartment were cluttered with drawings of emaciated, angular, knobby models, while Alice herself was full-boned and solid. Lea liked Alice because she was truthful, like herself. And she was generous, she did not take herself seriously, was always giving parties to help out impoverished friends; once every guest had come with groceries for a destitute Mexican couple, bags and bags of groceries, and the little apartment had been filled with people. Lea and Alice often sat up late together, talking.

"Yes, I don't condemn your mother. I think you misunderstand her," Alice said thoughtfully. "Your mother was trying to create a fixed universe. She tried to do it through owning things. But not just owning things—that would be trite—instead, through cataloguing and worshiping them. Right? You said your mother had a table worth eight thousand dollars. Frankly, Lea, eight thousand dollars isn't terribly expensive for an antique."

"It was an ugly, ghastly thing," Lea protested.

"How would you know? I don't want to criticize you, Lea, but you really don't know much about antiques. Or art. Or human nature. Because, actually, your mother in her selfish and confused way was an artist, and you didn't recognize it."

"Oh hell," Lea said.

"I sympathize with her desire for a closed universe. A self-sealing universe, like Spinoza's. Except he did it with theorems in imitation of mathematics and she did it with pieces of furniture."

"You don't understand," Lea said passionately, "what it was like to live there! My God, I couldn't touch anything, I couldn't play anywhere, can you imagine it? Everywhere all this crap! It was beautiful, some of it, but it was dead. Everything was dead. I thought I'd go insane sometimes, even when I was a child and couldn't have understood. With the misery everywhere, even our cleaning lady led a miserable, miserable life—with so much tragedy everywhere, my mother went into hysterics if something was scratched—she almost drove me crazy but she, she was the one who was crazy! She was the one! Don't tell me I don't understand my mother. I don't want to understand her. Terry says that simply to understand certain people—certain vicious people—is an act of collaboration. He's right."

"Isn't he exaggerating as usual?"

"No, he's right. Evil begins with compromise. A lot of kids my age who went away to college felt the way I did about their homes. Sure, we talked about it, not like this but we did talk—we talked. But they decided they could live with it, they loved their parents in spite of everything, they'd forgive their parents for being so—so dead—because they thought that peace was important. Living in peace! But I knew they were wrong. Now they're like everyone else, living in homes like my parents' home, they're married and their husbands are doctors or lawyers or businessmen— Evil begins with compromise. You can't compromise or you're dead. I knew that my mother and father were killing me, suffocating me, that I had to get out. In a way I loved them. I don't know. But I had to get out. I had to be free of them and not just free of seeing them, either, but free of them completely. Terry says I was born again this year. I really became myself. Until then I was half-alive, I'd been suffocated by *them*. . . ."

She had gone to a prominent girls' college in the East for two years, and then she had transferred to a large Midwestern university. In her senior year she was unable to study, unable to read—her eyes would not focus upon printed words—she was sick to her stomach, she was miserable, utterly miserable, and there was no reason for it. She and her parents could discover no reason. In discussing their breakdowns, years later, Lea and her new friends were emphatic about one thing: that "breakdown" was a term invented by guidance counselors and non-academic deans and parents, and that another term was needed, something like "vision" or "penetration." Because, of course, what had seemed to be a breakdown was in reality a building-up, but before any building could take place the clutter of twenty years of buried life had to be violently swept away.

"Now, Lea's experience was quite different from mine," Terry said. He was thirty-eight when she met him at the age of twenty-six. He was an instructor at a New York university, not a professor, not one of the permanent faculty, which he explained quickly and ironically to everyone he met. He was a poet. "She broke down rather negatively, I mean, her initial emotional experience was negative. Mine, crazily enough, was positive. It was fanciful. I was very happy—I was intoxicated. The meaninglessness of college work delighted me. I couldn't make myself read, just like Lea, but somehow this fact delighted me—and I was clever enough to get through my exams anyway."

"But how did you do that?" Lea asked.

"By knowing how to write, my dear. If you know how to construct a sentence, the academic world is at your feet. The academic world admires structures that look good. It has no interest in substance."

They laughed at this, but it was true. True, no substance, and true, a worship of structures. Forms without essence. Of the six or seven people in this particular apartment on this particular evening, all had attended college and three had quit in their freshman years.

Lea had managed to get a B.A. in something her university bro-chure called "The Humanities," and Terry had an M.A. in some-thing his university brochure called "Creative Writing."

"What you say is true, but still there was something pleasant about it," Lea said. (She was an attractive girl, but very fierce.) She hunted for the truth like a chicken pecking in the dirt for food. "I know it was blind and self-righteous. I know that. But the very sound of the tower bells, and the way the students shuffled in and out of buildings . . . and, oh, the way the professors droned on and on . . . there was something charming and safe about it, as if it were under a glass bell. . . ."

Terry smiled at her indulgently. "But to get the real thing, my dear Lea, you should commit yourself to a nuthouse. *That's* the real thing."

She joined in the laughter that followed this, not wanting to sit untouched and foolish. If she resisted, Terry would appear to be judging her, and she was afraid of his judgment. He sat on the floor, his shoulders hunched, his dark, bearded face cast in shadow. She loved him, but his judgment could be devastating.

By the time she was twenty-seven her cycle of stories about upper-middle-class life and college were polished and sophisticated but rather dead. She talked listlessly to a psychiatrist her father had begged her to go to, a Dr. Joris. He was a Park Avenue psychiatrist and really quite absurd . . . she found him amusing, terrifying . . . and in talking to him she felt everything go flat, all her anecdotes, her passion, her anger: "I don't know what I feel about them. My father, my mother. Are they important? I see faces. I could bring you photographs of them, if you insist on knowing about them. . . . I can't help you, frankly. My childhood? Yes, I had a childhood. I had a Siamese kitten. It was declawed. It tried to scratch the furni-ture, oh, it was hilarious to see that smooth little cream-colored cat paw desperately at the sofa and scratch, but nothing happened, over and over again its paws paddled and never caught hold, I re-member that quite clearly. . . ."

"And in your present condition, which you refer to as a kind of depression, what would you say is the dominating emotion?—what do you feel essentially?"

She thought for a moment. "Nothing," she said.

"Anxiety?"

"No. Nothing."

"Are you worried about the future?"

"The future?" she said.

II

After her setback in the last year of college she was a more serious girl. There was something radiant, even angelic about her smooth, handsome face: her high cheekbones suggested delicate dents about her eyes, her very manner was subdued and thoughtful. This was, of course, her essential self. She and her roommate could no longer get along because Lea had always been in disguise, all of college had been an occasion for her disguise as a college girl: a sorority girl, even, with cashmere sweaters and plaid skirts and a fanatacism for clean hair. Now the disguise fell from her. She returned to school after a month of having blanked out, back home and under the cautious hothouse alarm of her mother and father. Both her mother and father had talked with her for long, long hours, singly. They did most things singly. And, in listening to them, Lea had transcended the misery of her mysterious sadness and thought clearly: *Why, they are stupid people.*

Like her roommate and the others girls in the sorority, they believed in food first of all. Good solid food. They believed in the American virtues of eating the correct food, which would be transformed into the correct tissues. Secondly, they believed in good thoughts. Their beliefs were simple and blown-up, like a child's painful handwriting: easy to read, and yet senseless. They believed in sunlight, in opening Venetian blinds and adjusting rays of light so that they cascaded beautifully into Lea's beautiful room, onto her American antique bed that was like a magnificent boat about

to embark upon a mysterious stream. . . . They believed in talking
everything out, and yet in retreating to the shade of certain reserva-
tions, certain areas that are . . . not talked about, ever. When Lea
said, puzzled, "But how do you manage to keep going? I mean
every day, how do you manage? I want to know how you *manage*,"
her father seemed not to understand the question. He asked her
to repeat it. "How do you keep going year after year, Father?" she
asked. He thought a moment and said, "In my work there isn't
much time to brood over things, Lea. But I try to get in about six
hours a week of recreation, like tennis. You know. Nothing exaggerated, nothing neurotic. In work like mine it's very easy to collapse, I
know what you mean, it's very sad to work with some of my patients. . . . Very sad. . . . I try to keep a good schedule, that's about
it."

She had made the mistake of asking her mother if, really, she
loved her father. And her mother had been quite insulted. . . . But
it had seemed to Lea that her mother felt nothing except a superior
affection, almost a fond contempt for her father, and how was it
possible to remain married under such circumstances? Had they
always been so distant? Had they been in love at one time? "Was
there ever anyone you loved, I mean passionately? So that you
wanted to die?" Lea said. But her mother had been insulted, and
only Lea's feverish look had restrained her. "You're sick, and you're
saying sick things," her mother said.

And so when she returned to college there was nothing to say to
her friends there; it was all the same thing, she felt a violent, numbing sense of their *being liars*. And the sorority house, which was a
large, rambling white building with many beds, seemed to her only
another version of her mother's house. All houses were the same.
They closed you in, they confined you, trapped you. It was maddening. She promised herself that never, never would she own a house;
never would she own anything. She wanted nothing. She wanted
to be free.

At school she became acquainted with people who shared these feelings. She was still weak, she was aggressive and kept falling in love, when really there was no need to fall in love: her lovers told her that. One was a sociology instructor who was completing his doctoral dissertation on "Promotion Factors in Selected Public Relations Firms, 1960–1961." He believed none of his findings, though they were statistically accurate; he was brilliant and argumentative and attractive, and Lea fell in love with him in the summer and could not fall out of love. He was married, with one child. He invited Lea to the prefabricated hut in which married students lived, and he and his wife and Lea drank coffee and talked. They talked about freedom. "The only thing that matters is to be free, utterly free," he said. He spoke as if lecturing. "You, Irene, you know that. Lea, you claim to know it but I don't believe you. You're always enslaving yourself. You form these idiotic attachments, you make cow eyes, you bother people . . . when really people find you delightful, why do you hang on them? Irene and I have a relationship based on absolute freedom. We have other friends. We explore other relationships. But ultimately we choose to remain together, because we've decided that any one of a series of individuals is as valuable as any other, there's no 'progress,' and since we happen to get along intellectually and physically we may as well be married. We respect each other's freedom and, in choosing to live together, we are free. But you, Lea, with your terrible emotional dependence, you could never be free even when you appear to be free. Because you're always preparing yourself to latch onto someone else, someone stronger than you . . . you're not free, you're enslaved."

"But how do I get free?" she asked in desperation.

Husband and wife exchanged a look. "You have to live," the man said.

And so she left the Midwest and came to New York, where she got a job with a small publishing house. She was hired for a "project"—a yearbook to be called *Industrial Yearbook 1964*, though it really covered the events of 1963. The job paid $4500 a year and it was to be terminated when the yearbook was done.

Because she was fairly intelligent she could finish a day's work in an hour or two, and the rest of the time on the job she spent thinking, brooding. It seemed to her that every day was of crucial importance, that her life might end and would have come to nothing, had been worth nothing. She lived alone now. Her apartment was on the fringe of the Village, in what was to be called casually the East Village in a few years; she had the slow, confident, rather feline look of a certain kind of New York girl, though she was really Midwestern and easily shocked. Her hair, which was wound up around her head into a kind of heavy crown for work, could be unhooked and worn down around her shoulders the rest of the time; her clothes were plain and cheap, as if she realized that her youth was enough and that cheap clothing played up her face. She learned a new kind of laugh. It was staccato, rather breathless, and was intended to be a parody of itself: as practiced by certain men, it was a kind of bemused, incredulous cackle, a mockery of female laughter.

Her new friend Anthony laughed this way, and she thought he was very charming. He took her out to cheap Italian restaurants and they sat for hours in coffee houses, talking, arguing, making an impression on each other. Lea was elaborately dogmatic. "Please, I don't care what some mystic told you, there is no truth in religion. Absolutely none," she told him. With a few other young men who, like him, were vaguely interested in writing, he advanced the idea that the "religious" experience was of possible value; it established a basis for a community, a synthesis of separate experience. It was therefore valid. But no, no, Lea said scornfully, all that was just apologetic garbage!—it was like excusing the Nazis for their evil by saying that all men are fallen, we're all a little guilty, and so on. Anthony was exactly as tall as Lea, and quite thin. He wore working clothes though he did not work. He received unemployment checks.

He lived in a single room on a sleazy Village street and he liked
nothing better than to sit out on the front steps of his building and
stare at everyone who strolled by. There was something both adolescent and aged about him. After Lea had talked with him on two
consecutive evenings at parties, she looked him up, amused by his
chatter. She walked past his building and there he was, sitting . . .
it was a Sunday and there were tourists in the area, women who
might have stepped out of Lea's home town. She was stimulated by
their presence. She felt how powerfully, how violently she was
against them, and how her alliance was now with Anthony.

They fell in love in a certain fashion, and their relationship
lasted for six months. Later Lea was to remember with a kind of
desperate shame their long, involved, passionate arguments; with
them, arguing had achieved the quality of passion. "But you, you're
a hypocrite," he cried in his rapid, nervous voice, poking a finger at
her. "You work. You write to Mommy and Daddy. They send you
money and you take it!" "What about you?" she had said, furious.
"You take money from the city! You're a hypocrite yourself!" But
he said calmly, "I'm not a hypocrite because I have no illusions.
I know I'm stealing. But I have chosen this temporary degradation
because it's the only way for me to continue my writing at this
time." When angry, he had a peculiar trembling dignity. His hair
was blond, nearly the same fair, attractive color as Lea's, but his
beard was darker and rather scanty. When she hated him she concentrated her hatred upon this beard. It was too thin, it wasn't
masculine. It was an insult to her. If they were lovers he had no
right to advertise his weakness by wearing such a beard, it was
absurd. . . .

He took his writing very seriously, though he could not force himself to write often. In the evenings they walked out, over and over
the same route, to Washington Square and back, slowly, ponder-
ously. Though he was young, there were lines of worry on his forehead and on either side of his mouth. He sucked at his fingernails
unconsciously. The flesh beside his nails was unusually pink and

raw. He relaxed only when he took pills or drugs. Otherwise he did not relax even when he slept; his body remained rigid and apprehensive. She loved him, really. In the dark she would put her arms around him and try to soothe him, but as soon as he fell asleep his muscles went rigid. . . . She did love him, but there was something about the way he talked when he was excited, swallowing nervously, gulping at the air, that irritated her. But with him, she told herself, she never had to lie. It was always the truth, the truth. At a friend's party one night he had been drugged and dopey and had said to Lea: "That guy you're talking to, you want to go home with him? Go home with him. It's all right with me." And he had meant it, he had even wanted her to go with the man so that he could demonstrate his generosity. Lea was very hurt. She took pills that were offered to her, she did what the others did, but never noticed much effect; it seemed to her a put-on, a pretense. It seemed to her a kind of corny religious ceremony and she despised religion, she had no sympathy with it in any form.

Months passed in this way and her job came to an end, but one of the editors wanted to keep her on. She was pleased, strangely pleased. She went home to Anthony, who was still in bed—it was late afternoon—and woke him up to tell him about her news. But he only said, "Is that all? You woke me for that?" The tension rose in her at once. She hated him and his indifference, he was just jealous of her. . . . "You're very pleased, aren't you?" he said scornfully. "Somebody praised you!"

And, after that, she had to turn down the job. He was right that praise pleased her. She was that weak. She was enslaved to other people's opinions of her. And she turned her eye upon Anthony himself, who was increasingly sleepy and verbose, and she asked herself whether she was now dependent upon this . . . young man. This boy. The pattern of their relationship was exactly the same as it had been on that first night: combative. She was not necessarily female in the relationship, and he was not necessarily male. They were disembodied voices arguing with each other. Of course, they respected each other's intelligence, or the contest would have been worthless. When they were with other people they tended to defend each other, childishly. Perhaps they were brother and sister? They looked alike. Anthony's hair was long for a man, and his eyes behind his dark-rimmed glasses were the same deep brown as Lea's. He was not exactly ugly, but his face was long, brooding, ponderous. Lea, though a pretty girl, had the same exaggerated brooding look, and tiny lines had begun in her forehead.

She asked herself: *Am I emotionally dependent upon him?*

The question itself put her to shame. She had to work herself loose, be free. The loneliness that Anthony had assuaged in her life was only a memory to her now, and she was confident that she would meet other men. She already knew other men. And she had a casual, chatty acquaintance with some girls like herself, among them Alice Baumgarten, who was an "artist." She would not miss Anthony. She had a vague faith in him as a writer, he impressed her with his continual brooding and his long monologues about a series of novels he meant to write, but still she would not miss him. In the end, she coolly used his writing as a means of prying herself loose.

"I'm bad for you. I sense it," she explained. He was agitated at her tone, he was so nervous that his hands began to shake. "I don't think a writer can share himself with a woman, I truly don't. Everyone says that. If you were just a mediocre person like Sam Snyder, or Babs, it would be different. But you're very talented. I sense there's no room in your life for me and so I want to leave."

A kind of pseudo-joke between them, as lovers, was Anthony's "irrational genius" and Lea's "rational genius." For him, the glories of art, and for her, the more muted glories of practical life. She had gone along with this joke but had resented it bitterly, and now she turned it against him like a knife. She hated him; she did. She hated his not being masculine enough to shut her up when she was telling him such garbage. . . .

And so they parted. She spent a day or so in her bed, weeping, and she wanted to go back to him. It was a sickness, her dependence. But she told herself that she was finished with Anthony, she was free. If freedom was this painful, it would be a permanent freedom. She would be free. She would please only herself and she would be only herself, she would show no allegiance to anyone else. Already she had stopped writing home; she sent her parents' letters back to them, with their inevitable checks, and scribbled in brief answers. And she had definitely quit her job. She had no job at all now, she was perfectly free to lie in bed until noon, and she was pleased as the days passed at how unworried she was about the future. She would live in the present.

It was through her friend Alice that she met a man of about fifty named Pablo. Perhaps he was Spanish. He was heavy-set and very friendly, very charming. His dress was youthful though not extreme, he was not too obviously imitating the young people, and he had money. He took her out and gave her money and she mockingly accepted it, saying, "Now what does this make me?" But he assured her that it made her nothing, nothing! She was a beautiful girl, a pure girl! So intelligent and talented! She went with him to Florida but got fed up with him, he'd turned bullying as soon as they were alone, so she packed and left . . . and she thought it was all quite amusing. She and Alice and their other friends laughed about it. Strange people, all fascinating, came in and out of Alice's apartment, and Lea met them all. They were from every conceivable city in the country—it was strange how many of them were from small towns. No one was from New York City at all. Perhaps no one was born in New York City? Alice came home occasionally with older men, men who had the look of husbands, visitors to the city or commuters from the suburbs, and she and Lea went out to good restaurants and never said no to money that was offered them. Alice kept quitting her jobs and so she needed money, and Lea felt that it was immoral for her to accept her father's checks. So they both needed money.

Some of the parties lasted all night and well into the next day.

People kept showing up, strangers appeared, everyone was welcome. Sometimes the parties were legitimate parties and sometimes they were just imitations, given by people who were anxious to imitate a certain style. Alice had this style, though she was big-boned and healthy and looked like a Girl Scout leader. Lea, for all her prissiness, had the style too—she was delighted to realize this. Long-legged, languorous, irrelevantly profane, she was in "the style" and it was her new identity. The young men they knew had this style without seeking it, they dismissed everything that was beyond their world, they were gently scornful, they were really children. Men who worked at legitimate jobs tried to imitate this style but failed. One night a hilarious argument arose. A young man, who was in advertising but wanted to show how much he despised his work, attacked the American Establishment and the Culture of the Dollar. It was degrading, he said earnestly, to prostitute oneself to such horrors.

But the others said lazily that there was nothing wrong; what was wrong? Wasn't life beautiful?

Life was ugly!

A bearded man, new to Lea, said in a gentle, scornful, condescending voice: "Hiroshima is a poem. Vietnam is a poem. You are not an artist, you can't understand. You're a moralist. Moralists are dead."

"You think that our commitment in Vietnam is good? A good thing?"

"Vietnam is a poem," the man said. "Bombs are poetry when they go off. Machine-gun fire is poetry. Agony is poetry."

He was a little high, this man. He'd been taking something but he was in control of himself and Lea felt a sudden jab of desire for him, he was so much in control, so intelligent. . . . She stared at him. His hair was dark and his beard was full and nicely trimmed. He wore ordinary clothes, not trying to prove anything, but clearly he possessed that indefinable style. "You win! He wins!" Alice declared loudly. She yanked the bearded man's hand up into the air. "Oh, Terry's the winner, Terry's triumphant. Don't argue with Terry, you poor stupid bastard! Terry is a genius."

So she met Terry. They talked for hours, he and Lea, sitting on the floor in one corner of the white and gold apartment. He was rather high. He had an aggressive, soothing, sweet manner; she loved him. His accent was pleasing to her. He was from east of the Connecticut River. "And you, honey, you're obviously from Kansas," he said. "Not quite Kansas," she said sadly, knowing that to an intelligent man she would always seem provincial and second-rate. They talked about loneliness. They talked about the movies of Antonioni. They talked about their families, about the past. "The past cannot be escaped," he said. He played with her fingers, in his childlike, grave manner. "So many of the people think the present is the only reality, that the past doesn't exist. It breaks them up. They don't last. I understand, instead, that the past is more powerful than the present, and therefore it must be accepted. It must be transformed. Made into a work of art, into a poem. And then one can be free of it."

"Yes, free of it . . ." Lea said slowly.

"My wife killed herself. This was eight years ago. We had three children, three girls, they're with me now—beautiful girls. I love them. My wife was a brilliant woman but she broke down and was hospitalized, and then at Christmas she came out to visit us. She seemed better. But she killed herself, she hanged herself in the basement. This was in a rented house by the university where I was an instructor. . . . I was left with the girls. The impulse in such a case is to cut off the past completely, to forget about it, to deny it. To begin life again in a capsulized, antiseptic form. Right?"

"Yes, yes, I think so," Lea said, staring at him.

"But that's wrong. That leads to death. Instead, I transformed the past. My wife: I loved her. Is love bad? No, love is good, love is the only good. I cherish that love. She died: is death bad? She chose to die. It was a choice of hers. Her freedom was to die, and so she died, and I have no right to pass judgment on her. I think about this all the time, I relive the past and transform it, I make it beautiful. And now it's beautiful for me. My wife's death has become beautiful. I love her for her death, for being so free, I love her for her courage. . . ."

"You're . . . you're very brave," Lea stammered, in exactly her mother's voice. She was quite upset. She stared at him and the thought came to her that he was to be her fate. Everything in her fell toward him. Gravity shifted toward him. She stared into his face and thought he might do anything he wanted with her.

She expected to hear from him the next day, but he didn't call. He didn't come over. A few days passed, a week passed, and she was miserable. She began to go out again with older men, acquaintances of Alice's. She treated them with a mournful indifference. She took money from them, she was distant and greedy, having no shame. Why should she feel shame? Through practice she had become freed of it and, anyway, it was only Terry she wanted. So her relationship with any other man had a certain purity about it, the purity of the accidental and meaningless.

Then, at a friend's apartment, she finally met him again. They talked at some length; once more she was overwhelmed with desire for him. She said boldly, "Come back to my apartment with me." She couldn't help but say it, the words were out of her control. And she herself was a little high. He came back with her. He was a man in a way that Anthony wasn't a man, and yet he too was a writer, a poet. He taught English at a university in order to support his children, but his only interest was poetry. She loved him; the experience of love with him was devastating, overwhelming. Afterward, they talked for hours. They talked, they held hands. . . for the first time she was in love, it was unmistakable.

And if he left her?

But he didn't leave her. In a few weeks they rented an apartment together, sublet to them from a friend of Terry's. He had many friends, he knew everyone. She was proud of the people he knew.

And yet she was a little jealous of the girls he talked with. For the
first time in her life she felt hostility toward other girls. "It must be
that I'm becoming more female myself," she said. They talked
about themselves, the complexities of their feelings, for hours. "In
the past I wasn't really a woman because I hadn't a man, therefore
I liked the company of women. It was men who seemed a little
fraudulent to me. With most men a woman has to put on a little
act, oh, some kind of act . . . it's a sordid routine, it's enough to
make you vomit. But now that's changed. I don't feel that way.
Now it's women I feel edgy around, because I identify with them
so strongly, I know they're competitors of mine, I'm in danger of
losing you. . . ."

"Danger? There's no danger," he said. But he was pleased.

She was a little afraid of his daughters, just as she was afraid of
all children. The oldest girl, Clavdia, was eight; Marie was seven;
and Bettina was five. They were beautiful children, but oddly quiet;
when they played they could be silent for hours and then break out
in sudden hysterical shrieks, which Terry was slow to silence. Gradually, living with them, Lea felt something in her awaken . . . it
was like a flower opening, her love for these children. She pitied
them immensely. While Terry went out to teach, she played with
them, getting down on the floor with them. She toyed with the
idea of becoming a mother. Why not? She was a mother already.
These children were her children. . . .

She divided her time between the girls and Terry, between the
simple-minded routines of the apartment and the jarring, exciting,
but also simple-minded routines of the outside world. She was
exactly like a wife. She was a woman in love, she had a husband and
three children, she had found her place in the world. But her brain,
which had worked so fast at her job, seemed now to be unaccountably slowing down. She did not drink or smoke much, but she was
dependent on some blue-and-green capsules that Terry brought
home: strong tranquilizers for which he had a prescription. He also
had pep pills of another sort, bought from a contact. She took

these listlessly, having no will to resist him. Sometimes she didn't know what she was doing. She loved him and yet—yet the love was disembodied and somehow outside of her. She was a woman in love and yet it was a condition she could not quite feel.

Then, in April, he came home and told her shakily that his contract at the university was not going to be renewed. "What does that mean?" she said.

"It means I'm fired."

"Fired? Why?"

"Just fired."

"But didn't they tell you why?"

His face wrinkled into a malicious, mocking look. He seemed to be saying to her, *Why? Why? Are you that stupid, to be asking why?*

And yet she found that she was pleased, because he would have no job now. Like her, he would be free, unattached. He wouldn't meet so many people now, have so many friends. She tried to soothe him, like a mother, talking gently, rationally, pointing out how much he had hated his job and how hard he had worked, how they had exploited him—three composition classes! three!—and how much more time he would have now to write. He needed time, he needed leisure. Why should they exploit him and work him to death? Her words were soothing, deathly soothing.

With so much time, they began to sleep late. The two oldest girls got up and dressed themselves for school, and left for school, alone. Sometimes they weren't dressed warmly enough, and sometimes they forgot to eat breakfast, or didn't know where the food was, and the apartment was so cold that Bettina remained shivering in bed until Terry and Lea awoke. They were groggy most of the time, but pleasantly so. They went out often. Their friends gathered them in, sympathetic with Terry's bad news—which had been molded into an anecdote now, centering on Terry's "nonconforming teaching methods" and the fascistic administration of the university. Their friends seemed to like them more, now that Terry was fired. The world opened up, more people appeared, the circle grew loose and wide and Lea was madly proud of her alliance with this brilliant man. . . . Under his influence she began to experience a certain illumination, with drugs. The essence of the experience, Terry told her, was not physical at all, but spiritual. One had to be prepared for it. It was like love, it was mainly spiritual, it didn't work at all on an inert physical substance. . . . And she felt that the universe was truly opening up, she could stare into its secret workings, it was beautiful and intensely alive. . . .

"Everything is so beautiful," she said in alarm.

"It's beautiful," Terry said.

"I can hardly stand it, it's so alive. . . ."

"It's beautiful because you are beautiful. The universe shows itself in the colors of the mind that perceives it. Those who see horrors are horrors themselves. They're not beautiful. We're beautiful, we see the universe clearly, we understand. . . ."

Their friends sometimes asked Terry to talk to them in this vein. And he talked: gently, humbly, yet with a strange, fierce confidence. "The universe is a mirror. The reflection of the mirror is the universe. You look into water and see yourself, and in seeing yourself you see the universe. Everything. It splits open, the waters part, the beauty of it cries aloud . . . it's like pain, it's like love. . . . People fear beauty because it's painful."

But sometimes, in spite of everything, in spite of his faith, he went sour. And Lea went sour under his influence. Then they stayed in bed all day, they forgot to eat, they locked the children in a back room and forgot about them. Really, children could be exhausting. "Now, look, you understand that I love those girls," Lea told Terry. "They're my own children. I love them. They're under my care, but I don't have to put up with nonsense. I don't have to clean up their mess. Bettina knows enough not to wet the bed, she's five years old, therefore she does it out of spite. She does it as a sign against me. But I, her mother, choose to cut her off. I choose not to think about her. I X her out, my mind will not register her. . . ."

Terry loved the girls too but he didn't care to talk about them. He agreed vaguely with Lea. For hours he sat by the gritty window, staring. His eyes had a filmy, dreamy look. Lea knew enough not to bother him, but once he turned to her just the same and said mockingly, "You're attracted to Jews, eh?"

"Jews? What makes you say that?"

"Because you came right to me that night. Do you like Jews, is that why?"

"Of course not," Lea said.

"Back in Kansas there aren't many Jews, eh?"

"You don't even look Jewish, my God. . . ."

"Did you hang around with other Jews before me? Live with them?"

"No."

"I can check that."

"Oh, hell—"

"I'll check on that, sweetheart. And if you're lying, I'll have to punish you." He stared at her sadly. His eyes were a little swollen, his face looked pasty, puffy. "Yes, I'll have to punish you if you're lying."

She was rather frightened. But she said, imitating his squinting, sleepy, drugged look, which she thought charming, "Terry doesn't seem to be a Jewish name, I didn't know you were a Jew or care one way or another. . . ."

"We'll see."

Then one night when they returned from a dull party they heard screaming from their apartment. When they went in they found Bettina in the kitchen, screaming. The other girls were watching, helpless and terrified. Bettina was screaming like an animal, a high wailing whine, she had torn part of her pajamas off, spittle gleamed on her small, distorted face. . . . Terry tried to pick her up but she fought him. There was such a commotion that neighbors gathered out in the hall. "What's wrong, Bettina? What's wrong?" Terry cried. The little girl was crouching in a corner, like an animal. She was panting. Clavdia said that Bettina had told her her head was getting big. "Her head? What? What do you mean, getting big?" Terry said. Clavdia explained in terror that Bettina had said her head was swelling up, it was big and heavy, she couldn't hold it up. . . .

Lea, who wasn't high herself, understood. She called an ambulance.

In the kitchen Terry kept trying to pick up Bettina, circling in toward her, talking to her. There was a small noisy crowd out in the hall and Lea shouted at them, "I called the hospital, you can go away now! You goddam nosy bastards!" She slammed the door in their faces. Then she stood by the door, waiting. Minutes passed slowly. She knew what was wrong with the child. But she could not bring herself to tell Terry, who was himself high from the party, who wasn't thinking clearly. . . . If she hadn't loved him she would have left. Fled. This was too much, it was ugly and complicated. The police would arrive, the ambulance would arrive. A diagnosis would be made. Bettina had obviously eaten something of theirs, it was something "illegal," she was having hallucinations and was out of her mind, an animal. Lea thought dizzily that she would not have to love the child any more then, if she became an animal. That wasn't required. But she did love Terry. She was enslaved to him. Miserable as he was, idiotic as his voice sounded out in the kitchen—"Bets! Bettina! Come here!"—still she loved him and could not leave.

The child was hospitalized, and what Lea had thought turned out to be true. She and Terry were taken to a police station and they swore that the drug had belonged to a friend of theirs, who'd left it in their refrigerator without their knowing. . . . He would be around soon, they could identify him. . . . So they were released, they returned to the apartment. It was over. They were free. Terry sat in a stupor and Lea made the beds, tried to clean up the filth in the apartment. There were dirty dishes and food and towels and clothing everywhere underfoot; it was filthy. She had not known how filthy it was until other people had come in and she'd seen the look on their faces. . . .

Clavdia and Marie were turned over to a child welfare center. Lea thought with relief that she would not have to love them either; the universe was becoming simpler. But Terry sat and said nothing. He was pale, sickly, strange. There wasn't much that was beautiful about him. Lea stayed with him for another week, her mouth fixed into a hard, spiteful line. *Why don't you talk to me? It wasn't my fault!* she thought bitterly. In the mirror her face looked like another woman's face. The lines on her forehead had deepened. She felt she would go mad if he didn't talk to her, didn't love her. . . .

Finally she screamed, "You're driving me crazy! I'm leaving! I'm getting out!"

He turned his bloodshot eyes upon her in mild alarm, as if she were a stranger to him and . . . who was this loud woman? what was she doing?

"Oh, you're crazy, everybody is crazy," she muttered. "I'm getting out." She packed and prepared to leave. She screamed with sudden rage, throwing things into suitcases. She smashed dishes in the kitchen. She wanted to tear the place down with her fingernails, she still loved him and could not bear his silence. Why did he blame her? But he ignored her; he had retreated inside his skull and had no need of her. She ran out of the apartment with her heart pounding madly, she wanted only to leave him behind and never, never think of him again. . . .

After a few days with Alice, Alice told her she would have to leave. The excuse was that other friends were coming to visit. "All right, you lying bitch," Lea said. So she packed again and moved out. She moved in with six or seven people who shared a room somewhere, and they were willing to have her, they didn't argue. The filth and clutter of the room made her feel at ease. No one would judge her here. And the people were so dirty and eerily vague there was no danger of her loving them. She wouldn't love them. With Terry, love had been almost fatal, it was like a bog she'd nearly fallen into and drowned. A bog: stagnant and disgusting. The body: stagnant and disgusting.

She went back to Alice's apartment and sat on the floor, waiting for Alice to return. When Alice appeared on the stairs, with a man of about fifty behind her, Lea started screaming.

She didn't know what she was screaming; afterward she couldn't remember. But she remembered a policeman jerking her to her feet and pulling her downstairs. He yanked her off balance so that she fell and kept falling. It was crazy. He slapped her and wouldn't stop. She could not get her balance, the stairs were too steep, and he became outraged and struck her on the jaw with his fist.

III

She was being examined by a doctor. Her mind woke slowly, lethargically. Her eyes would not quite focus. She resented the examination, she tried to claw at the doctor, but someone strapped her down. That was that. *A doctor is tearing out my insides,* she thought in icy calm. *He'll put in something made of plastic. . . .*

When she was released, she took the money her parents had sent her to come home and leased a new apartment. Though she no longer took drugs, not even simple tranquilizers, she was still a little groggy. She kept thinking about something plastic inside her, pink plastic, a coiled spring of plastic. A birth-control device of the sort put in natives of India, helpless ignorant women . . . and why was it in her? Didn't they want her to have children? She shook her head to get rid of such garbage . . . she knew better . . . it was just that she'd had certain nightmares and could not get them out of her mind.

Her mother came and stayed with her. She played at being Lea Gregg. Sometimes she misjudged her performance and geared it too low: she was Lea Gregg back in high school. But most of the time she knew by instinct what was working and what wasn't. Her mother took her out to good restaurants, took her to Peck & Peck and bought her an excellent wardrobe, and begged her to come home. Lea refused. After her mother left, she did go to Dr. Joris, however, and paid him fifty dollars an hour to listen with a suppressed yawn as she talked about her home life of years ago, her school life, her experience here in New York, her new feeling of nothing, absolutely nothing.

"But you say there was a time when you felt everything was beautiful?"

"I think so. I was high then. But, yes, it was beautiful," she said.

"But that was an unnatural state."

"I think so."

"And now, for instance this morning, what did you feel?"

"Nothing."

"What kind of nothing?" Dr. Joris said. He had a faintly foreign accent, perhaps a pretense. He was certainly an immaculately groomed man in his fifties, a coldly handsome man. But nothing was in him too.

"Just nothing."

"Is it cold, is it dark? Does it give you a sense of horror?"

"No, it's just nothing."

"Does it confine you, is it pressing in?"

"No, I'm free inside it. I'm totally free."

"Is it a physical thing?"

"No, it's just nothing."

"Spiritual, then?" He glanced behind her, as if irritated. He was certainly a well-groomed man, patient and self-contained, and she was sorry to disappoint him. "Intellectual?"

"No."

"Is it just a word? Or a concept? Or a sensation?"

"It's just nothing," Lea said.

But when the hour came to an end she would realize in a panic how precious it was, how quickly it went—and nothing ever happened, nothing changed. The hour was a small bubble inside the larger bubble of her life. At the close of a session, perhaps to emphasize its close, Dr. Joris would begin smiling a certain sympathetic, practiced smile, and Lea got nervously to her feet. "I can't explain it any further," she would say in a rush of breathless words, twisting the strap of her purse. "It's just there . . . it's nothing. . . . I can't explain it. . . ."

And his smile italicized itself somehow, called attention to itself; it seemed to be telling her *Yes, yes, but next time perhaps we will make a breakthrough.* . . .

"I can't even think it through, I get mixed up," Lea stammered.

He stood. He smiled; he said, "Until next week . . . ?" and she snatched onto these words and stood for a moment trying to figure them out. Then she said, "Yes, until next week, good-by. . . ."

"Good-by, Miss Gregg."

She took these words home with her and broke them down into syllables and into sounds, looking for meaning. Though she was certain there was nothing to them, no meaning, still she puzzled over them as if she were dealing with secret emblems of a highly charged and complex universe. Only when she fell asleep sitting by the window did the slightly stale presence of nothing flow into her . . . she understood its coming, she met it, she opened herself to it and slept.

... & Answers

I remember the car, yes. I can still see it. It swerved off the road, it crashed through the guard rail, down the cliff and into the water. . . . I remember seeing the guard rail collapse. I don't think I could hear anything, except screaming. It was my own screaming. And hers. . . . I remember that guard rail. Yes, it had been painted white recently. The weeds near it were splattered with white paint, they must have sprayed the paint on, and I—

This was just before my own accident. Yes. Seconds before. I was staring at that other car, at the broken rail and the edge of the cliff —I was screaming, and—and I lost control of the car—

I have never understood it. I don't believe it. I did see that other car—it crashed just ahead of me, around the turn in the road. I don't believe the car wasn't found.

How? Maybe it belonged to someone who was so important, they wouldn't allow him to die. I mean the newspapers, the government. . . . Deaths can be kept secret, can't they? Anything is possible.

I don't want to talk about it again. My life isn't interesting.

I hate to repeat it, my life; I've answered so many questions, yes, I know you are being very patient and courteous, yes. . . . My life is an ordinary life. It isn't interesting. Nobody would write about it. I was born in San Diego and lived around here all my life. . . . What kind of events? I don't know what you mean by "events." I grew up without thinking about it, like a plant up through the soil—or a weed—just pushing its way through. I tried not to think about it. I never thought that I was unusual. . . . Which tests? High school? Did you look up those old records? Why did you do that?

But it didn't mean anything. I didn't believe it, I didn't allow it to change my life. We were tested one afternoon, all afternoon, complicated questions with multiple-choice answers, very confusing questions, some of them involving little shapes and designs and symbols, not the kind of questions we were used to answering in school. Very confusing, yes . . . some of the kids gave up and started fooling around and were asked to leave. . . . I was afraid to give up. I remember how strange the questions were, and exciting in a way, because they made me think about things I hadn't thought of before. . . . Yes, I was always afraid of tests and questions. There are so many questions to be answered! I used to be afraid of giving the wrong answers. . . .

But now I'm not. Why should I be?

Well, that was years ago. I don't think it means anything now. A week after the test we were called down to the principal's office, a few of us, called out of our first-period class by an announcement over the loud-speaker; you know how frightening that can be, to hear your name over a loud-speaker. . . . Two boys and myself. Everyone knew the boys were very smart. But the principal told us we had all done well on the tests. He was very pleased. I think he looked at me strangely. I was embarrassed. He said we were in the upper percentile of something, one percentile . . . ? I don't remember the terminology.

No, I didn't really believe it. It must have been a mistake.

How should I know? Someone else's score might have gotten mixed up with mine, how should I know? My life has been completely ordinary. I wanted it to be ordinary. I was married when I was nineteen and my husband is a very . . . well, you've met my husband . . . he is a very nice man, very kind. I prefer his parents to my own, in fact.

A little weak, maybe. But very kind. I've never regretted my marriage, no, not at all. We live in a very nice apartment, we moved there five years ago, right after Linda was born. It's a high-rise apartment building, the Northumberland, in the San Fernando Valley. . . . The ninth floor. It has a very nice view. It's a little small, so my husband would sit at the table in the dining alcove to go over work he brought home, and I'd sit there with him and do something, oh, I don't know, anything, mending or anything, and sometimes he'd ask me to check some figures for him . . . his work is very complicated, he's an income tax specialist . . . and I'd help him a little, the best I could. I can add up columns of figures quickly, in my head. And Linda would sit with us until it was her bedtime, playing, cutting out paper dresses to fit over cardboard dolls. Sometimes she would have trouble cutting them out carefully and I'd help her. Children get frustrated very easily when things don't go right. . . .

I don't want to talk about her.

I did see the other car. It wasn't a hallucination. No, I couldn't exactly see who was driving it, everything happened so fast, he was swerving off the road when I came around the turn . . . or she was, it might have been a woman. . . . The road is very dangerous all along the coast. They should do something about it.

Because I wanted to go for a drive. I wanted to show Linda how pretty it was, the northern part of the state. The ocean, and the rocks, and the sky . . . all those little flowers along the side of the road. . . .

From Sunday until Wednesday Linda had been sick in bed with the flu. I caught it from her. I didn't go to bed, of course. The week before, my husband had had sinus trouble, very bad headaches, so the apartment smelled of sick people—you know, Kleenex stuffed in paper bags, in wastebaskets, and the feeling of germs in the air, a sense of thickness. . . . When she was in bed Linda needed attention all the time, conversation, she was always asking questions . . . a thousand questions. . . . She was very quick, very curious. All the questions she could think of to ask! She was very smart for her age. We are very proud of her. . . . So she was better that morning, and I was going to take her down to the playground the way I always did when it didn't rain; there's a nice little playground by the apartment building, a concrete square with a pond and some swings and benches, where all the children play. I've gotten to know a lot of the other mothers there. It's a very friendly place. But a number of men have begun using the square, just sitting around. Not bums, no. I don't know how to describe them. They're not bums or alcoholics, the kind of men you might see in downtown squares, but ordinary men, middle-aged, in suits and neckties, just sitting around.

Maybe they lost their jobs . . . ? I began to be afraid of going there with Linda. So when she got over the flu and we were going down in the elevator I asked her if she would like to go for a ride; I thought of it just in a second, it came to me out of nowhere. It wasn't anything I had planned. No. No, my husband didn't know about it. How could he . . . ? I just thought of it going down in the elevator. Of course Linda wanted to go. We were both very excited, very happy. I don't know why I felt so happy. . . . Linda was so pleased she began to jump around the way she does, a little feverish, the way children are when they open presents, almost as if they're afraid of the presents. Of course they want them, but still they're afraid. I was like that myself. Linda gets very excited over surprises, even good ones. She's only . . . she was only . . . five years old. Surprises are disturbing to children, good surprises as well as bad ones.

No. Not really. I don't remember much of my own childhood.

If you could only understand how ordinary I am, and how simple, you'd see what a waste of time it is for you to construct these theories. . . . It makes me embarrassed. I'm not equal to you.

I said: I'm not equal to you.

Because you imagine something that isn't there. I did see the other car when I came around the turn. The other driver was speeding. I saw his car crash into the railing and go over the side, and I heard the screaming, and my mind went blank with fear, and all the confusion—do you know what it's like to feel your car go out of control . . . ? I don't remember anything after that.

I already told you: he was a famous man, maybe a politician, an important man, and his death has to be kept secret. So the police are keeping it a secret, out of the newspapers. *You* wouldn't know about it either. Isn't that possible? There are many secrets in the

world. I know that. Even when I was a child I knew that. The
world is held together by secrets.

. . . Then nothing. Nothing. I don't remember my own car going
over the side, I don't remember the water. I woke up and someone
was lifting me onto a cot—the ambulance stretcher—a Negro boy
in a white outfit was yelling for someone to grab my legs before I
slipped off. He was one of the ambulance attendants. But I remember this the way you remember flashes from a movie, without any
emotion, because they don't have anything to do with you personally. I don't remember being hurt. No. I don't remember the water,
or anyone screaming, either one of us screaming. . . .

What? Did I say that? . . . Then maybe I do remember it, it's
all so confusing and. . . .

If my husband says that, it must be true. I believe him. I wake up
and he's shaking me, he's frightened and seems ready to cry, he says,
Wake up! You're having a nightmare! He says that I scream at
night sometimes. I don't know I'm screaming, I don't remember
what I dream about that could make me cry out. . . . Once my husband began crying himself. I stared at him, I didn't know that men
could cry. I didn't think they could cry. My father certainly never
cried, he was a very hard, secretive man. Not big. But he gave the
impression of being big. He had many secrets he kept from all of
us, about work, and money . . . even from my mother, he kept
secrets. When he died, he tried to keep it a secret. He lied about
how sick he was and why he was going to the hospital. . . .

I'm not upset!

He told my mother he was going on a fishing trip with some men
from work. He worked in a factory. He said he'd be gone a few days,
but he was really going to the hospital. He died during the opera-

tion. None of us knew where he was. It was just after Labor Day, when school started, and my brothers and I were all confused and frightened. That was the kind of man he was: very hard, very tough. He joked a lot, but if you listened closely you discovered that he never said anything. You could never imagine him, what was in his mind; he liked to keep everyone guessing. I was afraid of him. But I loved him. Then a year ago I first began to notice, in my daughter, something strange . . . when she was very excited she would get nervous, fluttery, her eyes would narrow as if she were afraid of something, the way I had been with my father. As if she had inherited it from me. Is that possible, that children can inherit fear? Can you inherit fear, does it come along with physical characteristics like the color of hair and eyes?

I would never risk that. No. Not another child. Never.

Because of the fear that can be passed on. And all the questions that must be met, and answered, during a lifetime. . . . It's a terrible thing to turn a child loose into that, a world of people asking questions and poking and examining . . . asking questions, not believing the answers, taking notes, asking more questions. . . .

I'm not upset. I'm not angry. Is my face strange, do you see something in it that I don't know about? I used to be a pretty woman. But now my face is strange.

Yes, my face is strange.

I believe what you say, but it hasn't anything to do with me. I trust you. I know you want to help me, you have that goal in mind, yes, I trust you, I know you don't want to deceive me, and—

I'm not angry. I'm not upset. Sometimes my mouth turns up at the corners, sharply, but it doesn't mean anything, it isn't a sarcastic smile, it isn't any kind of smile at all. I only smile when people smile at me. That way I can be sure that a smile is appropriate. I wasn't being sarcastic. I know you're paid to help me or someone else like me, and I don't want to disappoint you the way I've disappointed everyone else. So when I say that I believe you I mean that it's easy for me to believe you, on the surface. I believe anything men tell me and I always did. On the surface. What men say to me, what they said to me before my marriage—when I was involved with several men—goes along the surface of my skin, like the passing of hands over my skin, caresses, but it doesn't affect me. So I do believe you. I trust you just as I would trust any man.

I don't discuss that kind of thing, not with anyone. Not even a doctor.

But I am an ordinary woman, an average woman. That doesn't mean normal, I suppose. I know I'm not normal because of the concussion—my headaches, the way my vision gets blurred at night —I'm not normal now—but I will be normal sometime soon. And through it all I've been an ordinary woman, because you can't change that. My soul is ordinary. It's just that I can't remember the accident. The baby is gone but I have to keep living. . . . No, I don't want to move to another building, it's all right where we are. One building is like another where we live. I have to keep living there.

I'm not crying. This isn't what I would call crying. I feel a strange vibration in my head, as if things were rattling. Or is that from trucks outside on the street? My father used to drive a truck before he went to work in the factory. He was gone a lot. He hated driving. After he quit that job he went to work in a factory that made precision tools or parts of tools, for one of the aircraft companies. But he hated that too.

No, I didn't know him at all. In fact, I never think about him.

Since the accident. People are always asking me questions. . . .
They are obsessed with making me remember certain things. The
way teachers want children to learn and remember certain facts,
but not others. The facts in books. *Learn what we tell you and
nothing else!* . . . But you are like that, aren't you? You want me to
remember certain things, the events of two or three minutes in my
life, that are all over with and will never come back again. But I
can't remember. And what I do remember you don't believe.

Yes, I want to be well.

According to your standards, and other people's standards. Yes.
I want to be well again. My husband wants me to be well. I want
to please you both. Women do want to please men, that's why they
remember things that are important to men . . . they learn what is
important, and after a while it becomes automatic.

Because of a certain fear. I don't know what it is.

. . . I told you: it came to me in the elevator, the thought of taking a drive. Instead of sitting in the square. Linda was very excited
about it. Once I mentioned it to her, of course I couldn't go back
on my word. You know how children are. And she needed fresh air,
she was pale and restless and I had the idea that. . . .

That she was an unhappy child.

That we were failing her—I told my husband that once, I don't
remember when. That her childhood was a failure.

The opposite of "success," I suppose.

Yes, I admit it's a strange thing to say, I suppose it is. But maybe
I got it out of a magazine I had happened to read . . . ? You don't

read those magazines. But there are many articles in women's magazines that help women, housewives, to organize their lives. They make you think seriously about your life. How to bake little cakes that can be fashioned into a train, for a child's party . . . or weaving rugs out of fluffy wool . . . or assessing your success as a mother, on a scale of ten. Maybe I got the vocabulary from one of those articles.

I'm not being ironic.

It might be that sick people sound ironic, because they're weak. Their voices are weak. But they're not ironic at all. They only want to please other people and be considered well again.

. . . So I asked him if he thought her childhood was a failure. If he noticed how frightened she was. . . . Of the street, of other children in the playground, of trucks . . . television shows, some of them . . . bad dreams . . . I don't know, what are children afraid of? Being lost, or kidnaped. I hated to see her so fearful. If we went shopping she was always afraid of getting lost; she stayed right with me. But my husband said he hadn't noticed.

No, no reason. There was no reason for her to be afraid. I would never have left her.

Yes, it's working out better at home now. Did he tell you that? I think it's better. I think I'll be able to sleep with him again soon, and eat breakfast with him again . . . it's just the early hour, the way he eats. . . . He didn't say anything? No, he doesn't eat noisily, he's a very neat, careful man. It's just the idea of it.

Of sitting close to someone who is eating; moving his mouth.

Sometimes I stay in the bathroom as long as I can. Or I say I'm not hungry. I don't want to hurt his feelings. Sometimes I make his breakfast, then take as long as I can to make my own. That way he might be finished before I sit down.

He doesn't believe me. No.

He just doesn't talk about it, none of it. He would never ask me about the other car. But I know he doesn't believe there was another car.

I don't have to answer that.

I resent that. I have never been suicidal.

I believe in God.

Yes, but I don't think about Him. I wouldn't know what to think about Him.

I believe in God the way I believe . . . in certain things . . . the way I believe in books I will never read, in their facts, in maps I will never see, in parts of the world I will never see. The way I believe in you; what you tell me. Because none of it is important.

You're angry . . . ?

Yes, you are angry. I think you're angry.

Because you expect something from me that I can't give you. But there isn't anything inside me, I don't go down that deep. I can't remember much about the accident because there isn't much to me. . . . One morning when Linda and I went to the playground we sat with another mother, her name is Mollie, a very nice girl I got to know, and while our children were playing we noticed a man watching us. He was really staring at us. I became very nervous and wanted to get Linda and leave, and I was terrified that Mollie would walk away and leave me there, and we kept talking and trying not to notice him, and finally I started to laugh, I told Mollie that we had an admirer; so it turned into a joke and Mollie and I laughed about it. We whispered and laughed. The man kept starting at us, maybe he didn't know what was going on or didn't care. Mollie and I laughed together because it struck us—*what did he want?* What could we give him? Women can't give men much of anything. A body isn't very important, it doesn't last, it isn't like God, and yet men expect something like God. They expect something. Then when they discover there's nothing there, nothing inside, they get angry. Like you. I think you're angry with me because you expect something from me that—

I don't want to talk about her.

She was only five. You know that. What could I expect from her? She was very pretty, with hair lighter than mine. She looked like me when I was that age. Looked like snapshots of me. She could read a little, story books and things, she was very curious and asked a lot of questions. She was always asking me questions: like what made cars run, why can you see through glass, how much water could come out of a faucet. I don't want to talk about her. . . .

No.

. . . Except once, in the playground. She was playing with some other children and they started fighting. Over a toy, I don't know what. I ran over to get her, and she was fighting with a little boy, the two of them punching each other hard and crying, and I grabbed hold of her to pull her away . . . and . . . and she was still angry. . . . I thought for a moment that I didn't know her. That this child was not mine.

The moment passed. I never thought it again.

I told you: that this little girl, who was struggling and screaming, wasn't mine. But the moment passed and I never had that thought again, not once.

No. In fact, I don't know what you mean by that.

But to be depressed you have to be happy too. Like a valley between two mountains . . . ? You have to be happy first. Then it changes and you're depressed.

I'm not being ironic.

Yes, I did request a change. Because I think a woman would be more tolerant.

When I say that there is nothing in me, nothing mysterious, she wouldn't be disappointed. Men expect too much. And yet even while I tell you this, and you nod your head, you're looking at me in a certain way. . . . I hate that look. I don't want it. I hate it.

When you were an intern you must have stuck your fingers inside women, didn't you? You wore rubber gloves! You did those things! You must have turned women upside down and inside out; you must have poked them and listened to their hearts and smelled their smells, which they couldn't help; you must have cut up the bodies of dead women; yet you still believe in the mystery, don't you? You still believe. But I don't. I looked at my daughter and it was like looking at myself in a mirror, but the mirror was dwarfed, and I could stare right into her eyes but I couldn't stare into my own in a mirror, but only at them. Because of the surface . . . the rounded surface. . . . I can't explain. Because of the opaque part of the eye. . . . I don't know.

I said I wasn't depressed. What does my husband tell you? It isn't necessary to move. I avoid the park, the playground, the other mothers; so they can't feel sorry for me. I don't think about it. We keep the door to her room shut, we avoid the subject of her, it isn't necessary to move. Linda would have left home sometime in the future. I knew I would lose her sometime.

Not a hard birth, no. You're the third person to ask me that. An ordinary labor and an ordinary birth. I was under all the time. I don't remember much. No pain, no. Sometimes a bulk like a mountain, the way a mountain towers over a small village, you know, taking up most of the sky . . . sometimes I see or feel a bulk like that when I remember giving birth to her, but I couldn't explain what it is. Maybe pain or the memory of pain. The fear of pain. I don't know.

Are you asking me if I killed her?

My pulse is always normal, like this. Check it. Check my head, my brain—wire me up again—go through all the tests again, those complicated little gauges! What can they tell you? Anything that I couldn't tell you myself? . . . You can't claim anything of the past except a few bodies and some crumpled metal. And you never found the first car and the first body! Where is that other driver? Why don't you look for him? All I did was follow him off the cliff; I lost control of the car and went right after him. When I woke up in the hospital that was the first thing I asked them—I didn't even remember about Linda—I asked about that other car. "Did he drown? Did he get out of the car in time? Is he safe?" I asked them. They'll tell you. Maybe it's written down. Because I wanted that other driver to live, didn't I? Because why else would I ask about him, when I had forgotten my own daughter? Why else would I ask? I must have wanted him to live, didn't I?

I Must Have You

I saw him. I crossed the street to him. I knew the face because I had cut his photographs out of papers—once, in a library back in the States, I had used a razor to cut the photograph out, slitting back and forth gently, gently.

I said—

I stammered and said—

He was wearing a long bulky jacket that came down far on his thighs. It had crude wooden things, like bullets, instead of buttons. Pain scattered up my left side, rib after rib electrified with pain. I hadn't eaten for a while. I felt my hair blowing savage around my face and I felt the pinched lips, my pale pinched lips.

"I—I want— I need—"

He stared and did not know me. But he did not draw away.

He was a doctor.

I shivered with pain, I was an emptiness electrified only with pain, like streaks of lightning—soundless heat lightning—illuminating an empty sky. I could not moisten my lips to say: "I need help, I need you, I must have you. . . ."

In spite of the wind that blew into my face and should have kept me erect, I felt myself going faint, shuddering into faintness. He exclaimed something. Then he caught me as I fell.

He was a doctor: he had been trained to catch people as they fell.

He said there was a certain kind of butterfly, a Monarch butterfly, that is blown from America to England . . . across the windy rocky Atlantic Ocean. "Oh, a miracle!" I laughed, as if he were teasing me. I feared miracles and laughed at them. I feared them. Coming upon his face in the street was a flash of a miracle, almost too powerful for me: the face absorbed all the others, all the faces of all other men I had known, drawing them together into one.

"There are no miracles. There is only nature," he explained.

Months before I had spread the cutout faces on a table, arranging them in a half-circle. They embraced me where I sat. I saw how the face changed, became altered gradually, around that half-circle: younger, older, lined and anxious, smiling, boyish, the forehead creased with the effort of a smile, grim again as if frightened of the photographer, who had been waiting for him on the sidewalk outside a London court. . . . That had been the most recent picture.

I half-knew I would love him. I half-know everything.

His face was an explorer's face. But thin, stung. Nicks from shaving on his jaw . . . tiny red nicks . . . invisible unless you were very close to him and loved him. My head rang as the faces blurred and became one, and I clutched at his hand and wept: "Oh I love you, it is a miracle . . . I came to you and it is a miracle. . . ."

"But there are no miracles, there's only nature," he said, and his voice meant that this was good. There was a gentleness in him, a harmony of sounds in his voice. *I must have you. I must have that.*

I bathed in the cupboard-sized bathroom, where the tub was jammed in beneath a sloping wall; I shivered and my flesh was afraid. From the other room came voices—no, a voice—it was his voice in its own harmony, half-singing, murmuring words I could not make out. He sang songs in snatches, not conscious of the words; sometimes they were in another language. I was too shy to ask.

The flat was very cold. He had me sit in the kitchen, and he turned on the gas oven and lit it and left the door open, and I sat in front of it, shivering. He fed me: it was soup stirred out of a dehydrated mix, tiny chunks and sandlike things springing into their own size. My hand shook; soup spilled onto the front of the bathrobe he had given me.

The first evening he talked with me, he was very kind, he looked at me and asked me: Why are you here? Why do you think . . . ? The telephone rang but he didn't answer it. The lines in his face were creases then. "I'm getting too old for this; I'm forty-one," he said. Then he smiled. He said: "I will have to get younger, then, obviously." I told him how I had heard someone talk about him . . . so long ago . . . out in the country, in the Berkshire Mountains . . . people wandering around, and an old dining room table had been dragged out of the house and some of us were sitting around it . . . and a man with a darting, raspy voice had spoken of him. . . .

He laughed and looked away. The kitchen had heated up; he turned off the oven and smiled strangely at the air, as if he could see the heat around us. "Are you warm now?" he said. My hands between his: warm. Warmed. Dreamily he said that he had half-known this would come, this moment, the kitchen warm and a young woman revived from death, her skin warmed, heated, her face revived like the faces of the near-dead when transfusions have saved them; he had known it would happen and that he must play his part in it, no matter how deathly he himself felt.

The first night we lay in his bed without undressing. It was very cold. The covers smelled musty, they were heavy and strange, and he embraced me as if from a distance, all silence, the two of us in an impersonal embrace. Something greedy leaped in me: I knew the universe was balanced now.

I had begun to love him, hearing that man; hearing his words until my mind shimmered, the words becoming my own. *I go far from him, but he's the center; I don't need to write letters to him or make transatlantic telephone calls like other people. I summon him back. And his face rises in my mind, I meditate upon it. . . .* It had been a Saturday, out in the country. People were arguing. But they were happy. This stranger with the raspy voice had loved, had loved. Loved. Had been loved. *His real face is beautiful; you can't judge from the photographs. He is beautiful. He is a saint.* The man I was with that day—a friend's ex-husband—tried to interrupt and ask about the arrest, the trial, the personal injury suit brought against Aaron by a woman, the raiding of his clinic— But no, no, it did not matter. No one heard. *We were lovers. We were. . . . We were so close that the halves of our brains could have been paired together, a right-handed brain, a left-handed brain . . . his and mine . . . we were twins in a single body. . . .*

And when he was my lover we were in the same body: not a man's body, not a woman's. I didn't recognize it. Its face was only a shadow and had no limits. The ceiling rose from us and showed how invisible the sky was, how one could rise into it forever. I cried with terror of it, I wept and clutched at him. But he said not to cry; not to be afraid; he would keep me from falling into the sky.

That was at the end of March.

A wind had blown me across the Atlantic. I had left New York with one suitcase and a winter coat, an expensive coat left over from the past. My mother had bought it for me one day, she'd come to where I was living, and she bought the coat at a nice store while I stood outside, then she went away again. Leaving New York, I felt my face prepare itself for the long flight, a dangerous journey, and when they told all of us we were in London, we were just outside London, my face had not changed for hours.

In the Underground I walked dazed from one platform to another. Someone approached me and asked if I needed help . . . ? It was a young Indian man, swarthy and handsome; I shied away. I had a map someone had given me at the airport and I made my way up to the street, past crowds of people—it was five-thirty here —and walked until I came to a street of small hotels. This was north of the University of London. The bed-and-breakfast hotels had signs on their doors:·*No Rooms*. But I rang a bell and asked the woman could I wait, and she glanced at my coat and at my shoes, which were good shoes, and agreed.

The room was on the fourth floor, and looked like someone's bedroom. The single light was distant. I stared out the window and down to a small square, which was green; the grass was green even though it was winter. I shivered. In the slanted mirror I looked older than I was, my skin looked sallow and used. It was that bad food people had given me all my life, the bad love they had pumped into me.

"These are events of the coming month . . . oh, it's last month. . . . Here is a brochure . . . did you want to go to Stratford, for instance? I hear only good reports about the bus tours. . . ." The landlady gave me more maps so that I could trace with my finger the curving streets, the near-invisible routes that would lead me to him. My brain jerked with energy, little lightning-spurts of energy that went nowhere. Then I did something wrong: I left her a pound note for a tip. She was too surprised to smile. I saw the thoughts rippling behind her skin, I saw how she wondered, wondered, her silence told me she wondered, and then she looked up and smiled and kept the money.

His square was off the Fulham Road and easy to approach. A main route, a back route, a curving side route. A dead-end street with an incomplete wall. My face got ragged from the wind. On the busier streets people bumped into me; the fast walkers wore sheepskin coats and high boots. I saw tall gloating figures. I heard American accents and turned away, fearing someone would call out my name; someone would seize me. It might be my father. He might shout at me again and his face would go red, the redness of heated-up skin, and I would be to blame for his death. His death again.

I approached his doorway and looked into the foyer where there were advertisements on the floor, a half-dozen cards advertising radio taxis, some undelivered mail. I smelled garbage but could not see any. Boldly, fearfully, I stepped inside and stared at the names above the mailbox: Warnes, Jansen, Cassell, Brook. I could have known from the sound of his name . . . *Brook* . . . I would have known him . . . I would have heard him inside the name.

A bare zigzagging stairway, the first half-dozen steps painted black, the next covered with cheap filthy yellow linoleum . . . and on and on, out of my sight. I did not dare go up.

But that day, it was that day, or it was a dark wet afternoon of another day, I saw him and he touched me in pity and said, "You'll be all right, don't be afraid, don't be frightened. . . . You're sick but you'll be well. Don't cry. Don't."

After the second floor the stairway changed again: bare wood. Outside the door of Flat 3 there was always a shopping bag of garbage, sometimes two bags, balanced carefully against the wall. The stairway smelled. From an enormous window came shattering light that meant nothing: openings of sky you cannot trust in this part of the world. Aaron kept the window open because of the odor, but someone else closed it. When he saw that it was closed he opened it again, saying nothing.

My eyes were darkened with fatigue, my cheekbones were too prominent. He studied me and said I had not led a generous life; I had not been generous to myself.

The sun set so early here, you could pass from one night into another without knowing. I slept shivering and could not tell if I slept or not: he sat on the edge of the bed and watched me. In pity he said I could stay. I could stay for a week. And then in pity he said I could stay longer. Drafts came to us from one of the windows. Outside, there were spires and chimneys and rooftops, buildings of dark brown brick, soot-stained, tear-stained, and all of it a miracle because it was his, his view, his design. . . . He had stared out at it while I had lived far away, not known to him. Now I saw his silhouette against the window, his arm thrust into a sleeve, the hand sliding deftly through the sleeve to emerge as a fist.

The way men dress, unobserved.

He was from Manchester, a city that was only a name to me. He had been a medical officer in the RAF and had become a psychiatrist many years ago, when I was still a child. It was strange to imagine the distance between us: the years and the Atlantic Ocean. When he spoke, his voice—his way of speaking—pushed out of my memory the way of speaking I knew, the accents of men in my own country, men I had lived with and loved. I could not even remember them clearly. Aaron had married his first wife when he had been quite young, in his early twenties, and his second wife when he'd been thirty-six, and she had come to him with three children from another marriage. "No one wishes me dead," he said. "I tell myself that. I tell myself that they cannot wish me dead because they need me . . . alimony, child support . . . eight children now who are dependent upon me . . . and two ex-wives who live only to hate me . . . but still they don't wish me dead. I tell myself that."

"Do you ever see them?" I asked cautiously.

But he did not hear. ". . . And the stories in the newspapers. . . . A woman I had never known, had never met, came forward and made claims against me . . . a personal injury suit that was thrown out of court . . . and a man tried to blame his wife's suicide on me, because she'd spent a night once with a patient of mine when we all lived at the clinic in Southwark. . . . If I could just get clear of them, if I could make my way through their hatred. . . ."

There was a constant wind from the window frame, a draft like the breath of something enormous and cold and very much alive. Rain was scattered against the windowpane as if flicked from enormous nervous fingers. Aaron walked around the room and the floor creaked thinly. It was a communication, it meant something. I did not have to interpret it. I stared at his face and wondered . . . *how do you love? What is there to do that you cannot do a single time and then multiply endlessly?*

He was talking about leaving the country: he wanted to go to the United States, where a psychological institute in New Mexico had offered him a research fellowship, but he could not enter the country because of an old marijuana conviction. "They told me to plead guilty, my lawyer insisted on it even though I was innocent . . . the bastard . . . his fee turned out to be larger than the fine. . . . I have to love them," he said dreamily, "because they are only forms of myself, acting the way I would act if I were them . . . but the bastards, the ruinous scheming bastards. . . . My colleagues' hatred was theoretical, but the hatred of the police was real. It sprang to life. Or maybe it was all the same hatred . . . springing to life . . . all of it the same. . . ."

He looked sickish, dazed. I remembered the photographs and the changing faces. "I don't hate you," I said.

He smiled toward me. "You won't betray me like the others, will you?"

"No."

"Like the others . . . ? You won't betray me?"

"I love you," I whispered.

He didn't seem to hear.

A steep way. A razor-like way. On the edge of craziness I whispered to him *No. No. I can't. No.* But he drove me that way, he forced me. Then he said, "Be generous. Be generous." But I could not interpret this. My insides were wild from him, and then trembling, echoing what he had done.

I told him I had never loved anyone else.

He told me that what I had loved was him, already him; in the bodies of other men.

No. I couldn't understand.

It was too strong for me. I couldn't memorize delirium. I heard myself scream and the screams climbed above us. My nails dug into his skin, but they were weak, and I saw later the white streaks they left on his back and shoulders. . . . Not sharp enough to draw blood.

I wept crazily. I told him he must not leave me.

He spoke but I could not understand.

"Don't leave me," I begged. "Don't leave. . . ."

It was April and still dark, still raining. A breakaway union at a university in the Midlands had invited him to give a lecture—to present his side of the case—they offered him £200 and he could not turn it down. He stroked my hair and said, "I'm behind on payments to both of them, I need the money, I dread facing an audience but I need the money. . . ."

So he left. I stayed behind and thought about saintliness: the secular way, the way he had to take. If the telephone rang I did not answer. Sometimes I unhooked it. I went downstairs once a day to get his mail, holding my breath as I hurried past the bags of garbage, and I studied the letters carefully, jealously; some I opened and skimmed, and then crumpled up; others I threw away without opening. I was protecting him, and spurts of joy and greed rose in me like tiny leaps of blood.

While he was gone three people came, saying they were friends of his. I let them in but I was frightened. Two men and a woman, Aaron's age, making their way into the flat and stepping around the boxes and scattered books and towels and linen. . . . I couldn't catch their names. . . . The woman wore a dark blue trench coat that was soiled. Its belt was twisted. Her complexion was rough, the cheeks reddened from exertion or from the cold. "I'm Harriet," she said. "Aaron's mentioned me, probably." She barely looked at me but strode into the kitchen, where the long, low table was heaped with Aaron's papers and books. She picked things up, looked into manila folders, nodded, muttered to herself, made a *tsking* noise with her lips. . . . One of the men, who wore a suede coat with wide, stylish lapels, pointed out something to Harriet: he tapped a thick, blunt fingernail on one of the scribbled yellow sheets. *Psychic phenomena*," Harriet muttered. "Oh, he's crazy, he should know his subject. . . ."

They hardly looked at me. They asked: Where was he? Was he—? Not sick? Not in trouble? Not hiding out?

The woman eyed me finally, as if reluctant to acknowledge my face. I saw her expression tighten. A *pretty American girl. Aaron has another pretty American girl.* She asked me about Aaron's health—was he sleeping now? Was he still fasting all day long? Did he ever mention anyone named Braganzi? "Think carefully, it's important," she said. "Braganzi is one of our enemies. He'd like to destroy Aaron."

I could not remember that name.

"Is he still so anxious, or is he calming down? Can he sleep at night without drugs? Or don't you know?"

"He can sleep."

"Without drugs?"

"Yes."

"Or don't you know? . . . You don't know," she said flatly.

She went into the bedroom. She stooped to examine a pile of books on the floor; she grunted, picking one up. "This is my book; Aaron borrowed it two years ago and never returned it," she said without looking at me. I wanted to protest. But she half-turned to me and showed me the cover of the book—*A Casebook of Psychosynthesis* by Harriet Lingard. "It's my book," she said flatly.

She was too old, too plain to be a wife of his; too manly to be a rival of mine. I pitied her. I hated her. She joked with the two men about something, and none of them really looked at me. She said: "Tell him Harriet got the U.N. grant for Indonesia and wishes him luck—hopes he'll get clearance to join us—can you remember that?" I told her I could remember. But she must have doubted me, because she scribbled a note for him and put it on the table, on top of his portable typewriter. "Here. I wish him well. Take care of him," she told me.

I threw the note away after they left, shredding it into the toilet bowl.

I was very hungry. Yellow-eyed as if with jaundice, with spite. He explained and explained but I could not hear; the words were not generous.

"Bonds are made between people that extend beyond their physical existences," he said. He was kind to me. But. "We don't have to live together permanently to love . . . to be united in love. . . . No bond of love is ever broken."

"Don't leave me," I whispered.

"People leave one another. People die. But the bonds between them are real," he explained. Like a professor lecturing: he spoke kindly. But. But I would not listen. Finally he said, "You want someone to sink into, to fall into endlessly! You want to be plowed into, pumped into, pushed down into a mattress . . . like a common grave . . . where other females have slept. . . . You're multiplied by millions. You're asleep."

"Don't leave me," I said.

An ex-patient of his met us on the street one day and began shouting at Aaron. Aaron faced him, trying to smile. The man shouted. He was immense, burly-armed, hatless in the rain; unshaven, he looked like a man half-turned into an ape. He shouted and Aaron faced him. *Liar! Murderer! You betrayed me! You betrayed us! You let the police break you! Murderer!* Finally he wept and backed away. He had not touched Aaron.

This happened on the street; then the man ran away, and it seemed as if it might not have happened. People stared at us.

"They love you. Too many people love you," I said.

I hated them all: I was beautiful when I hated.

*

Multiplied by millions. Unkillable as an ameoba.

I knew he wanted to leave me and I watched him as he worked: bent over the table, his shoulders raised as if with the effort of concentration. He had five or six books open before him at a time, reading from one and then the other, taking notes, scratching at his face. I washed the kitchen floor with a filthy, stiffened sponge mop I had found in a closet. The Ascot heater flared when I turned on the hot water faucet; small blue flames sprang into life.

The kitchen floor was covered with the same yellow linoleum that was on part of the stairs. It was very dirty. And the floor slanted: so the soapy dirty water ran in one direction, down toward Aaron's feet. This disturbed me. Then it seemed funny, so I laughed.

He glanced up at me, as if he had forgotten who I was. He smiled uncertainly.

"Oh, it's nothing," I said.

"What?"

"How strange you look. . . . It's nothing. I'm sorry," I said.

"What's wrong?"

"I'm sorry," I said.

I went out. I knew he would leave me, he wanted to leave me. But this would not happen. I ran down the stairs past the bags of garbage and out onto the street. It was chilly but not raining. I walked fast, very fast, to keep up with my heartbeat. I walked down to the Kings Road, along the crowded sidewalks, past antique shops, clothing stores, record stores. . . . I stared into an estates agent's window, reading the advertisements for flats, townhouses . . . *For let. Freehold.* It was too much for me to interpret: the many ways of living, the many bedrooms, beds, the couples who lay together in sleep, a woman's hand lightly pressed against a man's shoulder.

I wanted only to sink into him. Deeper, deeper. I could enter myself through him. I could feel it. I could shape my words with his lips. My name. I did not have a name.

He had a name: Aaron.

Yes, to be plowed into . . . pumped down into a common grave, a common bed . . . where other females have slept with their fingers half-curled in sleep, like a child sleeping. Innocent there, between the stale unclean sheets. Innocent. Multipled by millions.

When I went back to him I said: "Are you going to go? Going to leave the country?"

"I think so. Yes," he said.

I had been a guest here for many weeks. He looked up at me, distracted by his work. The same cup of cold coffee, from early this morning was at his elbow. I was anonymous, this man had sucked the life out of me! He had sucked me dry and now he wanted to abandon me. I had lived with him, I had been a guest in his life, and now he stared at me as if he did not know me.

". . . Can I go with you?"

"To Indonesia? I don't think so. Why should you want to come with me?" he asked. His hair was dark but thinning. I saw the chaste scalp through the hair. This made me forget his words. "You've been with me too long already," he said. "You should go back home."

"I don't have a home."

"Yes, you have a home."

"I don't have a home! I don't want a home except with you!"

"Now don't—"

"Don't! Don't!"

I seized his arm and the coffee cup was knocked over. I felt my nails dig into his skin, but helplessly, helplessly; not sharp enough to hurt. I began to cry and he stared at me, his face darkening, stern, the eyes shifting to break the connection and then refocusing again, staring at me. He was a famous man, a famous face. "Famous." I wanted to frame his face with my hands, to quiet him and myself, to lie down with him once more in that anonymous bed. . . . His face was like a map of an unexplored country and all maps frightened me.

I felt that I would go mad if he left.

"Don't leave me, I can't live without you, I can't live . . . I can't exist . . . I can't force myself to stay together, my mind to stay together, from one minute to the next. . . ."

I saw the pity in his face. He was a doctor: he had trained to be a doctor and that was his fate.

But he extricated my fingers.

Gently he said: "I can't give birth to you."

"What? What does that mean? What . . . ? I don't understand," I said.

"I can't give birth to you."

I went into the other room and closed the door. After a while I heard him leave—I heard him on the stairs—and I stood for a while in the bedroom, wondering what I would do. When I knew he was gone I went into the kitchen and a kind of flame, a blue flame, seemed to leap about my brain. I snatched up some of his papers and ripped them in two, I threw the pieces down . . . I pushed the typewriter off onto the floor. . . . But it was very quiet in the flat. Quiet. The noise of the typewriter falling was already gone.

Outside, a jet plane passed slowly, the sound building up slowly, slowly, into a terrible pressure. Then it too began to fade.

I laughed aloud at the ugliness of the room I was in. *I want you, I'm not going to lose you, I must have you!* But the flat was quiet, at the top of this old building. It maddened me, this quiet that I could not destroy. I felt a flaming girlish anger inside me, like an embryo. . . . If he would only come back, if he would only see me like this, my sorrow. . . . If he would only love me again. . . .

I picked up one of his books and tore a handful of pages out. I threw it down again and it knocked the coffee cup onto the floor— some cold brown liquid spilled onto the floor—I picked up something he had been writing and my eyes stung, tears of anger and love tried to blind me, *I'm not going to lose, not going to lose,* I skimmed the page and read something about "a quantum leap of soul," "sudden storms of meaning"—but I could not interpret this; my anger flared inside me like an embryo stirring with life—I tore the paper in half and let it fall. I was too excited, too angry, to rip it into small pieces. Next I snatched up another book and forced myself to read a few lines, so that I would know what I was destroying—

> *Darkness there was; at first hidden in darkness*
> *this all was undifferentiated depths.*
> *Enwrapped in voidness, that which flame-power*
> *kindled to existence, emerged.*

—and I ripped this page out, pages of poems; I hated them because I could not make sense of them, I hated them because he loved such things and did not love me.

Yet even then I was thinking that he might come back, he might see how upset I was, how he had forced me to do this because I loved him. . . .

But he didn't come back. Minutes passed. And I found myself thinking of how his clinic had been raided, of how residents in that part of London had demanded the place be closed . . . the headlines about Dr. Brook's arrest on drug charges, his trial, the six-month jail sentence. . . . The bastard. He had deserved it. The law never makes mistakes about people like him.

Feverishly I leafed through the telephone directory to the page of Emergency Numbers: I dialed the police. I began to sob. ". . . this man, this doctor . . . he did things to me . . . his name is Brook, Aaron Brook, he kept me here with him . . . kept me a prisoner here and experimented on me. . . . He forced me to . . . injected me with, with . . . with drugs. . . . I don't know the names of everything he did. . . . I want to accuse him . . . I want him to be arrested and to die, I want you to. . . ."

A voice in my ear was asking me to repeat: to go slowly. It was a man's voice, so my panic went down. A man's voice. *Repeat. Go more slowly. Tell us where you are and we'll come get you.* It was a man's voice and so I knew I would be saved, I knew I would be loved; I obeyed it and began to speak more slowly.

*M*agna Mater

"Where is he?"

"Why do you keep asking me that?—you know he's in New York. You were just there two weeks ago. Stop asking that stupid question!"

"But where is he right now?"

"Are you trying to drive me crazy!—Come on, Denny, we have to leave. Why are you wearing that sweater again? I asked you to put it out so I can take it to the dry cleaner's—please try to remember, honey."

"I'm not done eating yet."

"It's almost eight-thirty. . . ."

"I'm hungry, let me alone. I wake up hungry. You eat so fast, you're like the boys at school—the big boys—I told you about that

Sandler, the son of a bitch, didn't I, how he eats oranges just biting into them, all the nasty juice running down his face—I always peel mine and divide them into segments."

"Don't say words like *son of a bitch*."

"Everybody does. They do on television."

"We don't here—I don't."

"*He* did."

"Yes, he did. He did. And he also moved out when you were still sick—wasn't that thoughtful of him? You had a temperature of a hundred and three—But I didn't get angry, I didn't scream at him, I didn't call him names."

". . . where is he, right now?"

"Denny, please!"

"Well?"

"I have to get you to school, honey. It's raining so hard and you know I hate to drive when everything is slippery, I'll have to drive slow—and I have a committee meeting at nine-thirty at the University. Don't make us both late. Please."

"I asked you, Mother: *do you know where he is?*"

"—in New York, where he's been for the last four years, East Eighty-Third Street—I forget the number—why are you acting so childish, aggravating me when I have so much to do? And the way it's pouring out—If this doesn't stop, if you don't get over this, I'll have to make another appointment with Dr. Gruber."

"Like hell."

"—do you want me to leave for school alone? I won't be insulted —I'll just leave you here. You can't make me upset, Denny."

"You never answered my question."

"Denny, you're eleven years old—"

"And you're forty-five, so what?"

"You're making a mess with that cereal. Let me take the bowl away."

"All along, Mother, I've been studying you. Like you study your books. And you know what?"

"What?"

"You won't look at me when you talk about him. And you won't answer my question."

"He's in New York, I said!—with his wife!"

"No, he is not. He's in Capetown."

"Capetown?"

"So! You didn't know, did you? Him and Muriel, they both flew there for two weeks. You didn't know! You didn't!"

"Why Capetown? Why both of them?"

"Because he's interviewing somebody there and he wanted Muriel to come along. Because. Because."

"You want to destroy me, don't you?"

They never asked her about Theodore, her ex-husband. Or about her father, retired from Harvard many years ago, a widower, slowly dying of a brain tumor in a Cambridge nursing home. In the casual, groping, but very sensitive explorations that precede friendship, that determine what can be investigated and what must never be mentioned, they soon learned that only Dennis was a safe topic. *How is your brilliant, charming little boy? Is he over the chest trouble?* Of course. No one dies of bronchitis. *And is he still so precocious?— the violin lessons, the medieval history, the tutor in math—?* Of course. Of course. *And his teachers—so delighted with him?* Of course.

But that year she began to hear herself lying. She, who believed in truth, in an absolute commitment to all truths, began to feel the tension in her smile . . . which became, subtly, against her own desire, a smile meant to convince. It had been very difficult for her to refuse to shy away from the facts of the divorce, but she had faced them; she had managed to laugh, to shake her head and say, at parties or in colleagues' offices at the University, that it was one of the hazards of living in a rapidly accelerating society, in which utilitarian vehicles lost even their utility once they were outmoded, once they were challenged by newer, younger, more vital "models"—

and how grateful everyone was, to hear her speak like that, so
openly, so honestly! Of course, so many of them had been divorced,
remarried, and divorced again, so many of her old friends were
deteriorating in complex, sordid relationships they dared not challenge with the truth, that her assessment of her own predicament
allowed them to pity her and like her at the same time. And her
cheerful homeliness, her strangely domestic, comforting, plain face
and hair, even the way she moved her body—too abruptly and then
too hesitantly—allowed the men to be very fond of her, true colleagues, and the women to respect her, though of course they were
in awe of her reputation. That did keep them at a distance. She
accepted the friendship of her colleagues, which never developed
into anything too intimate, and she certainly accepted their respect
—she believed she had earned it—but her most intense pride in herself was a pride in her moral integrity, her commitment to the truth.
And now that seemed to be eroding.

Her maiden name was Akenside; one of her ancestors had been a
minor poet of the eighteenth century and she had once considered
doing a serious study of his work, "resurrecting" him, but decided
against it—his verse was poor, even for that period, and the entire
project might seem sentimental. Her mother's family could trace its
roots back to the Massachusetts Bay Colony, and all of them had
been Puritans—church members only, no ministers or theologians
among them. Though she was certainly not religious herself, she
often spoke of being a "Puritan"—half-jokingly, half-seriously. She
liked to work. She had worked most of her life—not at physical
labor, for there was no need of that, but at studying, learning,
memorizing, writing. Her father, Ronald Akenside, had taught
philosophy at Harvard for forty years; he had written a half-dozen
books, each wonderfully well-received at the time of publication,
though their influence on other scholars was not what one might
have predicted . . . one of the bitter disappointments of his life.
Nora's success as a scholar, her appointment at Radcliffe, even her
marriage to Theodore Drexler, had seemed to please Dr. Akenside

at first—then, inexplicably, he had lost interest in her accomplishments, had stopped asking her what research she was involved in, what plans for the future—she even realized, one day shortly before he entered a neurological clinic for brain-scan tests, that he had not even read her most recent book. It remained on a bookstand, exactly where she had left it. A terrible thought flooded her: *None of this will save us.* Afterward, she had no idea what that meant or why she had thought it.

Unfortunately, she had published three of her four books under her married name, Drexler; her reputation was linked with that name, which she had come to loathe; she could not return to Akenside, to the daughterly, chaste Nora of the early years, infatuated with books, willing to work ten or twelve hours at a stretch. So it was Drexler. Drexler. And she told the truth about him, she faced the shame of having been rejected: this made her seem very human, made even Theodore's friends admire her, accustomed as they were to shrewish, evil-voiced ex-wives. And since Theodore had not asked for Dennis, since his new young wife—twenty-four years old—certainly did not want moody brilliant Dennis, Nora had found good things to say about him, charitable words, adjectives. She knew how to use words.

And your little boy must be—he probably isn't little any longer, is he? Why don't you bring him over sometime? He and Roger got along so well that Sunday—Roger says Denny is the only boy he can really talk to. And I could ask the Swansons over—do you know him?—he's down here for the semester, from the Medieval Institute at Toronto—

But she could not: no.

—no? Why not, Nora? You've turned us down twice in a row—What's wrong?

Nothing was wrong.

Nothing? But—

Nothing, nothing.

*

"Isn't Grandfather dead yet?"

He followed her around the garden. He was still in his pajamas, though it was past noon.

"All that big damn noisy fuss you made, driving out there at seven in the morning—big deal!—thought the sons-of-bitches might send you an ambulance, the way you rushed around. And all a false alarm. And you woke me up and now I keep waking up before dawn and by the time it's time to get up, I feel like I could die. *I feel like I could die.*"

She rented a two-story townhouse in Cambridge, a modest house with a plain facade; fortunately it had a walled-in garden, small, beautifully-contained, hidden from her neighbors on either side. She hadn't known how she would love gardening until she moved to this house. That side of her had never been developed, not with all the long years of scholarship, then motherhood, then a decade of research, teaching, and motherhood madly combined, which had exhausted her more than she had cared to admit. She never complained: and she hadn't complained, not even then. That was to her credit. *He* had complained, not liking the hurried meals, her distraction when he spoke of his work—he specialized in a new, flamboyant area of psychology and linguistics and sociology, in which reputations rose and fell with the seasons, in which books were heralded as "revolutionary" and then forgotten a few months later—he hadn't liked the way Dennis began to shy away from him, afraid of his intensity, his barks of laughter, his growing impatience with Nora's "qualified assertions," as he called them. He, her husband, had complained even of her work: at first because it made her so distracted, and then because it made the name *Drexler* known in the Cambridge-Boston-New York area, as if it were truly her name and not his. Most of all, he complained about the drafty, ugly brick house on a boulevard sloping down from her parents' former home, and, even before he began spending most of his weekends in

New York, she had known the marriage was over, she would soon be living somewhere else, cast loose again like a daughter. . . . But a daughter with a child of her own.

How to begin again, in early middle age? . . . She did not begin again, but continued with a project she'd been working on for many years, a study of the poetic vision of old age, the peculiar numinous knowledge of the elderly poet as he confronts his death:

> . . . *Then he struggled with the mind;*
> *His proud heart he left behind.*
>
> *Now his wars on God begin;*
> *At stroke of midnight God shall win.*

–and the work took on a new, horrible meaning for her, with the onset of her father's headaches, his failing vision, his convulsions and slow numbing hideous disfigurement—his forgetfulness of her, of *her*, as new visions rose to challenge his mortality. Reading Stevens's "The Rock" to her graduate seminar at the University, she had become blinded by tears, unable to continue. One of her graduate students had acted swiftly, finishing the poem for her— but it was the very opening that had terrified her, for she seemed suddenly to hear these familiar words in her father's voice—

> *It is an illusion that we were ever alive,*
> *Lived in the houses of mothers, arranged ourselves*
> *By our own motions in a freedom of air.*
>
> *Regard the freedom of seventy years ago.*
> *It is no longer air. The houses still stand,*
> *Though they are rigid in rigid emptiness.*

Isn't Grandfather dead yet? She worked in the garden, kneeling on a magazine section from the *New York Times*, working briskly as always—pulling weeds, some of them very small weeds, putting everything in order. This garden had been a mess when she'd moved in. She hated untidiness, borders gone wild . . . she shared with Yeats and Stevens and others of her saints a need for assertion, for staking the claims of a particularity of being in a gross universe. And yet this chubby hectic child in the sweaty pajamas wandered around the garden, listlessly eating something—Ritz crackers out of a box—trying to drive her mad as his father had tried to drive her mad. She ignored his desperate little taunts. He wasn't well; she lied about him and to him. When Theodore called, back from Capetown and what had evidently been a successful visit—he'd interviewed a Nobel Prize-winning biologist for a men's magazine, of all unlikely places—she had lied to Theodore, telling him that all was well, perfectly well, as always. She felt ungainly even speaking to him over the telephone. They had been in love once. Decades ago. They had lain together many times, so many times it made her dizzy to think of it—no, she would not think of it. But now, speaking to him, answering his rather impetuous questions, she had the idea that they'd known each other as children, that they shared only the uncomfortable intimacy of a brother and sister, eager to be free of each other.

Eager to be free. . . .

Yes, his parting remarks were always perfunctory, as he backed away from her like a man backing away from her at a party: enough of this intellectual conversation, now for real life!

"Why don't you take me to see Grandfather any more?" Denny asked. Suddenly he crouched above her, a serious, stricken child. His uncombed hair rose from his skull in feathery puffs. "You used to take me. I miss Grandfather. I have a right to see Grandfather. The next time you go, Mother—"

"No, Dennis."

"—I won't be nervous and bad, Mother, I promise. I don't know what got into me—fooling around with the elevator like that—I promise I'll be good. I'll behave myself." He spoke urgently, with the immediate, rather brainless intensity of a child much younger than eleven. Evidently he had forgotten the terrible things he'd been saying all morning. "Unless Grandfather died and you're keeping it a secret. . . ."

"You know better, Dennis. Please."

". . . like you did with Father. . . ."

"What do you mean by that?"

". . . his plane could fall into the ocean, Mother, and you wouldn't give a damn. And you wouldn't tell me a word. You want to keep me all muffled up, you want to stick my head beneath the water. . . ."

"When Theodore telephoned I held the phone out for you, but you ran away," she said calmly.

He snickered.

"Honey, go get dressed. Please. What if someone drops in this afternoon?—You in your pajamas, a big boy in his pajamas!"

He wandered back into the house. She saw that he'd left the back door ajar. *Even our shadows, their shadows, no longer remain. The lives these lived in the mind are at an end.*

She looked up Gruber's telephone number but did not call. Days passed. Weeks. Sometimes Dennis was himself again—cheerful and eager to get to school, returning with news of the school's complicated networks of popularity and feuding and triumph—then, unaccountably, he would tell her the next morning that he was too tired, too fed up, to bother getting dressed. He stared up at her, groggy and baffled. *He was trying to destroy her.* And on those mornings he wept if she insisted upon going to the University, as she must—she *must*—telling him that an eleven-year-old child didn't need his mother with him even if he was ill, which she doubted; and he called and screamed at her from his bedroom while she dressed, her hands shaking, trying not to give in. On the second floor of the townhouse there were only the two bedrooms, with a bathroom in between. He banged on the wall of the bathroom when she was in there, shouting, evidently with his hands cupped to his mouth. *I'm sick! You can't leave! You can't leave!*

Then, the next day, he might be back to normal again: though perhaps a little too brightly normal, too eager to talk about the clever things his teachers had said that day, the high grade he'd received on a history test, the crazy funny things one of the boys told him, a boy he admired very much. Nora was cautious, careful not to be too quickly relieved. She smoothed his hair down, listened to his chatter, smiled, nodded, agreed, made him meals he loved— simple, blunt foods, the kind Theodore had liked, just ordinary grilled steaks or chops, ordinary mashed potatoes—and stayed home with him every evening. She made excuses if friends invited her out for dinner or to parties. She told them she was working quite hard these days, but happily, concluding the book she'd begun so many years ago . . . and this usually convinced them, since they knew that Nora Drexler worked all the time.

"Who's that on the telephone, Mother?"

She put her hand over the receiver. "It's nobody, honey, please don't interrupt."

"It's Gruber, isn't it?"

"No. Please don't interrupt while I'm—"

"Hang up."

"Denny, I'm warning you—"

"Hang up, you don't need to talk to anybody! Hang up!"

So she made excuses hurriedly, anything so that no one should know what was wrong. For hours afterward, for days afterward, she would be sick with worry, *What if Denny's voice had been overheard . . . ?* When she gave in so quickly like that, he was oddly pleased; he was absurdly and visibly flattered, like a child much younger than Denny's actual age, and yet unlike the child Denny had been at any earlier age. He came to her, pressed himself against her, sniffing, mumbling something about "being afraid," not exactly thanking her for giving in . . . a little ashamed of himself, hiding his face from her.

She took off his glasses and cleaned the lenses on the hem of her dress absentmindedly.

"It was only someone's wife, the wife of a professor in the department," she said soothingly. "No one I know very well, honey. No one important. No one at all."

Even if the call had been from an old friend, someone she wanted very much to see again, she said: "It was no one important, dear. No one. Please don't be upset."

Sometimes, when she was asleep, he roamed the house. If she woke up, terrified, she could hear his step out there—barefoot, but heavy, clumsy. "Dennis," she said, "Dennis—?" And he would pause, freeze. And then call back something about "checking the windows," "putting the night-lock on the door." Once he tried to convince her that there had been someone outside, in the garden. He put on the terrace lights and jumped about excitedly in the kitchen. "A prowler, Mother! I saw him! I saw him!" She asked him how a prowler could possibly have gotten in that way, through the Feuchts' or the Steiners' gardens?—and how had he escaped so easily, then? But Dennis was caught up in the excitement of a prowler, of actual danger, and seemed as the minutes passed to believe his own words. She sat wearily at the kitchen table, watching him. Why? What had gone wrong? He knew she was staring at him, and this pleased him, as any kind of attention did now— Dennis, who had been so wonderfully dignified as a young child, now turned into an exhibitionist, a show-off! Nora had always dreaded the company of her friends' children, because most of them were ignorant, silly boys and girls, chattering about their utterly banal interests, unlike *her* boy—cool and silent and courteous when company came—and now he giggled and chattered like the rest, exactly like the rest. Theodore would be pleased. . . . No, Theodore would not be pleased: Theodore too took pride in intelligence, though he had misused his own.

"I must call Dr. Gruber, honey," she whispered.

"Okay, call him."

"In the morning. I must call him and make an appointment."

"Make it for yourself," Dennis said airily. "*You're* the one."

*

Gruber's wife had been a graduate student of Nora's many years ago; she had done her Master's thesis with Nora—on Yeats's revisions of *A Full Moon in March*—but had never continued with her scholarly work, a disappointment to Nora. But Gruber was a wise, good man. Nora had dreaded meeting him, as she always dreaded meeting the husbands of women she admired—somehow they usually disappointed her, as the women married to men Nora admired disappointed her most of the time. But Gruber was a thoughtful, meticulous person, fifteen or more years older than his wife; he'd known Professor Akenside as a student, and he told Nora he was honored to meet her. Only later, after Theodore had moved out and Dennis first began to "act strange," had she called him for any professional reason: and then half-jokingly, half-fearfully, saying that she was certain her son was expressing normal grief and bewilderment, but perhaps. . . .

Gruber had been very understanding, very tactful.

She telephoned him from her office at the University. At first he seemed not to recognize her name—his receptionist must have gotten it wrong—then he spoke warmly, asking how she was, how was Dennis? "He's become very possessive," she said carefully. "Very strange. . . . He's as demanding as one might expect a child of four or five to be, but not consistently . . . at times he's fine, then at other times he's very . . . very emotional." Gruber listened sympathetically. She had closed her office door and, as she spoke, she heard with a kind of detached pleasure the orderly progression of her statement, her argument. How odd that it would have to be couched in the terms of an argument, not with traditional rhetorical points . . . not as a syllogism, certainly . . . but rather in the form of an Italian sonnet, graceful, precise, irrefutable. There was an art to critical analysis and assessment, though ignorant people believed that only creative writers were *creative*, were therefore artists; Nora knew the movements of that art from the inside, not instinctively—for she did very little by instinct—but as a habit acquired by conscious effort and labor over the years. When Theodore had chosen to "fight" with her, rather than to argue rationally, she had known in despair that all was lost . . . he'd picked absurd, trivial excuses for their quarrels, almost insulting her with the arbitrary nature of their disputes; he had been unfair, unjust. She detested injustice. But she had never accused him, as he'd accused her, of those made-up grotesque problems—she had never been angry with him, at least not in his presence. All that had taken place several years ago. And he had remarried almost immediately, of course. But he seemed somehow with her, as her father seemed often with her, invisible in this handsome, cluttered office, or in the classrooms or lecture halls she spoke in, the two of them listening, forced to be impressed, nodding in agreement, yes, *yes*, that was an irrefutable point . . . *yes* . . . step by step the argument advanced, unfolded, like a piece of rigorous music . . . yes, *yes*. One could not deny that point. Nor that one. Yes. . . .

She had been explaining to Gruber the unpredictable nature of Dennis's behavior; he asked if Dennis had actually accused her of anything. Accused? No, she didn't think so. "A few years ago, when you saw him . . . it seemed to do him a lot of good," she said generously. "Of course, you're busier now . . . I assume you're busier now . . . and you probably don't remember Dennis that well. . . ."

"At that time, Nora, there was a fairly good reason for the boy to be so frightened," he was saying, "but now things are different . . . he's had some time to adjust to a broken home, and. . . ." His voice continued, and she began to feel uneasy, hearing in it the same purposive, relentless movement she'd heard in her own. *Broken home?* That expression was so vulgar, so insulting . . . and now he was saying, yes, he was fairly busy, but he'd certainly make an opening for Dennis as soon as possible; in another week, perhaps, he'd have his secretary make an appointment. . . . "Tell me," he said, "what does he accuse you of?"

"Oh, it's absurd . . ." she said, reddening. "I really wonder if there's anything wrong with him at all, it might be that he craves attention, he resents my professional life . . . that sort of thing. . . ."

"Does he accuse you of anything at all?"

"I can remember only one thing," she said, not quite truthfully. She considered what she might say: Gruber would be listening closely. He would be analyzing her words. *He* would be analyzing *her*. ". . . the other time, I don't recall your asking me so many questions, personal questions," she said. "Of course you did ask me questions, but I don't remember them being quite so. . . ." She hesitated, not wanting to say *prying*. But he was a professional psychiatrist, an analyst turned child-psychiatrist, and a fine man, not as expensive as the psychiatrists her friends went to, or took their children to, but reasonable, really quite pleasant if one hadn't to deal with him like this. In her nervousness she had begun scratching at the side of her throat with her fingernails—an unconscious habit Theodore had brought to her attention—and she forced herself to stop, as if Gruber might see, or someone watching her might see. ". . . he's had, oh, these absurd fantasies or dreams . . . nightmares. I suppose they are . . . were. . . . They're not accusations, because there isn't anything he might legitimately accuse me of . . . the divorce was entirely my husband's idea, as you might remember. And . . . and so. . . . He's really very babyish, he says absurd things . . . he jokes and pretends I've killed Theodore, of all things! . . . and once, one night, oh it must have been three or four in the morning, he woke up shouting from a bad dream, something about my running water in the tub and waking him. . . ." She paused, but Dr. Gruber said nothing. Evidently his silence—his annoying, superior silence!—was meant to encourage her, but she felt only a dull resentment. It was difficult to keep her voice from sounding ironic, as it often became when she had to go over, point by point, the omissions and misstatements of a student's paper read to her graduate seminar. She was patient, yes, but barely. Polite, yes. But barely. " . . . the entire nightmare stemmed from a simple accident that happened when the child was no more than fifteen months old—I tried to calculate exactly how old he must have been . . . and

it was simply an accident. I was bathing him before bed, at the
other house . . . I don't think you ever saw our other house? . . .
well, I was bathing him and somehow he slipped beneath the water,
he was just a baby, really. . . . I remember what happened: there
was a kind of tray, a plastic tray, that I set across the tub . . . a big
enamel tub, an old-fashioned tub . . . and it had colored soap and
floating toys on it, that sort of thing, and something must have
happened, I can't remember exactly, but. . . . No, I really can't
remember exactly," she said.

"He claimed he'd heard you running water, and that woke him?"

"The dream woke him," she said carefully.

"Yes—"

"And nothing would do afterward but that I sit by his bedside—
a boy eleven years old, and with his I.Q.—he's in the upper one
percentile of—well—no doubt you have this information in your
records, if you keep records—So I sat by his bedside, of course. I
comforted him. He fell asleep finally and I sat there the rest of
the night, though I had three classes to teach the next morning."
Gruber sounded sympathetic, so she went on to say, resentfully, that
Theodore only saw the boy when he hadn't much else to do—which
was typical of him, of the turn his personality had taken in his early
forties. And when Theodore lost interest in, or failed to inquire
about, some activity or study of Dennis's—the wonderful work he'd
been doing on the violin, for instance—Dennis himself lost interest
gradually, without seeming even to know what was happening to
him. If she reminded him of his lessons, if she remarked that he
hadn't read a new book she had bought him quite so quickly as he
usually did, he seemed more baffled than ashamed, as if she were
speaking of matters he knew nothing about. The only activity they
did together now was eat—and she heard the heavy irony in her
voice and felt the corners of her mouth sag. She had always been
proud of being quite a good cook, but of course Dennis wanted only
American food, defrosted hamburgers were good enough for him,
minute steaks . . . or Ritz crackers, eaten noisily from the box, hand

over hand. As she spoke she remembered suddenly another of the odd dream fantasies he had disgusted her with . . . *a mouth* . . . he spoke of a mouth in the room with him, in the dark, *a mouth chewing and grinding and making wet noises.* . . .

Gruber was speaking now, saying wise, logical, superior things. She realized that he was speaking into the receiver of his telephone as if speaking into a mere mechanism, summing up, speculating, analyzing, perhaps with his eyes half-closed, shrewd and clever. He hadn't caught her irony, evidently, because he spoke seriously, even solemnly. She was not so nervous now; anger was clearing her mind. ". . . usually an awkward thing to explain, though in your case, of course, it's much simpler . . . the fact that there are actually no disturbed *individuals* as such. And never any disturbed children, of course. There are only disturbed households . . . environments . . . family situations. And so it would really be necessary, I think, for me to see both you and Dennis together initially, and perhaps after that separately . . . we'll see how the first interview works out. After a while, if the sessions don't seem to be helping your relationship there, we might even ask Theodore to come up. . . . But we'll see what happens. . . . Please don't be upset, Mrs. Drexler. I'm sure everything will be all right."

"I'm not upset," Nora said.

"It's quite normal to feel some apprehension, even anxiety, in a situation like this," he said in a maddening paternal voice, as if he had handled situations like hers a thousand times. *What an insufferable man.* . . . "But I think you should have confidence in your basic relationship with your son, whatever eccentric forms it seems to be taking at present, and it should certainly make you less upset to be told that I've dealt with a case rather like this once before, except the child was a precocious little girl and the mother a professional dancer, actually a famous woman. . . ."

"I'm not upset," Nora said.

After a few more seconds he handed her over to his secretary and Nora was able to say curtly that she wouldn't be able to make any specific appointment at this time; but she would call back, of course.

She hung up.

Where is he? What did you do with him?

Do you realize it's four in the morning? she wanted to scream. But she humored him. Stroked his damp, hot face. Yes, yes, he was feverish . . . yes, she wouldn't be angry. . . . A *mouth in the room with him, chewing and wet, the teeth grinding, chewing,* and she could feel his heart pounding, as if all this were real: as if he weren't imagining it all, inventing it all. If she didn't stay with him all night, he said, the mouth would eat him. He couldn't sleep. He couldn't let himself fall asleep.

. . . *things go into it, they get sucked into it,* he said.

After a while he calmed down, as usual.

She asked him if he'd like a sleeping pill, one of hers?—broken in half? She would put it in orange juice for him, grind the pill up so he wouldn't taste it . . . since he couldn't take pills normally, for some reason they made him gag. He hiccuped, sniffed. But agreed. He was really quite rational, if she spoke calmly enough, patiently enough, waiting out the hysterical nonsense he spouted. She wondered if perhaps it wasn't all a matter of words, of simply explaining reality to him—or to any child—repeating and repeating a few simple truths. But, though he was chagrined by his own behavior, Dennis still begged: "If I fall asleep now, you won't leave?"

"I can't sit up all night again," she said.

"But—"

"Dennis, please! The dream is over now, isn't it?—you're awake and in no danger, and when you fall asleep again you'll be perfectly safe—"

"Leave the light on, then. The overhead light."

"Isn't this ridiculous!"

". . . and leave the door to the room open too."

"Yes. All right."

"And the door to your room. . . ."

"Yes."

He shut his eyes obediently. He lay in the center of the bed, his head on the center of the pillow. She could see the effort he was making to be good, to be obedient, so she laughed as if nothing strange had really happened—she was determined not to infect him with her own intermittent anxiety—and said gaily that he would forget all this nonsense very soon, she was sure of it. "Maybe by this time next year," she said. Dennis's face showed no expression. "Maybe earlier than that . . . in time for your birthday, maybe," she said encouragingly. "And you'll be in ninth grade then . . . and you'll graduate from high school . . . and do very, very well, without any nightmares at all. . . . You won't remember this silly phase of your life at all, honey, in fact I'll remind you of it sometime years from now . . . the night before your wedding, let's say! . . . and we can joke about it and see how silly you were. . . ."

"Don't close the door to your room," Dennis whispered.

"I won't," she said.

Evergreens and forsythia shrubs and untidy bridal wreath lined the garden walls, which were made of old, weathered red brick; these had come with the house and were not very interesting to her. She had planted a few rose bushes at the rear of the garden and, closer in, close around the small brick terrace, beds of poppies and shasta daisies and primroses. Orange, white, pink. . . . But she was happiest about her potted things, exquisite arrangements of flowering onion and waterlily tulips, clay pots set inside clay pots to make designs everyone marveled at. How artistic Nora Drexler was! And though she rather resented the tone of these compliments—as if she, a distinguished scholar and critic, were *not* artistic—the words did please her, they were usually uttered so spontaneously, they were so genuine. In the academic and literary world, much of the praise that came her way was deliberate, even rehearsed. She was now on the promotion-and-tenure committee of her department, and it was generally known that she was a reader for a number of university presses, though the identities of these readers were always kept secret . . . and of course she did many reviews, ceaselessly, reviews not only of critical and scholarly books in her own field, but reviews of poetry and biographies. So whatever praise came to her might well be calculated. She accepted it, of course, since she detested the false modesty she noted in others, at times, but much of her innocent pleasure in this praise was tainted with the simple knowledge that there was often a personal motive behind even the truth. . . . Yes, even the truth could become tainted, in the mouths of certain people.

But her garden! That was always a surprise, even to her old friends, who seemed to forget from one visit to the next the variety of flowers and plants she had cultivated, and who were often delighted with what they saw.

"It must take you hours to keep all this weeded. . . . When do you find time?"

". . . the time this must take you, Nora! . . . aren't those daisies beautiful!"

"But what are these flowers?—I don't recognize them—*Chives?* Look, Mason, flowering chives, I didn't even know chives had flowers—And what you've done with this edging here—our terrace is bordered with weeds, it's just hopeless, and the boy who does the lawn just can't be bothered—It looks like lettuce—look, look what Nora has here—I never realized lettuce came in so many different forms and colors—Isn't this ingenious?"

She laughed, saying it was quite simple; she'd gotten it all from instruction manuals. Anyone could do it. But they told her *they* could never do it—their lives were always such a rush, projects imagined and never completed, then summer upon them and out to Cape Cod and that awful cottage and the awful people on either side—and when they came back in the fall, then there was school again, classes beginning—when was it this year?—the third week in September? "I can't get anything accomplished," a man named Colebrook complained cheerfully. He was stooping over Nora's "knot garden"; she had just explained to him that such tiny gardens, set in boxes, were very popular in the seventeenth century, complex geometrical designs made by variations of color, in this case by leeks, lettuce, and carrots. She was flushed with pleasure, though the Colebrooks had taken her by surprise—it was after three on a Sunday afternoon, rather late for anyone to be dropping in without having called, and she was wearing a shapeless dress, her bare knees unattractive—bulging—and her feet in sandals not very clean. But at least Dennis was dressed, and not bothering anyone. He was leafing through the *New York Times*, pretending to be reading.

Colebrook was a specialist in contemporary British literature, in her department; his wife, Nora's age, did translations now and then for a small Boston publishing house and had traditionally envied Nora her "freedom," as she put it—though Nora wondered what on earth the woman meant. Colebrook was a brilliant man, in his late fifties, the author of at least one excellent book, and, over the years, Nora had alternated between pitying him on account of his wife—she was so enthusiastic, so eager, but uninformed on most subjects—and sympathizing with him. Yes, she knew. Yes. She too had married someone not quite her intellectual equal. But today she halfway approved of Sarah Colebrook's exaggerated enthusiasm, since she *had* planned these container-gardens quite carefully and other guests did not really examine them closely enough. . . . So she was grateful when the Colebrooks agreed to stay a little longer, for cocktails.

A few yards away, Dennis looked up from the newspaper. He said nothing, but his expression showed reproach.

"We haven't seen you for quite a while, young man," Sarah said. "You and your mother have been in hiding, haven't you?"

Dennis shrugged his shoulders.

"He's tired," Nora said. "Sundays exhaust him, isn't it odd?—he insists upon reading that entire newspaper. It can't do much good for his eyes."

"Our Mark reads it too," Colebrook said. "Just likes to waste time

. . . what point is there in it, plowing through all those columns of print? . . . Sarah, sit down, you make me nervous. Let's relax. Nora's going to make us some drinks, eh? . . . and we can relax, that's next on the agenda."

Colebrook was always humorous, mysteriously witty.

She fixed them drinks, chattering through the screen door. It was surprising, how lonely she'd become for guests, for adult companionship. Her colleagues at the University were always in a hurry, and, now that the semester had ended, she found herself rather isolated. There was no one even to inquire about her work, or to congratulate her on an article or review that had appeared . . . fortunately, she corresponded with a number of scholars and critics and old friends, in the States and abroad; but that wasn't really enough. Now that classes had ended she was at home with Dennis most of the time.

". . . ran into Ted the other night," Colebrook was saying.

"Yes?"

". . . looking good, still the same. Exactly the same," Colebrook chuckled.

"Oh, I wouldn't say *exactly* the same," Sarah said.

"So you wouldn't. You didn't," Colebrook said bluntly and cheerfully. "Ah yes, thank you, dear sweet competent Nora . . . it's really good of you, you know, to put up with all this."

She sat with them. ". . . all this? What? What do you mean?"

Colebrook raised his eyebrows enigmatically. He was a man of moderate height who somehow seemed tall; perhaps because of the way he crossed his legs, exaggeratedly, the ankle of one leg resting casually on his knee. When she had first met him, many years before, he'd been uneasy, ambitious, far too eager to make an impression on his superiors . . . now, a full professor himself, he was cynical, outlandish, flippant, though always respectful of Nora. He wore tinted glasses with square-cut lenses and, though the day was warm and muggy, a light green sports jacket over a polo shirt. His wife wore a simple linen sheath and a few strands of pearls. And stockings. Nora noted this, thinking swiftly that they were on their way to a party, probably somewhere in the neighborhood . . . she wondered if the party was at the home of someone she knew.

"Benjamin Edwards asked after you," Colebrook said. "He said, Say hello to Nora Drexler for me! So hello, Nora. Aren't you flattered?"

Nora laughed. Edwards had done graduate work with her some time ago; he had attempted an ambitious, heroic study of the poetics of Pound, but the dissertation had never really taken shape, and so he'd drifted onto another topic, with another professor, and finally he had been asked to leave the program. Since then he had published a book of poetry, all of it coarse and sentimental, and he had even been invited back—by the creative writing department, not by the entire English Department—to give a reading. Nora had been unable to attend, because of Dennis; but, frankly, she would have found it impossible to sit through such drivel.

"He isn't so bad," Sarah said. "I like him."

"Oh, we all like him," Colebrook said.

"We never had anything against him," Nora said.

"Certainly not," Colebrook said. ". . . quite a satirical little bastard, it turns out. You haven't read the one on you, have you?"

"I? What do you mean?"

"Stop," Sarah said.

"*How Leda Got the Swan*," Colebrook grinned, rattling the ice cubes in his glass. "Nasty little genius, Benjie Edwards, too bad we didn't recognize it in time . . . in time to pulverize him, the little bastard. . . . If you hadn't been so rigorous with him, my lady Drexler, he might have written the definitive study of, of whatever the hell it was . . . Mauberley? . . . the Cantos? . . . and won the same awards you and I won . . . and that'd be the end of him. But with your high standards. . . ."

"Stop, Mason. Stop," Sarah said. She spoke calmly and mechanically, as if she had been prepared for this. Nora's heartbeat quickened, she looked to Sarah Colebrook as if for some explanation— the way she often glanced at the student in her seminar who was superior to all the rest, with whom she had established a kind of magical rapport, excluding the others. But Sarah did not quite fit this role, and she did not quite return Nora's look.

"When you frown, my dear, the most extraordinary creases appear," Colebrook said to his wife, "and in your neck the cords stand out . . . three of them, at least by my count. Most unflattering. Can't you imitate Mrs. Drexler, my dear?—be ladylike and gracious? —girdled in?"

"I hope nothing is wrong," Nora said uncertainly.

Neither Colebrook replied. Nora glanced over at Dennis—obviously not reading the paper, but hunched over it, almost squatting over it with the pages spread messily on the terrace; he leaned forward in the canvas chair, his plump legs pale, fuzzy, bulging out beneath his old khaki shorts. He was determinedly turned away from his mother and her guests. Overhead, the sky was a hazy blue-gray, the clearest one could hope for now, with so much pollution . . . and the garden looked lovely, Nora knew it did, especially the things she had planted herself. Yet there was something wrong. She knew something terrible was going to happen.

Colebrook cleared his throat and asked her about her work—speaking in his normal voice, a relief to her. She was absurdly grateful for the question, which she had come to fear might not be asked, and did not mind that Colebrook had asked the same question a few weeks ago, at a University reception for a visiting English poet. When she spoke of her work she seemed to move into another dimension entirely—she was not the overweight, perspiring, rather too anxious hostess, but a consciousness entirely freed of the body, of all temporal limitations, and it seemed to her the ultimate gesture of love—the ultimate *act* of love—when any man, especially so intelligent and gifted a man as Mason Colebrook, simply asked her the correct questions. *What are you working on . . . ?* At the age of twenty-seven she had published her doctoral dissertation, written at Harvard, on the poetics of Eliot, a 500-page work, heavily footnoted, which had as its thesis the vision of the poet as transcendent—triumphing over personality, over the limits of the body itself. For this book she had won an award from the American

Academy of Arts and Letters (Colebrook had won a similar award, for a book on rhetorical devices in the modern novel), and she had been offered excellent positions at various universities—though, of course, she would never leave the Boston area, would never have left the general environment of her childhood. Her marriage at the age of thirty had been an agreeable surprise to her; and she had loved Theodore Drexler very much. Whatever had gone wrong in their relationship had not been from her side . . . but it was pointless to think about it, to think and rethink it, when Theodore himself had obviously forgotten. . . . Marriage, a child, eventually a divorce, had not seriously interfered with her work; she had been promoted up through the ranks, she had published three other books since *The Poetics of Eliot*, and innumerable essays and reviews, though Nora Drexler's reviews were always review-essays, extremely thoughtful and lengthy, well-argued, at times rather cruel, but always with a detached puritanical zeal that forced the reader to agree, to say *Yes, yes, it must be, yes.* . . . As the years passed and new books were published on her subjects, on Eliot especially, since new biographical evidence was always turning up, Nora had had to defend her position vigorously—she had had to defend Eliot against those who sought to link his work with sordid, petty details of his private life, as if art grew out of ordinary, routine, emotional life, and not from a higher consciousness altogether! . . . though she suspected that other academic critics would give these books the devastating reviews they deserved, their impertinence being so obvious, she had, upon occasion, actually requested books for review so that she could dispose of them properly. And she did this with absolute detachment—a puritan schoolgirl, really, only defending the Church against outsiders.

She was speaking to Colebrook rather passionately. No, she could not believe that art meant much to most people—certainly it was the possession of a very few. Poetry, especially, was the possession of a very few, it satisfied a need that certain people are born with, to have words fall into place, perfectly, the best words in the best order. . . . As Hopkins said. . . . As Stevens said. . . . "Just as in music, when you see the cadences that please the public in music, which are always predictable and clear, just as the rhythm is emphatic, you really can't make any link, discoverable in a lifetime, between their taste and yours. It isn't possible!" Nora was flustered, girlish. It pleased her that Colebrook seemed to be listening so intently. He had the look of a man forced to think *I must admit that. . . . Yes. She's right.*

She went to the kitchen and brought back, for him, not only another drink but some salted peanuts, and he thanked her with a big smile. He could be so boyish, so charming, when he tried. Rumors about his cynicism, his lack of charity, were just like rumors about Nora . . . without foundation, sheer lies. He was nice enough, today, to refer to Nora's most recent review, for the *American Scholar*, a slashing rejection of one of those new psychological-poetic books Nora detested—*The Seamless Imagination*—even the title angered her for some reason—and Nora shook her head helplessly, saying that she had hated to write that particular essay, knowing how it would hurt the author, she had truly *hated* to say such blunt, irrefutable things about the intelligence that had written it—but unfortunately "Someone had to do it," she said. "The book might have been assigned to someone else who might actually have praised it. . . . Can you imagine? What a thought. . . ."

Colebrook chuckled. He was eating peanuts hungrily.

"It took three weeks for me to arrange my thoughts on that book, in the best possible order," Nora said. "A waste of time, I suppose, but I felt I *must* do it. Even though I have less and less hope for educating the tone-deaf into loving cadences. . . . I cringe at having to seem cruel in print so often, but as you know, Mason, we haven't much choice about these issues. I have visions of the floodgates opening . . . our universities vulgarized, destroyed . . . our programs infested with grotesque 'literature' written by all kinds of people . . . even oral literature, even . . . even illiterate work. . . . Unless we're courageous and fight these issues at once, we'll be teaching Pawnee bear songs before we know it!"

"Issues?" Mason laughed. "Where?—I just like to be a sadistic bastard myself," he said cheerfully. "There are no issues with *me*. I just like to—" and here he made clumsy chopping motions with the side of his hand, a parody of karate strokes. Perhaps he meant to be amusing, but neither Nora nor his wife laughed. He reddened, grinning stupidly at his own unfunny joke, and Nora realized that he was drunk. Something was wrong with him: he was either drunk or drugged. Sarah began asking Nora a question in an attempt to change the subject, but he interrupted rudely: "Is this salt or good old-fashioned dust on the peanuts?"

"Nora, just ignore him," Sarah pleaded. "I didn't want to come here, it was *his* idea . . . he said he wouldn't behave like this. . . . I know how you value your privacy, Nora, and you hate people to bother you . . . and . . ."

"But I'm delighted to see you," Nora said. She looked from one to the other, bewildered. "I've been working so hard this year that my social life has dwindled to practically nothing . . . and you know you're always welcome to drop in, please, at any time. I don't get out much myself, but I'm always happy . . . happy to have guests. . . . What did you mean by that, Mason? . . . what you just said?"

"Harmless little joke!" Colebrook said. "The peanuts. Every time we've ever been at your house, Nora, it's the same little snacks . . . the same nuts, the same ceramic bowl. . . . Don't misunderstand, I love them and I love you. . . ."

"No, I don't mean the peanuts," Nora said, almost angry. "I mean—"

"We'd better leave," Sarah said, putting her drink down on the terrace.

"Please—what's wrong? What's happening?" Nora said.

"Let's barge in on Nora! Give her a little thrill!" Sarah mimicked.

Colebrook scooped up a handful of dirt and threw it into her face.

Sarah lunged at him, screaming. Something was overturned—a small wicker table; a glass was shattered.

All this happened so quickly, Nora had no idea what was going on. One moment they'd all been sitting, quietly, though there was certainly some tension between the Colebrooks—the next moment, that awful confusion, Sarah's ugly shouts and Colebrook's laughter. He jumped to his feet, out of her range. He stepped back into a redwood container of flowering chives.

"You son of a bitch!" Sarah said.

He laughed, waving his arm at her. His drink spilled onto his sleeve. Nora got to her feet, stunned, and didn't know what to do or say—she simply stared at them, bewildered. *What was happening? What on earth—?* Then Sarah was apologizing, saying she was sorry, sorry, she should have known better than to come here with *him*, sick as he was, and half crazy; and Colebrook strode away, muttering *Go to hell, both of you.* He went into Nora's kitchen. Sarah said they had to leave, she grabbed her purse and followed him, wild-eyed, her hair escaping from a knot at the back of her head, glinting blond or gray-blond, while Nora hurried alongside her. "Sarah, what on earth is wrong? What's wrong?" she said.

"Nothing," Sarah said.

The front door was open; Colebrook was down on the sidewalk, rubbing his arm across his face. He swayed foolishly, like a man imitating a drunk. When Sarah turned to say good-by to Nora and to apologize again, he yelled back at her to shut up, why the hell was she always apologizing? "Nora's the same ugly old selfish sadistic bitch she's always been, she won't give a damn, will you, Nora?—eh? Nora and I, we understand each other—twins!—Mutt and Jeff!—come on, Sarah, let's go—"

"We're not separating," Sarah said, backing down the steps from Nora. "I know what people say, I know what the gossip is. But he isn't that well. I suppose you'll get right on the phone and tell everybody, but it's very misleading—it's very superficial. He's just acting something out. He doesn't mean any of it."

Nora watched them walk to their car.

She was still standing there when they drove away; Sarah was in the driver's seat, Colebrook slumped beside her. Nora stared after them in utter amazement, still holding her drink—*What had happened? Was the world insane, that such a horror had swept into her garden, into her life?*

Behind her Dennis was whining: "Mother? Mother?"

She turned.

"You're not going with them, are you?—to some party or something? Are you? You said we'd be home all day today by ourselves—you said . . . you promised. . . ."

She closed the door. She was trembling.

"I won't let you upstairs to change your clothes," Dennis said, sniffing. "You're not taking a cab after them, are you? . . . I don't like that man, I hate that man. I hate the woman too. I hate all of them, don't you? . . . I don't like living people. Muriel's pretty but I hate her too, don't you?"

"Yes, yes," she said, embracing him. An agitated, plump child . . . her son . . . she must protect him, certainly she must protect him against the madness of people like the Colebrooks. How rude, how insufferable! She felt almost betrayed, once again betrayed, by a man she had somehow believed . . . had somehow believed might admire her. "Yes, honey, yes, yes, it's all right, I'll stay with you. . . . None of them are any better than your father, are they? . . . yes, I do hate them, you're absolutely right . . . I hate them all. . . ."

". . . did you whisper some plans with them? To meet them later?"

"Honey, no. That isn't a sane, rational question, is it?"

". . . not going to school tomorrow, are you?—school's out now, isn't it?"

"School has been out for weeks, Dennis. That isn't a rational question either, is it?"

"But I . . . I'm so afraid—I—"

"Is it?"

"I guess not, Mother. I guess it wasn't rational."

She embraced him again, pleased at last.

At last.

Explorations

1 *Spontaneous Farewell*

"There's an animal of some kind out there—"

"What?"

"An animal, a rabbit—it looks like a small brown rabbit—"

"That isn't a rabbit, that's been there for weeks," he said. He came up behind me. "It's rubbish or maybe a dead bird—how the hell do I know?—I never go out there. That isn't a rabbit."

It was crouched beneath a wild, sprawling bush, an untrimmed forsythia at the rear of the yard. I could see it plainly. I saw it. But I had to imagine its small perfect ears bent back against its skull, and the rim of white inside the ears. Fritz was caressing my shoulders; he stood close behind me, his thumbs caressing me as if

210

from a distance. He was very warm. He was perspiring inside his clothes.

"Are you going to tell anyone?" he asked.

He nudged the back of my head with his jaw.

"Why would I tell anyone?" I asked tonelessly.

He released me and walked away. I didn't turn—I stared at the small brown shape, the shape of the rabbit, waiting for it to move. Then I would make Fritz see it.

"Well, yes, why? . . . why, why?" he murmured, talking to himself. "Women do strange things. Stranger things. Yes, they do indeed . . . I could tell you such stories as would convulse your soul. . . ."

My eyes filled sullenly with tears.

"But you're a lovely girl, a very sweet girl, and so on, and not to blame, as I hope you're instructing yourself, and I suppose you wouldn't tell . . . I suppose it isn't any more flattering to you than it is to me. . . ." I heard him sit down heavily. I turned: he was sprawling on the sofa, a strangely small, dwarfish piece of furniture, much too low, yet with armrests that were curiously high. He tried to smile at me. It came out as a mock-robust smile, the lips parted in a greeting that never exactly turned into a greeting but remained expectant, poised. The first time we had met, four or five months earlier, he had stared at me like that: he had approached me and asked my name with that smile.

I had told him.

"Are you going directly home from here?" he asked.

"Why do you want to know?"

"Because you look a little sick, frankly. Because if your husband is home—"

"He isn't."

"He isn't. Well, good, Well. Fine. Yes, fine. And so if he isn't there, well, fine, you won't disturb him with that look of yours, will you? . . . You know, Margaret, I have a problem, a little problem like a clot of . . . well, not poison, that's too melodramatic . . . a clot of phlegm, let's say, at the back of my throat, let's say; it gathers there and causes distress to me and to others. Therefore I'm a bastard, therefore I acknowledge myself as shallow and guilty and guiltier than you know, in fact guilty of being so cheerful and guiltless, so even my apologies are just something I clear my throat of and spit out. Also I have a weak stomach. Also weak eyes, but my glasses are misplaced somewhere in this dump. . . . When I first noticed your lovely blue eyes—blue?—yes, blue—I should have looked away immediately, but I didn't. And so. . . ."

He talked. I missed whole patches of words. I was listening, but the words didn't come through; weren't connected with his facial expressions. It didn't matter. I watched the face closely and saw what it had to tell me.

He looked like his photographs: the eyebrows thicker near the bridge of his nose, so that his broad, solid face looked squeezed-in, compressed. His forehead was lined with the tensions and mock-greetings of many years.

"Come away from the window, please, you make me nervous," he said. "Sit down with me. Be forgiving. Let me move some of this junk aside—what is all this crap?—letters, packages—this box is from my paperback publishers, but my stomach is too weak this morning; I can't face what they've probably put on the cover— Come over here and sit down. It makes me tired, the way you keep standing around staring at me."

There was something I had wanted to say or do—but I could not remember. Fritz looked at me.

I kept forgetting.

"I'm leaving," I said.

"If you insist," he said.

He reached around and snapped on the radio. It was a dismissal. Or it was the pretense of a dismissal. I saw how his face reddened. From the radio came a bright simple rhythmic song, a popular rock song, the strenuous chords of someone's guitar, music from a local radio station. "Tonight, tell your husband . . . your earnest angular young husband . . . tell him not to respect me so much, it's tedious and embarrassing. He and the other young instructors egg me on, they encourage me to excess by their half-witted adulation. Yes, tell him. Set him at ease. Tell him in metaphor how sick I am; and that I don't mind being sick. A sick monster is tolerated with affection."

The guitar music swelled suddenly. Fritz reached for the radio, irritated, and knocked an ashtray over. Cigarette ashes and butts and something else—it must have been pits of some kind—scattered over the sofa. He turned the volume down.

"Oh, you're leaving . . . ? You really are . . . ?" He sighed, half yawned, and got unsteadily to his feet. The colorful sports shirt he was wearing was too tight for him; his broad, heavy chest and stomach strained at it when he pushed himself up from the sofa. "The fact is, dear, the incontestable fact is that I met you two or three decades too late in my life, and it isn't your fault. Neither, of course, is it my fault. It's all exploratory, Margaret, don't you know? —it's not serious."

He followed me into the front room. He never used this room except to store books in loose piles and to toss there other things he didn't want to clutter up his life. Beneath all the junk were the solid, old-fashioned, slightly shabby furnishings of the professor who owned this house, who was away for a year; no one dared write to inform him of the mess Fritz Risner had made of his trim little home.

"Hard to believe it's March here, such balmy weather," Fritz muttered. It was his "conversational" voice—flat and unconvincing. "North Carolina is lovely, like you, but I came to it too late. You won't tell them?"

"Them . . . ?

"Any of them."

He was standing at the door, so I had to approach him. He stood with his hands on his hips, his stomach slightly protruding, in a posture of awkward gallantry. I loved him. And he stared at me through it, through my love.

"I want—I can't—" I began.

"No, no. Darling no," he said, shocked.

"But I—"

"Not one more word! You'll break my heart!" He pursed his lips, pretending to be upset. But his face sagged with weariness. He longed to be rid of me. "You'll break my heart, Margaret, just remember that it isn't so serious—"

"But it is serious."

My body ached.

"No, not at all. Not at all. . . . You won't tell anyone?"

I never told anyone.

2   Rite of Spring

He heard me saying something, but could not make out the words. Inaudible. Unimportant. *I am Fritz Risner, too old to be enduring another session.*

He said to my back: "What?"

My voice was frail and disappointing. "An animal—a rabbit—it looks like a small brown rabbit—"

No. No exterior substance, no sentimental distraction. She is trying to fix her emotion on something exterior. She is trying to make this session poetic. She is trying hard. But no.

He glanced over my head into the boring thicket of a rented and unexplored back yard; it belonged to a professor of history, "well-loved," away on sabbatical leave Fritz did not know or care where, and he saw a not-uninteresting filmy blur of the sort one sees when one opens one's eyes underwater.

He countered the poetic image by declaring forcibly his knowledge of the thing beneath the bush, which was probably a dead bird.

I struggled to reply. His firm hands silenced me, through certain fingertip pressures too subtle to be described. Bored, he walked away and noticed with approval the shelves of books, rising to the ceiling, that he had laboriously re-shelved, undoing the professor's meticulous and surely neurotic methodology. Here and there were books placed upside down, so that their upside-down letters drew the eye, like a brutal image in a line of poetry; the kind Fritz liked best.

I was an unabsorbed object. He was thinking he had had this conversation before. But when? With whom? My mid-Southern accent was not familiar. His wives were all northern, and the current wife was English, possibly even in England, for all he knew. He was sympathetic with my newly shampooed hair, the American sheen of that red-blond-brown burnished hair swinging loosely about the face, but in all fairness to him his stomach was queasy and had been queasy since Thursday evening when he had drunk a bottle of something unlabeled, discovered behind some telephone books in his host's kitchen cupboard along with a bottle of Windex and a soured bottle of Mogen David. So.

Terror suddenly: that he had had this conversation before.

Terror denied: he would not give in to such a thought.

But: he wanted desperately to alter the script, only he could not think how.

He forced himself to stare at me, pitying-loving. His demonic-moronic smile might save him. Beside him on the sagging sofa were letters, some still in their unopened envelopes; if I walked out, he would be left with those letters. One was from the dying-of-cancer editor of an English journal who had befriended him during his wretched year as Visiting Lecturer at a university best unnamed, and he did not want, oh he did not want to read that letter. Another was from an ex-wife, second in a series of five, who was as well an ex-student and ex-friend and ex-poetess, whom he hated but whose coarsening beautiful face terrified him, and therefore he forced himself to stare at me, sweating, the pores of his enlarged body itching with sweat and the pressure of more sweat, like tears anxious to be shed. I was a small girl-sized woman in her twenties—mid-twenties? —yes—and I was saying good-by to him, or, rather, he was trying to maneuver me into saying good-by. The alarming familiarity of the scene should have consoled him, yet still he sweated.

I was a pretty young woman. Some months before he had auto-graphed his novel, *Genocide*, for me, "for Margaret," with love and a trembling fumbling hand shaken by his excitement: all the old responses of his blood, the flashing-to-the-brain of the old Risner, believed dead, but restored to a fifteen-year-old's lust by a woman with an accent he half believed must be a parody. "Pretty" was a word he focused upon, though now I was not standing in very good light. And my voice was toneless and unmusical. But he tried to focus his attention upon the word "pretty" because it was a word that might save him . . . might flash to the brain a white-hot response that would unclick the programmed responses he knew, he knew were still there, but sluggish and. . . . Was it spring so soon again, in this balmy evil climate, must he go through once again his rite of spring . . . ?

"Margaret? Margaret?" he cried.

He seemed not to see me. Not to be seeing me. He stared, his face strained, dense with blood and the layers of years. He said faintly, "Margaret . . . ?" and I knew it was not my name he was pronouncing.

We stared at each other helplessly.

He was staring at a young woman with a skin that was precious to her. Did he know? It was a silky, delicate skin, too sensitive for his coarse skin; it had begun to change in small ways—a rash of very tiny bumps along my jaw, not visible from where he sat, and a flat but very sore pimple up near my hairline, not visible either to any-one except myself. But I saw, I knew. I took my skin seriously, I admired and feared it, this magical envelope of flesh that made me *pretty* and valuable to Fritz Risner, as he stared blindly at me. Shyly I saw how blotched, how thick and sagging his own skin was, liver-ish beneath his eyes. . . .

He broke the moment suddenly. He reached around to switch on a small radio made of red plastic; at once a stranger's sweet, breathy voice filled the air between us, murmuring some words that had to do with love.

". . . you'll forget me, you'll move on, you'll ditch your gawky husband and float away like the lovely fluffy pollen you are," he was
saying rapidly, as if he had said all this before and needed only to
move through the words, as the boyish singer was moving through
his words, accompanied by a heavy guitar, ". . . and, uh, someday
I'll write you a letter, desperate and pleading etcetera, and you'll
rip it to shreds and laugh. . . ."

Now to walk her to the door. Walk me to the door.

Now tenderness: ". . . you knew I was a satirist, you should have
avoided me. Women must always avoid satire; it denudes them.
When people are nude, love is a blank. But, but Honey-girl, but
remember this so you won't think ill of me: the satirist is absolutely
conservative in his innermost heart, dedicated to the eternal verities,
which he can't quite locate in anyone he knows. But his heart is in
the right place. . . . You're almost as young as my oldest daughter,
did you know that?"

The greeting-smile, blurred with fondness, a chaste tenderness.
He smiled. He was holding something—my purse—an object made
of a beige canvas-like material; I had to take it from him, he seemed
not to know what to do with it.

"I'll write to you . . . when my head gets clear again," he whispered. "I need to disappear for a while, then reappear in some un-
expected place—the tundra of Montana, maybe, or the death-deserts
of the Southwest. I don't know exactly. But I'll make a connection,
I'll start writing the next chapter of my biography . . . or revising . . .
or. . . . But God, how I hate to revise! In fact," he laughed, "I hate
to write. . . ."

I spoke. He shook his head. *No. No.* The fatherly-generous expression faded, another expression appeared: and with a curt
embarrassed movement of his head he indicated the rear of the
house, meaning the bedroom we had been in for those few torturous
minutes. ". . . well, not a word, not a word! Because—you see?—not
all explorations end with treasure, digging up buried treasure, you
see?—just remember that it isn't so serious—"

I heard someone's voice: *But it is serious.*

My body ached—the chafed skin of my thighs, the flesh of my arm that he had squeezed, pinched, torn at so angrily, not knowing what he did, in his fury, his desperation. *Oh you bitch!* He had wept, those eyes gone blind with self-sorrow, and even now he wasn't exactly seeing me, but looking toward me and completing another rite: ". . . But not a word of it, no apologies or tears or—Margaret?—no tears? You won't tell anyone?"

I never told anyone.

3   Zero & Sub-Zero

I went to the building we lived in, my husband and I, an apartment building on the east side of the campus, made of bright orange brick that was new but starting to crumble. I made my way along the toy-littered walk and to our door, with its curlycue "17" above the doorway, made of a luminous white material that would glow in the dark, and inside the apartment I drew water for a bath, even though he had probably stopped thinking of me by now and would not have thought *Now she will take a bath to heal herself. . . .*

Lowering myself slowly into the hot sparkling water: I smiled, to see a strange shape emerging beneath the surface of the water. It was distorted but not frightening. It was funny. There was something funny about it. But at first I couldn't laugh. But then I did laugh.

Years later I was staring at a cover of one of his books, a paperback edition. It was prominently displayed on a news-agent's stand in London, near the South Kensington Underground station. *Zeroing Under,* "a racy blend of science fiction and brilliant satire," "the masterpiece of America's foremost satirist," with a cover that showed a long-legged girl in a brief, metallic costume, her wild blond hair tumbled about her bare shoulders, a ray-gun cradled in her arms. The shape of her legs, which would have been lovely, since they were the shape of the legs of a beautiful woman, were cruelly hidden by red plastic boots that laced up tightly . . . tightly. . . . I smiled. There was something funny about this. I thought of how Risner had hated the covers of his books, and in fact the books themselves, and how he must hate this cover. . . . Then I thought: It isn't funny. I thought: He loves these covers. And it wasn't funny, but the shape of the legs and the shape of the body came to seem distorted, frightening. The woman was a man's goddess, trapped in that body. The news-agent was watching me. I wondered what showed in my face; I thought I should walk away quickly, not looking back.

I walked away quickly, not looking back.

My husband and I lived at this time in a second-floor flat in a row house, for which we paid thirty-five pounds a week, so that my husband could work at the British Museum: he was doing research for a book about the prewar correspondence of certain English literary figures who had confided doubts and hopes to one another without guessing that young men like my husband would one day scrutinize their letters and pass severe judgment upon them. The flat had only a kitchen, a bedroom, and a bathroom. In the bedroom were our books, most of them my husband's; but I had all of Risner's novels, the paperback editions.

Without taking off my coat I stopped and picked them up. I walked out into the kitchen. My heart was pounding. I looked under the table, where we kept the wastebasket, and smiled down into it, standing with the six books in my arms. They were very light. Very thin. The longest novel—*Genocide*—was only a hundred and fifty pages long. But the wastebasket was already filled with trash. I thought of how I would put the books into the basket, covering them with paper to hide them; then I thought of how my husband— who emptied the wastebaskets every few days, reluctantly enough— would discover the books. He would wonder about them; he would ask questions. So I thought of throwing the books away myself, taking them down to the basement. But the trash containers down there were always filled up with raw garbage. So. So I would take the books outside, throw them away outside. . . . My heart pumped with the excitement of doing this, but I did not move, and the thought of going back outside into the rain tired me, I began to feel very tired, my face was warm, hot, almost feverish. An old dull ache began somewhere in my body.

I put the books back. I took off my coat and sat at the kitchen table, as if waiting for someone. But my husband would not be home for a long time.

That was in December. One afternoon in February my husband came home at his usual time, about twenty to six, and handed the newspaper to me saying in a strange voice, "Your hero died. . . ."

It was *The Guardian*, which he bought every morning and sometimes left behind in the reading room, forgetful of me, but today he had remembered it. His hand shook a little with grief or with drama.

At the bottom of the left-hand column, a series of brief news items in dark print, was the headline *U.S. Novelist Risner Dies*.

The American novelist Fritz Risner, 54, was found dead Sunday morning twelve miles north of Cardston, Alberta. His automobile had evidently stalled and death was believed due to the low temperature ($-30°F.$). Risner, who has been associated with the University of Montana until last year, lived in Great Falls, Montana.

Famous for his bitter satires, which were compared by critics to works by Swift and Orwell, Risner was a popular figure in American literary circles. He was the recipient of many awards and honors, the editor of the controversial *New Fauve Review*, and during the academic year 1968–69 he was Visiting Lecturer of American Literature at Warwick University. His most famous novels are *Genocide*, *Sun-Speck*, and *Zeroing Under*.

Risner is credited with reviving serious literary interests in science fiction. He is survived by his wife, Mona, and his five children.

". . . I was shocked, I was really shocked," my husband was saying. I heard him explain: how he had come across the item, how he had read it, how he had been shocked. ". . . and, you remember, don't you, this Canadian scholar I mentioned . . . ? From Edmonton? Well, I went over to him and showed him the item and he told me how deadly cold it is up there . . . no one goes out in the winter, evidently, without a survival kit in the car. . . . So it must have been, I mean it must, it must have been . . . don't you think? . . . suicide . . . ?"

No.

And no. No. That he had died. That my husband was watching me so closely. That he had died like that, so much alone.

My husband was speaking gravely, yet with an air of quiet satisfaction. "Margaret, you're not upset, are you? I thought you should know . . . I remember how much you liked him, of course everyone liked him. . . . I liked him too. Of course, I don't mean I liked his writing, his writing is just trash. But . . . I thought I'd better tell you, since you would find out anyway. I'm sorry if I upset you. . . ."

"I'm not upset," I said.

My husband took the paper back from me. He frowned. He read the item again. "I suppose it might have been an accident," he said. "We heard those wild stories of how drunk he got, and how careless he was with himself . . . remember? . . . he might have driven up there without any purpose in mind. . . ."

"Yes," I said. "That's probably what happened."

". . . probably. It might have happened that way. You were very fond of him at one time, weren't you?"

"Yes."

". . . it doesn't say whether he tried to get help, whether he tried to flag down anyone. Or what. It's very brief, isn't it, very ominous,"

my husband said slowly. "We'll probably hear more details later. . . .
He did a lot of drinking, people said. Remember how drunk he was
that time, that one time at the Hogans, I think it was, the Hogans'
party around Christmas? Do you remember?"

I heard this question and recognized it as a question. But I could
not think how to answer it: yes or no.

I said *Yes*. This seemed to be the answer my husband wanted to
hear.

"There was such a cult of Risner, and I never understood it," he
said. "Of course he was personally very charming when he was sober
. . . and of course college students loved him. . . . You were quite
fond of him yourself, weren't you? But it was hard to get to know
him, wasn't it? That's what everyone said. . . . *Mona*. Is that the one
he was married to while he was in North Carolina, or was it . . .
wasn't it another name? . . . I think it was another name, wasn't it?
This woman, whoever she is, must have been his sixth wife. . . ."

"Yes," I said.

He continued to speak. I focused my attention upon him. We
stood in the wintry tundra, but the winds were still around us; perhaps we were at the sub-zero center of a storm. I focused my attention upon him. He had just come home, through the dark. The sun
set around four o'clock here, though it was difficult to tell; sometimes the sun did not appear at all, and it was evening all day long.
But now it was past five-thirty and genuinely dark. There should
have been nothing to fear about a genuine dark. Since he was speaking to me, I focused my attention upon him: he was living, he was
standing before me. His face was that of a pale, serious young man,
and his name was Tevsky, Mark (Marek), my husband of five
years. He had Slavic cheekbones and intense dark eyes that were
always a little suspicious. His parents had come to America from
Prague, and he had inherited from them a certain guarded dislike
of all Americans, though he was an American himself and married
to an American. With his birdlike talent for locating soft things, he

had already published several essays on the pre-World War II correspondence of Pound, Lawrence, and others. His own letters to our friends back in the States were very carefully written: cheerful, chatty, informative, ironic, usually containing one small twist, a comment or a rumor or a question, that was designed to hurt the person to whom it was written.

I have a little problem like a clot of . . . phlegm, let's say. . . .

He was talking to me, then talking to my back as I walked into the bedroom. His voice lifted with surprise. I half-heard it. He had not been talking about Risner any longer, but about the crowded underground and the singers who begged for money down there, who annoyed him very much, and about the trash in the building— he could smell it, the garbage, when he came in the foyer, and it sickened him, and—

"Margaret, what's wrong?" he called. His voice was shrill with surprise and vexation. I was walking slowly away from him but his need for me was so strong I felt it, the tugging, the ache in both our bodies, the pressure of my image on his brain. The eyes, the retinas of the eyes. The brain.

A woman walking away. A woman's back, and the back of her head. She is walking slowly. Unsteadily. The woman is myself, and the man who is watching her is someone else, someone apart from her. . . . I saw how it was in this man's head, in his eyes. I saw the figure of the woman. *I saw.* And I felt the thumping heartbeat of the male, watching, staring, I felt the tinge of despair and venom as the woman walked away . . . and, in my own body, I felt a sensation of alarm, an almost eager terror. I felt it all, I felt it and saw it. Around me were walls, a room I did not remember. A bedroom. The air was cold; a small thin draft edged in steadily from the window. I felt my strength drain out of me and into the chilly air of this room. I heard someone calling a name: "Margaret . . . ?

I stood there, helpless.

"Margaret?"

Yes, that was my name.

4   *The Death of Risner's Death*

"Margaret?"

"Yes...."

"Who's that letter from?"

"This?"

"Yes, of course. Who's it from?"

A Saturday morning in late March. We were still living in London. My husband had brought the mail upstairs—several letters for him, two for me, one of them from my sister; the other, forwarded many times, missent to an address a block or so away, was in a long manila envelope. The printing on the envelope was small and careful, not familiar.

The postmark was from Montana.

"I don't know, I don't know who it's from," I said, beginning to tremble.

My husband watched me. I was holding the envelope, staring at it. I was sitting in the cold dull light from the window, an unflattering light; I did not want him to observe me but he was there, close to me, watching. *Did you ever tell anyone?* No. No, I never had. No. Someone was speaking to me, curiously, irritably, asking me why I didn't open the letter—*It's all exploratory, Margaret, don't you know?—it's not serious—*

"That letter is postmarked Montana, isn't it?" my husband asked. But his voice was level, controlled. "You seem afraid to open it. Why are you afraid, Margaret?—don't you want me to see it? Would you like me to leave, so you can read it in privacy? Would you like me to leave?"

"No."

"Then open it. Go ahead and open it."

I made a motion to open it, a fingernail inserted somewhere, hesitantly, weakly, and then an eerie, impersonal chill enveloped me; I knew I must not read what he had written, I must not know.

It had been sent many weeks ago. Desperate, pleading . . . ? Or only more satire, another exploratory lunge . . . ?

"What's wrong?" my husband asked. Out of the corner of my eye, without wanting to, I could see that small nervous picking gesture of his—the nails of his middle fingers drawn against the fleshy part of his thumb. "Are you afraid it's a letter that came too late?—is that why you won't open it?"

I ripped the envelope in two.

"You shouldn't have done that," he said, surprised.

I ripped the pieces again, folding them over and ripping them slowly.

"Why should I have opened it?" I said.

But I was not speaking to him.

Small Avalanches

I kept bothering my mother for a dime, so she gave me a dime, and I went down our lane and took the shortcut to the highway, and down to the gas station. My uncle Winfield ran the gas station. There were two machines in the garage and I had to decide between them: the pop machine and the candy bar machine. No, there were three machines, but the other one sold cigarettes and I didn't care about that.

It took me a few minutes to make up my mind, then I bought a bottle of Pepsi-Cola.

Sometimes a man came to unlock the machines and take out the coins, and if I happened to be there it was interesting—the way the machines could be changed so fast if you just had the right key to open them. This man drove up in a white truck with a license plate

from Kansas, a different color from our license plates, and he unlocked the machines and took out the money and loaded the
machines up again. When we were younger we liked to hang
around and watch. There was something strange about it, how the
look of the machines could be changed so fast, the fronts swinging
open, the insides showing, just because a man with the right keys
drove up.

I went out front where my uncle was working on a car. He was
under the car, lying on a thing made out of wood that had rollers
on it so that he could roll himself under the car; I could just see
his feet. He had on big heavy shoes that were all greasy. I asked him
if my cousin Georgia was home—they lived about two miles away
and I could walk—and he said no, she was babysitting in Stratton
for three days. I already knew this but I hoped the people might
have changed their minds.

"Is that man coming today to take out the money?"

My uncle didn't hear me. I was sucking at the Pepsi-Cola and
running my tongue around the rim of the bottle. I always loved the
taste of pop, the first two or three swallows. Then I would feel a
little filled up and would have to drink it slowly. Sometimes I even
poured the last of it out, but not so that anyone saw me.

"That man who takes care of the machines, is he coming today?"

"Who? No. Sometime next week."

My uncle pushed himself out from under the car. He was my
mother's brother, a few years older than my mother. He had bushy
brown hair and his face was dirty. "Did you call Georgia last
night?"

"No. Ma wouldn't let me."

"Well, somebody was on the line because Betty wanted to check
on her and the goddam line was busy all night. So Betty wanted to
drive in, all the way to Stratton, drive six miles when probably nothing's wrong. You didn't call her, huh?"

"No."

"This morning Betty called her and gave her hell and she tried to say she hadn't been talking all night, that the telephone lines must have gotten mixed up. Georgia is a goddam little liar and if I catch her fooling around. . . ."

He was walking away, into the garage. In the back pocket of his overalls was a dirty rag, stuffed there. He always yanked it out and wiped his face with it, not looking at it, even if it was dirty. I watched to see if he would do this and he did.

I almost laughed at this, and at how Georgia got away with murder. I had a good idea who was talking to her on the telephone.

The pop made my tongue tingle, a strong acid-sweet taste that almost hurt. I sat down and looked out at the road. This was in the middle of Colorado, on the road that goes through, east and west. It was a hot day. I drank one, two, three, four small swallows of pop. I pressed the bottle against my knees because I was hot. I tried to balance the bottle on one knee and it fell right over; I watched the pop trickle out onto the concrete.

I was too lazy to move my feet, so my bare toes got wet.

Somebody came along the road in a pickup truck, Mr. Watkins, and he tapped on the horn to say hello to me and my uncle. He was on his way to Stratton. I thought, *Damn it, I could have hitched a ride with him.* I don't know why I bothered to think this because I had to get home pretty soon, anyway, my mother would kill me if I went to town without telling her. Georgia and I did that once, back just after school let out in June, we went down the road a ways and hitched a ride with some guy in a beat-up car we thought looked familiar, but when he stopped to let us in we didn't know him and it was too late. But nothing happened, he was all right. We walked all the way back home again because we were scared to hitch another ride. My parents didn't find out, or Georgia's, but we didn't try it again.

I followed my uncle into the gas station. The building was made of ordinary wood, painted white a few years ago but starting to peel. It was just one room. The floor was concrete, all stained with grease and cracked. I knew the whole place by heart: the ceiling planks, the black rubber things hanging on the wall, looped over big rusty spikes, the Cat's Paw ad that I liked, and the other ads for beer and cigarettes on shiny pieces of cardboard that stood up. To see those things you wouldn't guess how they came all flat, and you could unfold them and fix them yourself, like fancy things for under the Christmas tree. Inside the candy machine, behind the little windows, the candy bars stood up on display: *Milky Way, O Henry, Junior Mints, Mallow Cup, Three Musketeers, Hershey.* I liked them all. Sometimes *Milky Way* was my favorite, other times I only bought *Mallow Cup* for weeks in a row, trying to get enough of the cardboard letters to spell out *Mallow Cup.* One letter came with each candy bar, and if you spelled out the whole name you could send away for a prize. But the letter "w" was hard to find. There were lots of "l's," it was rotten luck to open the wrapper up and see another "l" when you already had ten of them.

"Could I borrow a nickel?" I asked my uncle.

"I don't have any change."

Like hell, I thought. My uncle was always stingy.

I pressed the "return coin" knob but nothing came out. I pulled the knob out under *Mallow Cup* but nothing came out.

"Nancy, don't fool around with that thing, okay?"

"I don't have anything to do."

"Yeah, well, your mother can find something for you to do."

"She can do it herself."

"You want me to tell her that?"

"Go right ahead."

"Hey, did your father find out any more about that guy in Polo?"

"What guy?"

"Oh, I don't know, some guy who got into a fight and was arrested—he was in the Navy with your father, I don't remember his name."

"I don't know."

My uncle yawned. I followed him back outside and he stretched his arms and yawned. It was very hot. You could see the fake water puddles on the highway that were so mysterious and always moved back when you approached them. They could hypnotize you. Across from the garage was the mailbox on a post and then just scrub land, nothing to look at, pasture land and big rocky hills.

I thought about going to check to see if my uncle had any mail, but I knew there wouldn't be anything inside. We only got a booklet in the mail that morning, some information about how to make money selling jewelry door-to-door that I had written away for, but now I didn't care about. "Georgia has all the luck," I said. "I could use a few dollars myself."

"Yeah," my uncle said. He wasn't listening.

I looked at myself in the outside mirror of the car he was fixing. I don't know what kind of car it was, I never memorized the makes like the boys did. It was a dark maroon color with big heavy fenders and a bumper that had little bits of rust in it, like sparks. The running board had old, dried mud packed down inside its ruts. It was covered with black rubber, a mat. My hair was blown-looking. It was a big heavy mane of hair the color everybody called dish-water blond. My baby pictures showed that it used to be light blond.

"I wish I could get a job like Georgia," I said.

"Georgia's a year older than you."

"Oh hell. . . ."

I was thirteen but I was Georgia's size, all over, and I was smarter. We looked alike. We both had long bushy flyaway hair that frizzed up when the air was wet, but kept curls in very well when we set it, like for church. I forgot about my hair and leaned closer to the mirror to look at my face. I made my lips shape a little circle, noticing how wrinkled they got. They could wrinkle up into a small space. I poked the tip of my tongue out.

There was the noise of something on gravel, and I looked around to see a man driving in. Out by the highway my uncle just had gravel, then around the gas pumps he had concrete. This man's car was white, a color you don't see much, and his license plate was from Kansas.

He told my uncle to fill up the gas tank and he got out of the car, stretching his arms.

He looked at me and smiled. "Hi," he said.

"Hi."

He said something to my uncle about how hot it was, and my uncle said it wasn't too bad. Because that's the way he is—always contradicting you. My mother hates him for this. But then he said, "You read about the dry spell coming up?—right into September?" My uncle meant the ranch bureau thing but the man didn't know what he was talking about. He meant the "Bureau News & Forecast." This made me mad, that my uncle was so stupid, thinking that a man from out of state and probably from a city would know about that, or give a damn. It made me mad. I saw my pop bottle where it fell and I decided to go home, not to bother putting it in the case where you were supposed to.

I walked along on the edge of the road, on the pavement, because there were stones and prickles and weeds with bugs in them off the side that I didn't like to walk in barefoot. I felt hot and mad about something. A yawn started in me, and I felt it coming up like a little bubble of gas from the pop. There was my cousin Georgia in town, and all she had to do was watch a little girl who wore thick glasses and was sort of strange, but very nice and quiet and no trouble, and she'd get two dollars. I thought angrily that if anybody came along I'd put out my thumb and hitch a ride to Stratton, and the hell with my mother.

Then I did hear a car coming but I just got over to the side and waited for him to pass. I felt stubborn and wouldn't look around to see who it was, but then the car didn't pass and I looked over my shoulder—it was the man in the white car, who had stopped for gas. He was driving very slow. I got farther off the road and waited for him to pass. But he leaned over to this side and said out the open window, "You want a ride home? Get in."

"No, that's okay," I said.

"Come on, I'll drive you home. No trouble."

"No, it's okay. I'm almost home," I said.

I was embarrassed and didn't want to look at him. People didn't do this, a grown-up man in a car wouldn't bother to do this. Either you hitched for a ride or you didn't, and if you didn't, people would never slow down to ask you. This guy is crazy, I thought. I felt very strange. I tried to look over into the field but there wasn't anything to look at, not even any cattle, just land and scrubby trees and a barbed-wire fence half falling down.

"Your feet will get all sore, walking like that," the man said.

"I'm okay."

"Hey, watch out for the snake!"

There wasn't any snake and I made a noise like a laugh to show that I knew it was a joke but didn't think it was very funny.

"Aren't there rattlesnakes around here? Rattlers?"

"Oh I don't know," I said.

He was still driving right alongside me, very slow. You are not used to seeing a car slowed-down like that, it seems very strange. I tried not to look at the man. But there was nothing else to look at, just the country and the road and the mountains in the distance and some clouds.

"That man at the gas station was mad, he picked up the bottle you left."

I tried to keep my lips pursed shut, but they were dry and came open again. I wondered if my teeth were too big in front.

"How come you walked away so fast? That wasn't friendly," the man said. "You forgot your pop bottle and the man back there said somebody could drive over it and get a flat tire, he was a little mad."

"He's my uncle," I said.

"What?"

He couldn't hear or was pretending he couldn't hear, so I had to turn toward him. He was all-right-looking, he was smiling. "He's my uncle," I said.

"Oh, is he? You don't look anything like *him*. Is your home nearby?"

"Up ahead." I was embarrassed and started to laugh, I don't know why.

"I don't see any house there."

"You can't see it from here," I said, laughing.

"What's so funny? My face? You know, when you smile you're a very pretty girl. You should smile all the time. . . ." He was paying so much attention to me it made me laugh. "Yes, that's a fact. Why are you blushing?"

I blushed fast, like my mother; we both hated to blush and hated people to tease us. But I couldn't get mad.

"I'm worried about your feet and the rattlers around here. Aren't there rattlers around here?"

"Oh I don't know."

"Where I come from there are streets and sidewalks and no snakes, of course, but it isn't interesting. It isn't dangerous. I think I'd like to live here, even with the snakes—this is very beautiful, hard country, isn't it? Do you like the mountains way over there? Or don't you notice them?"

I didn't pay any attention to where he was pointing, I looked at him and saw that he was smiling. He was my father's age but he wasn't stern like my father, who had a line between his eyebrows like a knife-cut, from frowning. This man was wearing a shirt, a regular white shirt, out in the country. His hair was dampened and combed back from his forehead; it was damp right now, as if he had just combed it.

"Yes, I'd like to take a walk out here and get some exercise," he said. His voice sounded very cheerful. "Snakes or no snakes! You turned me down for a free ride so maybe I'll join you in a walk."

That really made me laugh: *join you in a walk.*

"Hey, what's so funny?" he said, laughing himself.

People didn't talk like that, but I didn't say anything. He parked the car on the shoulder of the road and got out and I heard him drop the car keys in his pocket. He was scratching at his jaw. "Well, excellent! This is excellent, healthy, divine country air! Do you like living out here?"

I shook my head, no.

"You wouldn't want to give all this up for a city, would you?"

"Sure. Any day."

I was walking fast to keep ahead of him, I couldn't help but giggle, I was so embarrassed—this man in a white shirt was really walking out on the highway, he was really going to leave his car parked like that! You never saw a car parked on the road around here, unless it was by the creek, fishermen's cars, or unless it was a wreck. All this made my face get hotter.

He walked fast to catch up with me. I could hear coins and things jingling in his pockets.

"You never told me your name," he said. "That isn't friendly."

"It's Nancy."

"Nancy what?"

"Oh I don't know," I laughed.

"Nancy I-Don't-Know?" he said.

I didn't get this. He was smiling hard. He was shorter than my father and now that he was out in the bright sun I could see he was older. His face wasn't tanned, and his mouth kept going into a soft smile. Men like my father and my uncles and other men never bothered to smile like that at me, they never bothered to look at me at all. Some men did, once in a while, in Stratton, strangers waiting for Greyhound buses to Denver or Kansas City, but they weren't friendly like this, they didn't keep on smiling for so long.

When I came to the path I said, "Well, good-by, I'm going to cut over this way. This is a shortcut."

"A shortcut where?"

"Oh I don't know," I said, embarrassed.

"To your house, Nancy?"

"Yeah. No, it's to our lane, our lane is half a mile long."

"Is it? That's very long. . . ."

He came closer. "Well, good-by," I said.

"That's a long lane, isn't it?—it must get blocked up with snow in the winter, doesn't it? You people get a lot of snow out here—"

"Yeah."

"So your house must be way back there . . . ?" he said, pointing. He was smiling. When he stood straight like this, looking over my head, he was more like the other men. But then he looked down at me and smiled again, so friendly. I waved good-by and jumped over the ditch and climbed the fence, clumsy as hell just when somebody was watching me, wouldn't you know it. Some barbed wire caught at my shorts and the man said, "Let me get that loose—" but I jerked away and jumped down again. I waved good-by again and started up the path. But the man said something and when I looked back he was climbing over the fence himself. I was so surprised that I just stood there.

"I like shortcuts and secret paths," he said. "I'll walk a little way with you."

"What do you—" I started to say. I stopped smiling because something was wrong. I looked around and there was just the path behind me that the kids always took, and some boulders and old dried-up manure from cattle, and some scrubby bushes. At the top of the hill was the big tree that had been struck by lightning so many times. I was looking at all this and couldn't figure out why I was looking at it.

"You're a brave little girl to go around barefoot," the man said, right next to me. "Or are your feet tough on the bottom?"

I didn't know what he was talking about because I was worried; then I heard his question and said vaguely, "I'm all right," and started to walk faster. I felt a tingling all through me like the tingling from the Pepsi-Cola in my mouth.

"Do you always walk so fast?" the man laughed.

"Oh I don't know."

"Is that all you can say? Nancy I-Don't-Know! That's a funny name—is it foreign?"

This made me start to laugh again. I was walking fast, then I began to run a few steps. Right away I was out of breath. That was strange—I was out of breath right away.

"Hey, Nancy, where are you going?" the man cried.

But I kept running, not fast. I ran a few steps and looked back and there he was, smiling and panting, and I happened to see his foot come down on a loose rock. I knew what would happen—the rock rolled off sideways and he almost fell, and I laughed. He glanced up at me with a surprised grin. "This path is a booby trap, huh? Nancy has all sorts of little traps and tricks for me, huh?"

I didn't know what he was talking about. I ran up the side of the hill, careful not to step on the manure or anything sharp, and I was still out of breath but my legs felt good. They felt as if they wanted to run a long distance. "You're going off the path," he said, pretending to be mad. "Hey. That's against the rules. Is that another trick?"

I giggled but couldn't think of any answer.

"Did you make this path up by yourself?" the man asked. But he was breathing hard from the hill. He stared at me, climbing up, with his hands pushing on his knees as if to help him climb. "Little Nancy, you're like a wild colt or a deer, you're so graceful—is this your own private secret path? Or do other people use it?"

"Oh, my brother and some other kids, when they're around," I said vaguely. I was walking backward up the hill now, so that I could look down at him. The top of his hair was thin, you could see the scalp. The very top of his forehead seemed to have two bumps, not big ones, but as if the bone went out a little, and this part was a bright pink, sunburned, but the rest of his face and his scalp were white.

He stepped on another loose rock, and the rock and some stones and mud came loose. He fell hard onto his knee. "Jesus!" he said. The way he stayed down like that looked funny. I had to press my hand over my mouth. When he looked up at me his smile was different. He got up, pushing himself up with his hands, grunting, and then he wiped his hands on his trousers. The dust showed on them. He looked funny.

"Is my face amusing? Is it a good joke?"

I didn't mean to laugh, but now I couldn't stop. I pressed my hand over my mouth hard.

He stared at me. "What do you see in my face, Nancy? What do you see—anything? Do you see my soul, do you see *me*, is that what you're laughing at?" He took a fast step toward me, but I jumped back. It was like a game. "Come on, Nancy, slow down, just slow down," he said. "Come on, Nancy. . . ."

I didn't know what he was talking about, I just had to laugh at his face. It was so tense and strange; it was so *important*.

I noticed a big rock higher up, and I went around behind it and pushed it loose—it rolled right down toward him and he had to scramble to get out of the way. "Hey! Jesus!" he yelled. The rock came loose with some other things and a mud chunk got him in the leg.

I laughed so hard my stomach started to ache.

He laughed too, but a little different from before.

"This is a little trial for me, isn't it?" he said. "A little preliminary contest. Is that how the game goes? Is that your game, Nancy?"

I ran higher up the hill, off to the side where it was steeper. Little rocks and things came loose and rolled back down. My breath was coming so fast it made me wonder if something was wrong. Down behind me the man was following, stooped over, looking at me, and his hand was pressed against the front of his shirt. I could see his hand moving up and down because he was breathing so hard. I could even see his tongue moving around the edge of his dried-out lips. . . . I started to get afraid, and then the tingling came back into me, beginning in my tongue and going out through my whole body, and I couldn't help giggling.

He said something that sounded like, "—won't be laughing—" but I couldn't hear the rest of it. My hair was all wet in back where it would be a job for me to unsnarl it with the hairbrush. The man came closer, stumbling, and just for a joke I kicked out at him, to scare him—and he jerked backward and tried to grab onto a branch of a bush, but it slipped through his fingers and he lost his balance and fell. He grunted. He fell so hard that he just lay there for a minute. I wanted to say I was sorry, or ask him if he was all right, but I just stood there grinning.

He got up again; the fleshy part of his hand was bleeding. But he didn't seem to notice it and I turned and ran up the rest of the hill, going almost straight up the last part, my legs were so strong and felt so good. Right at the top I paused, just balanced there, and a gust of wind would have pushed me over—but I was all right. I laughed aloud, my legs felt so springy and strong.

I looked down over the side where he was crawling, down on his hands and knees again. "You better go back to Kansas! Back home to Kansas!" I laughed. He stared up at me and I waited for him to smile again but he didn't. His face was very pale. He was staring at me but he seemed to be seeing something else, his eyes were very serious and strange. I could see his belt creasing his stomach, the bulge of his white shirt. He pressed his hand against his chest again. "Better go home, go home, get in your damn old car and go home," I sang, making a song of it. He looked so serious, staring up at me. I pretended to kick at him again and he flinched, his eyes going small.

"Don't leave me—" he whimpered.

"Oh go on," I said.

"Don't leave—I'm sick—I think I—"

His face seemed to shrivel. He was drawing in his breath very slowly, carefully, as if checking to see how much it hurt, and I waited for this to turn into another joke. Then I got tired of waiting and just rested back on my heels. My smile got smaller and smaller, like his.

"Good-by, I'm going," I said, waving. I turned and he said something—it was like a cry—but I didn't want to bother going back. The tingling in me was almost noisy.

I walked over to the other side, and slid back down to the path and went along the path to our lane. I was very hot. I knew my face was flushed and red. "Damn old nut," I said. But I had to laugh at the way he had looked, the way he kept scrambling up the hill and was just crouched there at the end, on his hands and knees. He looked so funny, bent over and clutching at his chest, pretending to have a heart attack or maybe having one, a little one, for all I knew. This will teach you a lesson, I thought.

By the time I got home my face had dried off a little, but my hair was like a haystack. I stopped by the old car parked in the lane, just a junker on blocks, and looked in the outside rear-view mirror—the mirror was all twisted around because people looked in it all the time. I tried to fix my hair by rubbing my hands down hard against it, but no luck. "Oh damn," I said aloud, and went up the steps to the back, and remembered not to let the screen door slam so my mother wouldn't holler at me.

She was in the kitchen ironing, just sprinkling some clothes on the ironing board. She used a pop bottle painted blue and fitted out with a sprinkler top made of rubber, that I fixed for her at grade school a long time ago for a Christmas present; she shook the bottle over the clothes and stared at me. "Where have you been? I told you to come right back."

"I did come right back."

"You're all dirty, you look like hell. What happened to you?"

"Oh I don't know," I said. "Nothing."

She threw something at me—it was my brother's shirt—and I caught it and pressed it against my hot face.

"You get busy and finish these," my mother said. "It must be ninety-five in here and I'm fed up. And you do a good job, I'm really fed up. Are you listening, Nancy? Where the hell is your mind?"

I liked the way the damp shirt felt on my face. "Oh I don't know," I said.

*T*he Voyage *to* Rosewood

This happened when I was sixteen:

I was walking down our road to the highway when two motor-cyclists drove by. They were out on the highway and far away; they didn't bother to glance down our dirt road to where I was walking, nor did they glance at the kids who were already waiting for the school bus at the crossroads. Why would anyone bother to look at us? Every school day we waited out here for the bus, anywhere from eight o'clock to eight-twenty, a bunch of homely ordinary country kids—our faces still dark from summer and oddly bright against the landscape of early winter. Seven or eight of us had been waiting for the bus at this corner every school day for the past three years, since our one-room school had been closed. We knew one another and our families and everything about our lives, we knew one another's houses, farms, dull scandals and shames and the illnesses of the old, which were perpetual. I was now the oldest because when boys in Oriskany were sixteen they quit school; now the boys who had been in my class were gone and their younger brothers remained, loud and profane and always jostling one another. Once at school we two girls—Sally and I—fled from them, desperate to be free of their noise. We were so ashamed. . . .

Never mind those boys: imagine clouds of breath shot from their sneering mouths, imagine Sally (with pale freckled face, heart weakened by rheumatic fever, and therefore the most delicate of us) standing a little apart from their eternal scuffling, imagine the boys' lunch bags propped up against their books, lying on the ground, imagine me—but you are inside me, inside my skin, and so you can't imagine me. Imagine the cold morning light of early November and the roar of the motorcycles fading away, and imagine the raw marveling admiration of the boys for those mysterious helmeted motorcyclists, speeding off to a great city sixty miles to the north, exposed to the frigidity of our country air. . . .

Now the school bus arrives. You know its dark yellow color: we can see it approaching far down the highway. We get on. The driver—a woman in man's overalls—has a gritty look about the eyes, as if she has just awakened. "Come on, come on," she says, impatient with two of the boys who are still fooling around. Sally and I sit together. The bus is very warm, it reminds me of my chair at the table at home, right by the register. Sally and I do not talk much. She is only fifteen and a year makes a big difference. I feel older, slyer, more abrupt and confident . . . her books are wrapped neatly in brown paper; mine are scuffed and dirty.

A twenty-minute ride to school. A long ride, with innumerable stops. How did I shut off my mind all those mornings, how did I endure them? The bus gets hotter, kids crowd on, some have to stand in the aisle with their books clutched up against them, fooling around, laughing—every year there are new, shy children or the bratty sisters and brothers of kids already riding the bus. The boys are writing nasty words in the steam on the windows. Oh, let them write anything! I am thinking instead of . . . the motorcyclists. . . . I am thinking of the way they roared past our crossroads without seeing anything. Something in me leans out after them, and the feeling is a dangerous tingling one: like leaning too far out a window, and then leaning a little farther. We lived a quarter of a mile from the highway, down a dirt road called Creek Road. Many roads were called Creek Road; the creeks had names but we didn't know them—if there were names on maps we never saw the maps; our creeks were just Mud Creek and Big Creek and whatever people wanted to call them . . . it would be years before I thought, Is there a name for where I live, a name other people might know? Is it on a map? Does anyone ever look at that map, running his finger along the thin little roads, and pause at the junction of that highway and that "Creek Road"? Living a quarter mile from the highway was too far. I wanted to live right on the highway. I wanted to sit on our front porch and watch people drive by, trucks and Greyhound buses and motorcycles and people without faces speeding by in cars in the early morning, every morning, before sunrise. . . . Oh, everyone was heading north! North to Derby! It seemed to me that a smaller number of people bothered to come back.

Now houses are more frequent; we are passing out of the country and into the outskirts of a city. Not much of a city, but good enough for us: Brockford is large to country kids, its children are privileged and oddly superior. Its adults seem more confident than our adults. The big gray building that is school approaches us and Sally wakes from her slumberous trance, getting ready for the chatter she'll need in her sophomore corridor where city kids think she "isn't too bad" when you consider where she lives. What do they think about me? Always I am anxious about the opinions of some five or six girls in my class, but today I don't give a damn, I hurry past them on the stairs and get to my locker and put my books away. A relief. My lunch, in its much-used paper bag, catches my eye and I squeeze it a little to fit it into my pocket. A faint, delirious sensation rises in me

at the thought of being here, safe, with everyone ordinary and predictable, lockers opening and being slammed shut, the usual noises,
and back home, before I left, the usual noises—the cat yowling to
be let in, the seven-thirty news my father always listens to with his
chin uplifted as though he were peering through the static to get at
something real, some truth—all these things that are familiar I
think of as things in a dream, my own dream, and I am waking up
without mercy or kindness and leaving them all behind.

Now I turn the wrong way in the corridor and brush past my
classmates, and on the stairs I am the only one going down, hurrying, and at the front door—the front door no one uses!—I am the
only one and I have to fight the impulse to run and lose myself out
on the street. I walk out the sidewalk slowly and the school tugs at
me: those corridors smelling of wet wool and wet leather, all the
chattering voices, the friendly bent shoulders of my homeroom
teacher who is also my English teacher, standing in the doorway in
her beige dress, neat and nervous like a big beige bird—they are pulling me back but I think, To hell with them! "To hell with them!"
I am a girl who never swears, out of squeamish delicacy, but I say
this aloud and, having said it, recoil with a sort of delirium from my
very words, as if it is myself I am recoiling from and leaving behind.
Yes, yes, I think, my words mixed in with the strange beating of my
heart, yes, let's leave everything behind, let's leave the crossroads and
the old farmhouse my father fixed up (there's nothing he can't fix
up!) and my room upstairs, cold in winter and hot in summer, let's
leave it all behind and go far away where my name will be lost. If
anyone were to call out, "Marsha, where are you going?" I wouldn't
even notice.

I waited down the road for a bus and in a few minutes one came
along. There is something about Greyhound buses that still excites
me—just the big blue-gray bulk of them, the tinted windows, the
gritty impersonality of the aisles and the white pieces of paper
tacked on the tops of the seat backs to protect one passenger's head
from another's germs. I jumped up the steps and handed the driver

some money, flushed with excitement. He was a small man in a silvery blue uniform. He said, "Where are you going?" The sign on the front of the bus had said "Chicago" but I hadn't enough money for that, I didn't dare Chicago. For a moment it seemed everything might end, and a few people were looking at me. But I thought of the name of a city some distance to the west and told him that; it was a magic incantation to get the bus going again. He must have been pleased with the word. He took my dollar bill and gave me some change and I turned to find a seat, my heart pounding. I was so young that day! Everyone on the bus was an adult and I did not trust adults. My mother and father talking late at night, no, not even them, not my mother and father whom I loved, their hushed urgent talk coming up from the kitchen late at night—worries over money? what?—or my mother fixing herself up before that mirror of hers on what she called her "dressing table," getting ready for my father to come home from work as if she were still a girl!—I didn't trust them in their private worlds, marked off from me by certain glances and certain intonations I did not understand. I had heard, once, my mother making excuses for me to my father: "Marsha has cramps today," my mother said, and I felt my backbone go straight and hard as if it had turned into steel: why did she say that? How shameful, how ugly to betray me like that—thinking nothing of my embarrassment, my shame—Adults talked to one another in their own language and so the hell with them too!

I found an empty seat and sat beside the window. What a wonderful thing a Greyhound bus is, pushing on through slush and fog and rain, a monster nothing can stop! I looked out the window at the impoverished outskirts of Brockford slipping back, the beginnings again of the "country"—mailboxes out by the road—and, later on, the real, deep country, hills and ditches stiff with frozen weeds, and miles and miles of fields with broken corn stalks that seem about to gesture as you ride past—and the farms—all the landscape of my life, suddenly distant from me and part of a world I was leaving. I felt a little feverish. Those gray heavy skies, those empty

fields! Those haystacks beside rotting barns, and the meager shape
of a farmer opening a door and peering out at the sky—what
wouldn't he give to be like me, cast free of the manure piles and
the sick cows and all the ugly, bitter drafts that belong to an old
farm, winter and fall and spring alike! Under doors, around windows, through what looks like solid wall—always cold drafts easing
in to embrace you and what can you do about it?

Only what I was doing.

At the thought of it I was seized with a strange impatience. It
was as if something were about to happen and I was far from it,
hurrying, and these people in their dark, grim winter clothes, with
their destinations marked on their tickets, were holding me back.
To calm myself I looked down at my feet and legs. I wore gym
shoes, sneakers that had once been white but were now filthy: this
was Brockford style. I wore dark blue wool socks that came up to
my knees, thin wool and therefore chic (not like the coarse socks
my mother knitted for me and I never wore), and they had already
begun to fray at the heels. My tan coat had a blurred vulgar resem-
blance to the real camel's hair coats the very special girls in my class
wore, whose favor I demanded even while I looked down at
them. . . . Sixteen is empty as any other age, but the very kernel of
my being has never changed—nameless or named, I am always
Marsha—but the outside of my face was plastered with a pink-
toned cosmetic that would cover up any blemishes on my chin or
forehead, and dark pink lipstick, and a hard, knowing, rather slut-
tish expression that meant nothing, I suppose. My hair was dark,
and I had a habit of brushing it back from my face as if it annoyed
me. That year I wore it down to my shoulders and on my forehead
in puffy bangs, the style of a senior girl whom I hated and envied.
Under my coat I wore a dark blue sweater and a plaid skirt. The
sweater had been bought after weeks of saving—$6.98 up at the
Brockford Sears Roebuck's—and my grandmother had made the
skirt for me. I remember opening the box, on Christmas or maybe
a birthday, and seeing the skirt there, delicate in its tissue. "Why

do they love me? Why is it like this?" I had wanted to weep. Looking up at them—my mother, my two grandmothers—I had felt that morning what I was to feel at certain helpless times in my life—a sense of indefinable entrapment, imprisonment in a fluid and sweet and fragrant element. Now, outside, the meager November landscape was a world opening slowly before me, great distances the same color, textures that varied only gently and never upset the eye: farms with rainwashed and humble buildings, aged haystacks, cats with their fur blowing in the wind close to the road—and here, in this world that had once enclosed me and was now only something for me to look at, nothing was confining or threatening, what limits could I see?

Across the aisle a mother was whispering to her child. The loving urgency of her manner touched me; there was this possibility of love, of loving and being loved, and I would realize that possibility.

My heart began to beat rapidly. I found myself thinking about my room at home that morning, waking up so abruptly and knowing I was awake. When you wake like that, with a jerk as if you've just jumped into the daylight, you know you can never go back to sleep. I was hot on the bus so I unbuttoned my coat and glanced over my shoulder uneasily. Somewhere nearby a vent shot out waves of heat. . . . A man was sitting behind me, leaning forward in an odd way. My glance caught his. He was middle-aged and had a long, sallow face. He smiled and said something. Frightened, I inclined my head toward his, with the sudden frozen politeness that was always beneath my brazen look, and asked him what did he say? "Just like that Mrs. Murphy," he said, grinning. This made no sense to me so I nodded vaguely and turned away. I put my sneakered feet up onto the back of the seat before me, like a child, earnestly like a child, as if I wanted that man to see how young I was. . . .

My skin was always pale; the backs of my hands looked bluish. When my hair was messed—it was always messed, that was part of my style—my eyes looked wild behind the strands of hair, the brown eyes of an animal surprised but not yet frightened. I was famous for my hard curious stare, which I turned on weak teachers and substitute teachers, and occasionally, just to tease, on the favorite teachers everyone liked; I looked hard and I wanted to be hard, but when a boy once referred to me as a little bitch, I had burst into tears. This passed rapidly through my mind, as if it were evidence to be held against me—my willfulness and my stupidity. The man in the seat behind me must have leaned forward suddenly and knocked against my seat; I was jolted.

And now, glancing across the aisle at the mother and her child, I saw with surprise that the woman had a brittle freckled face, red hair (dyed?), sharp little lips, and that the child, lying sideways with its head on her lap, was restless and feverish. The mother's eyes shot up at me; who the hell are you, you little bitch? Her glance wove around to take into account the middle-aged man behind me and she seemed to approve of his interest in me, that was just what she'd expected, just what I deserved. I wanted to get her on my side, say something hard and knowing and flat about the bus and that character behind me . . . but, confronted with the real thing, my hardness softened and turned itself inside out. My cheeks were burning.

It seemed to me that I had to get off this bus. We were approaching a small town and I got out into the aisle, swaying, afraid the man behind me would offer to steady me—but no—and I made my way up to the front. Behind the driver, I stooped a little as people do, as if making sure that they are in the right place after all. "You can let me off here," I said.

"Thought you said Shepherd."

"I changed my mind."

"Changed your mind?"

He chuckled and looked at me through the big tinted rear-view mirror, as if he had never heard of such a thing. "Pretty cold day to be changing your mind, eh?" he said.

"I guess so."

"Guess so? Don't you know?" he said. I kept waiting for the bus
to stop but the driver seemed always to be heading for some spot he
had in mind, then changed to another spot. Finally he did pull the
big bus over to the side of the highway and let me out. The door
opened with an immense sigh. I started down and he said, "Hey,
you—girl—" Terrified, I jumped down to the ground. "Hey, you!"
he said. "You got some change coming!"

I heard those words but was too confused to know what they
meant. Change? What change? Was something changing? I made
a certain gesture to indicate he should drive on, forget about it, and
that was that. He did not argue. Only when the bus was out of sight
did I understand what he meant. I had fifteen cents coming, maybe.
I patted my pockets and discovered my lunch had fallen out somewhere, onto the seat probably. The man behind me—whose face I
could not recall—was probably eating it. "That bastard," I said
aloud, and saying this encouraged me; I turned to walk back to the
center of town.

This town was Remus. There was a fireman's picnic or hot-rod
races or something here in the summer; people often drove up.
Remus. The name pleased me, I'd never been here before. . . .
There were few people out. Cars parked before stores were tilted
off the edge of the highway. A truck. A diner, a gas station. In a car
parked nearby a man moved suddenly as if coming awake; he was
sitting behind the wheel, waiting for someone. His face startled me.
I thought of the man back on the bus but of course it wasn't the
same man, though they were both middle-aged and had a certain
slow, meticulous, unhealthy stare. Not the same man, I knew that.
The cold air met my warm, perspiring body and I thought of that
man on the bus. What had he meant by "Mrs. Murphy"? Who
was Mrs. Murphy? Why had he bumped against the seat?

I walked past the man in the car without looking at him. This
was Main Street. I looked in windows—a children's shoe store, with
shoes arranged dustily amid bright cardboard cutouts of roosters and
rabbits guiding one's eye; an expanse of wall that meant nothing;

then the door to this building with a sign that said Dr. William Cleere, M.D. It gave me confidence to think of a doctor in Remus, after all. One could not die mysteriously in Remus. I looked around at the other buildings but did not seem to see anything. Here I am in Remus, Remus, and my eyes began to throb with the profundity of that fact—which did not seem to mean anything—there goes a pickup truck driven by a kid my own age, and the sky is getting overcast and heavy, it looks like snow. Where am I, what am I doing? Thinking so much makes me tired. I was warm but now I am shivering; bodies change so quickly. I think of my room at home, the familiar unfinished walls—just some panels my father picked up at the lumberyard, they look like cardboard—and how, if I am sick, I can lie downstairs and watch television with the "sick quilt" over me—a quilt heavy and very old and musty, and not very clean. . . . A man in an overcoat and a hat (men do not wear hats around here, not often) is just crossing the street and he stops to look at me.

"Miss?" he says.

My heart is pounding rapidly. He seems to know me. All the vast world—the countryside with its furry grays and blacks—is far from me now and there is just this world of human beings who use words to talk, and who always talk and ask questions.

"Miss, are you looking for somebody?"

He can see I do not belong in Remus.

"Are you going somewhere?"

"I just got off the bus," I tell him, muttering, as if that means anything. He glances down at my socks. These dark blue socks, so chic in Brockford, maybe mean nothing here—maybe mean something I don't know about.

The man tries to smile. His overcoat looks expensive, he belongs here, he is speaking for Remus like the mayor of the town and nothing is personal. "Well," he says. "Looks like snow."

I turn away but I have nowhere to go and maybe he can see that. I wonder if he will follow me. Past the shoe store, on a board sidewalk, I blunder on, walking fast—a hardware store, closed—and there, back in a kind of field with a wide muddy drive, is a tavern built of cement blocks. The mud is hard. I stand here for a while, waiting and trying to think, because whatever is happening is not quite right but I do not know what should be happening in its place. . . . It occurs to me that I am alone. Terror cuts through my bowels at this thought, but I force it away. There are a few cars parked up at the tavern, even this early in the day. A stripped-down car with rusty fenders that has the same arrogant frightened look I have catches my attention. I think, What now? What now? My pockets are empty, only a used crumpled Kleenex. My purse hasn't much in it. My lunch is being eaten by a stranger, miles away. . . . I stand by the side of the road and look at the tavern. At night that neon sign—Cole's Corner—might look flashy, but now it looks lightly caked with dust. A wind rises out of the north and sweeps down straight along the highway.

Inside the tavern the darker air is a relief. A few men are standing at the bar. The television set is on and flickering. There is an odor of something harsh and the glass on a framed picture dazzles my eyes. It takes me a few seconds to make out that the picture is of a moose, standing in a few feet of water and looking at a hunter who is about to shoot him. The men turn around when I come in. Another man, in a plaid wool shirt, is sweeping some dirt out a side door. He stares at me.

"How old are you?" he says sourly.

"None of your business," I hear myself saying.

One man at the bar chuckles at this; I have a friend.

The man with the broom looks sullenly away. He goes out the side door.

The man at the bar who has laughed continues to watch me. I sit by the door in a rickety chair because my legs are suddenly weak. I feel sleepy. This man has a canvas jacket and eyes the same fuzzy green of the jacket. There are things I should be thinking but I cannot think of them. I cannot get them into focus. It is as if the world for me is the man who jostled my seat and the woman who didn't act like a mother, judging from her nasty look. How they have hurt my feelings. . . . The man at the bar has a cowboyish look and I know why—those boots. Something stirs in me, a memory. Boots? But these are stylish cheap boots, not like the overshoes my father wears in the winter. And no boys at the Brockford school wear such boots. They are tan and have a design worked into them, outlined in black but partly chipped off.

He glances over his shoulder at me. The other two men, farther away, ignore him. They are older—they have heavy, serious, middle-aged faces, they are a little embarrassed. They are fathers. This man, watching me with a smile, is not a father. He is young and boyish, ready to go. He says across the dingy room, "You on your way through town or something?"

"I'm going to Shepherd."

He makes a snorting sound. "Shepherd! What the hell's there?"

He seems to be asking this seriously, in spite of the sneer, so I tell him in a fast, urgent voice: "There's some work for me there."

"Yeah, what work?"

"Somebody's house. They need a girl to help out."

"Help out with what?" he says, snorting merrily.

The man with the broom comes back. He says, not looking at me but only at the cowboyish young man, "You can get out of here, both of you."

"What the hell? She ain't no friend of mine!"

"You heard me."

"I heard him. Did you hear him?" this man, my new friend, asks. He takes two big strides to get to "my" table. There are creases in his cheeks, it's sad, he isn't more than twenty-five but still there are lines in his face that will never go away. "He's kicking us out. Honey, you got me in trouble and I don't even know you."

I've never thought before of what a building is: walls and a roof, something to keep you warm. It keeps warmth inside. Through the windows light comes . . . that is a revelation. Asked to leave this building, my body is struck for a moment by a pang of despair; this has never happened to me before.

"Get going and keep going," one of the men at the bar says.

He addresses my presence, as if my presence were a halo radiating outward for me; something unmistakable. In this building made of concrete blocks I have an identity the men all recognize. It is a struggle for me to understand.

"I'm going through Shepherd, myself. Just a hole. You know Randolph?"

"Who?"

"Randolph. Sure you know him!"

I don't want to deny this and so I stand, patting my pockets again as if trying to figure out where that lunch has gone. No lunch. At the bar three people are carefully not looking at me—the man with the broom, who is the bartender and has set the broom aside, and the two fatherly-looking men. They have given me up and good riddance.

"No, I don't know Randolph."

Outside on the muddy drive his walk is bouncy. He has a lot of energy, he taps on the rusty fender of his car. I knew this must be his car. "Randolph is the craziest, weirdest maniac you'd ever want to meet. Can get away from any cop in the county, that's how fast he drives," he says. "No, this side. That's wired shut—had a little accident."

So I get in the car on his side and slide across. Like our car at home, it's cold in here, very cold, with the deep still cold that accumulates inside objects. He leans around to glance at himself in the mirror, then he looks at me. "I'm Ike. Where're you going in Shepherd?"

"I told you, somebody's house."

"Yeah, who?"

The demand of his voice stops me; I realize that he knows everyone in Shepherd.

"Yeah, I thought so!" he chortles. "You're just bumming your way through. You run away from home, kid, I bet!" He starts the car and this pleases him, as if he didn't expect it to start so fast. Backing it out the drive is a game to him, and when the car dips into mudholes he laughs to see me thrown against the door. "Look, those are just bastards in there, I could tell you a thing or two . . . that one of them, the fat one, that's my uncle anyway; some kind of an uncle. Randolph's my cousin. Where are you from?"

"Brockford."

"You know Sonny Wheeler there?"

"No."

"Everybody knows Sonny. Don'tcha know him?"

"No."

"What are you, from high school or something?" he says, sneering, but with such disbelief that it occurs to me I am not any longer a high-school student, that I'd better wake up and get things straight about myself. I can see the hole in the heel of my sock, just beginning to show.

"How long you been bumming around?" he says.

"A week."

"From Brockford, a week?"

"No, I wasn't from Brockford."

"I knew that. You didn't fool me. Those snooty Brockford girls, I could make them look kind of surprised if I wanted. . . . So look, what's your name?" He gives me a little push, meaning nothing. "You look sort of like Marilyn Myers, you know her?"

"No."

"You don't know nobody!"

He snaps on the radio suddenly, as if he has just thought of this, something important. As he talks I try to fasten onto everything he says, but his words get by me. Then we are stopping in front of a house, then another young man is running out to the car, down a driveway that had once been so muddy they had to put planks in it. But the mud is frozen now.

"Henry, look here," my friend cries.

Henry is a fawny, mousy boy with buck teeth. He stares in at me. "Who's that?" he says.

"Surprise! She's going to Shepherd, she says. I'm driving her."

Henry looks at me without understanding. He is wearing a green canvas jacket not warm enough for him and his longish hair is ruffled in the wind, like cat's fur. "You want me to come along . . . or what?"

"Why do you think I stopped?"

"Well, I don't know," he says resentfully.

Henry too has to get in the car on the driver's side. Our friend gets out to let him in and so Henry sits in the middle, awkward and nervous. "You're always fooling around, aren't you," he says when Ike gets back inside.

"Don'tcha want to go to Rosewood?"

"Last night you said. . . ."

"The hell with last night. Hey, honey, what did you say your name was?"

"Linda."

"That's Linda. Linda, this is Henry. My name is Ike."

Silence. Ike says, "She don't talk much, she's snooty. Said she was from Brockford and there's some people in Brockford got money, so they think. Hey, is your name really Linda?"

He is driving so fast the fields and houses look startled. Henry sits beside me with his arm held rigid so that he doesn't touch me by accident. Ike gives him a push and says, "You believe her name is Linda, Henry beast?"

"Oh, the hell with that."

"With what?"

"You fooling around."

"Who's fooling around?"

"Where didja pick her up?"

"They kicked her out of Cole's. I don't know. If we're going to Rosewood, did you get the money?"

"I got it," Henry says sullenly.

"I can swing around and take her to Shepherd, why not? She looks a little like Marilyn Myers, don't she?"

Henry, uncomfortable, glances at me sideways and crosses his legs.

"Hey, don't you press her leg or anything!" Ike laughs.

"You leave me alone," Henry says furiously.

"Linda, why don't you talk to us? You listening to that music or something?" He turns off the radio. "Linda, you say something. Be nice."

"What should I say?"

"You go to school, or what?"

"I did."

"You quit?"

"Yes."

"Say something they taught you in school. Henry and me both quit—Henry's older than me. You believe that?"

"Oh, quit fooling around," Henry says.

"No, look. Seriously. Say something they taught you in school."

This releases a slow flood of words. "*Macbeth* is a blood tragedy. It depicts the rise and fall of an ambitious man. . . . Near the end of the play, everything subsides. Death is approaching."

"That's nice," Ike says. He pauses, as if strangely subdued. Then he says, "Now talk about maps. I like maps."

"There are parts of the United States farther north than parts of Canada."

"Hell," Henry snickers suddenly, "anybody knows that."

"Henry beast, you did not know that."

"I did know it."

"You did *not!*" Ike says, punching his upper arm. Poor Henry cringes back against me and whimpers. "You're lying like hell. Apologize."

"I used to like maps . . ." Henry says defensively.

"Apologize to that pretty little girl."

Henry sits miserable and vicious. I don't like to look at his pudgy hands—on their backs blond hairs grow thickly. My eyelids feel a little gritty, grainy. I think of that morning on the bus, or was it many mornings ago? The woman bus driver in overalls and the boys fooling around. . . .

"I said apologize. Kiss her."

"You stop fooling around! Last night you said—"

"I said kiss her and make up, you bastard," Ike says in a whooping friendly voice. He is so interested in us that the car swerves. "Do it! Do it right now. Linda is waiting and you hurt her feelings."

"I will like hell."

"I said kiss her," Ike says, punching him again. I can see Ike's teeth framed inside his grin, and he is still cowboyish and bouncy— the problem is that this car just isn't enough to keep him down. He has too much energy.

"Ike, please," Henry says, his voice breaking, "you always kid around and that hurts, my arm hurts—" For his pains he gets punched again and almost bursts into tears. This blow silences him for a moment. Then he says in a dogged childish voice, "My grandmother gave it to me and won't tell *him* anything about it, only I got to get it back, she says, by Christmas. Okay? Ike, don't kid around so much, okay? We got to be serious about this. All the way to Rosewood—"

"We're going into partnership on something, Linda," Ike says.

"Yes, that's nice."

"A big motorcycle. You like them?"

"Yes."

"I'll take you out then, first time. Henry can wait."

I can hear Henry breathing quickly and shallowly beside me.

"Henry can sit in the car here and wait for us to come back, sweetheart, he's good at waiting!" Something about this statement amuses Ike, for he makes a sound like "Zzzzt!" and at the same time, out of his nervous exultation, cannot keep his fist from punching Henry's shoulder. "Been waiting around for lots of things, ain't you? He wants to be a goddam carpenter's helper so he can steal nails or something. That's Henry for you! Looking at us, Henry beast and me, it's easy to figure out who's getting a good job. My name is coming up at Farley's—you know."

"Farley's make goddam shitty little paper clips or something," Henry says.

For this he gets another jab, falls against me, and rights himself with frigid dignity. "Farley's makes steel. Girders or something," Ike says. "They don't take just anybody." He looks around to see if that impresses me—he has a big coarse face, skin pale as mine but tough, and eyes that are not feathery with lashes like Henry's; they seem to be staring boldly and seeing everything. "Honey, you are a cute girl. That's real nice lipstick—what does it taste like?"

"Nothing."

"I told Henry to kiss and make up and he wouldn't, he's afraid. Aren't you afraid, Henry?"

"Why do you always fool around? You know I—"

"Honey, pull your hair out a little. The other side. I want to see how long it is," Ike says. I shake my hair loose so that it falls over my shoulder. Dreamily it occurs to me that what I have worked at sloppily and sluttishly before my bedroom mirror has been loosed into this strange winter day and the raw ovals of Ike's eyes. A faintness rises in me. Ike says, "That's pretty hair but you should bleach it or something. Look here—look at me. Wouldya believe that I had blond hair when I was a kid? I did. Now look . . . it's just brown like everybody else."

He keeps on talking. He turns the radio back on. After a long while I notice that we are stopping at a motorcycle shop, a kind of junk dealer's place; I must have dozed off. "You stay here, Henry baby, and watch the girl," Ike says, getting out. Henry moves away from me and says nothing. Ike goes inside the grimy little shop, brushing his hair a little nervously with the flats of both hands. A few minutes pass. Henry gets impatient suddenly and mutters something I don't catch and gets out. I am alone.

The door is wired shut on my side, I see that. In a kind of daze I slide over behind the wheel and test that door and, yes, it opens, and now I am standing outside on a street in Rosewood. I have heard of Rosewood but know no one who lives here. The wind is colder in Rosewood than it is in Brockford. I button my coat back up, my hands are nervous, I keep pushing back my hair but it whips in the wind—I should be watching for Ike to rush out the door but I keep forgetting. Instead, there is something else I want to remember. What is it? There are five or six old motorcycles parked outside, some without wheels. . . . What do I want to remember? Those overshoes of my father's and brother's out by the side door, and the smell of rubber? Yes, there is rubber burning here; smoke rises slowly from a dump on the other side of the shop. And the memory of someone brushing past, moving past our dirt road and heading into the vast countryside . . . who were those people? Have I caught up with them? I search my numbed mind and cannot remember exactly. I do not know why I am here, in Rosewood (but I cling to this beautiful name desperately), what I am doing, where I am going, but I know I should be going somewhere. So I start walking. I am in a neighborhood of warehouses. Something smells—water? A river? Oily water, a factory? There is smoke in the air and grit underfoot, yes. I put my hands in my warm pockets and walk along, watching the sky anxiously. Last night at supper my father declared it would snow today; the newspaper said so. But the seven-thirty news didn't say so. The thought of snow terrifies me suddenly. . . .

I am down the block and crossing a street when someone whoops behind me. "Linda girl!" It is Ike running after me with great angry strides. Seeing him like this, his hair flying and his canvas jacket unzipped, makes me want to run from him. "Where're you going? What the hell? Sweetheart, are you sneaking away?" He grabs my arm and swings me around; no matter if a man is just driving by in a car and watching us. Ike is very tall and leans over me like an angry parent. "Going off and leave Henry like that, poor kid, don'tcha want to be nice to him?"

Henry is approaching us slowly. He has an ugly white face, a puckered forehead, as if he is witnessing something he does not want to see, not quite, but can't resist. I know that look—it's the way I look when mangled animals appear on the highway rushing to our car.

"Hey, I don't like you. I don't like your face," Ike says. He makes his "Zzzzt!" sound and suddenly my face has been slapped. There is his hand, jumping away. With a wide fast gaze to see who is watching—this is at an intersection with a large street and there is some traffic—Ike decides that he is safe and grabs the collar of my coat. "You, Henry, you come here, I'll show you how to treat them. They're all afraid—" I am backed against something, a wall or a fence, and though I stare at Ike's white face right by mine he doesn't see me but is tearing and punching at my body, ripping at my coat, my clothes, and the blows seem to have so far to come that the pain itself is distant and weak—Ike mutters something, passing judgment on me furiously, and Henry with his furry look is watching in silence, and then, with the air rocking about me, I am alone on the sidewalk and they are running away. . . .

The scene stops there and picks up again in a police station, me confused and warm again and knowing that I should cry but unable to cry. How can you cry in front of strangers? A man is asking me questions. What are you doing here? Where were you going? I sit mute and terrified, not knowing what to say, expecting to be slapped again. Everything is jumbled, but yet not really—because I know what has happened but cannot make sense of it. One event, another event, two and three more following rapidly—and here I sit, bedraggled and not seriously hurt, trying for a tomboyish style that will let these men know I am "okay." Men like tomboyish girls, I know that. I finger my bruised knee with a kind of curiosity—it's just a kid's accident, I must have fallen down. In another room I was encouraged to lean forward to stare into a mirror at a strange little dot on my temple—bloody tips where several strands of hair had been yanked out, looped around Ike's strong fist—but I won't think of this. It will go away.

They have telephoned my father. Now there are muffled voices, a woman's voice in another room: "I did take that driving test, I passed it already." The wait for my father, the long wait into early evening, and it crossed my mind as I sat in the Rosewood Fifth Precinct with papers scattered about me and floor-model ashtrays on either side of me, and high old-fashioned ceilings fly-specked above me, that if my father did not come I would never be able to find my way home again and, if I did find Creek Road again at the intersection with the highway, there would be no home there, no house—everyone moved out, the house itself abandoned. Or maybe I would come at the wrong time, years too late—everyone dead and gone, the house taken over by another family. What then? If he didn't come? I would lose my way and fall off completely, and never, never would I find my way back again to whatever it was that was my life.

We waited. Telephones rang, doors opened and shut. They were running a business here. "He should be here by now, shouldn't he?" one policeman said to another, past my head. I was not worrying. I waited and did not think.

"You think we better call again?" someone said.

No, I wanted to tell them, no, don't call. Don't put me in danger! The connection between me and those people in that house is so precarious that no one, no one must tamper with it. . . .

And then, finally, of course my father did arrive.

Muttering, frightened, he explained why he was late, as if these policemen would rip the truth from him in another moment. "The damndest thing, halfway here I had to stop and throw up, I had to stop the car . . . I was throwing up and dizzy and didn't think I should drive. . . . That never happened before," he said, ashamed to tell them and nervous of their embarrassed faces, looking at me, coming for me. They talked to him. Someone handed me my purse, which I had kept hold of all the while . . . "just like a woman." Father and I left the station. He was my father, yes. No mistake. At our slouching car—it always seemed to be leaning to the right, about to fall—he turned and stared at me. He slapped my face but not as hard as Ike had slapped it. "Why did you do this to us?" he sobbed.

Waiting

"I wouldn't be here except for them kids," Mr. Mott said.

"Your children?"

"No, them kids, like I said, them kids out of school," he explained, flushing. He was in his late forties and had a narrow, sullen face. From time to time his eyes lifted to Katherine's suspiciously, as if he were checking on her. Was she nervous, why hadn't she remembered about the kids who were out of school now, in June, instead of thinking Mr. Mott was talking about his own children—?

"Yes, I see," Katherine said. "The boys who work part-time."

"Hires them part-time and kicks me out, on account of that—that whatdayacallit, a law or something. He didn't have to pay into the thing, that state thing, with them. With me it's different, but I asked him, was that my fault? He pretended he was laying me off and it was only temporary—"

Sometimes these people brought to Katherine nuances and turns of speech that startled her, making her realize they did come into contact with other people. "Only temporary." That wasn't Mr. Mott's expression and, having taken it on, he used it with a certain defensiveness. Now he would talk on, some little peg in him released. Suspicious, sour, an odor of something unwashed and sad about him, he had the look of a man who is always silent, just as they all did; but, like Mr. Mott, they all began to talk after a certain mysterious point. . . . Mr. Mott did not look at Katherine but at the papers on her desk. He had to make certain facts known. He would not be back on welfare except for—In two weeks, then he'd be all set—He had this bill he owed, over a year now, and couldn't he try to pay it back?—he knew what the rules were, but—He talked rapidly, no longer squinting up at Katherine but staring at the papers. All Katherine's people were like this. Their respect was for papers, printed matter, records. They had outlasted other social workers and they would probably outlast Katherine. The flies remained. It was necessary to talk rapidly, muttering certain important points, so that the strange intricate process—it was now done with a big machine, which had already broken down that winter for an agonizing two weeks—would keep their checks coming.

Katherine was the fourth in her family, the third girl. By the time she was old enough to take the bus downtown to the library and return home again with books cradled in her arms, she was able to see the way her parents' house looked and the way her parents looked, inside it. Her father was retired. He wasn't very old but he was retired; he spent the day in the parlor, reading newspapers. He never wore shoes. When she had been little enough for him to kiss, she had shied away from the smell of his stained, uneven teeth— poor Pa! Now he did not kiss her. Making supper, she and her mother could hear him muttering in the parlor; the news made him furious.

When she took the bus downtown she went to Thirty-fifth Street, but when she came back, the other bus let her off on the Boulevard.

That meant she approached her house from the back. Coming up on it like that, sneaking up, she could see her mother's laundry hanging limp out in the back yard, and something always ached at the corners of her eyes. Her mother was a heavy, panting woman. She had to get everything done at once: dishes washed and dried, pans scoured, rinsed, put away, towels hung to dry, laundry done twice a week. It was necessary to bang back and forth through the back door, thump up and down the steps, to get all this done. Once, returning from the library, Katherine saw a bulky woman in an ugly dress descending the back-door steps in a queer rushed way, as if she were running with water to throw on a fire. But there was no water and no fire. She was carrying pieces of laundry to hang on the line. There was always something on that line, Katherine thought, recognizing the laundry and the woman together.

She had two older sisters and an older brother, who joined the Navy like all his friends. After their father died—a stroke killed him in an hour—Katherine's sisters moved out; first Lenore, who was a stenographer downtown, and then Jackie, who got married. Left with her mother in the big empty house, Katherine understood that her sisters had given everything to her. Everything! An hour after the funeral she heard her mother thumping about upstairs, back in her old Red Cross everyday shoes; she was moving furniture around, panting as she reached with a rag for a half-visible cobweb, new since that morning. . . .

She kept on with school, knowing how important that was, and after graduation she went to work. Her mother took half of her weekly salary, and the other girls gave their mother money too, and after Ed returned from the Navy and started work in a parts factory nearby he gave her money, so, as she said to the elderly female relatives they visited on Sundays, she "didn't have to worry too much." Katherine saved most of what was left of her salary and in two years she had enough to start college; it was just the community college, not the University, but think of all the money she was saving! Her mother talked about the money she was "saving" as if it were actually accumulating somewhere. And after two years at the community college she transferred to the University and went into "social work" because she wanted to help people and because there was something humble and accessible about the School of Social Work building; it was on the old downtown campus, far from the suburban lawns of the new campus, and the bus ride was familiar, everything was familiar and not very expensive. She had such a good average, her mother bragged to everyone, that they practically begged her to come—gave her a five-hundred-dollar scholarship!

In her senior year she met a young man who was studying dentistry. On their first date he told her about a girl he had gone with for years, who had rejected him. Watching his serious, melancholy face, Katherine had not smiled, nor had she allowed her heart to sink in her chest, behind the lacy blouse she had bought for this date. No, she stayed with him, she waited until his awkward recital came to an end; anyway she was fond of adjusting ashtrays on tables in restaurants and cocktail lounges, waiting for him to stop. She waited. Her relationship with him was to fall into two periods: the first part, when he made bleak and sarcastic references to this other girl, as if wanting Katherine to know everything and yet to know that there had once been someone valuable, someone worth mourning; and the second part, the long part, when he forgot about the girl and they fell in love, shyly and quietly, on a series of Saturday-night dates to dinner and the movies.

She began to know, in his presence, that there was something of value about her pale brown hair, her large, rather prominent eyes, and the narrow jaw that was almost too narrow but not quite; she had, in certain lights, a doll-like appearance. The young man became her fiancé and still they went to dinner at the Chinese restaurant across from one of the movie houses, and still Katherine's mother dusted and polished furiously before he came. When he and Katherine sat in the living room (once called the parlor) she liked to join his frequent silences and imagine them married—in another setting, a living room of their own that was somehow different—though she could not quite imagine the difference—the young man more talkative, his shoulders less stooped than they were now. Behind them, in the kitchen, she could sense her mother's poised, bulky body, not sitting, not at rest, but coiled like a big spring ready to fly at a speck of dust, a grease spot, or some bold ugly sound from the "living room."

One evening she announced that their wedding plans would have to be postponed a while—her mother was going to be operated on. He was concerned and sympathetic. No, Katherine assured him, the operation was a minor one. Her mother would recover in a few weeks.

But the operation turned out to be a vast and complicated affair. It covered two worlds—home and hospital—and miles of trafficked pavement in between. It stretched over many sleepless days and nights. It brought out many people, not just Katherine, but bunches of female relatives who had to be told everything: Her gall bladder was fixed up just fine now, Katherine's mother announced cheerfully, just fine! But somehow the "operation" had drained her the way a legal battle drains people who wait to be called to court but are never called, draining them of energy by the very idea of what they are involved with . . . something too vast to be survived.

By this time Katherine had begun her social work; she has a caseload of forty families! Forty families in her care! She and her young man went out on Saturday and Sunday and occasionally during the week, and whenever they talked about the wedding—about finding an apartment—about how her mother would go to live for a while with Jackie, then Lenore—Katherine felt a guilty sensation, keen almost to the point of nausea. And her work frightened her. If she tried not to think about her mother, she had to think about her job. "They're so unhappy. They have so many problems," she said. With her young man, she sometimes burst into tears over the ugly lives of her "people"; with her mother everything was going along well, the people were good sports, they weren't what the papers hinted—chiselers. Her mother was suspicious of Katherine's cheerful reports, waiting for the necessary ugliness and sorrow, but Katherine told her nothing. When her mother asked about the young man, about the wedding, Katherine managed to talk and yet say nothing. In this way months passed.

He began to have trouble with his studies and called her up every night. Hunched over the phone, in her bathrobe, with her hair in curlers, Katherine sometimes mixed him up in her mind with her "people"; she caught herself sighing over the impossibility of it all. What could she do? That evening during supper her mother had had a seizure of some kind. The pain or the surprise had made her face go white, so Katherine knew she was not pretending. "No, they don't know what's wrong with her," Katherine told her fiancé, as if "they" were a team of specialists instead of old Tom Trixby, who was seventy now.

"But when are we going to get married?" he began to ask her.

In the end, he spoke of their relationship as bleakly as he had spoken of his relationship with that other girl—when had it been, three years ago? Three years! He and Katherine had known each other this long when they decided it would be best not to meet again. Katherine had prepared her little speech for days, miserably, hating the momentum drawing her to it and dreading the half-bitter acquiescence of her fiancé; why did he give in so readily, so humbly, his chest more hollow than ever with this new defeat? Katherine wept hysterically that night, hating him for his weakness. She sensed her mother listening in the darkness, but she did not care.

But what kind of people were they? her mother wanted to know. Morning came, work came, another day rolled around, and it was an ordinary day after all. When Katherine returned from work her mother was always greedy for bad news. Sometimes the old woman was bedridden for weeks at a time, at least while Katherine was in the house. Though she had the idea her mother got out of bed when she was gone, she never dared ask about it. What kind of people were they on welfare? How did they act?

Katherine, now twenty-six, was conscious of herself as young and oddly clean compared to this old woman. Yes, her mother had become an old woman at last. Finally, to amuse her, she told stories of the "hillbillies" (an expression Katherine never used down at the Center, though other people did), who used all the wrong words, who couldn't keep jobs, who had such pale, washed-out, sad, humble, dangerous faces. . . . Mr. X's son, who was twelve, had gone into a drugstore and asked for some cream; and when he was served he was given *cream*—in a glass! (He had really wanted ice cream, Katherine explained.) So he lost his temper and started a fight, because everybody was laughing at him.

"Oh, those hillbillies! There's some of them right on this block," Katherine's mother said.

And what about the niggers? her mother wanted to know.

"The Negroes," Katherine said carefully, ". . . the *blacks* . . . are polite and quiet. They don't want any trouble."

"Hadn't better want any," her mother said. "*Blacks!*" She snorted; she seemed pleased.

But after the bad news subsided, after the promise of gossip dissipated and there was nothing left except the musty bedroom, Katherine's mother sometimes began to talk of her husband. It was with a jolt that Katherine remembered her father, that old white-haired man in the front parlor, with so many corns on his feet he couldn't even wear shoes . . . had he really been her father?

"He was so good," her mother sobbed, pulling at Katherine's hand, "you don't know . . . you girls and Ed never knew . . . all that he done, how hard he worked. . . ."

Katherine sometimes wanted to lay her head down beside her mother's so that the two of them could sleep. If only her mother would stop babbling! She loved her mother, but, over and over, that same story, the three babies no more than ten months apart and no help at home, no money, and how good their father had been, how good. . . . While her mother talked, Katherine tried to relax. Her life now was trying to hide somewhere, relax in some corner of her mind while people talked at her of their sorrow. She still felt young, though she was now twenty-seven and there were tiny lines of worry about her eyes. But why did she feel young? What was she waiting for that kept her young? "When I'm gone you'll meet a real nice man. That man—that one—he wasn't good enough for you. I never said anything, it wasn't my business. But he wasn't good enough for you," her mother said angrily, as if Katherine had almost disobeyed her. Nudged by her mother, in a way given permission, she began to dream about the man she would meet. She had money now, she could buy nice clothes. Her skin was clear; she was a pretty woman. It did not hurt to admit it. Men smiled at her but were balked by something timid and heavy in her. But she couldn't help it, Katherine thought, what could she do? How could she change?

Some days, her mother looked well enough. Some days she looked ghastly, her flesh turned flabby and yellow. But she had "nothing wrong with her." Dr. Trixby died and no one missed him, Katherine thought bitterly (for how he had wasted their time and money), and now a new doctor appeared; he teased the old woman as if she were a baby or a dog. Katherine was disgusted but her mother liked the new doctor. "Strong as a horse, listen to it yourself," he said cheerfully, offering the old woman the rubber tips of the stethoscope.

Every visit of his, Katherine thought, equaled so many hours of her job.

She went on "investigations." Her visits took her to homes not too far from her own—their neighborhood was changing, like all city neighborhoods—and so perhaps that was why, nervously and archly, she dressed as well as she could, wore expensive shoes, carried gloves, and had a purse without a torn lining. (So many women, pawing for tissues down at the Center, opened their purses to show a torn lining!) She was polite and pleasant. Wasn't she, maybe, from a well-to-do family, dedicating herself to helping people? And wasn't she pretty?

Some of them, the older women, marveled at how pretty she

was. "I used to have hair like that," an old cronc would say without any envy, as if Katherine clearly belonged to another species. These compliments—this coarse flattery—made her blush; she was still too girlish for the job, everyone teased; but when it came to assessments, she was already professional, they had to admit. "What? What about it, a bottle of grape juice? Why can't I buy that? I didn't know it was forty-five cents, the price wasn't marked," her scraggly witch-faced female clients screamed, caught in a lie. Gentle and shy as she was, Katherine could always recognize lies. Lies were to be expected from everyone, from the meekest to the most brazen, and on each level a lie was distinct from the truth by a certain false ring: emphasis upon the wrong words, a sudden odd tug to part of the sentence, a shrillness, a righteousness the truth never needed. With frightened people, lies were obvious because they never looked up at Katherine; with the bold and brazen, lies were obvious because they tried to stare her down. The only people who puzzled her were those who couldn't remember the truth, who didn't know themselves if they were lying.

It was sometime in her twenty-eighth year that she stopped re-running these conversations in her brain. She left the file in her desk and left its people there, and never again did she take them home and cry over them alone in her bed. When she thought of the man she was yet to meet she felt no self-pity but only a kind of amused, cynical wisdom: the wisdom of Clara, whose desk was pushed right up beside hers at the Center. She didn't act like Clara, but perhaps Clara's loud good humor was good for her. "Oh, listen to this, this is a hot one," Clara would chortle. " 'In business for twelve years. In bicycle business.' How the hell do you like that, in *bicycle business*?" And, foolish as it was, unfunny as it was, she could get Katherine to laugh. "Oh, those bastards sit around dreaming up this stuff," Clara would say.

Katherine's voice began to take on a clearer, more confident tone when she talked to her applicants. She explained the purposes of the Welfare Department, her eyelids drooping as if this were as familiar to the nervous, rather outlandish people on the other side of her desk as it was to her: "The aim is not to encourage the applicant to a lifetime on welfare, but to restore him to a condition of self-support. You have no relatives who are legally responsible?"

They squinted at her, breathing in shallow gasps, and seemed to be snatching in the air at certain significant words of hers—"self-support," "legally responsible"? What did it mean? They wanted to hear "yes," and only "yes." Their eyes sought out the shape her lips would take when she said, "Yes—"

With those *certain women* Katherine always felt nervous and vaguely ashamed. "How can you account for not having applied for welfare until now?" she asked. The coarse, lined faces of these "certain women" were like masks, a variation on the same mask they all wore.

"I borrowed money. There were some friends. My brother-in-law—"

"Did you borrow money from last January until now?"

"No."

"Were you employed?"

"I told you, no."

"No means of support except borrowing? No income?"

The woman would begin to sweat.

"I told you, some friends of mine—"

"I'll have to take down their names."

Silence.

"But I have to have their names. It's the law," Katherine said. The tension between her and the woman would increase until Katherine, like the woman, could look only at the papers arranged so neatly on her desk. In the silence—filled with the woman's coarse breathing and the noise from the rest of the bull-pen—Katherine felt an eerie, drugged dreaminess in which the woman's cheap perfume grew stronger. Or was that her own perfume?

"Miss, I need money. I need it right now, I'm not trying to fool nobody or nothing," the woman said. Her low voice threatened to veer out of control. Katherine looked down, licking her lips. Behind the woman's grayish face were six other "candidates," waiting in their hard-backed chairs with the kind of stilted, unreal look of people being photographed. They wanted to show Katherine that they were not listening. "I need to eat. I need emergency money. They told me to come here, you people'd take care of me—I ain't well—"

"I have to know the source of your income since January."

Another gritty moment of silence.

Then the woman began screaming. She jumped forward and screamed into Katherine's face. "What am I going to do? You dirty ugly bitch! You bitch!" The papers flew out onto the floor as if terrified by such violence. Katherine thrust her chair backward and it was over in an instant—there were always patrolmen at the Center, and two of them ran over right away. The woman was led out, swearing and weeping, trying to jerk away from the boyish policemen as if they were suitors she hadn't time to bother with.

Katherine walked slowly back to the women's restroom, avoiding Clara's offer of help. Everything happened so fast—how could you rehearse it? Right there in the great crowded smelly office with its high cracked ceilings and its battered desks and filing cabinets and chairs, and all its people, always the same people—such a thing had happened! It was as if the preposterous facts in those files could spring into life. In the restroom Katherine was sick to her stomach, and she thought of her mother all alone at home; what if her mother was dying? "My God, don't let me get like that," she pleaded, afraid to see herself in the mirror, "don't let me get old like that, don't let me change into that. . . ." Her mind was so jostled, she didn't know whether she was thinking of her mother or of the prostitute. There were monsters in the world roaming loose, Katherine thought carefully, and you must avoid them. What was terrible about the monsters was their ugliness; you couldn't love or pity them. Your stomach went dry with disgust for them, and nowhere, nowhere in yourself could you find pity . . . that was what they did to you finally.

When she returned to her desk, Mr. Mott was sitting in front of it, in the chair the screaming woman had used. There was something about him she always remembered, though she now had sixty-five families in her file; he always wore a suit and tie, never looked afraid, though he always looked sullen, and he asked no pity from her. "Yes, Mr. Mott," she said faintly, taking her seat while everyone watched. As soon as she was seated, everyone looked away. Mr. Mott, when he spoke, showed uneven teeth that reminded Katherine of something; she saw his lips moving for a moment before she heard what he was saying. Her mind was slow and dreamy today. "I wouldn't be back again," he began; and so they all began their refrains, "I wouldn't be here." "The reason I'm here is—" Katherine looked through her papers on him. The Mott family. Unemployment, no savings, of course, five children—one of them mentally retarded, two with Juvenile Court records—the wife couldn't work, she had a bad back. But Mr. Mott was saying something important now: "Yeah, she took off back to her folks in Tennessee. Run out with the kids. So it's just me now and I'm gonna get a job, but I got to wait two weeks—it's just two weeks and then this guy that I mentioned before—"

His recitation made her dizzy. In his record was a notation of Mr. Mott's job in a grocery store.

"Did you lose your job?"

"I told you. I wouldn't be here except for them kids."

"Your children?"

He stared at her with a kind of scornful dignity, flushing. "No, them kids, like I said, them kids out of school. My kids are gone back home. Gone back. *She* run off and took them, went on a Greyhound bus. I mean them school kids out of school now, looking for jobs. He hires them part-time, then lets them work longer—"

"Yes, I see," Katherine said. She was shakily aware of him judging her while he talked, and she wondered if the screaming woman had opened in her a wound everyone could see. Mr. Mott talked on and on energetically. There was something stubborn and vengeful in what he said, though it was pitched in the same low whining tone all these people had.

"She's gonna have another baby, she said," Mr. Mott said, leaning forward with a sudden vicious little grin, "so let her go. Who's she kidding? Let her go to hell and the rest of them with her, I can take care of myself now. In two weeks."

"Yes," Katherine said weakly.

In December of that year her mother began to die, at about the time Katherine was promoted to supervisor. She was moved down the corridor to another room, a smaller room, with high drafty windows looking out onto the concrete playground of a Catholic grammar school. She shared the office with a bald man who cleared his sinuses constantly, snuffling and snorting as he worked, and a sharp stylish woman in her forties whose glasses were gold-rimmed. Katherine's mother wanted to die at home, but her children, and what remained of her relatives, and her young pink-faced doctor told her this was just nonsense, she wasn't going to die anywhere. "Here in the hospital there's nurses for everything," Lenore said. "The hospital is best for you right now." Lenore had grown into a stout woman with rouged cheeks; her husband worked in the same factory with Ed. Alone with Katherine, her sisters turned into harsh whispering storks, tugging at Katherine's sleeves as if she, once the youngest sister, had become suddenly the oldest and strongest. "My God, he says it's all through her, it's everywhere—poor Ma—" they cried in sibilant voices, staring at Katherine as if she were somehow in power, she with her superior education, this career woman in her expensive suit, responsible for the terror and knowing the secret of how to vanquish it.

"Yes, poor Ma. It's terrible for her," Katherine said as they wept, but her body was drained dry of sorrow. An anchor dropped through her hollow body would fall forever before it sank into any emotion, sorrow or pity or even fear.

But her sisters' tears stopped when they learned, after the death, that their mother had left "everything" to Katherine—the old house and the furniture and the furnishings and the bills. They hired a lawyer to get out of the "estate" furnishings equivalent to the amount of money their mother had vaguely owed them, for running errands years ago, for bringing food over, for whatever miscellaneous tasks they and their husbands claimed to have performed, and Katherine, amused at their lies, gave them what they asked. She did not want anything active to remain in them for her: not love, certainly, and not hate. Now their hatred for her would subside into a blank, inflexible resentment, but it would have no life. She was free of them.

She put up the house for sale with a white real estate company, though the salesman told her there wasn't much hope. "Nobody's buying down there except colored," he said. For three months the yellow For Sale sign remained out front to greet her when she left for work in the morning and returned late in the day, and when the period was up she decided not to list it again. She did not want to sell to "colored"—why not? Because of her mother. But her mother was dead. Well, because her mother would have been humiliated to know that her house was of no value to anyone except "colored," meaning people who couldn't buy anything better. . . . But her mother was dead. Yes, yes she was dead, Katherine knew that, but kept expecting to see the old woman bustling around with her broom and dustpan. At the end she had thought of her mother only as the person who had kept her from marrying, but she had not hated her for that. She had not hated her or resented her or felt anything for her at all. But she did not move out of the house.

For years she had not understood her job, and then it suddenly became clear to her that the people, who were names in caseload files, were not customers; they were the opposite of customers. When the job was done well, the caseloads were lightened. It had nothing to do with the people at all. As a supervisor Katherine understood, when her workers came in, sweating and nervous (outside, a client might be in hysterics, and these young people were just out of college), that the job for which they were being paid was to keep the numbers down. Taking a file from one of them, Katherine could glance through it in a second—she'd seen so many —and at once catch on to the lie. "Look here, from May until July they were off welfare. Didn't you notice that? Who was supporting them, if she can't work? She's got a man somewhere giving her money, ask her about it. Here, take the file. No. No emergency funds."

She did not meet the candidates now, so it was nothing personal. She didn't dislike a woman's expression, a man's bad breath. It was nothing personal at all; it was simply her job. She might have been glancing through names in a telephone book, deciding by the very look of the name whether it could be crossed out—some names looked humbler than others and would not complain. Others, how-ever, might yell and try to start a riot, and, though no riot would start, the commotion would look bad; it was wise not to annoy these names. What was strange was that the "names" were attached to people who waited in line for hours down the corridor, in the pen, motionless and sheep-like in their overcoats. Sometimes this thought made Katherine a little dizzy, the way she had felt in high school when confronted with problems in mathematics that were beyond her comprehension.

She was in her thirties now and still thought of herself as young; after all, the people in her office were older. The house was old, so dark and drafty that the mere glimpse of her rather slim body in the hall mirror assured her she must still be young. And her mother's presence was so vivid that she, Katherine, must still be the little girl of the family. . . . Though she no longer bought nightgowns and bathrobes with the vague expectation of their being "for her marriage," she had not yet stopped thinking of the man she was yet to meet. In her secret mind she waited for him. Never, never did she think of her fiancé, who had died along with the woman who had prevented that marriage. From time to time female connections got Katherine together with awkward, polite bachelors, but nothing came of this. Sometimes they were teachers, sometimes "in business for themselves," sometimes they were a little bolder than at other times, but always the good-by at Katherine's front door was a final good-by.

Then, one afternoon in September, a few days after Katherine's thirty-fourth birthday, she was on her way to the bus stop when a man stepped out of a drug-store entrance and surprised her. After an odd hesitation he grinned and said, "Miss Alexander!"

It frightened her, being recognized like that; "Miss Alexander" belonged back in the Center on Fourth Street. She stared at this man. This wasn't one of her people, was it? Not a case worker, and not a client. He was a rather tall, narrow-faced man with thinning hair, about fifty, perhaps; he wore a dark suit of a shiny material, exactly like the kind advertised in all the fall magazines. "Don't remember me, eh?" he said. He smiled and showed crooked teeth.

"You aren't—Mr. Mott?"

"Mister, hell. Bob. Bob Mott, pleased to see ya," he said, a little embarrassed by this formality. "I mean, pleased to see ya again. Been a long time."

"It's nice to see you again too," Katherine said awkwardly.

In his new suit, with such fine polished shoes and such a firm, energetic face, he was clearly in charge. He was a man. Katherine, never certain of herself in high heels and clutching her purse too tightly, tried to think of something to say. Mr. Mott motioned for her to step aside and avoid someone hurrying past, and in doing this she felt she had relinquished something important to him.

"Everybody's in a big hurry down here, gotta get home," he said cheerfully. Katherine was amazed at how young he looked. "Me, I'm not in no hurry, why should I? Last time I saw you I toldja about the new job, didn't I? How her and the kids took off? Well, look, I still got the job, only it's better now, and boy did she beg to come back, but I told her—well—I mean, I told her it was too late. I'm on my own now. I like it. I ain't been back to Fourth Street for years, I'm all finished with that. But it's real nice to see you again. I was always kind of hoping—you know—I might run into you, by accident. But I didn't want to go back there."

Katherine stared at him. He looked like a salesman; was that his new job?

"You were real nice to me," he said, smiling. "Some of them other bastards—well, forget it. I don't want to get mad or anything. But you were real nice. Hey, are you going somewhere?"

"I'm going home."

"You drive?"

"No. I take the bus here—"

"I'll drive you. I got a new car. C'mon, I'll drive you home."

She thought this must be a terrible mistake, and what if someone saw her? But at the same time she felt something in his voice, some command, that she had been waiting to hear all her life and had not heard.

On their way to his car he chatted about his job. He kept interrupting his talk with quick, energetic chuckles and frequent glances at Katherine. "Yeah, I wouldn't of minded running into you—but—I wasn't going back to that dump. Never again."

"Are you still married?"

She blushed; the question sounded more personal than she had meant. She had been thinking of the application form back at the Center. . . .

"Gonna be straightened out one of these days," he said quickly.

His car was indeed a new car. Katherine let her fingers touch it the way models on television commercials touched cars, as if unable to resist them. Mr. Mott was obviously proud of his car. "Just got it the other day. Look at the mileage—ever seen one of them that low?"

She told him the car was beautiful.

"I like a good car. I like good things, you know? Since I got on my feet again I get good things. If I want a suit I get a good one, not just junk like in the old days. And nobody can tell me how

much to pay for it or how many razor blades I can have in a year!"
This last was said with a bitter, buoyant humor, but when Katherine looked at him he was smiling as before.

"I'm very happy for you," she said slowly.

"Well, sure."

They were both embarrassed.

He drove her home and she had the idea that he was disappointed when she told him where to turn off the Boulevard. "Here?" he said. In the warm September sunlight groups of black children were playing in the street. She pointed out the house; he said, "That house?" And, seeing it from his car, through his flawless windshield, Katherine had to admit it wasn't much—she had resisted for years any move to fix up the outside, though the paint was peeling and the front yard was just weeds. Her life had been one long gradual entrenchment against complications. She felt obliged to apologize to Mr. Mott, saying, "My mother loved this house. She died a little while back. . . . I stayed with her and took care of her."

"Gee, that's too bad. That she died, I mean," he said. A certain ready-made alertness in his voice told her he hadn't caught her meaning exactly. And she alarmed herself by saying carefully, "I had to stay with her. She wouldn't leave this house."

"Oh," he said, and this time he got it. His mouth showed sympathy.

When he parked before the house there was the terrible moment she had awaited, not knowing what she would do. But some festive air about Mr. Mott—it might have been his birthday—told her it was all right. So she said, "Would you like to come in a minute and chat?"

And he agreed at once, as if he'd been expecting this.

She was grateful, when they were inside, of the habits of cleanliness her mother had instilled in her. The living room, though shabby, was free of dust and had the look of a museum room, its very look of irrelevancy pointing toward something quietly important.

"Nice and quiet, just like home here," Mr. Mott said. He sat on the sofa before she invited him. But he didn't know any better, of course. Katherine hesitated, still holding her purse. She ought to offer him something, a drink. Wasn't that what people did? But perhaps Mr. Mott did not know what people "did." And anyway she did not have anything to offer him except tea, which was all she drank. Tea and milk. So she put down her purse and sat, facing him, in an easy chair whose sunken cushions seemed to have been expecting someone else's shape.

Mr. Mott's eyes roamed the room. All the light from the windows seemed to be flowing toward him. Katherine straightened her skirt and pulled it down over her knees, trying to think of something to say.

"Too bad about your mother," Mr. Mott said.

"Well, that's how it is."

"I'll say. People dropping like flies," he agreed.

"Do you—uh—live downtown?"

"On the west side."

"In an apartment?"

"Yes."

"I was thinking of an apartment myself," she said slowly, and then was surprised to hear how she had aligned herself with him. Had she done this to make him feel more comfortable?

"Ya mind if I smoke?"

"Go right ahead."

"There's no ashtray—"

"Oh, that's all right," Katherine said quickly, not knowing what she meant, "don't worry."

So he lit a cigarette and did not worry.

"Like I said before, I was hoping I'd run into you sometime. But you know how it is—people don't like to go back to the Center once they're off."

"I understand," she said quietly.

"People really hate that place, you know."

"I suppose they do."

"Some little bastards in our building use'ta tease my kids about it. Little bastards. Just like they was any better themselves!"

"That's . . . too bad," Katherine said.

"Of course, the program does a lot of good," Mr. Mott said. He paused. After a moment he said, "One of them investigators, I forget his name, he was a real son of a bitch." He glanced at Katherine as if he were saying something daring. Her silence encouraged him. "Some guy in the building, he was pulling out and ast us if we wanted his teevee set, it wasn't no use to him. So we took it. Then this investigator bastard, what's-his-name, with glasses, he came along and saw it there and tried to say I bought it myself. The bastard! Almost got me kicked off the roll for that. The goddam set never worked right anyway. . . ."

Katherine could think of nothing to say. She watched the ash growing on the end of his cigarette.

"Well, I'm out of it now. Phew! I'm my own man now," he said. He flicked the ash off onto the rug without noticing.

"I'm so pleased to hear that. . . ."

"Are you pleased, Miss Alexander?" he said. "Are you?"

"Of course."

"Really?"

She felt her face reddening. "What do you mean?"

Mr. Mott smiled at her and the smile turned into a grin. "I'm just kidding. Only I thought, driving up here, that maybe you weren't doing too well yourself—you know—your stocking's torn or something right there—"

She drew in her breath sharply but, childlike, could not stop herself from looking at her leg. Yes, there was a gash in her stocking. She must have snagged it sitting at her desk.

"Don't mean to be rude or anything," Mr. Mott said. "But this here house too, and this neighborhood's mostly nigger. What's that funny smell?"

"What? What do you mean?"

He smoked his cigarette as it if were a luxury. "Course, like you say, you had to stay with your mommy who was dying."

"I don't understand—"

"Everybody's mommy dies, you ever notice that? I noticed it a long time ago. I never was stupid, Miss Alexander. I had bad luck but I never was stupid. I seen that everybody's mommy and daddy dies and they got to stick around and bury them, so I lit out when I was seventeen. Wasn't I smart to do that?"

Katherine's heart had begun to pound. Mr. Mott's words were coming at her in a slow, smiling drawl, his Tennessee accent growing stronger all the time. "Wasn't I smarter'n you, come to think of it?" he said slyly.

Katherine got to her feet, trembling. Mr. Mott did not rise. He looked up at her with raised eyebrows. "I don't mean to make you mad or nothing, but I'm just saying how things are. I never was stupid. You got to give me credit for being smart. Kicking my wife out was the best thing I ever did, because if I hadn't—what then? I wouldn't be here right now and sure wouldn't have no car out front. Right? I figured it all out from people like you, Miss Alexander."

"What do you mean, from me?"

"I use'ta get there nine in the morning, when the dump opened. Then in we'd go—sometimes she was with me, with one of the kids —and wait in line without being able to take our coats off, then around noon we'd get up past that whatdayacallit, where the chairs begin, then we could sit. And all them hours sitting there I just watched you and learned lots of things from you, like how to talk, and how to smile when you're really telling some poor bastard to go to hell. That one day when the dame started yelling—I saw that too! I saw you! You really put the needle in her and you didn't let up till she was finished—you old ugly dog-faced bitch!"

"Get out of here!"

He made a laughing sound that was like a snarl and, as if she'd been tugging at him, he jumped to his feet. He took hold of her arm and twisted it. "If I couldn't get you, it would of been all right," he said, speaking right into her face, "one bastard is just like another down there! For six years I been waiting to run into one of you—" Katherine struggled and he struck her in the face, cleanly and deliberately, as if counting the strokes. When Katherine cried out, he slapped her again, harder. "You shut up or I'll tear your hair out. Lady, I'll kick you in, I'll smash you in pieces! Shut up or I'll drag you all over this smelly room and leave parts of you everywhere— you hear?"

A blow struck the bridge of her nose, and she fell. Sitting, her legs helpless, she looked up at Mr. Mott. A thin strand of hair had fallen onto his flushed forehead. He was panting. He wiped his hands on his thighs as if brushing off dirt. She saw his lips moving and could tell, from the glint in his eyes, that he was saying now what they were all saying, though silently—and she stared up at him, paralyzed, until she was staring at nothing and she was alone.

She waited. The numbness around her eyes began to ease and turned into pain, so that she was able to weep. The sobs were violent, like blows, and her chest heaved with the effort of giving them passage, letting them free. She had not wept for years. There was a lifetime of weeping before her but she did not know why. The secret of her pain seemed to her to be in the long procession of sallow-faced straggly witches and broken-down men, or in this house, in the memory of her mother and father, or out dawdling along the sidewalk from the Boulevard, Katherine herself a child again with an armload of books—but she did not understand it. She did not understand Mr. Mott's hatred and she did not understand the power he had, to make her feel such pain.

The Dying Child

The Arkin family lived in an old wood frame house, three stories high. At one time the house had been painted white, but for a decade it had been the soulless melancholy color of sparrows in winter. During the long winter months snow shot viciously against its gaunt unprotected height, slashing its windows; in fall and spring, rain was dashed by the wind against it, running sleekly down its smooth-weathered clapboards, overflowing its rusted and leaf-clogged gutters to spill out onto the ground. The old house had a veranda that sagged and on which, in warm months, Arkin children of various ages had been seen for years, staring out at the road, small children growing up, slowly, older boys and girls disappearing, very old people disappearing; and now there were only a mother and three children in the house. Anyone driving by on the road was taken by surprise, seeing the ancient house in a barren patch of land that seemed hollowed out of the woods on either side of it, the house itself having the raw and unused look of timber far out in the country, undomesticated by fences or roads. There were bales of rotting hay dragged up against the house, and over several windows on the unused third floor there were cardboard strips to make up for cracked or broken panes. Behind the house was a small barn now used as a garage, and an old log low building that had once been a chicken coop, and everywhere around the house were weeds and splotches of ground where nothing would grow, as if the soil were cancerous.

Late one afternoon in October the Arkin girl, Jean, watched the house emerge out of the scrawny woods on either side of it and wondered what she was to do with her life. She was being given a ride home by a boy two or three years older than she; he worked at the gas station in town and she had been working, now, for almost five months at the post office. Both had dropped out of school for their own reasons. Jean's father had been killed in a stupid accident on his tractor, tipping it over on an incline and lying pinned beneath it while he bled to death; that had been last spring. Now Jean sat in the dirty car and watched the last of the trees pass and the old house appear like a wooden skull.

"What's Timmy doing these days? Still like it at the mill?" the boy said. He was tall, big, clumsy, and hard; Jean felt his presence as a kind of perpetual danger, a tedious danger. "I guess so," said Jean. Timmy was her older brother; he was eighteen. "He going in the Navy?" the boy said. "I guess so, sometime," said Jean. She sat up suddenly. In the front yard was a car—the car that belonged to her mother's boy friend. "If she can spare him," Jean said slowly, "if she gets money from someplace else. . . ." She stared at the car and her lips moved silently; she was mouthing profanities. Her heart was pounding. "That what's-his-name, huh?" the boy said. He was grinning. Only eighteen, and already there were little wrinkles on his face, edged with dirt or grease. His teeth were poor, his skin coarse, the very shape of his head brutal and awkward, and yet Jean knew he was handsome somehow, some part of her responded to him and had no care at all for her hatred. "Do you think it's funny?" Jean said. "Hell, I didn't say anything. That guy, Wallace, he's okay as far as I know," he said. Jean felt her face getting hard. There were probably wrinkles about her mouth. She did not want to get old, not so quickly. Now that her mother was "in love" again, Jean felt herself aging while her mother got younger. Her mother sang in the kitchen, and went around with her hair twisted up into tight ugly little curls. . . .

"At least my mother doesn't drink," Jean said.

The boy's face stiffened. Jean said, "She doesn't drink, at least. Bitch as she is. Her and Wallace go out for a drink sometimes or have beer at the house, but her favorite treat is frozen custard in the cone. What's wrong with you?"

"Why did you say that?"

"What?"

"You know what."

She had known this boy for as long as she could remember. She did not think of him by name, did not think of him at all. He lived several miles down the road in a house not very different from theirs. Most houses in the area were like theirs, though in better condition; it was the new paint, the rebuilt garages, the flower beds that Jean hated. She had wanted to fix up their front yard but had never gotten around to it. Rake up the junk, drag her brother Andy's old rusted sled around back, maybe plant some flower seeds around the edge of the porch. . . . She had never gotten around to it, and, besides, her father had died that spring. "*He's* got no right in there," Jean whispered.

"Huh? What?"

"I wasn't talking to you."

"You're going nuts, you know it?"

"Shut up."

"Look, you can walk to town if you're so—"

"Let me alone."

"Look, he ain't so bad. That guy in there."

The flippant, familiar nod of the boy's head infuriated Jean. She reached out and was going to slap him; then, confused, she pressed her cold hand against his cheek and dug in gently with her nails. "You don't know anything about him. You said before you didn't," she said, pretending impatience. "What do you know about him?"

"From the Rapids, got a farm all paid for, what else? How should I know?"

"Your sister knows everything. All the gossip, everything. Who told you that?"

"My sister."

"What was that about his old mother?"

"Cancer, honey."

She stared at him and saw that he was uneasy—the word "cancer" had upset him. Because he had tried to soften it with another word, she felt a sudden rush of affection for him. Perhaps he was like her, after all. Perhaps she had never stopped to look at him, because he had always been around, one of the big boys she had always feared. . . . But now when she did stare at him, waiting to see someone new, she saw only the same old handsome-ugly face, the eyes that feigned sleepiness as if it were an important pose. "Then maybe he'll get it too," Jean said.

"Hell—"

"Timmy's at work, Andy's out playing. She tells him to stay around after school and play. That's so they can be together, do they think I don't know that? I know everything. . . . When I come in now, they'll be sitting in the kitchen. They'll look at me like I don't live there but walked in by accident, *her* especially. And he's always clearing his throat and swallowing it again; tries to do it quiet so nobody will notice. . . ."

"Hell, he ain't bad. It's a good idea."

"I wouldn't have to hate him except for *her*," Jean said. She slapped her thigh for no reason. Often she felt buoyed up and pressured by energy that had no direction to flow in, like lightning bottled up somewhere. She sang the words to a sleazy popular song: " 'If I didn't love you, what would I do. Spend my whole life crying for you'. . . . When are you going to get your radio fixed?"

"Tomorrow."

"This is a goddam crummy car, you know that?"

He shrugged his shoulders. "Good enough for me."

"Well, not for me."

"You want to walk, then?"

"No."

"What's wrong with you?"

"You know yourself it's a crummy car."

"It's better than nothing."

"He doesn't pay you enough over there."

"Look, you need to get married or something."

"What?"

"You need it. Like my sister did, Betty. Do you some good." He began to grin, thinking of something. Seeing that look, Jean shivered. "You can fight with your husband then, not me."

Jean looked past him, out the window. Across the road the trees were violent yellow against gray, leaves parched and dying with fall. Farther back were oaks, their leaves red-brown; Jean's gaze flicked on them without interest. Everything she looked at was precarious, mere temporary surfaces upon which she focused her eyes while inside her brain feelings and half-formed ideas demanded her attention. She had felt always, not just since her father's death but always, since her early childhood, tense and edgy, her nervousness pushing to the surface sometimes in the switching of slight, fragile nerves beneath her eyes. She wondered if a nerve was twitching now; she always hated the sensation but was fascinated by it, as if a part of her body had come alive by itself and was defying her. She slid over and turned the rear-view mirror down so that she could see herself. "Think nothing of it, help yourself," the boy said sarcastically. Jean stared up at her reflection. She had blond hair that darkened every fall and winter, cut short and falling straight down to the tips of her ears, but her skin was not really the skin of a blond's. It was dark, as if permanently tanned; in a certain light it even looked olive, which she hated. In any light there were deep rings beneath her eyes, sometimes dipping down to nearly the middle of her cheeks, so that she looked perpetually tired and impatient. She touched her skin; nothing wrong. She was satisfied with herself. She was not beautiful and had no interest in it—then she would have to take care of herself. She would have to wash her face carefully every night, she would have to wash her hair more often. As it was, she had a hard, indifferent face, the set of the features somehow right, almost pretty, so that she did not care. She was shaping the word "bastard" to herself, watching her lips move in the mirror.

"Fix the mirror and let's go," she said.

"What?"

"Drive out of here. For Christ's sake, this dump gets me down, I don't want to go in yet. What's the matter?"

"Where do you want to go?"

"Out in the woods, in a field. In a ditch."

He looked at her sullenly. His eyes became sleepier than ever. He hid from her whatever he felt because he did not trust her, and she had no time for it. "You're a hick just like me," Jean said. "Stupid back-country hick. Your teeth are just like his . . . when you get his age they'll be worse."

"Are you getting out or what?"

"I said no."

"Are you serious?"

"Don't make me angry," Jean said. She covered her face helplessly with her hands. "Please don't make me angry. I don't like . . . I feel so hot then, like I'm dying, my heart beats so fast. . . . Bob, please. If I could keep quiet, if there was someone to keep me quiet. . . ."

"You want me to drive away?"

"Yes."

He put the car in gear and drove on.

Jean rubbed her eyes. Her face felt so tense, so old. When Timmy had come running in with the news about their father she had not cried, and not even later, though her mother had lurched about the house with puffy eyes, looking ugly as hell. . . . The boy turned onto a dirt road, and Jean watched blankly the monotonous fields gone dry with fall, the ugly barbed-wire fences that dropped from wooden posts, part of the ·landscape she had been seeing all her life. She would change her life, she would leave this land, but where would she go? Everything ran back to that old house with the bare yard around it, and even this was being lost to her, for when her mother married they would sell that house, surely, or board it up. And she could not live with them after the marriage. . . . He stopped the car and they got out and kicked their way through piles of leaves back into the woods. "You were listening to me, huh? About getting married?" he said. "Are you going to marry me?" Jean said. She pushed against him, smiling a sudden rushed, shameful smile, just as she had smiled at some of the bad things the boys had said to her years ago when she knew it was wrong to smile and yet could not stop. "What's your cute little girl friend, the one with the fat hips, going to say? Huh?" she said. "She hasn't got fat hips," he said. "What do you call it, then?" said Jean. "The hell with her," he said. "Shut up."

When they returned to the car Jean was silent and cold. "Going to get hell from her, being late for supper," he said. But he too was awkward and uncertain; they did not know how to look at each other. Jean kept thrusting between them the thought that this did not count, she did not mean it, she had not even cared. She cared about nothing. He glanced at her small, set, rather mean face, her secretive eyes and pursed lips, and must have wished to see something else—some look of regret or shame, at least—but could see nothing. He drove back to her house and she got out without speaking. "See you tomorrow," he said. Jean walked slowly up the drive to the house. Lights were burning in the kitchen but the rest of the house was dark. Just at the veranda steps she stopped, grimacing with pain. Her insides had been torn, she thought in panic, something had happened to her. . . . But the flash of pain passed. She thought to look around behind her, at the road; but the boy had driven off without her noticing.

At the kitchen table sat her younger brother, Andy, her mother, and the Wallace man. He smiled at her and the grinding of his jaws slowed. In the unflattering kitchen light he did not really look ugly—only homely in a familiar, amiable way, like a dog. Her mother was always solid and hard: her face keen as if sharpened by sniffing at something no one else noticed, her eyes dark and witchy. "Sit down. You're late," Jean's mother said. She pushed a bowl of string beans toward Jean's place. Jean wanted to go to her room, wanted to hide from them for fear the pain would return, but at the same time she felt a mysterious hunger, a desire to sit with them and eat with them. While her mother and the man talked—her mother talking mostly—she sat, dizzily, and felt the seat of the chair hard and reassuring beneath her, as it had always been, her own chair and her own place at the table.

While the others talked, Jean ate quickly. She felt hunted and mean, like a wild animal rummaging in a garbage pile. Andy talked; for a child of nine he talked too much; why had he none of the bitter dignity Jean had had at that age? Jean's mother talked, as always, her words rushing in upon them with a rowdy, chatty gusto, enlivened by a man's presence; and the man himself talked from time to time, but clumsily, with that waiting hesitant smile of the meek. . . . Jean felt herself suddenly allied with him, this Wallace, this convenient incidental man whom their mother now "loved." It was clear that he was happy to be at this table, happy to be with them, as if he could not sense her scorn. Jean's mother wondered where Timmy was; he had not come home for supper; and the man wondered also, seriously and profoundly, though Timmy had never bothered to speak to him. Where was Timmy, what had happened to him? Jean's mother, who would have spat out profanities any other night, now mused wryly upon boys and young men who led lives of their own. Jean could barely swallow the food in her mouth; she was conscious of Wallace looking at her. They were all looking at her. "Huh?" she said, blinking. Her face was small and passive; the bones must have looked rigid beneath her stubborn skin. "What about Bob?" said Jean's mother. "Bob?" said Jean. She forced a look of stupidity onto her face. "Yeah, *Bob*, he say anything about Timmy? Did he see Timmy today?" Jean's mother said. "No," said Jean, looking down. Jean's mother waited a moment. Jean could feel the woman's anger; it seemed to vibrate out at them, frightening them. "Maybe you want to eat in your room?" her mother said. Jean didn't answer.

After supper she had to help her mother with the dishes, while Wallace sat in a chair by the stove, thinking or pretending to think. He smoked a pipe. Jean, who could not keep her contempt out of her face, did not dare to look at him; if she did, she would see only his shy, gentle smile, for how did it happen he was here? Here with a "family," with "love," absolved evidently of his loneliness? But it was a lie, Jean thought bitterly. We are all alone here. She thought of her mother as a force, like wind or rain, something that pushed into corners and tugged at things, getting them loose, toppling them over and devouring them. Yet Jean's father had been no better than this man—just as slow, as gentle. They had never argued; Jean's mother had only yelled at her father. At first Jean had hated her mother for this, for keeping on despite her father's silence, but in the last several years she had begun to see that it had been her father who was cruel—not cruel but something else, lacking something, a failure perhaps. But now he was dead; Wallace was sitting here smelling up the house with his pipe, what did it matter? Jean had given herself to that boy, to Bob, so that she would have something else to think about, something to worry about, but it had not worked. No strategy of Jean's could overcome her mother's strength.

She had gone to her room and was listening to her radio when the front door was opened and someone ran in. She heard Timmy's voice. She sat up; something was wrong. At once she felt her body stiffen as if preparing itself for pain. Timmy was yelling something in great excitement; Jean could not make it out. She ran out and collided with him in the dark corridor. "What's wrong?" she said. "Somebody killed," her brother said. He pushed her aside and went down to his room. The others were following him, Wallace last of all, hanging back. "What is it? What happened?" cried Jean, pulling the collar of her dress tight across her throat. Timmy ran out again with his rifle. He was a tall, thick, pleased-looking boy. "I'm going back down there, there's some guys waiting for me," he said. "We're gonna be authorized to go look for the killer. The sheriff's there and everything." "But who was killed?" Jean's mother cried, yanking at his arm. Her face was angry. "One of the Shaefer boys," he said, "that little one, what's-his-name, *you* know him," he said, poking Andy in the chest. "Freddie. Freddie. He was killed by somebody, they don't know who it is yet. He was found by a ditch in a lane behind his house—we're going to be authorized to go out and—" "He was *killed*, that little boy? Killed? Why?" Jean's mother said. "Yeah, killed, cut up with a knife. Real bastard that did it, that's what we're trying to find out. The little one, Freddie Shaefer." Timmy was trying to get past his mother. "You all come along, then," he said, "come on, you can see us sworn in and everything. They got dogs there. You want to come along?" Wallace started to say something, but Jean's mother cut him off. While Jean stood back against the wall and watched, they hurried in a group out to the front room. The house vibrated with Timmy's energy. Timmy was saying loudly, "He wasn't even dead when they found him— that was another kid that found him, a dog led him—And not even dead but just dying, all cut up and everything— He was dying when the kid found him but couldn't talk sense—"

Jean went back to her room and turned the radio up higher. For some time she thought of nothing. She held herself stiff and mindless, as if she were no more than an object in her little room with its tilted roof (a stairway led past next door, over her closet) and its perpetual smell of mustiness. Finally she allowed herself to say out loud, "Nobody I know did that killing." As soon as the words were out, her eyes shifted to the black window in which her own vague reflection lay lazily, watching her.

A few hours later they returned, Timmy's voice carrying in from outside with that damp clarity noises have at night. Jean heard certain words—"sheriff," "men," "guys," "kid"—but did not understand anything. She did not get up. They entered the house, loud and arguing about something; she listened closely to hear if Wallace was still there—perhaps he had gone home, it was late—but yes, there he was, some little murmur identified him. They sat in the parlor as if this were a holiday. Jean still did not get up, and after a few minutes Andy came in. He was licking a frozen custard cone. "You sick or something?" he said. "Get the hell out of here," Jean said viciously. He made a sound with his mouth and slammed the door. Jean, as if exhausted, did not look around. She fell asleep with them still in the front room and her radio on, and only late at night did she jerk awake suddenly to the radio's ugly static. Then everything was peaceful and familiar and even the watery, frightened reflection of herself in the window was reassuring.

At the post office the next day she had to listen to conversations about the murder. Over and over, everyone talked of it, their faces pinched with grief and wonder; the old woman who worked with Jean, sorting mail that soiled their fingers, knew everything and told everyone all she knew, over and over. The child had been nine. Nothing like this had ever happened, not ever, that other killing last year had been a regular fight and they were drunk, so it did not count; nothing like this had ever happened; he had still been alive when found, dying, but could not talk, was groaning and drooling blood, dying right then, dying right when the other boy found him. The sheriff knew more than he was telling, that was certain. He was tricky and smart. Nobody could fool him. . . . The boy was nine, that was the Shaefer boy who was sort of runty, not the other one, Bill, he had a bicycle and came in the store after school and got in the way, but never meant any harm. (The post office was in a small grocery store, one long counter at the back.) What was strange was that the boy's dog, his own dog, was sleeping in the house all the time and never warned anybody....

As the hours passed, Jean felt more and more perplexed, not at the story of the murder, but at herself. She was weary, sleepy, vague. Her hands moved slowly. Once Bob came over to see her and she could think of nothing to say to him. He said indifferently, "Think they'll catch him?" "Catch him?" said Jean. "The guy that killed the Shaefer kid." "Oh, yes, sure," Jean said. "The sheriff's s'posed to know something new," Bob said awkwardly.

Bob left. Others came in. Jean listened to the old woman's eager, spiteful voice, hating her and hating her own slow, cold hands. Something was wrong with her. Something was happening. She knew what the Shaefer boy had looked like and so she kept thinking of him, his shadowy little face, like a reflection in a mirror or window somewhere that had not the substance to define itself further but stayed forever blurred and out of focus. Certain words came to her again and again. "Not dead but dying. Not dead but dying." The word "dying" impressed her. Why had he not been dead, why had he been dying? Had he been dying long? Jean closed her eyes and clutched something before her—the edge of the old counter— and thought that she could not endure living if she did not know the answer to this question.

Bob drove her home that afternoon, trying to talk to her about the killing, about new things he had heard. Someone's car had been seen down that lane, the Shaefer kid had thrown a stone at someone a while before, the Shaefer kid's father was drunk again.... "Stop it, shut up," Jean said, turning away. He said no more. At her house she jumped out of the car and ran up the drive without looking back at him. Wallace's car was not there, that was good, but then her mother was not home either. Andy was not home. She wandered through the house, climbed the stairs to the second floor and stood listening up the drafty stairs to the third, though nothing was up there except junk. And suddenly terror overcame her, for was it not possible that the killer was in this house? Having run through fields, woods, hiding finally in this house? Jean went down and sat in the parlor, her hands in her lap. She was helpless before the threat of the killer, before his mystery and power. She was sitting there, like a visitor who had been forgotten, when Wallace and her mother and Andy came in a while later.

Her mother's face was flushed from the cold. "So, you beat us back. Any news?" she said. "No," said Jean. "We went out for a drive around there, lots of other people were out too," her mother said. Wallace had wiped his feet carefully on the old ragged mat on the veranda; now he came inside. Jean saw that his expression was strained and weary—he looked frightened. Like herself. She held his gaze for a moment before she turned away. "Honey, are you okay? Got cramps or something?" her mother said. It was always that sudden kind voice that made Jean impatient. "No, nothing," she said. Her mother felt her forehead with her cold hand. "Maybe a little fever. But I guess I'm cold from outside." "Too much excitement going on here," Wallace said gently. "Yes, that's it," said Jean, grateful for him. "Well, they ought to get the bastard in a day or two, if they're going to get him ever," Jean's mother said.

But days passed and nothing happened. Nothing changed. Jean stayed home from work one day, lying languidly in bed, safe from the chatter in the store, safe from everything except the incantation of "dying," "dying." She rummaged through her memory for pictures of that child—why had she never bothered to look at him closely, never paid any attention to him? She recalled him on a bicycle, his face pale with effort as he tried to catch up with some other boys; nothing more. Why was he now so important? Maybe it was because of Andy; Andy might have been killed instead. But no, she thought, that was not it, for the death that was the boy's could have been no one else's, it was his alone. It was unthinkable that it could belong to anyone else. . . .

Timmy came home every day with more news, but it added up to nothing: rumors and speculations, hints that the sheriff knew something secret, but never the man's name, never the name that would end everything. Jean had no appetite, could not sleep well, lay with her eyes open in the dark and sought out that child's face, that ghostly face, and tried to figure something out. What was it, what was wrong? In another day, someone said, they would have the killer. Something about license plates. Jean imagined an automobile by the lane, a man running out of it with a knife, the act of murder itself blurred and uncertain, the man fleeing in the car but someone seeing him: his face, the license plates. There it was, ended. In another day or so. The sheriff was perhaps questioning the man right now. Timmy knew everything that wasn't confidential. He had searched all over with other boys, all of them with their rifles ready, but no one had found anything; they had only trampled down grass and startled up pheasants. Someone had shot a rabbit, out of season. The Shaefer man, the boy's father, had knocked someone down in a tavern. Nothing more. Jean would not come out to the table to eat until the killer was found, so that she would not have to listen. For what would these things matter when the final truth was discovered?

She tried to explain this to her mother, who was angry. Always angry. But this turned to something else—a nervous warmth—when Jean's face flinched with pain. But the pain came out of nowhere and vanished at once; there was certainly nothing wrong with Jean. Her mother came to sit on the edge of the bed. Because Wallace was out in the kitchen she had to speak softly. "Are you in trouble?" she said. "Is that it? Don't lie." "I'm all right," said Jean. "With Bob or somebody?" her mother said. "Don't lie to me, huh? I can't stand that. Anything else but that." "I'm all right, I just feel sleepy," Jean said. "But is that right, to feel sleepy all the time? You must be sick. Goddam it, sick with something, that's all we need. . . . Does it hurt anywhere?" she said. "I feel . . . I don't feel. . . . I don't feel *alive*," Jean said. "Now what kind of talk is that?" said her mother. "I don't feel alive," Jean said. "Well, we're all dying, if that makes you happy," her mother said with a smirk. Jean noticed a cheap imitation silver bracelet on her mother's wrist.

That night Jean dreamed that the killer had been found.

But the next day brought nothing. No change. The ride in with Bob, their silence. Once in town, Jean looked eagerly to see if anyone stood about, groups of people perhaps; but nothing. "Why don't they arrest him?" she said aloud. Bob made a grunting noise that indicated he had not heard her or had no answer. All day, in the post office, Jean stared at each piece of mail as if she did not know what to do with it. So much mail, sent deliberately from people to people, a network of names carefully learned by heart . . . and among them, surely the name of the killer himself. How surprised everyone would be when they found out his identity! It would be someone they all knew, some man. Jean's eyes narrowed. It would be someone she knew well, perhaps. Bob? Bob's father? Her own brother Timmy? The man at the gas station, the man at the coal yard? At the tavern? That man there, coming in the door? Or some stranger they would have to go to another city to get, one of the cities to the south, whose name would mean nothing to them . . . ? That would be better, Jean thought. Some stranger. A name that meant nothing. But if it would only come soon, she thought, very soon, and written up in the newspaper with a picture of the killer; then it would be all over. The boy could end his dying. . . .

She was clumsy that morning, got ink on herself, said a word she had only heard boys say in the past; she was pleased to think the old woman heard her. But at once a dazed, languid feeling overtook her, as if poison from some rotted part of her body—a tooth perhaps —were seeping everywhere inside her. She could not get right. She could not even get the focus of her eyes right. If something should happen and they should stop their talk—though this last day they had talked of other things, that was true—then she would be herself again.

And when someone did come in and said nothing at all about the killing, a curious fear seized Jean. She would stare at the person and think, Is he the killer? When the man from the gas station came in to buy something, Jean herself had had to ask him about the killing. No, no news he had heard of. He was silent a moment and then went to a counter and pawed through something—winter gloves. Jean stared at his back. Was it possible he did not care? Was *he* the killer?

The next day brought no news, little talk about the killing. They were talking now about the flu. Several families had it, everyone had to watch out. Jean seized upon this. She was probably getting the flu. That was why she felt so weak and strange. So she left work early and walked home, two miles home through a damp wind, her lips forming words in an argument with herself that she did not quite follow. She did not care. The road was empty, wet. Down to the left, on a dirt road that led into this one, was the scene of the killing. She thought of going down to look at it, but why should she? She looked instead at the ditch by the road. She stopped and looked in it. Any ditch would do, any ditch. The murder could have taken place right there, just as easily; so she would look at that. She would imagine the boy . . . his face . . . his "dying." How long had he been dying and what did that mean? If he had not known he was dying, then was it "dying" for him, or was it something else? If a person did not know he was dying, then he was not really dying, in his own mind, where the terror would be. Someone coming upon him would be the one to say the word "dying." "Dead." "Death." It would not mean anything to the dying person himself. . . .

Jean looked around. Had someone called her name?

It had begun to rain. Drifting, dreary, languid rain that was nearly silent told her nothing. She was alone. No one was here, no one she could see. Perhaps he was hiding somewhere, awaiting her. Behind a tree, crouched in a ditch, peering at her through the cattails. She lingered, she walked slowly, though she was quite frightened. If the killer was nearby, waiting for her, then at least she would see his face. She would *know*. . . . But nothing, no sound, only the familiar stretch of woods and then the crossroads where, often on weekend nights, boys drove their cars so fast and so recklessly that the noises could be heard all the way down at the Arkins' house. There were accidents out in the country often, because the roads were so empty, so inviting—the boys could get their cars going up to nearly a hundred miles an hour—and even older, more cautious drivers sometimes risked accidents by speeding through four-way stops. When there was an accident it was usually a terrible one: closed caskets, rumors, horror, a peculiar, clumsy embarrassment among the next-of-kin. And Jean's father had died, of course. And. . . . And of course everyone died, somehow and in some manner, so it should not have fascinated her, the murder of the child, the fact of his dying. She could not understand what was happening to her, to her mind. Why did it frighten her, why that particular death?—as if the deaths by accident did not really matter, precisely because they were accidental and therefore innocent, unplanned; as if the deaths by disease did not really matter either, because they were natural, the body's natural wearing-out, and innocent as well, not ultimately frightening even to Jean. She did not fear death: she had heard aged relatives of hers speak comfortably of dying, of being ready for it, of having no quarrel with whatever happened. . . . No, it was something about the boy, the child, the murder, the murderer, that seemed to have come between Jean and her own self, the old toughness she had cultivated, imagining that this would somehow determine the world for her, forcing it to be less frightening than it really was.

By the time she arrived home, she was sick. Her clothes were wet, her face burning. "Jean, what the hell . . . ? Why did you walk home?" her mother asked. She was so surprised she must have forgotten to be angry. She undressed Jean and put her to bed, and Jean did not protest. Then she stood in the doorway, staring at her daughter, rapping her knuckles against the door—a habit of hers—not conscious of how fiercely nervous she looked. Finally she asked, in a whisper, if Jean was certain that she wasn't . . . wasn't in trouble? With Bob? With that Wreszin boy, maybe, who had always seemed to like her? She hoped that Jean would not lie to her; of all things, that was something she couldn't take. Jean swallowed and closed her eyes. *Bitch*, she thought. She remembered Bob and forgot him in the same instant. That did not matter, not *that*. How unimportant, what had happened between her and Bob or between any two people, compared to the boy's death, set aside his murder! . . . Jean hated her mother, that she should reduce everything to *that*. " . . . they didn't get him yet," Jean whispered. "They don't know who it is. Not yet. Nothing is changed. . . ."

"What?" her mother asked.

" . . . the killer. The one who—"

"The killer!" her mother said scornfully. "Is that all you've got to think about? Look, Jean, I'm very worried about—"

"Somebody said that tomorrow they want to . . . they're going to—"

But she was too confused to remember. A detective from the city? —a team of policemen?—but maybe it had just been talk; maybe she had imagined it. Her mother struck the doorframe irritably with the back of her hand, so hard that it must have hurt. Jean flinched. "For Christ's sake," her mother said, "they'll probably never get him, don't you know that? A few years ago there was a . . . well . . . I don't want to go into it, it wasn't very nice—a woman with her throat cut—in fact, someone your father had known, I mean before we were married," Jean's mother said flatly, hurriedly, "and—and whoever killed her wasn't caught, though a lot of us had a pretty good idea—Look, honey, what's the difference? I mean *what's the difference to you*, goddam it? —I want you to stay in bed. I'll make you some chowder, that thick chowder you like . . . I'll bring you some tea . . . spend a few days in bed and the hell with your job, and you'll be better."

Jean was noting her mother's thick, dark eyebrows, noting how strangely handsome her mother's face was in spite of so many things wrong with it—the coarse skin that she didn't bother to care for, her long nose, that expression of perpetual baffled anger and impatience everyone in her family had. Her mother was sometimes loud, sometimes soft. You could not predict. Before her Jean felt herself weaken, as if she were in danger of being argued out of something very important, though she didn't know what it was. She began to cry. She cried for the first time in years, while her mother gaped at her. "You're lying," Jean heard herself whisper, like a child. "You're lying. About that and everything."

"What?" her mother asked. "I *what?* —I can't hear you."

"About that man—"

"What man, the killer? Are you still talking about him?"

"I—"

"The hell with him!" her mother said. "How many kids do you think die in a year, in the world, and it's nobody special that kills them—they just die—what the hell are you going to do about it? Curl up and die yourself? Just wait until you—"

"You're lying all the time and I hate you," Jean said. She sat up in bed, her face burning with the shame of crying. So hot, so dizzy! She shouted at her mother: "I hate you for saying that! How can you say that! That makes you like *him!* He's there, they're going to find him, what the hell do you know about it? You think you know everything, always know everything, the hell with you—leave me alone, get out of here! I can't stand your face! They're going to find him!"

Her mother slammed the door. Jean heard her out in the hall, walking quickly. Then, in the kitchen, she paused. Thinking of what, doing what? Jean could not stop crying. She felt shattered, overcome, as if she had opened her own closet door and found in there something terrible—something ugly and dying—Blood, blood around its mouth, why were they all made up of blood—Why did this blood flow so precariously through veins and arteries? Why were people shot through with blood that could leak out through any tiny slash? Her breath came in shallow, rapid gasps. Her heart pounded as if at any moment something was going to jerk clear to her vision, and suddenly she would *see*: what?

When Wallace came in later that day, she got dizzily out of bed and put on her bathrobe. She heard her mother talking to him, a low voice; talking about her. As if hypnotized, Jean buttoned the big cloth-covered buttons of the robe, remembering how much she had liked it when it was new—but now it was part of the world she had to grope her way through, something that was no more than a function and did not matter because it could tell her nothing. If she could grope her way through the confusion she saw around her, then perhaps she would be safe; she could look back at such things and be able to like them again. . . . She went out into the corridor, hearing their voices in the kitchen. Did he know who the killer was? Was he the killer himself? But of course he was not—everyone could not be the killer.

She had not known when she came to the kitchen door what she was going to do, but when she saw him it came to her. He was wearing a green and black checked shirt made of wool, a little faded, dark trousers, short boots, his hair was sandy but thinning, receding, his skull meek and defensive beneath his coarse skin—and he was smiling at her with that surprised smile that reminded her of dogs or cats trying to smile, the corners of their dark-lipped mouths turning up as if in imitation of man. He was fifty or more. His hands were square and thickened from work, while her mother's were long and bony; when Jean came to the doorway the two of them moved apart, as if embarrassed by Jean's presence. *But they were going to be married.* Jean was trembling, still sick, not knowing why she was sick or what would happen to her. She stared at her mother, whom she had never really seen before: and at that man, that stranger in the faded shirt, with the coarse sallow skin and that tentative smile. Suddenly everything seemed to Jean so vulnerable, how could it be lived?—all of life as vulnerable as the dying child, whose death was never complete and whose murderer would never be caught.

"I'm sorry," she whispered. She did not know what she meant— whether she was sorry to have intruded upon them or sorry for something else. She raised her hand uncertainly, as if she were reaching for them. "I . . . I want you to be happy. I want you to be married. I didn't understand—"

But she fell silent, bewildered. Only now did it strike her: what if her mother and this man should not marry after all?

Narcotic

I

The thought of her brushed against him, flimsy as a whiff of some faint, faintly disturbing odor. It came and went, somehow in rhythm with his walking quickly along the hospital corridors or taking the stairs down, fast, two or three steps at a time when he was really in a hurry. It was not quite a thought of her—he stopped himself before he mouthed her name—but the idea of her, the abrupt unsettling image of her face, which he did not really know well. In a crowd she might not be recognizable to him. He did not know her at all.

At five o'clock he hurried outside, thrusting his arms into the sleeves of his coat, eager to get ahead of the crowd of nurses and orderlies who were leaving. They left by the rear exit, which was

also the Emergency Entrance. He saw that one of the ambulances
had been left at the door, parked hastily, its big rear doors still
flung open. The ambulance was empty, the stretcher taken out. The
door on the driver's side was still open, as though the driver had
jumped out in a hurry.

He was an orderly himself, but he walked apart from the others,
avoiding their conversations. They emerged into the queer, orange-
toned air of a winter afternoon that was really a twilight, a premature twilight; already the Christmas lights that had been strung
loosely upon evergreens in front of the hospital had been turned
on, so that the day seemed cruelly abbreviated, cut short. He
glanced at the sparse yellow lights irritably. All that day—in fact,
for several days—he had felt jumpy, disoriented, irritable. He kept
thinking of *her*, his mind turning mechanically toward her as toward
any distraction, any comfort. Yet he did not really know her and he
did not want to know her.

"Pretty, aren't they?" one of the older nurses said, meaning the
Christmas lights.

"Yes," Neil said.

He was always lying; it had become an art. Working with the sick
was itself an art.

At first he had liked his work. He had liked it well enough. Then,
after the first several months, which had passed quickly, a kind of
dizziness had begun to bother him: not a physical but an intellectual
dizziness, a sense of disorientation, a rejection of certain ideas. Yes,
he was jumpy, nervous, but he didn't mind that—it was the inability
to understand certain things that disturbed him. The idea of health;
the idea of sickness. *Health. Un-health.* Living tissue and dead
tissue. *Tissue.* The names of patients and their problems, which
were also names, some of them very complex—in fact, a secret language. A *secret language.*

It was a shock to keep remembering that the hospital was run by
people, and that its dreary corridors and rooms and offices and laboratories were populated by people who shared certain ideas of

health and un-health. These people were states of mind. Together, they were an intricate organization of states of mind; he was one of them. When he tried to comprehend this he felt that his mind was breaking down. Then he felt that it did not matter, all this thinking; then he found himself thinking of the girl, even allowing himself to think of her name, and a kind of warm, reckless indifference passed over him. He would be all right. It did not matter.

He was one of a small army of orderlies, young men with strong arms and strong stomachs. Not all young: there were two older men, very efficient and cynical. The orderlies were all called by their first names, which were simple, one-syllable names like his, Neil, and the interns and doctors were called Doctor, so there was no confusion between them and the orderlies. Neil wore a uniform that was never white for long. His name was Neil Myer. He knew this name was not important, but sometimes he discovered himself repeating it, over and over, mechanically fascinated by its sound. *Neil Myer.* A combination of shrill shrieking sounds that were muffled by the "N" and the "M" but were not really silenced.

Then he rejected his thoughts angrily. "Come off it. Forget it. Get to work," he said, and forced his attention upon other people: patients wheeled down for X-rays and brought back again, patients whose bodies had to be kept clean outside and in, or they would break down and someone would be blamed. He had to talk to these people, in spurts of good-natured bantering, a lot of joking. They liked him. He was careful not to like them too much, that might be bad luck. In the beginning he had liked all the patients on his floor and had regretted it; now he knew better. But though he kept himself busy, that dizziness bothered him. Even while he talked and laughed with other people his mind worked rapidly against him, accusing him: *You are still Neil Myer.*

He decided to walk, not wait for the bus. He didn't want to stand with the others, didn't want to share in their camaraderie and odd, defensive cheerfulness. They were all good people, the nurses and the orderlies, sturdy and hearty and brave, but he felt he could not manage himself with them. He could not respond normally. At the same time he hated this in himself, this fastidiousness, this disdain for other people. Terror was like a message in code. If you didn't try to decode it, you didn't know it existed.

He thought of her face again, stark and pale. It had seemed an accusing face, but why should it have been accusing? It had been turned away from him, the face of a near-stranger, a girl lying in a hospital bed like any other bed.

Paula Shapley.

His lips shaped her name involuntarily. Something was going to happen to him, he thought suddenly; it was time for good luck. For health, for exuberance. For life. You didn't work in a hospital for long without believing in good or bad luck; it was as simple as that.

But nothing was going to happen. He didn't know how to make it happen.

He walked the mile and a half into the city. Traffic rushed past him, most of it headed out. The peculiar orangish twilight had darkened into a true twilight. The air smelled cold and slightly soiled; in a way it pleased him after the disinfectant of the hospital, all that cleanliness, that sterility. He washed the unresisting bodies of patients all the time. He washed the heavy, cold, lardish bodies of the dead, which did seem to resist; even turning them over was sometimes a struggle, getting them out of the beds that no longer belonged to them and onto carts, ready to be rolled down the corridor and to the elevator and downstairs. He washed them with strong disinfectant, and though he wore rubber gloves he could smell this disinfectant on his hands. It burned everything clean and sterile. Germs could not grow where it touched: nothing could grow.

The most disturbing thing that had happened to him today was the sight of a new admission, a twenty-six-year-old boy, really a "boy" because he was so slight, so ravaged. Brought in for tests, partly paralyzed already; he had collapsed on the street somewhere, his legs had given out. The boy's thin, angular, shadowed face had looked to Neil like the face of death, and he had turned away with tears in his eyes. He was twenty-six himself. But that was not why he felt so agitated. He didn't know why. He didn't want to think about it. He felt a peculiar envy for the boy, who was doped up already with a legal, powerful narcotic. What could he find to narcoticize himself?

The girl had been brought in because of an "accident," an overdose of narcotics. Neil had recognized her name because he had known her husband slightly and had met her once. After a session in the emergency ward she had been brought up to the fifth floor, where she was kept for ten days in a room with two other patients, both old women. Neil had asked about her from time to time and had gone up to look in at her, to walk past her door. He didn't know her well enough to go in. And he feared seeing her up close, feared the ghastliness of her face. She was about twenty-two or twenty-three, but small as a child, very thin, silent. Neil asked one of the nurses about her and the girl said, with a look of repugnance, "Nobody came to visit her. Not one person."

Then she was discharged from the hospital and he believed he would forget about her. It was pointless to think about her: he did not approve of her life, he did not want to get near her. He wished her well, yes, but he feared her. He had not even wanted to recall her name, Paula Shapley, and that she lived only about twelve blocks from his parents' home.

His hands felt heatless, clammy, as if still covered with those loose-fitting rubber gloves.

If he did not go directly home he would have to telephone his mother. By a coincidence he saw a telephone booth just ahead, adjacent to a drug store. So it was decided! He would telephone his mother, make an excuse. . . . "I won't be home for supper tonight," he said. "I'm working late." His mother believed anything. She believed anything he told her, any excuse, just as she believed anything Neil's father told her: late at the yard, an overnight trip to Toledo, complications. She had never learned to read more than simple signs and familiar advertisements, she was easily hurt and easily confused, accustomed to being laughed at by Neil's father. Neil loved his mother, but he thought of her only reluctantly, guiltily. He did not love his father. He liked him, maybe, as an idea. His father made money out of scrap iron and other junk, enough to support a family of six children. At a distance, as an idea, Neil's father was excellent. Neil could admire him. But in person he was bullying, rather hateful, always a little drunk. His father always asked, "Why don't you work for me? Why at that hospital with all the sick people?" He teased Neil about wanting to be a doctor, though Neil had explained to him many times that you didn't get to be a doctor that way. But he was blustering, he didn't listen to other people. He went around with a foolish, aggressive, dazed grin, not listening to what people said. Neil explained that he worked at the hospital for the same reason he lived at home—to save money. "It's the only work I can get. *I need the money.*" That seemed to set him apart from the hospital, to mark him as untouched, free. For years his father had taunted him about saving money, half-arguing with him about working at one of the junk yards or driving a truck; he'd even lend Neil the money for college, he said, if Neil would ask. But Neil wouldn't ask. He had had to drop out of college in his second year, but he wouldn't ask his father for money.

His mother said she would leave something in the oven for him.

"No, don't bother," Neil said.

"It's no bother. . . ."

He felt a thrill of anger at her acquiescence.

"No," he said.

He left the telephone booth and walked over toward the Shapley apartment. It was strange how crazily eager his body was now! Yet he did not want to see her, he dreaded seeing her. She had been brought back from the dead. What she had done was sick, ignorant, selfish, stupid. . . . He could imagine what she'd looked like, brought in the ambulance, dying from an overdose of barbiturates. He had seen other young people dying like that. He did not want to remember them. Yet his legs carried him swiftly along and his arms swung easily at his sides, as if he were going to meet an old friend, someone who would give him comfort. He had played basketball in high school, and he'd never been able to forget the extreme satisfaction of those evenings when he had performed, his limbs coordinated and shrewd, his fair, handsome head carried nobly in a crush of opponents. He had played well. But now there was no time limit to the exertions he had to endure. He had to perform, to force himself into performances, yet there were no rest periods or audiences or scoreboards.

No one was keeping score.

II

"Who? What did you say your name is?"

"Neil. I'm a friend of—I was a friend of—"

She stood very close to him, peering out over the latched chain. The door was open only a few inches.

"Neil Myer . . . ?" she said.

"Yes. I was a friend of Fred's . . . I didn't think you would remember me."

She was silent, looking at him. He wondered why he had said that: *I didn't think you would remember me.*

"You don't have a message from Fred, do you?" she asked after a moment.

"No."

"Did you know him from night school? Those business courses? I can't remember when he brought you over here. . . . I'm a little mixed up but I remember you." She paused, but because of the light behind her he could not make out her expression. "It's because of the way you look; you look polite. It's that night-school politeness," she said oddly, as if taunting him. "What did you say you wanted?"

"Just to visit."

"You haven't heard from Fred. . . ?"

"No. I don't know him very well."

"You know he went to California?"

"I heard he left town . . . he went somewhere. . . . I didn't know him very well." He was standing in a dark, unheated corridor while she stared at him, studying him. It had been a mistake to come here. His face stiffened with resentment for her slow, almost sluggish manner. This slight, plain, pathetic girl, someone's cast-off wife!

Yet he felt he had carried something heavy, an invisible crippling weight, all the way to this door, and he must set it down on the other side.

"Could I talk with you for a few minutes?" he asked.

He was pleased at the sound of his voice, its unhurried, undisturbed authority. His voice never betrayed him, never showed any nervousness or panic. The girl looked at him, thinking. Her hair fell to her shoulders, yet was wavy all over, even frizzy, illuminated by the strong light behind her. Like feathers, like the fluff of milkweed. She was shorter than he remembered. He wondered if she were barefoot—she'd been barefoot the evening her husband had invited him back for coffee—but he did not dare glance down at her feet.

Finally she unlatched the chain. Her movements were abrupt and reckless.

She let the door swing open and backed away. Neil entered shyly. He felt suddenly very tall and awkward. The girl was barefoot, yes, and very small—a head shorter than Neil. He stared at her, his eyes leaped eagerly to her face. There was something in her face he yearned to see. As if knowing this, she allowed him to look at her, her smile small and perfunctory and mocking.

"You're very confident, to come here," she said. "To think I'd remember you after a year and a half—or two years, however the hell many years—"

"I didn't think you would remember me," Neil said.

"Maybe I don't. Sometimes I remember names but not people. I remember names that don't even have people attached to them. . . ."

But your face, your polite face, you look like someone I met once. Someone Fred dragged home. From night school, huh?"

"Yes. Introduction to Business."

"Oh, yes. Introduction to Business. Fred tried that for a while, then he left town. He yearned for a milder climate, he said. Sorry he isn't here tonight."

She folded her arms tightly across her chest. When she raised her eyebrows mockingly there were sudden, deep lines on her forehead. Her face was still pretty but it was going to wear out soon. "So you heard Fred walked out. What else did you hear?" she asked slyly.

"That you've been sick."

"Oh. Sick."

"I work at the hospital—where they brought you. I'm an orderly there."

"Oh. You work at the hospital. I didn't remember that."

"I've only been working there a few months. I wasn't working there when I knew you before."

"Knew me before," she repeated. "Knew me before. But did you know me before?"

Her smile was insinuating and mocking. But he faced it, he didn't let his disappointment show. And she stepped back as if acquiescing to some power in him, an authority he shared with her ex-husband —also very tall, also an ex-high school athlete. She seemed to do this unconsciously.

"Well, sit down. If you don't mind the mess in here. This is a kitchen, underneath everything. See the sink? See the table? Sit down, please, you're so tall you make me nervous."

They sat down at the table; Neil thanked her self-consciously, and saw that she had taken for herself a chair that had a rough, splintering back. The table was cluttered with dishes and silverware and a small pile of newspapers. An extra-large carton of cereal, with a giant panda on its front; tweezers, a soiled hairbrush with nylon bristles, books from the neighborhood library with yellowed plastic covers

The New England Beach: Drawings & Photographs. A Pictorial History of the Adirondacks. Religious Ikons: Gods and Goddesses of All Lands. She saw him glancing at the books and said with a smirk, "I need healthy images in my head. It's the first step toward rehabilitation."

"You look all right," Neil said. It was abrupt and clumsy, but he had to continue. "You look good. How do you feel?"

"Take my pulse if you're so interested," she said, thrusting her arm out at him and then jerking it back. She laughed. He felt pity for her, for her sad shapeless unclean dress, for the straggly hair, the meekness of her shoulders and head. He had not remembered her hair so light: it had looked darker on the pillow, almost black. But it was really a light brown, his own color. Her forehead seemed rather low, perhaps because of her jumble of hair and because of her continual mockery; her eyebrows were raised into those premature wrinkles. "Yes, I'm better. They discharged me. All the laboratory tests agree that I'm better."

She drew her feet up under her, mechanically, unembarrassed. Neil saw the immediate tension of her leg muscles. It was a little shocking, this unconscious and intimate movement of hers; he looked away. "Does Fred know about it?" he asked.

"What? The laboratory tests? Their agreement about me? No, he doesn't know. He doesn't even know about the tests and their initial reports, all that fuss," she said ironically. "Since he didn't send me back any address, I couldn't very well let him know the good news, let alone the bad news. Could I?"

"I don't know. No."

"Why did you come here?" she asked bluntly.

"To see you."

"But why tonight? I mean, why tonight especially? Is it your birthday, or is it maybe my birthday and I forgot? Sometimes I forget things like that."

"I just wanted to see you."

"To see what I look like, come back from the dead?"

"I see dead people all the time. It doesn't mean much to me any more," he said.

She drew in her breath sharply, as if this remark surprised her. For a while she did not speak. Neil watched her; he was excited by her, by the easy reckless intimacy of her talk, her behavior, even the way her hair looked, as if she'd just gotten out of bed. But at the same time he was a little disgusted, repelled. His mind raced freely ahead as if anxious to get to a time when he would not be *Neil Myer* but an anonymous young man, twenty-six years old, in anonymous good health, making love to an anonymous young woman.

"Then what does mean much?" she asked slowly.

"Everything else. Life. Health. Control." He spoke in a frank, open voice. He had learned to imitate the older doctors at the hospital, who answered the most hopeless questions in brief sincere replies, always looking the questioner in the eye. Everything frank, open. Healthy. It was important to make connections, fearless connections.

"Control, fine. I'm in control," she said. "If I'm not, someone else will be; I'm not worried. I might never worry about anything again. . . . Were you there when they brought me in?" She straightened some of the things on the table suddenly, as if she were alone; Neil understood that she was very serious. "Tell me what I looked like. Don't spare me."

Neil had not been on duty then. He had not seen her until the next morning, and then he'd seen her only from the doorway of her room.

"You didn't look bad," he said slowly. "Very pale. You were breathing hard. You looked very . . . very defenseless, like a child. . . . Very delicate. . . . Everyone wanted you to live."

She had picked up the large cereal box, as if distracted by it, and she reached around to set it near the sink. As she turned, Neil could see the movement of her skin over the small bones of her throat.

"Everyone wanted me to live . . . ?"

"Yes."

She smiled evasively, nervously. Neil felt a sudden, unmistakable sense of authority here, at this table, with this young woman: as if he had come home.

"So they brought me back by magic," she said.

"No, not by magic. By the usual methods."

"Is there much change in people when they're brought back? I mean, people who are very sick, almost dead . . . can you see the change in them as they're brought back? As the life comes back into them?"

"Yes."

"It must be like magic," she said softly.

"There's no secret to it. It's mechanical—it's very easy, in fact, if the doctor has the equipment he needs. A stomach pump, fluids to be hooked up to the patient, a few shots of some chemical solution—and the person begins to look better, sometimes his color returns in five minutes and he begins breathing normally—It's mechanical. It's very wonderful to see," Neil said.

"It wasn't my fault that it happened," she said.

"No."

"You believe me, don't you? It wasn't my fault. It was an accident. It won't happen again. He got me on drugs, you know, Fred, he could handle them all right, he got me started and then he ran out. He said I was too emotional. He said I was sloppy and that I dragged him down, I spoiled his mood. Did he complain to you about me?"

She didn't seem to understand that he had not known her husband well; but he said, "No. Never."

"He could handle them. He only took light doses. It wasn't until he left that I got really bad; I felt sorry for myself, Jesus, I'm such a. . . . I'm a natural addict, it's in my blood. I knew that before the doctor explained it to me. It's in my blood to need things . . . like I used to smoke a lot, and when I was a kid I liked chocolate candy, and I always needed . . . well, I needed people, I mean friends, I needed a close girl friend all the time I was in school, I mean I really needed a girl friend, and then I . . . I needed a boy friend. . . . I need things. I can't control it. In the beginning we were both the same, I mean emotionally, Fred and me, we were both in love, and then it started to change . . . it was like a teeter-totter . . . when I needed him more he needed me less . . . and it kept going that way. He got me started on drugs. Then he ran out," she said bitterly.

Neil thought of her husband, the burly dissatisfied young man who had sat near him in that night-school class. He had answered the instructor's questions in an alert, falsely humble voice, though he told Neil and others of his contempt for the man. So much love, so much sorrow, expended on such a man? She had wanted to die because of him? His expression had always been petulant, expectant, as if he were passing judgment on everyone. Neil had not liked him. Yet he had wanted to be friends with him; for some reason he had wanted Shapley's approval.

"Your husband was a cheap bastard," Neil said.

She laughed. She laughed too quickly, too eagerly.

"You wouldn't say that to his face."

"I would."

She smiled so that her lips drew back from her teeth, an oddly exaggerated, starved smile, as if she were alone, grinning unconsciously. Neil wanted to stop her, to caution her—don't twist your face around like that, don't make yourself ugly! He squirmed with desire for her. He did not want her to destroy that desire.

"Why did you do it?" he said.

"Because there was no reason not to. Because I watched my hands getting it all ready and I was curious to see what my hands would do; to see if I was serious or just bluffing. . . . And you were there in the hospital, you were there, all the time . . . but you didn't come to see me, not once. No one came to see me, did you know that?"

"No."

"Why didn't you come? Because I looked so bad, I looked so sick?"

"I didn't think you would want to see me."

". . . when I saw myself in the mirror, the first time, I started to cry when I saw what I looked like . . . because then I knew I was in for it, the rest of my life behind that face. I am about a teaspoon of protoplasm somewhere inside my skull, and I can't get that protoplasm out and into any other skull. I'm stuck here. I even failed at destroying the protoplasm, because it's hard to kill. I discovered that. It must be a scientific fact that other people know, but I had to discover it myself. It's very hard to die."

"How are the nights now? Can you sleep?"

"No, but that's all right. I'm not taking anything now—you know —I promised the doctor I wouldn't. Did you know no one came to see me while I was in the hospital? That must be a record of some kind."

Neil thought of his nervousness, the strange despair of the last several weeks; the taunting voice in his head that told him he was *Neil Myer* and could not escape. A teaspoon of protoplasm? He wanted to tell her about his own fears. He wanted to confess to her. But he hesitated, as if confessing to this girl would contaminate him.

"Dr. Kohler—do you know him?—gave me a solemn lecture. It was based on God; it was about the ethical commitment to life, and all that," she said with an ironic smile. "Lots of references to his children; he has three children. I don't know what that had to do with me. He told me I had no right to destroy life, even my own. I had a duty to maintain life. What do you think about that?"

"I believe that," Neil said.

"My brother sends me money but he didn't come down to see me. He owns a farm up north, he's thirty-nine, almost doesn't seem like my brother; he's so much older than I am. He doesn't want me to visit him; maybe he's afraid I'll contaminate the children or something. Why do you look so surprised?"

It was the word *contaminate* that had surprised him. But he said, "That he would . . . wouldn't come to see you. What about your parents?"

She shrugged her shoulders.

He wanted to ease the tension in her face. "I live with my parents, still," he said. "In the same house I was born in. I'm trying to save money, trying to get started again in school. . . ."

There was a long silence. He saw that her gaze was evasive, that she was a little confused. Probably she was wondering about him. And, as he sensed her confusion, his own composure began to grow. He was a healthy young male, six foot three, with a strong, intelligent face and clear skin. Always his skin had been clear, never bumpy or marred. That had been good luck. He felt himself humble in his attractiveness, chiseled as a figure made of ice or stone, his eyes on the girl, watchful, cautious, shrewd. His mind spoke bluntly to him as if daring her to overhear: *You don't need this. You don't need her. You are Neil Myer, sitting here, Neil Myer here instead of somewhere else, that's all. You can't change anything.*

But he wanted to put his arms around her and press his face against her, he wanted to burrow himself into her. And then perhaps she would fold her arms over him, her small childish hands on the back of his head.

"He said . . . he said to be careful of living alone, of thinking too much," she went on slowly. "Of thinking about myself. He said I should avoid emotional things, getting involved emotionally. I laughed and said I was an addict that way, couldn't keep clean; other people were like narcotics to me: like Fred was. Then I got serious and said okay, I'd try."

She got to her feet, staggering a little, off-balance. She smiled shyly at Neil. "I got an idea: I'll make us something to eat. I'd like to do that."

"That would be too much trouble," Neil said.

"I'd like to do that, please, I haven't made anything to eat for a long time . . . I mean for someone else beside myself, a real supper. . . . All right?"

He was very hungry. Yet he hesitated, staring at her.

"I'll make supper for the two of us. Oh, I'd like to do that," she said excitedly. She opened one of the cupboard doors and stood on

her toes, peering inside. She was breathing quickly and Neil wondered if she was a little drugged, in spite of what she had said. She
was slight, thin, and yet now she seemed energetic, her face coloring
with pleasure. She fascinated him—there was something trim and
sullen about her body, even a tough attractiveness he had always
noticed in girls of a certain type, city girls, hanging around the
streets in the slum neighborhood near his own. They were boyish,
quick with insults, sometimes pretty and sometimes ugly, but always
quick, clever. With soiled, knowing faces. Sullen and joking. He
had noticed them for years, knowing himself superior to them. Yet
he had been attracted to them, as if wanting to submit himself impulsively to their judgment, their cynicism, the way he had courted
Paula's husband.

"Oh, this will be a party. This will be a private party," she said
eagerly. Here's a can that says 'fancy pink salmon,' how do you
like salmon? . . . I have four eggs left in the refrigerator, somewhere
in here in all this mess . . . and some bread . . . and for dessert
peaches, canned peaches . . . yes, there's a can back there. . . . Can
you reach it?"

Neil got up to reach into the cupboard. He handed her the can.
Then he put his opened hands on her, on either side of her body;
he felt the stark ribs beneath her thin dress and the rapid pounding
of her heart.

She drew away from him. "Don't touch me. Please," she said.

"I'm sorry."

"Sit down, please. I'll make us supper. I can make a nice supper
out of these things. . . ."

He sat down again, embarrassed. He wanted to apologize but he
dreaded the sound of his voice.

"It makes me confused to be touched. I'm not ready for that,"
she said.

And then she began to prepare supper: to perform. Her cheeks
glowed as she worked. Neil was reminded of the color that flowed
back into the faces of the near-dead at the hospital. She moved

slowly about the small, cramped kitchen, but very competently, as if performing a ritual she knew well. Her movements had a kind of rhythm that was very pleasing to watch. Himself, he sat quietly and watched her. He knew there was a humility in his sitting like this, a valuable humility, because she had rebuked him and he had accepted it. And this pleased her, his obedience. As she stirred the ingredients together into a large frying pan and held it over the burner, her face was closed, concentrated, warm. She might have been any woman, cooking in any kitchen, being watched by a man —Neil's mother, cooking for him or for his father, in a trance of peace, of certainty, because she was safe in this performance and could not be criticized.

III

They were silent as they ate. Neil was very hungry, surprised by his hunger. And she had been so efficient suddenly, absorbed in her role, so competent, she had surprised him as well. He had knocked on her door, a near-stranger, and she had opened the door; and he had walked through the doorway and sat down in the center of her life. Now she had prepared food for him. She had given him more of the meal than she had taken for herself. . . . Her face was warm, still abstract from the performance she had just completed.

"Do you like it? Are you sorry you stayed?" she asked, raising her eyes to his, still a little mocking.

He told her it was very good; he was embarrassed not to have spoken sooner. But she had forced him into a kind of awed silence.

He felt overlarge at the table and was afraid of knocking something over. She was so slight, so close to him; her intimacy was unsettling. He could not quite interpret it. He studied her, the sallow tone of her skin, the slight hollows beneath her eyes, the frizzy, curly brown hair, the deep fleshly pink of her lips, which were full and rounded. . . . He was strangely close to her and could not think if she was attractive or not, as if he were trying to assess his own face, or the face of one of his sisters. *You don't need her. You don't need any of this.* Suddenly he remembered how she had looked in that hospital room, seen from the door: a slight body, a face that seemed almost featureless, hair spilled against the glaring white pillow. Too much white in that room, white reflecting white. Paula Shapley, a young woman who had almost died; she had shot a solution of barbiturate powder into her vein, something Neil had never even heard of before, and she had almost died. But she had not died. They had brought her back to life there, ordinary and conscious again, in one of the hospital's hundreds of uniform beds.

He wanted to tell her about the young man who had been admitted that morning, partly paralyzed. A dying young man his own age. He wanted to tell her about his own alarming thoughts, the mocking voice in his head. But he hesitated.

They ate the canned peaches out of coffee cups, because she had no more clean dishes. The peaches were almost tasteless. Suddenly Neil had no more appetite; his mouth was dry.

"Do you know Dr. Kohler?" she asked.

"No. I mean yes, a little, not very well."

"When he talked to me I started to cry and embarrassed him. At first I laughed, then I started to cry. I said I didn't want to cry the rest of my life because it hurt so much. So he told me: *Pull yourself together.*"

Neil laughed sharply, in surprise. "*Pull yourself together . . . ?*"

She laughed with him, shrilly.

Then they fell silent and she rose to clear the table. Neil got to his feet at the same time. He embraced her, at first experimentally, his mind racing with questions and little taunting shouts: *Now what? Now what are you doing?* She pushed him away weakly.

"I don't—"

She tried to laugh again, in embarrassment.

"I don't want—"

He held her and pressed his face against hers, bending so that his cheek was flat against hers. He would say nothing. He would say nothing at all.

He felt the tension in her rise, and he caressed her, stroked her, all in silence. She could not draw away from him, not now. He sensed the time for that had passed and that now she was surprised, baffled by its passing, not having recognized it. Not quite having recognized it. As he embraced her he saw in his mind's eye the boy admitted for tests, so pale and doped-up, and the image faded to Paula herself, one body among many. Then he saw nothing at all.

He urged her into the other room, half-walking with her, half-carrying her. She moved along with him, unresisting. She was very warm. The bedroom was darkened but they left the door to the kitchen open; Neil was aware of closeness, clutter, a narrow room with a window near the bed. He felt a draft on the back of his neck.

Her flesh resisted him, then gave in. He sank deeply into her.

Then he became aware of himself again, the draft from the window, the girl's damp, heated flesh, his own breathing. The room was chilly. *What are you doing here, what do you want?* He could sense her mind racing, beating like his own. The space between them was suddenly cold.

After a short while she pushed herself up from the bed. She picked up her dress from the floor. There was something defiant in the way she put back on the same dress she'd been wearing, as if canceling him out; she tugged it down impatiently over her head. Turned from him, still silent, she brushed her hair back from her face in brief hurried gestures.

"You can leave now," she said.

He stared at her back. Stooping to get his own clothes, he stared at her rigid back. She had folded her arms tightly across her chest again, still turned from him.

"Get out," she said in a flat, toneless voice.

"Why—What do you—" he began.

He dressed quickly, watching her. She would not look at him. And he would not go over to her, not like this.

"Why are you angry?" he asked.

He was careful to keep his voice neutral, innocent.

"You can leave now. Please. It's all right to leave,"she said. Her voice was toneless.

He felt a dark glow deep in his stomach, an echo of the sensation he had felt a few minutes before, sinking himself into this girl. It came back to him strongly. In his mind this same glow unfolded, a certainty about something, a sense of peace. He did not quite understand it. His face was open, questioning, innocent, as he waited for her to look at him. He would let her speak, he would not touch her. He watched her as if obedient to her, staying where he was.

"Get the hell out," she said.

"You won't ... won't do anything ...?"

"Just get out."

He did not move at once, as if testing her. Then, obeying her, obeying that harsh flat voice, he went into the kitchen. The air was warmer. The odor of food was warm and pleasant.

"Just get the hell out and don't come back," she said.

She stood in the doorway to the bedroom, hugging herself, her shoulders raised. Everything about her was stiff, ugly. Her face had become rigid.

"I can take care of myself," she said. "Don't worry. Don't worry about me."

Again he felt that surge of dark, abrupt joy. He groped for the doorknob, watching her cautiously. She was forcing him out of here, out into the corridor—very well, then, he would obey her, he would leave! His own expression was composed, grave. He said, "You won't do anything to yourself ...? You promise you...."

"Get out," she said.

He left. Going down the stairs he listened for the slam of her door, but wasn't sure if he heard it or not.

The door had opened to admit him, and now it had closed.

Out on the street he felt a smile distort his face. His mind played back what he had said, lightly and mockingly: *You won't do anything to yourself, you won't do anything? Anything? You won't do anything?* He did not understand his exhilaration. Everything had changed: the world itself had changed. He felt very free, very pleased. "All right, then, I will get out, I won't worry about you, all right," he murmured, as if giving voice to a certain rhythm in his head, "all right, Paula, the hell with you." It was the first time he had spoken her name out loud: it was an abrupt, pleasing fact, like the closing of that door.

A Girl at the Edge of the Ocean

One dark April afternoon a girl and her aunt were driving toward the ocean. The girl, Tessa, sat with her trench coat bunched up around her, staring out the windshield. She was nineteen. Her face had the pinched, distracted look of a convalescent, the intensity that seems to agitate the muscles around the eyes while the eyes themselves are slightly out of focus, baffled. From time to time she wiped at her nose with the back of her hand.

"Are you catching a cold, Tessa?" her aunt said.

"What? Oh, no."

She turned to smile nervously at her aunt. It was a mistake to alarm other people, these adults who loved her so much. This aunt, Caroline Guttmann, was Tessa's favorite aunt, the woman she admired most, the woman she had wanted to grow into. . . . "I didn't mean to do it," Tessa said, remembering now that she had been brushing at her nose for miles. She was ashamed. "I didn't realize I was doing it."

"That's all right, Tessa."

"I mean, I must look like such a pig. . . ."

"That's all right."

Packing her suitcase that morning, putting her things in one by one, with great care, Tessa had had the giddy sensation of putting her life into a small leather container, a leather coffin. But she had finished the job. She had pressed the top down and snapped it shut. Now, many hours later, she and Caroline were approaching the family house on the ocean, and she felt a sharp, perplexed curiosity about what was going to happen to her—it would be strange to live in this house out of season. It would be mysterious to see the beach deserted, to hang up her familiar clothes in the closet of her room, everything familiar and yet coldly curious, out of place.

Outside, the landscape was misty, dreamlike, as if lazily imagined. Most of the trees were stunted. Tessa felt they had driven a great distance and that it would be difficult for anyone to get to her now. If anyone came up from the city for a weekend this early in the year, Tessa's aunt would keep them away. *Tessa is up here for a rest,* Caroline would explain.

"It's too bad your father wants the telephone connected," Caroline said. "But I suppose he's right."

Now they could see the house. It was near the beach, yet on a rise of scrubby, bleached land, some distance from the houses on either side. Along this stretch of ocean, for several miles, all the summer homes were large, solid, private, and quite expensive. In the dim wet air of April the house looked black and battered. A target for something. Tessa gathered her trench coat up around her, shivering.

"How do you feel, Tessa?"

"Fine."

"As soon as we get in we'll fix up your room for you. You can lie down."

"That would be nice," Tessa said.

She smiled at her aunt gratefully, then hesitated—perhaps it was wrong to smile so much.

It was very windy when they got out. The cold went through Tessa, weakening her. Yet she felt a sense of pride, looking up at the big shingled house—this house belonged to her family, only to her family. No one else had a right to it. In other parts of the world, in other parts of the world only a few hours away, people lived together, cramped together, lying and sleeping and eating together, their faces and voices getting all mixed up, ugly and hopeless, driving them mad . . . but out here, on the ocean, on this lonely strip of beach, she and her aunt would be alone for weeks. The wind whipped her hair and she stared from the house to the ocean and to the sky. Late winter, early spring. It grew warm slowly this far north. . . . Something ran across the path in front of her, a cat, a stray blond cat. "Oh, what was that?" she cried.

"Just a cat," Caroline said.

Inside, the house was cold. "I'd better get this place warmed up," Caroline said. Tessa, still shaky from the cat, moved out of her aunt's way. She felt like a guest here. Caroline snapped on the lights; everything became clear and familiar, very quiet. "Well, here we are," Caroline said. She smiled at Tessa. She wore a dark blue trench coat and tweed slacks. Shorter than Tessa, not so thin as Tessa, she had a deft, urgent precision to her; even her hair, pulled back and knotted into a large, heavy, handsome knot, looked precise.

She was the widow of Conrad Guttmann, a minor Presidential aide. The legend was that they had been very happy together—so Tessa believed. She wanted to believe it. . . . But did that mean, perhaps, that she could not possibly believe it?

"I'm so happy to be here . . . that you could come here with me. . . ." Tessa stammered.

Caroline waved this aside. She had begun to put groceries away. She was busy, always busy; Tessa, feeling like a child, wandered over to the kitchen window. The ocean was furious, yes. She had not remembered it quite like that. She wondered if the pounding of the ocean would work its way into the pounding of her heart, her head. Would it help her sleep? Or would it keep her awake?

Tessa went out to get her suitcase. It had started to rain and she was afraid of slipping on the steps and cutting herself. But nothing happened. She dragged the suitcase back into the kitchen. "Tessa, is that too heavy for you?" Caroline asked, staring at her. "No, not at all," Tessa said. The suitcase was heavier than she remembered, but she managed to get it upstairs to her room.

Her room. The bed, the mattress. The cold bedsprings. She pulled the mattress back into place and steeled herself to see something ugly. . . . Nothing. She opened the suitcase. Right on top lay her green bedroom slippers, sole to sole, pressed together.

She went downstairs to help her aunt. Putting cans away, straining to reach up into the cupboards, she could not remember how old she was—ten years old? Six? Or nineteen? Nineteen was the oldest age she could remember, it was a limit to her imagination, an end; she must be nineteen. "Now we can make up your bed," Caroline said. "No, I can do it myself. I'll do it myself," said Tessa. The house was warming slowly, rays of warmth were radiating from the ceiling, from hidden panels in the ceiling. . . . Tessa felt as if the sun were shining upon her, mysteriously, secretly.

"Do you like it here? I think it's beautiful," Caroline said.

"Oh, yes. It's beautiful," said Tessa.

Her aunt carried another suitcase upstairs, and Tessa, lingering in the kitchen, went to her own purse, which lay on the kitchen table. It was a large, crudely-shaped purse of dark leather. In it Tessa carried a jumble of things. She picked with her fingers at the torn lining, pulling gently so that it would not tear any further, and peered inside. Nothing. With her fingertips she explored that secret pocket . . . nothing. . . . Of course, nothing.

She went upstairs and she and Caroline made up her bed. She felt oddly buoyant now, like her aunt. Perhaps she was imitating her aunt. "This has always been one of my favorite places in all of the world," Caroline said. Her emerald ring flashed like an exclamation point. Tessa wondered at her aunt's coolness, her self-containment. If she had suffered, if she suffered still, no one knew. . . . Tessa wanted to be a woman like that, a female like that. Her body would be slim, contained, a dancer's body. She would not stumble, she would not damage herself . . . no scars on her face, no yearning inside her face, just the smooth, hard, cool complexion of a woman who needs no one.

"Now, why don't you lie down? I'll make us some dinner," Caroline said.

She lay down. She was alone. In her slacks and sweater, flat on her back, she felt immediately for her ribs, her pelvic bones—prominent bones, like marks of identification. Her teeth too, set hard into her jaw, would be another mark of identification. She sat up, alarmed. This was no good. Thoughts scrambled in her head, made her eyes water . . . she knew that if she tried to read something now she'd be unable to read, the words would jump all over the page . . . she wouldn't be able to make out the numbers on dollar bills. . . .

She forced herself to lie down again. The room was freezing, but such air was good, it cleared the senses. She stared at the ceiling. Few girls had a room like this. And at home, outside Boston, she had another room, a better room. She lived in these rooms, inside their walls, and could lie down at any time on "her" bed, closing her eyes, sleeping, while the house expanded about her, any house her father might own, and she might feel how completely it protected her, like a fortress.

She jumped up and ran to the window.

The ocean was gray, many shades of gray, very wild. *That is our ocean*, Tessa thought suddenly. The beach was deserted and yet cluttered: debris had been washed up onto the sand—the bodies of dead things, branches of trees, boards. Tessa's eyes watered. Something moved farther down the beach, but she couldn't make it out.

A piece of paper . . . ? A stiffened, muddy piece of paper suddenly lifting itself, as if to catch her eye . . . ? She stared. If someone appeared on the beach, a man, what would she do?

No, I am indestructible, she thought.

The wind blew wildly about the house during dinner. Tessa ate slowly, watching herself. She wanted to please her aunt. She watched her hands, her fork lifting food to her mouth, moving slowly. "The telephone will be connected tomorrow," Caroline said. In her voice was a note of apology that Tessa seemed not to notice.

Tessa went to bed early. She cleaned her face with cold cream. Her toilet things were arranged on the bare shelf in her bathroom, looking new and out of place. It was strange that it was not summer, and yet her things were here in this bathroom, on that slightly warped shelf. She took a single sleeping tablet and went to bed, safe with the tablet inside her. The room was both dark and light. The wind seemed to make shadows. Tessa did not think about her father. She did not think about her mother. She did not think about her room back home, or about her other rooms, those many other rooms in which she had lain, like this, flat on her back. She did not think about the telephone that would be hooked up tomorrow. That was tomorrow. She did not think about . . . about Ginger Dolly . . . and suddenly the words shaped themselves in her skull, *Ginger Dolly . . . Dolly Ginger . . .* that scarecrow of a girl, her shrill laugh and her shrill crazy face. . . .

She made her skull empty. Everything flowed out.

She did not think of. . . .

She did not think of. . . .

She woke up, suddenly. It felt very late. She remembered at once that they were at the shore, she and her aunt, alone. No panic. Still, her heart was pounding dangerously. The tablet had worn off. *Goddam it,* she thought, sickened by the darkness she had to confront. *Son of a bitch. Bastard. Shit.* She lay without moving, feeling the anger rise and subside in her, feeling herself betrayed. She had told that bastard Dr. Stuckey these pills weren't good enough.

Wide awake, hours before dawn . . . how was she to get through these hours? Her mind was very sharp. After a sleeping pill her mind was always very sharp and she hated this, this alertness, it was not truly herself. She got up and went barefoot to the window. Her beach. Her ocean. The waves moved without stopping in the night, even while she slept, while she slept here or back home, miles away, safe from the ocean. And the beach was always deserted, out of her sight, safe from her sight . . . she stared boldly at it, as if prepared now to see someone down there, unafraid.

Nothing on the beach.

She lay down carefully on the bed. Her body was a vessel containing her life, her conscious self: she had to lie down carefully. Once flat on her back, she must hold herself in tension, waiting to sleep. But perhaps she would not sleep. Perhaps she would lie awake for the rest of the night. Trying to keep down panic, she lay carefully, feeling the warm blood beating in her arms and legs, soothing her, murmuring her name, *Tessa Hunt*, which was an incantation that would keep out of her mind other names she must not recall . . . *Ginger Dolly . . . Peter V. . . .* She opened her eyes. Was that a noise on the beach? It was more than the wail of the wind, it was something stubborn and distinct, a human voice. . . . Didn't it call out *Tessa?*

But she would not listen.

In the hospital they had fed her with needles and tubes. Her stomach was pumped out once a day and filled up the next. Green fluid. Oh, the juice of plants had brought her here again, to her ocean, her private ocean and her private life, the memory of her childhood indestructible within the walls of this room. Down there the waves were moving like shadows, shadows made solid. She did not understand the ocean. She did not listen to it because she might hear, instead, a voice calling out to her, stubborn and sly, lifting over the waves—*Tessa, Tessa!* Her father had kept saying, "You can go to the ocean with Caroline! You can rest! Everything is all right, already everything is forgotten! To the ocean with your aunt

—you love the ocean—remember?" Filled with stinging fluid, she had nodded at him, loving him, loving them all, feeling love fill her up like green fluid or like the poisonous colorless fluid of impregnation, a magic that had not worked upon her. Yes, she loved her father. She had always loved him. Her mother, evil-eyed with headaches, bossy and too pretty to be this girl's mother, her mother was another case, don't ask Tessa about her mother yet. . . . Yes, she loved them all. And the ocean, which was their gift to her, this house a gift, everything in the world a gift from parents to their children, to keep them safe.

Out on the beach a voice lifted morosely, sullenly: *Tessa.* . . .

She did not get up to look because she knew no one was there. But she could not sleep; she lay awake until dawn, and energy built up in her, panic and energy. When she heard Caroline in the bathroom next door she jumped out of bed. Her head ached with excitement.

She took a cold shower. She dressed. Her movements were rapid and clumsy, she might have been dressing at the age of six, anxious to get outside in the sun. There was no sun this morning. Anxious to get out in the ocean then, to wade in the stinging ocean. . . . But no wading today, the ocean was too cold. Even so, nothing could slow her down. She struggled with zippers, buttons, ran her fingers through her hair and stared at the face in the mirror, having no time to look at it. Eat. She must eat a meal called breakfast. And then out, out for a long walk, maybe she could run along the ocean. . . .

Hurrying downstairs, barefoot, she stumbled at the bottom of the stairs and caught herself on the railing. Caroline was in the kitchen making coffee. "Why are you in such a hurry, Tessa?" she said gently.

"I'd like to go outside."

"Let me make you some breakfast. Would you like an egg?"

Tessa's stomach seemed to come loose, jerking with revulsion. "Thank you, no," Tessa said politely. On the tile floor her toes curled warmly, yet she suspected the floor was probably cold. "I don't want to trouble you. I'd like to go out for a walk, that's all."

"It's drizzling outside."

"Oh, I like weather like this, I like this part of the world," Tessa said happily. She could not sit down. "Everything is misty here, things don't shoot out at you and hit you in the eye by surprise. Everything is prepared. The ocean is the same for miles. No people, no towns. All the houses are boarded up for the winter. There's no one here except us. Is someone coming to hook up the telephone? I'd like to walk out there, I'd like to run . . . I could run for miles. . . . I feel as if I could run for miles this morning. . . ."

"You must have slept well last night."

"Yes."

"You look a little tired, dear."

Suddenly she was tired, yes. But she hated these adults with their observations, seemingly so casual, running her through. She continued pacing the kitchen, though her strength was flowing out of her second by second and her feet began to feel cold. "No, I want to go out. I need to go out," she said. Even her blood felt distant to her now.

"Tessa, sit down. I'll make you some oatmeal."

As if a hand were pressing down on her shoulder, she sat. Caroline boiled oatmeal for her. The smell of oatmeal filled the kitchen. Tessa felt her mind ready to somersault backward, she felt her eyes preparing to go out of focus. No, it would not happen. She was indestructible. Then, rubbing at her eyes, she saw a figure pass before one of the kitchen windows. . . . When she looked again, the figure was gone.

Should she cry out to her aunt, *He's out there, he's come to get me?*

But her panic did not get loose. If he had come for her, Peter V. with his love, how could she resist? She would slip outside to him. They would run along the beach together; how could she resist? She watched the window but saw no figure again. Her head ached. Her face was sore, the very roots of her hair sore. There was no one outside. If Peter V. did come for her she would call the police, as they had instructed her. It was an easy matter to call the police. It was her duty and she would call them.

She poured milk and sugar onto her oatmeal, fascinated with its sweet babyish smell. Caroline poured coffee for her. In the morning light Caroline's face was kindly, but marred with wrinkles. It was a human face, aging. A man had loved that face, had rubbed his own against it for twenty years, and now he was dead; had died. And now what? A woman abandoned, meticulous at pouring out coffee for her niece, her trim body enveloped in an expensive woolen robe. . . .

The figure appeared again, suddenly. Its shadow grew black at the kitchen door. Tessa jumped up from the table, screaming.

"Tessa, what?" cried her aunt.

Someone knocked at the door. It was the telephone lineman.

Caroline hurried to him. Tessa, trembling, had bumped into the stove and her thigh pounded with pain. She closed her eyes and waited for Caroline to come back. She thought of nothing. She thought *pain: green. Green: lawn. Lawn: home. Home: home. Home: home.* She shook her head angrily to get off that. *Home!* What next, wasn't there anything next? Front door. Front steps. The newspaper. Unfolded newspaper: the front page. But the front page was blank because she must not see any papers, not any local papers.

. . . *An unidentified mulatto girl of about sixteen known only as Ginger Dolly . . . no family . . . no fixed address . . . known to be a drug-user . . . found executed "gangland" style . . . forced to her knees and shot in the back of the head. . . .*

Caroline returned. "I'm sorry he upset you," she said.

Tessa sat and finished her oatmeal obediently. She poured more milk onto it. Tiny bits of oatmeal floated in the milk. As she swallowed each mouthful she felt it congeal inside her body, thickening, growing hard and heavy and hot in her stomach. Perhaps it would harden into rock there. Perhaps she would become petrified. A woman had shot into her own eyeballs, so the story went, and the eyeballs had turned hard, to stone, but maybe that was just a scare-story. Who the hell made up such lies? Tessa wanted to laugh, thinking of all the lies made up to scare her.

"When your father telephones, do you want me to speak to him?"

"No, I can handle it. Thank you."

"I'd be glad to. . . ."

They sat for a while in silence. Tessa thought it was a mistake this woman was not her mother—why not? Instead of that other one. Why not Caroline? Why were things determined so abruptly and so permanently, but without sense? "Do you think," Tessa said slowly, "there are some things no one can ever forget?"

"What do you mean?"

"Just a few things in a lifetime . . . ? Once I saw a certain picture in a book, I won't say what the picture was, except that it was in a nursing textbook at college, my roommate's book . . . it was a . . . it was a picture of a . . . a womb, I think, a womb where hair had grown wild, I don't know why . . . hair, hairs . . . frizzy hairs grown wild . . . I can't forget that, I will have to die before I can forget it . . . frizzy dark hairs in a woman's womb . . . the picture, the photo-graph was taken I don't know how . . . I kept staring at the picture . . . I would look at it when my roommate was gone . . . I stared at it . . . I kept staring at it. . . ."

"Tessa, don't frighten yourself."

"And, and . . . and this boy I knew, this Peter V. . . ."

"I don't think we should talk about this," Caroline said.

She was chaste and cool, with her kindly aging face; she was eas-ing the door shut in Tessa's face.

"I know. You're right. I won't talk about it," Tessa said. She looked down at her hands. "But I'm afraid my father will say some-thing I can't forget. I can hear him talking to me when he's not saying anything, I can hear his voice, I know what he's saying. . . . I feel that I'm filling up with things I won't be able to forget. For years I lived without remembering anything, it didn't stick in me, but now I seem to be sucking in hooks, fishhooks . . . everything catches in me. . . . I remember my mother crying once, about a year ago. She was very angry. She was angry and hysterical, her face was streaked with tears and she looked ugly . . . she kept saying *I don't love anyone! Not anyone!* Someone told me, a girl friend, that my mother had broken up with some man. Everybody knew about it, her and that man, except me, I guess . . . but she'd broken up with him, she'd told him to go to hell for no reason . . . because she didn't love him, she didn't want to bother with him, she didn't love him or anyone, it was too much trouble . . . it was something that struck me as true, hearing her say it . . . there was this pretty woman, almost a beautiful woman, screaming at me because she couldn't love anyone . . . I understood her. I'll never forget that."

Caroline looked embarrassed. "Your mother is a strange person."

"She always tells the truth. I can depend upon her," Tessa said slowly. "And there are other things I can't forget . . . certain shapes, geometrical shapes that keep changing. And colors. They get burned into your eye, deep into your mind . . . like the hairs growing in that womb, inside a woman's body . . . I wonder how she began to feel them, what it was like. . . . It must have been like a strange baby growing inside her, all those frizzy crinkly hairs . . . and my mother screaming like that, it's inside me . . . and Peter V., what he did to me. . . ."

The telephone rang.

"Would you like me to answer it?" Caroline said.

"Thank you, I'll be all right," Tessa said. She picked up the telephone and immediately knew that it was Peter V. contacting her, as he had promised. But when he spoke it was in another, deeper voice—her father's voice.

"Tessa? Hello. Can you hear me?"

"Very well. I can hear you perfectly."

"I'm at Kennedy Airport. I've been calling you every ten minutes, honey, and I never thought I'd get through—how is it up there?— it's pretty foggy down here."

"It's nice here."

"How are you, honey? You sound good."

"I'm fine. Wonderful."

"And Caroline?"

"Fine."

"Did you have breakfast yet?"

"Yes, we just finished. We're going to go for a walk now."

"Did you sleep well? Are you all right?"

"Yes, fine."

"Make sure you get plenty of rest. I'm flying to Montreal, then to Chicago. It's a crazy week!" He sounded overloud and cheerful. Tessa grinned into the receiver. "Bundle up real warm, honey! Don't catch cold. Sleep a lot. How's your aunt, doing okay? How is the old place? I wish to hell I could join you. . . ."

"Everything is fine."

"You're sure you feel all right?"

"Yes."

Silence. She heard him shouting at her, silently, *You little whore —why should your mother speak to you, why? Why should anyone speak to you?*

"And how is the ocean, sweetheart? How's the beach—need cleaning up?"

"A little. We're going out now for a walk."

"I wish I could join you . . . this week is really hectic . . . I'm flying to Montreal and then to Chicago and probably out to Los Angeles if all goes well. . . . It's pretty foggy here, must be bad there too, eh?"

"It's clearing up. The sun is coming out."

"What?"

"The sun is coming out."

"Yes, well, keep warm—take care of yourself—Could I speak to your aunt?"

"Good-by, Father."

She handed the receiver to Caroline.

That was finished. From now on the day would disintegrate into mild, easy bits, no threat. She smiled. It was true the sky was clearing up; the sun was coming out. She would go for a walk barefoot. She opened the door and went out onto the porch, feeling the splintery wood beneath her feet. Good, it was like summer. Like childhood. Behind her Caroline spoke quietly and Tessa's attention, as if released, flew at once to the farthest point of the ocean—a stormy dark-blue sky, bunched clouds like fists. And the beach was dirty, yes. Debris lay everywhere as if thrown down in rage.

She followed the path down to the beach. Around her, everywhere, birds screamed. She was not welcome here. She smiled to herself, thinking of the innocence of sand and scrubby grass, how the forms of nature remained innocent, never aging. Year after year she had run along this path, barefoot, and the form that had been herself had passed away; she walked now in another form, which was a sign of what she was now. To live out this form, to bring it to its conclusion, she had to keep going, she had no access to the past, nothing could help. The form of her skeleton was spare and anxious on this chilly April morning.

The stray cat approached her. It made a mewing, questioning sound, yet it remained cautious—only hunger encouraged it—there was something ugly, wicked, uncanny about the cat's bony head and clear, staring eyes, its prominent ribs. "Kitty, here kitty," Tessa said, reaching out toward it. "Kitty, be friends . . . ?" Absurdly, she was afraid of the cat. Yet she wanted it to come to her, she wanted to stroke its shabby blond fur. "Are you hungry, kitty? What do you want?"

The cat backed up, distrustful of her hand. "I'll feed you. I'll give you something to eat and we'll be friends," Tessa said. But the cat turned and ran around the corner of the house. *I must remember to feed the cat,* Tessa thought, fearful of forgetting and already forgetting, coming to a stop. It was a mistake to have come outside without shoes. She was shivering. The wind from the ocean was hard, harsh. She hugged herself and looked up and down the beach, squinting in the sun. Such sunlight might be bad for her. Glaring light might produce hallucinations. Mirages? Miracles? She turned from side to side, too tired to move her legs, twisting her waist to look up and down the bright, pale beach, looking for a sign.

No one.

It he were coming for her as he had promised, why had he not come? Three weeks in the hospital, two weeks at home. Lying on her back. Sleeping, waking, living in the body of Tessa Hunt, unable to get out of it. She had strained to get out of it, to flow into someone else—into her aunt, even into her mother, into any female whose flesh hadn't been brought to the breaking point as hers had.

But now she was not in love: she was beyond that.

Her aunt joined her. "Tessa, why are you barefoot?" She looked genuinely startled. "Honey, don't you know it's cold? Shouldn't you go back and put on some shoes?"

"I'm sorry. I didn't think," Tessa said, ashamed. "I guess I'm trying to rush the season."

She hurried back to the house. It was good to be told what to do. Go back, put on some shoes. She hurried up to her room and some accident of shadow caught her eye—she turned and faced a sunny white wall, a blank wall. Nothing.

"Is there anyone up here?" she called out, trembling.

She crossed the hall and looked in her aunt's room. Of course, the bed was made. The window was open a few inches, chastely. A neat, handsome room, an ordered life. Tessa caught sight of her own wasted body in a mirror and grinned at herself.

"No, there is nobody in this house," she said aloud.

She wandered back into her room. Why was she up here? . . . was she supposed to get something? Down on the beach her aunt was strolling, enjoying the sunlight. Tessa spied on her. The sky was an enormous fist except for where the sun had boiled through. Really, the sky was ugly, frightening, ponderous. Its colors were the colors of bruises on women's thighs—dark blue, greenish blue, a rotten orangish yellow.

Tessa stared at the figure on the beach and saw clearly that it was not her aunt but a man—a young man—strolling casually along the beach as if owning it.

Her first vision of Peter V.: strolling along a sidewalk. In late summer, Peter V. with his chestnut-red hair bouncing about his head, his fuzzy neck, his round, hard, clever face. He wore a light green shirt open at the neck, showing his fuzzy chest. He wore white trousers, always clean. *My name is Peter V.*, an announcement that was musical to her, fatal. Peter V. between her and the sunlight. Laughing at him, aware of the soft roll of fat about his stomach, aware of his stylish, shrill, overdecorated absurdity, yet she felt him step between her and the sunlight, her laughter faded, she forgot herself. Peter on the sidewalk, bouncing in the open air. Peter slipping something into her pocket, a gift from him. Peter rubbing his tongue along the back of her neck, murmuring *I'm going to be a famous man. Be famous with me.* Tessa, standing at the window, felt Peter's arms around her, his tongue prodding her, his breath raising her skin in tiny gritty bumps. . . .

She had to lie down. She was shaking. Better to lie down, lie still.

She must have fallen asleep. Caroline called her gently, it seemed to be much later in the day. Tessa was lying flat on her sore backbone. She began to cry. "I'll never get well," she said.

The next morning her father called again. They had the same conversation, except that now her father was in Montreal, at the Queen Elizabeth Hotel, and he was flying in two days to Chicago. Afterward, Tessa and Caroline went out for groceries. The day was warm but overcast. While Caroline drove, Tessa kept hearing her father's voice, the voice beneath the telephone voice, crying clearly *Why didn't you die! Why are you back in three dimensions with the rest of us!*

They took some time shopping, and back at the house they took time putting things away. They talked about food. It was good to talk about these things. Basics of life. Then, when everything was put away, they went outside for a walk. This time Tessa wore shoes and a scarf around her head. The walk did her good. When she returned to the house it was time for her nap. She slept. When she got up it was time for her bath, a before-supper bath, and while she ran the water she began to hear music, rising up through the water, inside its splashing. This did not alarm her. She lay in the hot water, resting, thinking of the form of *Tessa* and that other, elusive form of *Peter V.*, and of how those two forms, now so distant, had come together in love, desperate with the need of love, their faces and hair entangled, their teeth grinding together.

The water grew cold. She stepped out of the tub unsteadily.

When she came downstairs, feeling a little feverish, she discovered that the music was real—her aunt was listening to the radio. Tessa sat and leafed through old magazines, *Newsweek* and *Fortune* and *Reader's Digest*, taking them from a heap by the fireplace. The furniture in this room was comfortable, splotched red and yellow, very cheerful. The cheerfulness grew heavy. It hung down from the windows—yellow drapes—it hung down from above the big stone fireplace, an abstract painting in red and gold. Tessa's mother had picked all this out one humid afternoon, having nothing else to do. She redecorated both houses often, every two or three years.

Tessa tried to concentrate on the magazine in her lap. She could not read well. She seemed to be reading a feature story about a composer, a famous man who lived with eight elegant Borzoi dogs, his dark hair combed down brutally onto his forehead in thin damp strands, his eyes dark, brutal, vivid, mad, and, behind him, over his gigantic fireplace, an abstract painting in bright colors. Red and gold. *Music that breaks through the pores of the skin . . .* he wanted to compose such music, evidently . . . *music that exhausts the body. . . .*

It was difficult for her to read. Her mind broke up into little spangles of light. One evening she had stood between Peter V. and another man, a man with hair combed down onto his forehead, and Peter V. had reached out to push her gently forward toward this man, and she had been unable to move her feet and, except for the

man's embrace, she would have fallen. *He can love you in my name,*
Peter V. had said on his way out in a hurry; *he can take my place.*
Remember me, love me, don't think evil of me! But that time he
had returned. It was the next time he did not return. She lay on a
mattress somewhere, in a room, for several days . . . sweat had con-
gealed on her face and body, even in the lashes of her eyes . . . she
had soiled herself, the tops of her legs were raw with filth, bright
red, on fire. . . .

She turned the page and looked at an advertisement for Steuben
glassware.

"Tomorrow we'll have to get the camera out," Caroline said.

"Yes, I forgot all about it," said Tessa.

They worked together in the kitchen, experimenting with a
chicken dish. Chicken with curry sauce. Shredded coconut sprinkled on top. Tessa liked the smell of curry sauce, so she said. They
made the dish, they ate it, they rinsed the dishes afterward and put
them in the dishwasher.

Tessa looked out the window and saw a figure appear in the distance, where the shoreline bent outward from a clump of patchy
trees. She said nothing to her aunt. The figure approached the
ocean, walking slowly. It stopped as if to pick up something from
the beach. But Tessa could not see who it was, a man or a woman
wearing slacks, or a child . . . she shaded her eyes, waiting, a girl
waiting on the edge of the ocean, in silence. It was nearly sundown;
the sunlight broke up into sordid, painful slivers, hurting her eyes.
The figure in the distance seemed to glow about its edges, as if light
were illuminating it from behind. *Come and touch me, touch me*
again. But the figure did not heed Tessa; it disappeared.

Evening. Another day of sunlight completed.

In the morning, just before breakfast, the telephone rang. Everything was timed. Tessa had been leafing through a handsome,
glossy magazine, pausing to admire the advertisements: *An ice*
bucket of the King Francis Collection, heavy silverplate . . . a Nor-
wegian blue fox coat . . . a pulsar stainless steel time computer

(touch the button and tell the time) . . . *a crystal frog with 18-karat gold crown, again by Steuben.* How lovely! Tessa accepted the receiver and began to speak to whoever was at the other end, easily, without alarm, happily. How lovely it all was, yes, this was Tessa speaking and she was keeping warm and the day was lovely, no not foggy, she was sleeping well every night . . . yes, yes. . . . Would he like to speak to Aunt Caroline?

Now she was free. She put on a sweater and hurried outside. Fresh bright air. Too bright. She squinted; couldn't see the road, which was hidden from the cottage. Stunted, humped-over trees . . . bushes with the look of aged human beings, everything listening for her footsteps, listening. The road was far away. If Peter V. drove up to the mailbox she would not even see him. If he drove up the lane . . . ? She would telephone the police. She was not going to think of his fingers closing about her face, so loving, so gentle, but hinting at their power to squeeze her face out of shape . . . not going to think of his matted eyelashes, his curly hair, the golden-red hairs growing out of his ears with such comic health. Singing, muttering to himself. He came alive like music, but it was both sly and percussive. Ginger Dolly had once crawled up into his lap and tried to press her eyeballs against his, eyeball against eyeball, giggling. But that was past. Giggling. If he arrived she would telephone the local police, would slip her finger into the proper dial hole and dial, dial. . . .

She inspected her fingers suddenly. Should the time come, how would her fingers operate? If she stuck only one finger in the hole it might snap off. What then? She must remember to stick two fingers in.

She walked along the beach. Glancing back at the house she was surprised at how large and empty it looked. It was a fact that the world was underpopulated; nothing existed. Silence. Only the wind and the gulls, which were not human though they eyed her like human beings, curious and knowing. *Tessa is getting lots of rest, this vacation is good for her,* Caroline was saying in the kitchen.

Tessa could hear her this far away, or she imagined that she could hear her. Good. It was true: she was getting lots of rest.

Her body was floating in a glow of sunlight. Every cell of her body seemed to sparkle, well rested, healthy. She saw the blond cat approaching her, stepping delicately along the sand. It ran toward her, then hesitated. "Here, kitty," Tessa said, bending down. "Don't you want to be friends? I'll take you in the house and feed you." The cat stared at her. Tessa took a step toward it and it cringed, hissing. "No, be friends. Please be friends," Tessa pleaded. The cat's tail twitched. Moving suddenly, Tessa snatched the cat up in her arms. It began to fight at once. It snarled and clawed at her, raking her wrists, the backs of her hands, digging into her sweater. She screamed. "Stop it! Stop!" The cat squirmed viciously in her arms, a sudden slash across her cheek exploded with pain, yet she could not release the cat—she screamed at it, the two of them struggled together and would not give up, screaming—until finally the cat leaped away. Tessa stood in the sunlight, looking down at herself. Blood ran from a dozen scratches on her arms and the backs of her hands, a deep slash ran diagonally across her left thigh, through the material of her slacks, blood welled up there and on her face; how could she stop it? She felt something filling up her eyes, ruining her eyesight. She could not see. She stood there, waiting, while her eyes filled up hotly with this mysterious fluid. Everything was silent.

Unpublished Fragments

Here is a northerly city, where the sun sets at three-fifteen. Some of us live here. I drifted to the window (I was in X's apartment) and stared out at the streams of traffic down below. X was calling out to me, halfshouting from the bedroom; talking about the cruelty of one of his son's teachers, who had forced a seven-year-old boy—not X's son—to stand in front of his classroom with his trousers down around his ankles for half an hour, punishment for "saying bad things. . . ." I looked out at the darkening sky and thought for a moment that it was almost night, then I remembered that it was only a few minutes after three o'clock.

What do you do in such a world? You think. You drift to the window and stare down at the streams of traffic as they slow, slowing as you watch, slowing as if hardening, coming to an impatient rest. It takes too much effort to imagine the people who drive each automobile, because there are so many automobiles. The buses creep by, overloaded. Too many people. People crowded on top of people. And then it darkens as they stare helplessly ahead, trying to see past one another to where the traffic is blocked, because it must be blocked . . . they cannot believe that this is only normal traffic. Yes, it darkens as you watch them, it darkens gently, soothingly, the sun withdrawing behind its usual bank of clouds.

For some reason I was waiting for the street lights to come on. I was a little nervous, waiting for that magical instant when they would light up—little fake shouts, bursts of clarity. If you can predict the exact instant when something will happen, that is an important power. It expresses a truth about you. I stared down at the traffic, the hundreds of cars come to a single, unified halt, the stalled buses, all so docile and patient with their red turn lights signaling—*let me out of this lane, let me into that other lane!*—and at the hazy leafless trees over in the park, and I licked my lips nervously, waiting for the precise moment when the lights would all come on. Then I could wait no longer: I whispered *now* to myself.

Now.

But the lights did not come on; I had been too impatient. No magic this afternoon. No. None. I checked my watch and it was three-twenty already, but no lights yet.

That meant I was safe for another day.

X came out of the bedroom, knotting his tie. He said: "What would you do to a woman like that, even if she is sixty-one years old? What could you do? What punishment would be terrible enough? What punishment could you invent?"

2

The sex is in error: a reversal. I had to endure that from the beginning. I was a woman, all along. But to get back close to nothing, to pare yourself back to nothing, you must be a man first—and then nothing. The maleness is also a confusion, but it is not so bad. It is not a contamination. Think of the maleness of all skulls, the maleness of wind-ravaged obelisks, those photographs of Stonehenge against a sunny, stormy sky.

3

R said to me: "But why do you say your sex is wrong? What does that mean, what should that mean to me?"

He laughed, lying on me. His heavy warm shoulders were pinning mine down.

"A soul by itself . . . by itself . . ."

But I could not think of what I wanted to say.

"Oh what, what? You say such crazy things!"

"You shouldn't laugh at me."

"Are you serious?"

"Yes."

"No. I don't think so."

He laughed.

R was a young doctor who had finished his internship and had his medical degree, but was doing a year in our city as a highly paid advisor to a state committee investigating abortion clinics, legal and illegal. He was always talking about all the free time he had—how wonderful it was, after his year as an intern. Having so much time, he intruded upon my time, but sweetly, and not seriously. He was always laughing.

"No. I can't take you seriously," he said.

"If I should die?"

"Oh why, why would you die? Why you?" he laughed.

4

It is the solitude of marriage that redeems it. The inner silence, all the noise emptied out and the elbowing, the jockeying for position, the shouting of names and numbers: my marriage was noisy and kept moving in spurts and surges, not always forward, sometimes backwards or sideways. *My marriage*, as if it were a possession of mine; it wasn't. It wasn't *his marriage* either. We kept pushing it back and forth between us, as if we were playing a game.

I know there is that solitude, that inner grace—in someone, in lovers married or unmarried—I know it exists, but I can't find it. It is hard enough just to be a face, an approved American face. That can be the work of a lifetime, just that. I did accomplish that. But isn't there more?

"Yes," X said slowly, "yes, in my marriage . . . in the beginning. . . . Yes, we were happy. We were very happy. It does exist."

"Then what happened?"

"Then we went into a kind of second marriage, a secondary marriage. I can't explain. And the first marriage was lost. You know," X said apologetically, "there is no marriage like the first. . . . Even for you, even you, there can't be. It isn't repeatable."

I was afraid to ask him, *What does your statement mean?*

5

There are easily identified people I am not: Mrs. Howard Cooper, a large, red-haired woman recently arrested by police when she tried to drive through a roadblock a few miles north of the city. She refused to give any reason for driving her car into the barricade, which had been set up to catch a 29-year-old Puerto Rican who had beaten up someone and stolen someone else's car. Mrs. Cooper had also swung her purse at one of the sheriff's men and was reported to have "used profane language." Her husband told television reporters that she had been in a bad mood all week.

6

Another person I am not: the 29-year-old Puerto Rican, arrested this morning by state police over near Ft. Rollins and indicted for second-degree assault and having stolen an automobile; with resisting arrest; with having failed to reregister under the Aliens Registration Act. He was given a Legal Aid attorney, but when the young man tried to shake hands with him, he struck the attorney in the face.

7

Lying in bed, listening to the radio, to a distant station. . . . It was like listening to the past, to someone trying to speak to me across many decades. What if my real lover, my real husband, had died before I was born? A century before I was born, or only three decades? What if I had never met him . . . ?

My husband had talked excitedly about certain semisecret fantasies of his (which he was later ashamed of, which he hated me for having learned): he believed that someone, an acquaintance of his, was writing about him . . . writing him down . . . writing down parts of his life, exploiting him, manipulating him . . . not presenting him with love, or charity, or even any real interest . . . but only jotting down fragments about him.

"My life is too important to be just a fragment," my husband used to say, laughing. But he was serious.

I never told him about my conviction that someone might have loved me perfectly, might have understood me, might even have invented me . . . and I would not have minded, no, why would I have minded? Being a fragment in a great man's head? No.

In that marriage, no risk of noise, elbowing, pain. No playing at strangling. *When you play at strangling, the play sometimes gets rough because the hands are in charge, and the hands are the most experimental part of a man's body.* So my husband told me, joking, but not joking, when he came home one night doped-up on some exotic combination of powders. He had a cool, haughty, almost regal charm, a man ruined for life by all the prizes he'd won in his boyhood, the big scholarships, the big grants.

Half asleep, half awake, I thought suddenly of a boy who had been punished by standing naked before his class. Had this really happened, or had I imagined it? Was the boy my husband or someone else I knew, a man I knew . . . ? Or was it something I'd read, just a snatch of information, a fragmentary news item I had begun to forget as soon as I read it?

8

I was lying in bed, listening to the radio. In the past, before my husband left, I had to get up early with him; now I can lie in bed for hours. . . . Important experiences come to you in bed, if you are alone. I am beginning to remember the mysterious kingdom that a bed really is, which I had known as a child.

A soprano joined me in my half-sleep, a lovely voice descending to me, illuminating me. *This is your essential voice, the voice of your soul.* The voice was reed-thin but not weak. Thin as a knife blade. Beautiful. It came to me from a great distance, as if from the past . . . and then the radio station faded, began to blend with another. . . . I woke, startled, and tried to adjust the dial. But I couldn't get the station back. Its place was taken by the sunny, Midwestern voice of a local announcer, giving the weather forecast for every part of the state and temperatures recorded at various airports. I couldn't locate the other station, couldn't find the singer again.

The beginning of a February day: no magic, no expectations. Therefore I was safe for another day.

9

You make the choice of days yourself. You mark the calendar at the end of a certain segment of time—the end of March, the end of a week. You put an X on that day, not to cross it out but to make it sacred.

In infinity, nothing is sacred. Too much distance, too much time. The soprano's voice would echo forever, without meaning, drifting helplessly across all that space. The audience becomes restless, yawns, forgets. The voice is sacred because you must struggle to hear it, you must feel terror at the thought of losing it, and then

you must lose it. *Your essential voice, the voice of your soul.* But
when you put an X on a day, any ordinary calendar from the bank
is transformed into a sacred document.

And all the days between today and that X are sacred.

10

Monday morning on the bus, after the hour when people who
worked would be using it; no men my own age, only one other
woman, no children. My eye was drawn to a wild white-haired old
man who sat across from me, but nearer the front of the bus. He
had something in his right hand that he kept moving around his
jaw and chin. He was disheveled, he hadn't shaved for several days.
Muttering to himself angrily, he kept moving this thing around his
stubbly jaw—it looked like a small pair of scissors—he kept clicking
at his jaw, muttering, very much alone, fierce and unseeing. I stared
at him, though I was afraid he would turn to glare at me.

You—what do you want? What do you see? he might demand.

Because I had twenty-five days left, I had to look for signs, hints.
I got off the bus when another woman my age got on: it seemed
right, to be keeping a kind of balance. I was on a street corner
downtown, in a fairly good section of the city, and from this corner
I could look in four wide directions and make my choice of streets.
It was very windy, wet. People hurried by me. Something in my face
must have attracted them, because they glanced at me—that look
men give to women, startled, recoiling a little as if looking into a
beacon, too much unwanted light, and then going neutral again,
very civilized.

Music drew me somewhere. At first just the throb of music, and
then the scattered sounds of it, mixed up with the wind. I walked
along a row of buildings until I came to a dress shop; the music was
from this shop, piped through a loudspeaker. It was a recently remodeled store, the front window edged with glaring chrome as if it
were a canvas, and the display inside made use of chrome tubing

and starlike shapes. It was a shop I would never have gone into in real life.

I was suddenly very happy. I asked to try on a dress with a long, heavy skirt made of dark velvet. In a three-way mirror I examined myself critically for the first time in months: I had begun to forget myself. Yes, that was I. It was still the same face, the same unmistakable eyes. That person had existed independently of me all the while my mind had been measuring off days and weeks, watching for signs.

That was the beginning of a March day.

11

The next evening I was in X's car and he was driving out along the highway, approaching the junction with the interstate expressway. I was wearing the long dress. I was in a kind of ecstasy, my face glowing, my brain cautious, watchful, looking for a sign. This happiness could not endure another twenty-four days. I could not endure it. I thought suddenly, as if a voice had come to me from a great distance telling me something very simple: *I don't want to die alone.*

X's face was no longer clear. His words, his angry gestures—he was always angry about something—his presence, my own presence beside him—Always there had been a division between us, a confusing, inert area, like neutral land between two warring nations, yet nations that were not actively at war, not at that moment. Now the inertia between us was almost gone. I almost loved him. I would wait for a sign, I would wait for him to fall silent, and then I would take hold of the steering wheel and turn it to the left, so that the car would speed into oncoming traffic. . . .

But he was talking. And gradually the words slowed down so I had to hear them. I tried to keep the fierce glow about his face, my own sharp, keen, painful ecstasy, but gradually it faded and I began to hear him. . . . He was talking as usual about his former wife. A jinxed woman: her hearing had begun to deteriorate, though she was only thirty-six years old. Her father, in and out of mental hospitals, telephoned her several times a day and accused her of wishing him dead. She had trouble with the people who lived above her in her apartment building; they were very noisy and would not discipline their children. And she had become involved in a complicated, vexing court case. A co-worker of hers at the county welfare office had been fired, as a result of his having been arrested in a raid on a homosexual bar; he was bringing suit against the welfare office and against the city, charging them with discrimination; the police had dropped all charges against him, he was guilty of nothing, and yet he had been fired and now could find no employment anywhere. . . . X's former wife had been subpoenaed by the plaintiff and was miserable because she would have to tell the truth. . . .

I waited for him to fall silent.

I thought: When the precise moment comes, I will know.

Obedient, docile, I sat beside this man, X, and waited as he drove along the highway, overtaking slower cars, swinging out into the left lane to pass other cars, trucks, a sluggish heavy-duty truck with a load of white turkeys, crates packed tightly together. But he kept talking. He was angry, bewildered. He was still married, in his imagination. He kept talking about his wife.

That night I put the dress away in the closet where I keep my off-season clothes.

12

At the back of the classroom were men of all ages, listening to my lecture. They weren't registered in the class. They were very enthusiastic, though; they laughed and even applauded from time to time, while my own students just took notes. They liked poetry best—I read Poe's poems, emphasizing the rhythms and the rhymes. Very good. Applause. The class usually began at any time after ten and ended at eleven-fifteen. My registered students would start to come in the room after ten, and by ten-thirty they would all be there, taking notes, serious and unsmiling and vacuous; these other men, all ages and all sizes, would begin to appear a little later, and they would remain until the end of the class. Sometimes they were less interested than at other times, they would fidget and yawn, but they never walked out.

Then one day I kept the class a few minutes longer, finishing a lecture on Hawthorne, and all these men walked out at the same time! I was stunned, humiliated. I found it difficult to finish the lecture. When the class was over I asked one of my girl students, and she explained to me that the bus must have come, that was all.

The bus?

Yes. The room opened out onto the street, and there was a bus stop there. The men at the rear of my lecture room were waiting for a bus. That was all.

And this was quite a shock to you? a surprise?

Yes. I never got over it.

Your vanity was so hurt?

I suppose that's all it was, vanity, I suppose. . . . But I thought the men had come to my lectures because . . . because word had gotten around that I was a good teacher . . . or that I could teach simply enough for them to understand English, even to like the poetry . . . or . . . or even because I was an attractive woman and in their culture women don't often appear like that . . . in public . . . as a university lecturer . . . and. . . .

And your vision of yourself was altered?

I don't know.

Your vision of reality was altered?

. . . we were all fragments, pieces of things . . . we were crowded together for a few minutes, but not the same few minutes. . . . I don't know, I can't explain. . . . I. . . .

Did you feel estranged from the students after that?

From all people.

13

Someone is telling me important facts: that the recording I am
going to hear of the *Sonata quasi una Fantasia* ("Moonlight Sonata") was made in 1939, one of the few remaining records of the
pianist Vanouch; it was made when he was seventeen. "In spite of
surface noises, this is a superb recording," the announcer says. "No
one has ever played this piece more beautifully than Vanouch."

Half asleep, half hypnotized, I listen to the music: the slow progression of notes, which are soft, gentle, unstoppable, almost building to a climax but then drawing back, restrained, like a breath that
gradually gains power. The sound is grave, sonorous. It is too pro-
found for beauty. It is somehow like memory, not erasable, too deep
for beauty; a piece played out of memory, but rigorously correct. No
surface errors. . . . Then the Allegretto, which is filmy, insubstantial,
unbelievable; as if the pianist, the boy pianist, cannot believe in it
but continues to play it, experimentally. And then it becomes clear
to me that this section is only a way of getting from one part to the
other, from the beginning to the end; it is a transition, with soft
trivial crescendos, a minuet tempo, a caress. . . . The last section
leaps out at me, suddenly very fast, with an almost ethereal light-
ness, but masculine, hard. There are no trivial moments here, no
caresses. The music gathers power, leaps into being, the rapid notes
growing stronger as they echo earlier sounds, becoming distinct,
hard. There is no freedom inside this music, only the absolute do-
minion of a great mind; a tyrannical power that bears down upon
the boy pianist and upon me, a stranger to him, a woman listening
to his work thirty-three years after he executed it.

The sonata ended. I was freed, but immediately struck by a sense
of loss. I sat up in bed. I was both older than the pianist, and
younger. I was older than the seventeen-year-old boy who had played
the sonata, but younger than the pianist now, today, this morning.
And in our heads, in his and mine, were the terrible imprisoning
notes of that music, which someone else had invented. . . . I turned

up the volume but the announcer was now talking about something else. *No, not so soon! What about the pianist? What about Vanouch?* The announcer was telling me to stay tuned for a half-hour of Australian bush music, which would be presented by an anthropologist-musicologist from Columbia. *No, wait—*

But time moved away. Rushed away. I lay back in a kind of inertia and began to hear twangs and shrieks and incomprehensible sounds, said to be human—I lay as if paralyzed, sodden with laziness or a failure of all muscles, especially the muscles of my brain—what about the young pianist, what about that recording, what about his life? How was his name spelled? What had happened to him?

He was like myself, dispersed in time, fragmented, tugged apart and flung in all directions, unseriously, seized and honored for a while and dropped again, rushed through an impersonal ritual, a series of rituals performed with good will, without evil. . . . Without permanent evil, anyway.

14

"You let it die."

"I didn't let it die. I didn't do anything."

"You let it die deliberately."

"No."

"Yes, deliberately."

He was sitting behind the wheel of the car, staring. Not at me. At the dusty windshield, at the cluttered rear of the garage.

"The battery is dead. Of course it's dead, after so long."

The garage was colder than the air outside. I shivered. I looked away from his pale, tense, hating face—I studied the debris in the garage, this rented garage, and felt a tug of something like affection, for this was not my property and yet it reminded me of my parents' property, the big garage back home and its accumulation of boxes and piles of newspaper and rags. Junk is a universal language.

"You deliberately let it die," he said sharply.

"No. I didn't do anything."

"You didn't do anything. Of course. That means you let it die, deliberately."

"I didn't know you were coming back."

He laughed.

From the side, he appeared to be smiling.

"You didn't want me to come back," he said.

". . . didn't think you would be coming back," I said, feeling faint.

He looked at me: a white, ravaged face, not a face meant to be shown to anyone.

"You would let me die, like the car. Wouldn't you?" he said.

In our marriage he had spoken often of "areas of life, like areas of the brain" that must always be untapped, not brought into consciousness. He had seemed to worship these "areas." And yet he might allude to them, teasingly, as if to draw me into a terrible mistake.

I looked at the junk in the garage: all the boxes and crates, the piles of newspaper bound neatly together with twine. In terror I stared at these things and realized they could not save me. Why? What was this? What was all this?

"Well, if you ever need an abortion yourself," he said with a sudden laugh, "you'll be in good hands. . . ."

I tried to speak. But he interrupted: "You won't need an abortion, though, will you? Not you! Nothing could get planted in you, not in _you_," he said with his old, stylish, almost conversational hatred, cheerful enough to be displayed before friends. He had never quite finished his graduate work in history so that he could become a "historian," a "professor of history." And yet he spoke as if superior to his own expectations, freed and witty and ironic; he could not be categorized. But as he spoke I realized that he was not speaking to me. He was not even looking at me. I felt the excitement of his hatred dancing around someone, an image in his brain he thought was me but was not me: his sister, that vicious beautiful older sister? or his mother, who had loved the sister so much? I had not met them, but he had told me about them. And now, staring at me, an ex-wife, an ex-lover, an ex-friend, he was not able to concentrate in the ecstasy of his rage and I felt him losing me . . . I felt how he let me go, how he grasped for me and yet let me go, desperately, carelessly, just as in our lovemaking he had let me go, coming to a quick, private finish himself and not able to imagine me any longer. And, since I could not be imagined by him, I returned to substance . . . to flesh . . . and he to substance, to flesh . . . two separate bodies.

Suddenly I realized a truth: that he could not love me and I could not love him, love was not possible unless people imagined one another fully, ceaselessly, unselfishly—but all I said to him, all I could say, was "Don't leave me!" And he misunderstood; he stared at me, incredulous. "Don't leave me—I mean—I mean don't forget me— Please don't forget me—"

"What? What are you saying?"

"If only you could concentrate on me, on *me*—even if it's only to hate me—if you could see me and not other people in my place— other women—If—"

He stared. But he did not see me: he stared through me and saw someone else.

15

That was our marriage.

Yet was I so innocent in other relationships?

One of the shocks of my life was having learned, by accident, through acquaintances who were not even being malicious—only helpful—that a friend of my early twenties, a young man who had never been my lover but simply a friend, a casual friend among many, had been telling everyone who would listen to him how vicious I was: how I had betrayed him, had cut him out of my life as soon as I had fallen in love. . . . Circumstances had made him mean, a little crazy. He lived alone; had been forced to collect unemployment insurance; had never gotten a job, though he had a Ph.D and had worked very, very hard. . . . So the bitterness made sense, in a way. And yet he had focused upon me to hate. He had focused his hatred, his wild disappointment at life, on me, I who believed myself so innocent of having misused others. I had not torn him into fragments; I had simply forgotten him. I had married, had moved away, had stopped writing him . . . had not cared to remember him . . . had come to believe, abstractly, that the man had died, that he had died for me. Two years later and he was still thinking of me, still dreaming, fantasizing . . . inventing a young woman in his imagination to explain the humiliating chaos of his life.

I ran to my husband with the news of him: "He gets drunk, he says he'd like to murder me! Can you imagine! Says he'd like to murder me with his bare hands because I betrayed him. . . ."

My husband was not a jealous man. Consciously, he had no emotions at all.

He laughed.

"Betrayed him, did you? How did you betray him? With *me*?"

"I don't know," I said, breathless, beginning to weep with the absurdity of it—that someone should hate me who no longer knew me—that he should wish me dead—should gloat about murdering me! "They said he gets drunk and says the most disgusting things about me—he's made up stories about me—says I borrowed money from him and never paid it back—says I forced him to drive me all over town—And I don't remember him. I don't remember him any longer, except for the name."

"Who is this person?" my husband asked.

I hesitated. "Why do you want to know?"

"If my wife is being insulted, shouldn't I know about it?— shouldn't I do something about it? After all, my reputation is involved too."

"His name. . . . His name. . . ."

"Unless you want to protect him even now," my husband said.

I knew he was joking. But I said, faltering: "I don't remember his name even. I've forgotten everything about him. . . . In fact, I had the vague idea that he had died of a drug overdose or something."

"Evidently he didn't oblige you by dying," my husband said.

16

On page 502 of the *American Directory of Musical Arts*:

> VANOUCH, THADDEUS. Born 1922, Philadelphia, Pa.; of a musical family; studied piano and composition with David Frima of the Connolly Institute, then with Philip Wrexham at Yale, where he made his debut with the New Haven Symphony at the age of 10. After an extraordinary career that took him to resounding successes in New York, London, and many of the capital cities of Europe, Vanouch withdrew from professional musical life at the age of 23. He is believed to be living in France.

No photograph of Vanouch.

I tried to recall the sound of music, but could not. The ears have no memory. The eyes have no memory. Pure sound is reduced to soundlessness and then to nothing. After the piercing sensation of love, its absolute certainty, after the muscles contract and go crazy, after that there is memory: but it puts you to sleep.

But I didn't want to think about love.

I turned the page and saw a photograph of a young man. It was a dramatic, arranged photograph, a man's face shown in sharp contrasts of light and shadow. His hand was posed on the strings of a cello. Delicate, very delicate, those fingers. His hair was black, but highlighted with streaks of light. His eyes were large, intense. He was staring off to my left, not dreamily, but with an alert critical precision: those eyes frightened me. He wore a shirt and a sweater, no tie. He looked very young.

> VAN WYCK, STUART. Born 1947, Chicago, Ill.; of a musical

family; studied the cello with R. F. Aronson at Juilliard and with Pablo Casals in Prades, France, and Marlboro, Vermont. VanWyck received a grant from the French Government in 1970 and now lives in Paris, where he is studying with Andre Navarra. In 1971 he was the only cellist from a Western country to be named a prize-winner in the 5th International Tchaikovsky Competition in Moscow.

I stared at Van Wyck, the contours of his strong, critical face, the black hair, the gentle hand with its smallest finger extended straight, the others bent, that single finger tense, listening, listening very hard.

After a while I came to myself. I saw that I was sitting in a library, an ordinary branch library; sitting by myself at a table beneath a dim light. At the next table sat an old man who muttered to himself. He looked familiar. He was running his hand swiftly around his chin and jaw and throat, all the fingers moving swiftly and angrily. On the table before him was an opened newspaper from the rack, but he was not reading it. His hand leaped about his face, checking for something, spasmodically, angrily. . . .

I thought: Are we fragments?

I thought:—being forgotten even while we complain about being forgotten?

I closed the oversized directory and returned it to its place on the shelf, because a sign warned me that a book misplaced is a book lost and I did not want to lose anything.

17

On March 27 I received a letter from my mother.

She explained that my father had had a series of eye operations for the removal of cataracts; that they had not wanted me to know about the operations; that the trouble was over, my father much better, and that they planned on coming to visit me the first week in April.

I began to weep.

I let the letter fall and wept for my father.

I wept for the letter: for my mother's lovely handwriting.

I wept for that terrible uncharted time beyond March 31, an infinity of time I would have to face.

18

April 4, ten in the morning, and I am on the bus for the airport. I will meet them there and the three of us will take a taxi back, since my car doesn't work. My mind is thrumming, thrumming: *the eleven-o'clock flight from St. Louis.* It is a very important flight. I am happy and keep checking my watch.

Dressed a little lightly for this time of year, having miscalculated the sunlight. . . .

The bus stops and a woman gets on and veers toward me, a grand-motherly woman carrying two shopping bags. They are made of red plastic, with firm black handles. She gives me that inquiring, apologetic look people flash on buses—May I sit with you, please, with you?—and I smile to tell her yes, why not?

Her cheeks are naturally red. She breathes huskily. She settles herself in the seat beside me, heavier than I had thought. The shopping bags are heavy. One on the floor, the other on her lap and partly on me.

I think of the eleven-o'clock flight, and of the door of the plane opening, and of my parents coming down the steps. . . .

The woman begins to speak, in the middle of a sentence: ". . . my daughter-in-law . . . with the radish-top, I call it . . . she thinks she can cut me out just by changing the telephone number . . . isn't that a laugh? My single problem is Iris. My problem is this: should I withdraw from the constant tension and abandon Iris to them, or should I report them? Report my own son? He is my own son. Iris is nine years old and has never for a day had the use of her own legs, never any sensation in them . . . the doctors can stick pins in

her until she's bleeding from a dozen places but what good does
it do . . . ? Isn't that a tragedy?"

I am going to say something, but she keeps on talking:

"If I abandon her to them I'll have her on my conscience all my
life, because they can't love her the way I do . . . they are short-
sighted and cruel and not people I would pick for my own
friends. . . . Isn't that a terrible confession to make? Isn't it? I love
Iris and I know she loves me, far more than she loves them, and of
course they're jealous and try to hurt her. . . . They don't help her
with her hobbies the way I do."

The woman has a faint Scottish accent. She does not look at me,
but inclines her head toward me. She smells of strong soap, like
disinfectant. The shopping bag has eased onto my right knee and
thigh. It is quite heavy.

". . . what kind of hobbies?" I ask shyly.

"Collects autographed pictures of the singers . . . you know," the
woman says, making a sudden gesture around her head, as if describ-
ing mounds of hair, ". . . has half a dozen shoeboxes filled with them,
in alphabetical order . . . it's a waste of time, I know in my heart,
but it cheers her up . . . her parents are so cheap, I have to bring her
stamps myself. I don't mind. Her other hobby is collecting marbles.
Oh, all kinds of marbles, all lovely beautiful kinds of marbles . . .
they really can be beautiful, you know, if you take the time to look
at them. And just down the street, I mean at the first house but not
the new one now that they had to buy on their high horse, just to
show off, on Sutherland, at the corner there was a little boy who
came to play with her . . . real good for her to have a friend like
that . . . he was real cute, only about four years old, but smart as
a whip, and he'd play marbles with Iris where she was pulled up to
the card table. It was so wonderful for her, you could see the joy
of it in her face. Then, afterward, he sold the marbles back to me,
the ones he won, it was like a game all three of us played . . . until
they moved . . . and now the telephone business, I don't know what
to think. . . ."

I notice that the bus is going very fast. It is almost time for me to pull the cord.

The woman is saying, "There are legal means to bring a couple in line, aren't there? I know there are. Injunctions and lawsuits and that Battered Child committee . . . that thing in the paper . . . you remember all the publicity about it in the paper. . . ?"

"Excuse me, I have to get out here. . . ."

The woman doesn't seem to hear me. I get to my feet and the shopping bag tilts, falls over, and onto the floor spill handfuls of marbles—an avalanche of marbles—They bounce and roll everywhere, bouncing down onto my feet and rolling out of sight, and still the cascade keeps coming, helpless, in a crazy rush, and I stare down at the marbles and try to think—

No. Stop. Wait, wait—

A Premature Autobiography

BREUER AT THE SISLEY ACADEMY, 1954

Anxiety in him—his tense body, his gesturing hands, his eyes that dart everywhere about the auditorium, not finding a place to rest. Impossible to imagine the color of those eyes. I am sitting too far away.

Behind me a man begins coughing.

Breuer speaks softly and rapidly. His smile flicks off and on, not touching us. Why is he so anxious? Why is he apologizing for himself? Drably dressed. Round-shouldered. He is speaking of Schoenberg and Webern and then his voice fades into nothing . . . behind me that man coughs again, and in one of the front rows another person begins coughing.

Breuer begins again. A rapid, uncertain flow of words . . . Breuer is like a man leaning forward, falling forward. He pronounces certain words with special precision, making them sound like small precious weights dropped clearly and cleanly through water, unique combinations of sounds, priceless sounds. It is a world of unique combinations of sounds! Priceless sounds!

Yes, his voice is like his music. I can hear that now.

From this distance I can't see Breuer's features clearly, but I can see slight shadowy pouches beneath his eyes, and other shadows, hardly more than lines, that mark his cheekbones. His hands float to demonstrate something to us—the fingers outstretched—the performing of magic. "It is to reverse the usual procedure, my third piano sonata," he says shyly. "It is to attempt a simple version of the theme, which comes in second place, secondarily . . . to make it a variation of itself . . . you must hear and understand the variation first. But I am doubtful of it now. The harmony is too much a skeleton."

It is September: humid everywhere, the park surrounding the Academy's buildings humid and silent, a small oasis that keeps the traffic of the city in another dimension. But the heat is here with us. I feel it rising in me, into my face. I am alone and there are empty seats on either side of me, setting me apart.

In the first row Dr. Taggart sits with his abrupt listening look, a man with savage white hair cut close to the skull, shaved up the back of the skull. He has brought Herbert Breuer here to the United States, to Buffalo, New York. He nods as Breuer speaks; short, impatient nods of the head; and as Breuer concludes, he nods more fully, as if relieved. How painful this hour was! Now we all begin to clap and the clapping causes Breuer to recoil slightly, as if he senses how we want to drown out his words, which have not made too much sense.

I follow the crowd out into the foyer. Being so alone, I feel unreal. People seem to look through me. Mr. Reiff, one of my teachers, waves at me but he is too far away—I can't be expected to talk to him. There is a reception in Breuer's honor now. Everyone is moving steadily along, talking, agreeing with one another. Without anyone to talk to, a person is not quite real. Sounds are very important—we are like bats tapping at each other with sounds, making sure there is someone there, groping along. Sounds. Syllables. The beat of music. It is all a curious flowing, which you can hear only when you are silent yourself.

Dr. Taggart will expect me to come to the reception, to be introduced to Breuer, but I am not able to cross the square, to follow these people along the walk and into the hall. It is too much for me. Instead, I go quickly into the women's restroom, which is empty. A sad, dark smell about this place. The Sisley Academy is sad, dark, shabby . . . everywhere about it the city of Buffalo is noisy and ominous. Too many buses, too many cars. The mirror above the sink here vibrates from all the noise of Buffalo. In the sink there are several strands of long black hair that seem to be vibrating too, drawing my eye to them in loathing.

BREUER AT THE FOUNTAIN, ROBSON MEMORIAL SQUARE

My heart pounds and sends me up the stairs to the studio, hurrying. It is Monday morning. Somewhere a piano is being played —it is mixed up with my pounding heart—keep on going, keep on, there is no way to turn back! The door is open. A whiff of warm air—the odor of familiar mustiness, books and papers on high dark shelves, the odor of the Academy itself. Mr. Reiff is talking with Breuer and they both turn to me.

Introductions. Breuer shakes my hand: his own hand is strong and damp.

"So you are the student of such scholarship! I am deeply honored," Breuer says.

I can see now that his eyes are blue, very light. His face is thin. Yes, he is thin, his clothes are too big for him, as if he were wearing another man's clothes. Very restless. The raw structure of his face is prominent beneath his skin.

"I am anxious to meet you. I have been reading these—" Breuer indicates some papers. Suddenly I feel faint. Sunlight falls in a cascade around us from the big window that faces the park, and it is too bright for me. The bits of dust that whirl in the light are like my own thoughts, atom-sized and agitated.

"They are all so highly pleased with you here, it is a pleasure to meet you," Breuer says formally.

We are alone together. He is looking through a sonata I wrote a few months ago. It is this sonata that won me these particular lessons, instruction with Herbert Breuer as an advanced student . . . but I can't remember the sonata, I couldn't play it now. I stare at Breuer's face as he bends over the score as if nearsighted. He nods and makes agreeable noises to himself. "Yes, like that. Yes. I can see that. It is all very cold, what you have done." He looks up at me and smiles. "But that is a bad word, *cold?* I mean it is logical, it is not very like a girl. It is not to be expected, this kind of thing. You are a daughter of Bach . . . ? Sit and play this for me, talk to me about it. Talk to me on the piano."

I start to play for him—then I must stop. I am too nervous.

Breuer walks around the room, behind me. I think that he is anxious for me to do well; he is anxious to make agreeable noises along with my music. And this holds me back, this paralyzes me "Why are you waiting?" he cries. "Why are you afraid? Four times now you have checked that scarf that ties your hair back—it is all perfectly neat, it is very pretty, now you can forget about it!"

I start to play again and yes, there it is now—the music is there, waiting for me. It is my own language. The eight or ten minutes I live through now are my own language, my music, even Herbert Breuer is not important to me—

"You have said all that? That is a great deal, what you have said." Breuer exclaims.

"Thank you. . . ."

My hand darts happily to the back of my head, to the scarf tied into a small bow . . . I have survived this first meeting, I am Herbert

Breuer's student! All my life I will have been Breuer's student, one of his American students; my life has propelled me quietly to this moment and now it will propel me away, and yet my life has been changed.

"Now we must sit down and figure out how to expect more from you. This, and this, and this," he says, tapping the score, "it is all too tight, inside itself. I will teach you. You will teach me also. Here—in this city—I will learn things, I will take them back with me. Or maybe I will never go back? We will see what to expect from ourselves."

The lesson lasts more than an hour; it is getting late. Breuer talks swiftly. His smile is darting and fastidious, not touching me. He leans over the piano and with his bony fingers taps something out, talking to me, but the notes go nowhere and his words go nowhere; they are like stairs leading up to nothing.

Breuer wipes his forehead. He seems very tired.

"Now lunch. We will have lunch."

"Isn't someone coming at eleven?"

"No, it is time for lunch. We will leave here. I am up at five o'clock every day, it is time for lunch now."

I get to my feet slowly. "Won't someone—"

"No, no, the sun is only out for a little while here in Buffalo. I must get out in it," Breuer says. For the first time I hear a pressure in his voice; it is not so gentle or musical. "You will walk with me."

We cross the park and no one sees us. It is a mystery, my walking with Herbert Breuer in this early fall sunlight, the two of us passing through the heavy air like swimmers. I think suddenly *We are like swimmers* and the thought puzzles me. I feel ashamed of myself. Herbert Breuer is walking besides me, a man of ordinary height in an ordinary suit. He is talking rapidly, almost feverishly, and I can't understand everything he is saying. There is something flamboyant about him, now that he is free of the studio . . . and in myself something flamboyant arises, a sensation of bubbles rising in the blood, recklessness. I am sure that someone is due up in that

studio . . . he will knock on the opened door, peer into the room
. . . maybe step inside, puzzled. Where is Herbert Breuer?

At an old downtown square he stops. The fountain's waters are
thin; the fountain is encrusted with layers of filth and green mold—
I think it is mold, perhaps it is moss. Breuer stares at this fountain.
"There is a photograph of my wife by a square in Rome. A fountain.
It comes back to me right now, it is very powerful . . . she was your
age then. It was before we had met."

He tugs at his necktie. He opens his collar, and his shirt takes on
a jaunty, dissolute look.

"Marriage—all that is ahead of you. You don't understand. At
your age it is all ahead of you, life. Why are you so embarrassed
of me? We must talk frankly to each other if we are to work
together." He stares at me, smiling. "My wife and I—there is not
much between us. She will go her own way now. I think that will
happen."

"I'm sorry. . . ."

"Why am I embarrassing you? But yes, yes, it is too personal, all
this," Breuer says sourly. "It is too soon for us to be friends."

Breuer in the hazy September light. Breuer at that old fountain,
a man in his early forties, old enough to be my father. I feel the
rawness of Buffalo around us, pressing us together. I see us through
the eyes of the five or six old men who sit around the fountain on
park benches, silent and shabby and staring. Together this man and
this girl are an oasis.

BREUER'S SECOND CONCERTO FOR PIANO AND ORCHESTRA

The music is a flood. It is furious and demanding. Cycles pass,
pass again, repeat themselves. I hear the hint of a melody I had not
heard before. Something unknown presses upon us when we hear
this music—the unknown of the great composers—a terrifying presence that is somehow not frightening. It is very formal. That is

why it is terrifying but not frightening. It is made into music for us, so that we can listen to it at peace.

We are at rest inside the music.

Violent outbursts, like seizures. Then the assimilation into the structure, the architecture. Yes, I know very well that the adagio makes us think of Mahler . . . a descending octave jump . . . and then all this power, this loneliness. But it is Breuer's music.

I am listening to this record in my room on an evening in October. On the record cover—it is a Columbia recording, made by the Symphony Orchestra of Baden-Baden—I read about Breuer's life, I have read about it again and again, and the only words that strike me are: *This work was dedicated to Eugenie Halbreich, later to become the composer's wife.*

At the school we never saw Breuer's wife. She was in Buffalo for a while, so it was said, but now she has left.

Breuer at a rehearsal of one of his string quartets: sitting in an overcoat and galoshes at the back of the auditorium, very still. Dr. Taggart directing. A few of us scattered around, conscious of Breuer behind us, so very still, and Dr. Taggart's growing nervousness. In Dr. Taggart nervousness and fury run together.

Buffalo is making strange bruise-like smudges on Breuer's face.

My lessons with him three days a week—excitement, the pounding of my heart, his vague hazy eyes. I play for him. I play to him, talking to him. A theme slightly his own, taken from an early piece of his; he understands this. "Ah, my friend," he says, laying his hand on my shoulder, "you are so good for a girl, it is not predictable. Why do you want to be so good? There is no future for you to be like me. You must marry, you must have babies."

I smile quickly and helplessly at this.

His hand on my shoulder.

Breuer is not working out well here at the Academy: he skips classes, he is "not healthy," he is "overtired," he is "not in the mood," he is missing. But he is always up in the studio for my hour with him at nine o'clock, he always has coffee for both of us, he says happily when I come in, "Already I have been awake five hours! Now we will have breakfast together."

And so we drink coffee together, this troubled man and I, a famous man and an unknown girl, a man of forty-two and a girl of eighteen, together. I don't think yet of the time when he will leave the Sisley Academy, on his way to another part of his life, another set of students or a commission or something unknown. "What are the rumors you hear about me this week?" he says with his sweet-sour smile. "Tell me all their secrets. Your Dr. Taggart, please betray him to me!"

"I don't hear anything."

"You are too good, my sweet little friend. You do not want me to be ashamed."

Now I sit on the edge of my bed, listening to his music. He is here in the room with me, explaining the movements to me, taking my hand in both of his . . . leaning toward me, gentle and ragged and sweating, a man who is falling apart and whose face has become hawkish. . . . I know he is almost a famous man, and yet if we walk somewhere together people glance at me, not at him. Men glance at me. I hate their looks, that casual resting of their eyes on my face, my legs . . . it is the manner of men in cities, staring openly, staring at women as if women cannot see them in return. As if we are only objects to be looked at. Breuer passes through their vision: he is really nothing. In the wind his overcoat flaps about his legs.

My mother opens the door to my room. "Are you playing that again?"

"I'll turn it down. . . ."

She has a frizzy, harassed look, my mother. The two of us live alone in this house, which is a one-story house not far from Delaware Avenue. She works in a bank during the day in a position of some responsibility, though she will never get anywhere. No background. No special training. She is a woman alone, a woman whose husband left her years ago, and the fact of this betrayal has made her mouth bitter; even her clothes have a bitter used look to them.

"Turn it off, I'm tired. I want to sleep," she says.

I turn off the phonograph. The music comes to an end.

My mother is a woman who has finished her life. It is lived out, completed. She never thinks of men and will live out the years of her life without thinking of them; her life has been completed for her.

BREUER ON THE TELEPHONE

One winter morning I hurry up to the studio and it is empty. No one. Two days in a row Breuer has not been here.

I go to the piano and sit down automatically. This is the center of the room and the center of my life. Breuer's presence is here, the smell of him, his urgency. I say to him: *Should I come to you today?* From a room on the second floor comes the sound of a violin, a piano, a violin. Stop. Begin again. The two sounds together, beginning again and stopping. For music there is always time—forever. Space stretches. Time stretches.

After a while I go back downstairs slowly, and outside into the wind, and across the park to the street. Into a drugstore. Breuer and I: we are wound around each other, the two of us. It is music that flows between us. My music written to him, out of him, my way of speaking to him. Already I have written several pieces, very rapidly; it is not like me to write so rapidly; I am working on a longer piece, dedicated to him. I will dedicate everything to him! When I write I am not myself, not this girl who is small and dark and frightened; I am the very clarity of the notes themselves, a voice, free. There is power in everything I do. Even my own piano playing is not equal to it—I go beyond myself, I am powerful beyond anything I can explain.

I telephone Breuer and listen to the ringing on the other end.

He is somehow in the phone booth with me, pressing close—his smile flicks on and off, his hand lightly brushes mine, leaning over me he brushes my back with his chest, accidentally. This is a mysterious moment: the telephone ringing, Breuer's presence, the absence of sound that is a part of music most people never hear.

He answers the phone. "Yes . . . ? Yes . . . ?"

And so I came to Breuer on that morning.

BREUER IN PRIVATE, FEBRUARY 1955

He is stalking me through these four rooms. The rooms of his apartment: four familiar rooms.

In one of his trunks I found a photograph in an old-fashioned gilt frame, under some unpacked clothing. I take it out to look at it. *Eugenie, 1941.* Breuer says, "Put that back. Why are you always looking at that?" She is a young woman posing in front of a car, dark and pretty. No, she is not really pretty. I turn the photograph from side to side so that the light catches it, glaring on the glass.

"Put that back. You, you are not like that," Breuer says. He is still not quite well. He takes my hand and brings it to his lips and it seems to me that I can feel the dryness of those lips, their heat. "You are a girl in a Renoir painting, one of his young girls . . . you are not like *her*." But it is a fact that I am like this woman, I am dark and slender and pretty, and I keep staring at the photograph in spite of Breuer's impatience. "What is it, are you hateful of her? Or of yourself?" Breuer curves his arm around my neck and forces me to look at him. So close to this man, I am not real; I fade into him; I flow into him and there is nothing left of myself.

I never had time to tell him that I loved him. He was always this close, pressing against me—first in the telephone booth, then up here in his apartment.

"No, with you it is all music. It is beautiful, what you bring to me," he says slowly, as if assessing a piece of music I have written for him. He is my teacher, he is Herbert Breuer. He assesses me and I stand close to him, staring at him, my heart pounding. "You are a beautiful young girl and you do not know it, not really. Good. But I know this. And from the beginning I know what you say to me in your music. I was never young as you, I was never the age when I did not know myself. Always I have known myself. I am tired of

Breuer, that man!—now I know that I will live through this year because of you, only because of you. And you will come with me to this new place. . . ."

I close my eyes.

"Yes, you will come with me," Breuer says. He presses his face against mine. I am bathed in a flood of warmth, of love—and yet I am isolated in it, too frightened to move. For three months now I have come to Breuer's apartment, loving him. And yet I am too frightened now to move. I close my eyes and see us like this: embracing, Breuer and a girl; the girl is wearing a blue and white dress, her hair is smoothly drawn back from her small, pale face, tied with a blue scarf, so that the part is clear and white in the center of her head, a white brushstroke. She is too young for this, she is not even this man's wife!—and yet her body bends to his body, it gives in to the stress of his hard, precise fingers.

My heart pounds to the breaking point.

And then afterward he stalks me again, picking at me with his voice. "You love me and so you will come with me. What is Buffalo to you, this place? Yes, you will come with me. I must leave here. It is impossible here, where they want to kill me. So you will come with me."

I am dry-eyed from too much crying. I sit down on a chair—the chair is in the middle of this cluttered room, in the middle of nothing—and say to Breuer, "I can't come with you. I can't come with you."

"Yes. You will come with me."

"I—"

"Do you want me to be sick again? To lie in bed like I was, dirty and sick? Do you want me to die *here*, here in this place, this city of yours?"

I put my hands to my face and shake my head slowly, no. No.

"And so today, this very day, you will explain it to her. You are of an age to declare yourself free. Tell her. Tell her you belong to me and no longer to her."

"I can't—"

"Why are you so afraid, always so afraid! You disappoint me."

If I open my eyes I will see Breuer's haggard impatient face, the face that was pressed against mine only a few minutes ago. It is the same face still. It is always pressed up close to me, burning me, so that when I am alone, hurrying here to this building through the snow, or washing myself afterward back in my own room, I feel the imprint of his face on mine, the skin rough against my skin, wearing me out.

"If I try to talk to her she'll scream at me," I say. I am speaking to Breuer through my hands. "She'll slam doors on me. We'll be up all night. . . ."

"Women should not live together. It is unhealthy for them both."

Breuer puts his hands on my shoulders and slides his arms slowly around my neck. Yes, I love him . . . yes, it is a fact. When he touches me like this he releases love inside me. He presses his warm forehead against the top of my head and makes me bow my head slightly, giving way beneath him. He stands over me. "You love me, do you? Like before?"

"Yes."

"And you are not angry with me about Dr. Taggart and those others?"

"No."

"Do you think I am being bad to them, to walk out on them?"

"No."

"Because it is a fact that this climate is destroying me. First, the United States is not good for me, but Buffalo is very bad for me. I am not thinking only of the money. In New York they have more money, but I am not thinking of that. I am thinking only of how I must survive. You are the only thing that helped me live— you saved my life—that is a fact we both know. You saved my work. Now it will finish itself, I am confident of that, I will not die. And so you must come with me to this new place."

He caresses my face with his fingers. He is outlining my face so that I can see it: I can see us together, Breuer bending over me, me bending backward, a girl with a face being outlined just so, precisely.

"Your wife—"

"My wife, what! Why do you always talk of her?"

I am silent.

"If you would let me go to New York alone, if that is truly in your mind, then you would be weeping now," Breuer says shrewdly. "But you are not weeping. If you would want to leave me, to let me go away from you like we are strangers, you would never be here today with so beautiful a dress! And your face, so beautiful a face! It is small, delicate, it is something that belongs to me—you are not going to leave me, eh? For any young man, ever? For the rest of your life?"

"No."

"For any man?"

"No."

"Because you have saved my life. In December you saved my life." He is speaking feverishly, loudly. His voice is too loud. Why is it so loud when we are standing together?—"So beautiful, like silk, a young girl is white and fine like silk . . . you are just a child, you belong to me . . . you will move out of that house where everything is ugly, where that woman is ugly, and you will come with me to this new place, where I will be treated with respect. I am Herbert Breuer, after all, should I pretend I am nobody?"

"But your wife—"

"What of my wife? She is not here! You are here, only you! Why are you always asking me about my wife?"

What I want to say to him can't be said. He is too close to me, he is pressing down upon me. His weight is very warm. I feel myself give in to him suddenly: yes, I will go with him, I will begin a new life with him.

When he releases me I see that I am in his apartment, in the large front room, sitting in a chair. The walls are empty and white. The floor is bare; boxes and books and papers are pushed back against the walls. The piano is heaped with things. A clutter. Breuer walks out of the room on his way to get something or on his way to the bathroom.

BREUER IN NEW YORK, APRIL 1955

And now he says to me angrily, "But your opinion is important. The others, what is their concern for me? Only you are concerned for me in myself. You must come!"

"They all stare at me—"

"Of course they stare, you are a beautiful girl! What of that?"

But I am lying in bed. The air is too thin outside, in this vertical, rising, dizzy city. Everything is too high. When I am out in the street alone my eyes shoot up to the tops of the buildings and I feel I am going to be sucked up.

"Get up! Get dressed!"

Breuer throws something on the bed; I don't turn to look at it.

"And then we will talk of some things. We will go to the rehearsal and afterward for something to drink and we will have a talk, the two of us."

Breuer will be leaving me.

He goes into the bathroom and I hear water run. Angry water. Something is slammed shut. I wait for him to relent, to come back out again and take my hands in his, as he has often, and to say to me, "Forgive me, I am joking. I should not joke with you ever." But he won't come back out and say this, he won't take hold of my hands in that way again. I think that part of my life is over.

Breuer's picture on the cover of the *Saturday Review*: that straight urgent nose, the cheekbones, the eyes that are both suspicious and gentle, a light blue. No, this is not anyone who will take my hands in his.

He flushes the toilet and hurries out, into this room, getting dressed. "You lie there! You are sick and want to make me sick again, like before, like in Buffalo!" But he is not looking at me, he is on his way out; buttoning his shirt; clapping his hand against his chest angrily, the fingers outstretched.

When Breuer smokes he lets the ash grow long on his cigar. It is silken and fine, that ash. It is beautiful. He lets the ash grow long and watches it, and then with his forefinger he taps the cigar and down the ash falls ... !

Alone in the apartment I imagine myself wandering outside, alone. I will walk along Forty-eighth Street, toward Park Avenue. I will stare at the lovely buildings, those buildings of glass and metal and space . . . and then I will look up at their tops, my eyeballs sucked upward, and I will be lost. A girl without Breuer. Lost. Without him I will be sucked up to the tops of the buildings, having no weight! So I lie in bed here and stare at the space where Breuer stood only a few minutes before, the ghostly outline of Herbert Breuer. . . .

Breuer is going to leave me. I think, judging from the telephone calls I have overheard, that his wife is flying to New York.

BREUER IN ENGLAND, 1955–1956

My stationery is light blue. I am back in Buffalo, but I am still Breuer's beloved. I write to him every day.

He is in London.

One evening he telephoned me, the telephone rang at eight-thirty in Buffalo. "What are you doing? Where are you? Your health—what is your health?" He seemed to be shouting at me across the ocean, and yet his voice was very small. "Yes, yes, I will be coming back in a few weeks! Soon! It is a triumph here, did you read about it? I am very happy at last! I am sorry you are not here with me—but your health? What is your health?"

He fears the sickness in me, his own sickness that passed out of him.

The doctor tells me, "The electrocardiograph shows nothing. Spasms like that are not organic . . . there is nothing to be afraid of . . . you are not going to die. . . ."

I am not ever going to die.

My mother tells me the same thing. Short, harassed, frizzy, ironic, in a hurry—she wears spike-heeled shoes, the latest style, and the linoleum in the kitchen has hundreds of tiny dots in it, so small they can hardly be seen. I put my hands over my ears, hearing her footsteps.

"What did you eat today? Are you taking care of yourself? Are you thinking about *him* again today, why are you moping about *him*? Your life isn't over just because *he* left you—"

It is not true that he left me, not exactly. He is not living with his wife.

"Should I make another appointment with Dr. Bart?"

I dream of a sky, clouds parting. I dream of being sucked up into the space between those clouds, in that delirium of love I once lived in for five months. Five months. But it is a dream that belongs to someone else, a life that belongs to someone else, to some other girl.

BREUER ON BREUER, 1969

The book is six hundred pages and it weighs me down on one side, like a drunken woman. I am tempted to laugh aloud! Walking to the bus stop, a woman in her mid thirties, feeling a little drunk. *Breuer on Breuer.* It is a precious weight I am carrying and not like the other books and papers and my purse, which I always carry.

I teach music at State Teachers', piano and theory to young women who will teach music in high schools and junior high schools and lead choruses and choirs and play piano as children troop into assemblies in the schools of this city. It is a safe job. It pays well, since the very articulate lobbyists for the State University of New York agitate to get raises for all college teachers in the state. . . . When I think of my job I think automatically of the future: of promotions, of tenure, of a pension, of retirement. My life is prepared for me.

It is a cold, dry day in December.

Why am I so frightened? This book. This book I ordered weeks ago, greedily, as soon as I saw the advertisements for it. And, in the Doubleday book store, when the saleswoman handed me the book (a week before it is to be officially published, as if this copy is a special gift for me from the author himself!) I felt dizzy, faint. . . . I felt feverish, thinking of this book and the secrets it will tell me about Herbert Breuer.

A few women wait with me for the bus; difficult to figure out who they are. What they are. Saleswomen, maybe, but it is a little early for them—only quarter to five. Shoppers? Married women with homes to get to, children to tend, husbands . . . and yet they look as isolated as I do, shivering in their coats, knowing that Buffalo is always cold.

Buses come into sight, but they are not the right buses. They don't stop at this corner.

Finally the bus comes. I try to relax, I am really feverish. My first class was at nine this morning, and all day long I have been working, talking to people, hurrying from place to place . . . then down to Doubleday's to pick up this book . . . now on my way home. When I get home my mother will telephone me, as always: *How was your day? Are you tired? What did you have for lunch? What are you going to fix for dinner?*

It has been years since I moved out of her house, across town and out of her house.

Teasing, the book lies on my lap. A striking cover of white and gold: *The Premature Autobiography of the Great Composer.* A photograph of Breuer, mature and balding; his eyes encircled with shadow; but he looks intense, strong. His head gleams slightly beneath the fringe of hair. *Herbert Breuer.* On the dust jacket there are words that swim in my head as if a chorus of voices were trying to get my attention: *frank and uninhibited! a real surprise! the public and private life of a genius!*

The faintness rises in me like love.

When I get home I walk slowly up the stairs. It might be dangerous to hurry, to speed things up. *Breuer on Breuer.* But once inside

my door I sit down and leaf shakily through the book. My eyes
jump everywhere—I am terrified that I will come across my own
name too quickly. What if he tells of all the things we did together?
The things he did to me? But the lines of print jump by, page after
page, and nothing makes sense. The top of page 348: ". . . the ten-
day Roman sequence passed without further event. . . ." I turn to
the back of the book, looking for an index. No index. The back
flap of the jacket: "Herbert Breuer, born in Berlin in 1911. . . ."
Born in 1911! The world has become so much younger, everywhere
there are people now who were born in 1950, in 1969 . . . and I myself, though I am not young, am much younger than Breuer.

I sit in the darkening apartment, leafing through this book. My
mind is filled with whispers. Words. Sentences out of the book,
phrases in neat black type, very clean. Not much emotion to the
look of these words. I try to read the book from the beginning, but
the early chapters about Breuer's father and his large, musical,
quarreling family confuse me . . . and I begin to skip, paragraphs
and then pages . . . Breuer in the Twenties, Breuer in the Thirties
. . . a strange sentence on the top of one page, which leaps out: *In
everything I was growing at this time in my life—the universe
expanded around me—I could feel myself growing into it, becoming
myself*—That is Breuer's voice. Unmistakable.

And now I come to the chapter called "Breuer's Americanization,
1954–55." He speaks of himself in the third person, then in the
first person, then in the third person again—why? He holds himself
at a distance, critically. But behind the detachment is his persistent
pride, his ego—*Breuer*, always *Breuer!* At what point in his life
does a genius realize he is a genius, that he must give himself over
to this other personality that inhabits his life, his body? He must
name it absolutely, irrevocably—giving it the name that will become
famous, whether that name is Breuer or something else.

Here, the Sisley Academy. The stench of Buffalo. Yes, yes . . .
and brief mention of his colleagues here . . . *the late Lawrence
Taggart.* . . . And what of . . . ? My heart is pounding violently, I am
really feverish now. . . the lines leap and twist in my eyes . . . what of

me, what will he say? The words arrange themselves in small shouts:

> Breuer in Buffalo had to fight to survive. He drank excessively,
> he got sick and could not even wash himself, there was no
> question of work. Weeks passed without work. The Concerto
> for Violin and Orchestra lay untouched; only the first move-
> ment was completed. But this first movement. . . .

I skip over to the next page:

> At this time Breuer was nursed back to health by a student
> from the Academy. He recalls this young girl as very talented
> and very devoted to Breuer, and in a way he owes all the work
> he accomplished at this time (and after this time) to her.
> In fact, from time to time Breuer says to himself: "I will try
> to recall that name. I will try to recall that face."

I turn the page, which is like metal, crackling. But no more. Only
this:

> What can we say about the people who have saved our lives,
> in forgotten parts of our lives? It is a mystery, those X's we
> make with others. We make the X, we observe and honor
> each other, and then we pass on.

I turn back and read again: *Breuer in Buffalo had to fight to*
survive. He drank. . . .   . . . this young girl was very talented and
very devoted to Breuer. . . . So this is myself! I sit with the book on
my lap, blank. I cannot think what I have read. There is no use
to read further, my name will never appear . . . but in a minute I
leaf through the book anyway . . . other names, dozens of names,
hundreds of names . . . precise names. . . .

But sometimes Breuer thinks to himself: "I will recall that name.
I will recall that face."

And now a sense of peace comes over me.

It is completed, finished, my life with Breuer. The book fixes it
permanently. He will never write to me, he will never call me. He

will never even dedicate one of his compositions to me, since he cannot remember my name. And yet I entered his life at one point, at a certain time in his life, and perhaps I did bring him back to health, perhaps it is true that all his work after that time is because of me, my devotion. . . . The feverish sensation has passed from me now. I am completed.

For years I tried to hate Breuer, and then not to think of him at all, but now I can see that I loved him then and that I love him now. I love him now. My destiny was not to compose, myself, or even to develop my piano technique to any unusual degree, it was not even to make a normal life for myself with a husband and children, but only to cross into Herbert Breuer's life at a certain point, an X, and then to move out of it again forever.

There is a joy in such certainty. It cannot be disturbed. I glance through the book's final chapter, pausing over the photographs of Breuer and his second wife, the violinist Esther Kovenski, a woman twenty years younger than Breuer—a striking woman—and I am not disturbed. Everything is completed now, it is certain. This is my being. Throughout my life I lived like other people who are still fairly young—waiting *to be*, to *become* something—but now I know that I exist completed, in certainty. I am. It is my essence, my being.

The telephone is ringing . . . ! I wake to the apartment, the dreary December light, the ringing phone. Who is calling me? I am still sitting here with my coat on! I stumble to my feet, as if waking from sleep, cowlike and blinking . . . who is telephoning me, who is interrupting me? Then, as soon as I pick up the phone, I know it is my mother; of course it is my mother. *Hello?* she says. *Why didn't you answer for so—*

I put the receiver back gently. I can't talk to her now—not right now. She wouldn't understand my happiness. I couldn't explain it to her. How can a woman explain to anyone else how her life is finished, lived out, completed? How she is free of anguish, needing nothing for the rest of her life, knowing that her life has been completed for her?

Psychiatric Services

—For T. Weisman

". . . not *depression*, then?"

"I wouldn't define it that way, no. That's listless, indifferent, isn't it, that's all-life-drained-out, like some of my own patients. . . . No, it's a confusion of all the genres, I've sifted through everything I know, I use my mind on myself but I can't come to any diagnosis. . . ."

"Whom do you fantasize killing?"

"I can't come to any diagnosis."

". . . what fantasies do you have?"

". . . .I don't have time for fantasies."

"What fantasies might you have, if you had time?"

"Haha, that's a very good line. . . . Well, we all have had fantasies, haven't we, of murdering people? . . . other people? That must go back into my childhood, it must go back, oh, Jesus, twenty years . . . doesn't everyone have these fantasies?"

"I don't think everyone does, necessarily."

"Didn't *you*?"

"I'm a woman."

". . . What bothers me is the suicide fantasies, which are new."

"What means do you use?"

"Not that programmed."

"What is it, a thought, an emotion . . . ? A cluster of thoughts . . . ? Is it something that hasn't yet coalesced?"

"I'm sure it has, when I've been asleep, but when I wake up I can't remember. . . . When I'm on duty over there I wake up and can't remember anything about myself, anything private . . . if I'm being paged I hear the name, a code name, *Saul Zimmerman*, but they could be paging anyone, they could be reading off numbers; all I know is that I respond . . . getting like a fireman: the way I suppose firemen must respond. All body."

"What means would you use?"

"Hypodermic? No. I'm too young . . . it was a rumor, Edward Aikley killed himself, did you know that? . . . must have been a hypo, if anything. No, it's something stronger . . . violent . . . *visual* somehow . . . not with pills, like the poor crazy poisoned kids they bring us. . . . No, God. Did you know of Dr. Aikley?"

"No. . . . When did you begin your residency at County General?"

". . . It isn't procedure, is it, to notify them? . . . My supervisor, uh, you're not going to notify him, are you?"

"Who is he?"

"Feucht, and he knows about some of this, I mean I've talked with him a little, he's fairly nice . . . he's interesting . . . says I'm tired."

"But you disagree with him?"

"Agree, disagree, what does it matter? You know how it is . . .

who's your supervisor? . . . agree, disagree, it makes no difference whatsoever. The disturbing thing is that I'm not as tired as I should be. Everyone else is worn out, but I keep going . . . especially in the last few weeks, when I think of *it*, I mean a kind of doubleness comes over me . . . right there in the emergency ward, doing all the things, a kind of double sense, double vision . . . uh, I would define it as a mental-visual hallucination, but the word hallucination is too strong . . . hey, don't write that down! . . . No, it's too strong; there's nothing visual about it. You didn't write it down? Okay, I'll tell you: I feel very . . . I feel very powerful at those times, when I think of *it*, because it's, uh, the secret . . . that nobody else knows. The mess in there! . . . 900 people a day we get . . . most of them are black, of course . . . how is it over here? . . . of course, you get more students; black or white, they're better patients. But Christ, the mess. . . . So it occurs to me that *I* know the way out, the way they're all groping for but can't discover . . . *they don't know enough.* So in a crazy way . . . don't write that down, please, in a peculiar way, not serious, not intellectually *serious*, in a peculiar way I feel superior to them and even to the staff . . . even to my supervisor. . . . I think of *it*. The means wouldn't matter. Messes carried in here are instructional . . . I never got such specific instruction at Northwestern, where I went to medical school . . . I mean, it's so clear how and why the poor bastard blew it: some of them shoot themselves in the forehead at such an angle that the bullet ploughs up through the skull, or they try for the heart but shatter the collar bone . . . *they don't know enough.* And the ones who take poison take too much or too little. . . . So I feel very, I would say very superior . . . and I feel very masculine . . . so I don't get tired the way my friends do, which is good for my ego, I feel very masculine and I feel young again."

"How old are you?"

"Twenty-eight."

"Yeh, fine. Okay. A scrupulous detailed report, nice handwriting.

But I read between the lines and am not impressed: an exhibitionist."

"But he did seem very nervous. . . . He talked rapidly, he kept making small jokes and grimaces and asides . . . he looked as if he hadn't slept for a while. I asked him if he had been taking anything and he said a little Librium, but it didn't seem to help and—"

"Who's his supervisor?"

"He didn't say."

"So? So ask him."

"I . . . he. . . . He was out in the corridor waiting with everyone else . . . dressed in old clothes, he hadn't shaved, looked sullen and frightened . . . no one would have guessed who he was, I mean that he was a resident. If they had guessed, someone else would have grabbed him, but as it was I got him. . . . I had the impression he was disappointed to draw me."

"Why, because you're a woman?"

"Yes, of course."

"Ha! The little whiner, the bastard, he wants sympathy and someone to talk to, of course he prefers a woman . . . you'll discover it to be a life-pattern in certain personalities. . . . How tall is he?"

"Medium height."

"Innocuous. All of it is innocuous."

"He's twenty-eight."

"I can see that here. . . . Okay, fine. Now who's this, what is this? *Deller?*"

"Yes, you remember, she was the—"

"I don't remember. Stop trembling."

". . . black woman, in the school system here . . . teaches fourth grade. . . ."

"Jenny, does your behavior with your patients resemble your behavior with me?"

"I. . . . I don't know."

"Do you sit there on the edge of your seat, are your lips bluish

with fear? . . . do you lower your head like that just very very slightly
—no, don't move!—so that you can gaze at them through your
lashes? Don't be offended, Jenny, why shouldn't you show yourself
to your best advantage? Have you sense enough to determine what
is your best advantage, however?"

"Dr. Culloch, I . . ."

"You're an attractive woman, why shouldn't you live your life to
the fullest? . . . However, there's no need to be so nervous with me;
what are the rumors, eh? . . . what have you heard about me, eh?"

"I wish you wouldn't laugh at me, Dr. Culloch."

"Who's laughing? . . . this is chuckling, sighing, this is a sympathetic noise from across the desk. But you! If you're angry, go red
instead of white in the face . . . much healthier. Nothing wrong with
healthy anger."

"I'm not angry. . . ."

"Nothing wrong with healthy anger."

"I know, but I'm not angry, Dr. Culloch."

"*Aren't you?*"

"No. No."

"What is all that passion, then?—all that trembling?"

"Dr. Culloch, I wish you wouldn't do this—"

"Are you happy here?"

"Oh yes. Yes."

"We treat women better here, better than the boondocks where
you interned; this is a livelier place in every way, do you agree? . . .
So you're happy. So stay happy."

"Yes, Dr. Culloch."

". . . no, you're not disturbing me. . . . What time is it?"

". . . You were asleep, weren't you. I lose track of the time myself . . . it's probably around two or three . . . my watch is untrust-
worthy and I can't see any clocks from here. . . . I'm sorry for waking
you up, did I wake you up?"

"It's all right. It doesn't matter."

". . . been wanting to call you all evening, but I didn't get a break until now. I'm on the fourteenth floor, staff lounge, do you know the layout here?"

"No."

". . . The thing is, I feel awfully shaky and embarrassed, I mean about the official nature of it. . . . You aren't going to report back to Feucht, are you?"

"Who? . . . No."

"Okay. Jesus, I'm sorry to wake you; I'll hang up now."

"No, wait—"

"And the reason I didn't show up for the second appointment, I didn't even remember it until a few hours later—a friend of mine was sick, I had to take over for him off and on—I wanted to call you and explain but so much time went by I figured what the hell, you'd forgotten. . . . I'll hang up now."

"No. How are you? Do you feel better?"

". . . I would say so, yes. Sometimes I feel very happy. That sensation of power I mentioned . . . it's rather encouraging at times. I realize this is absurd, I realize how crazy it sounds . . . God, I hope nobody's tapping this telephone! . . . I know I should hang up. . . . The reason I called you is, I feel a little strange. There's this sensation of power, of happiness, like I used to have as a boy occasionally, and when I was in high school, playing football, occasionally I'd have it also . . . a surge of joy, a pulsation of joy. . . ."

"Euphoria?"

"Euphoria. Do you know what it's like? . . . Being carried along by the pulse of it, of *it*, whatever *it* is. . . . So much excitement, so much life and death outside me, carrying me along with it, along with the flow of it. One of my patients died on me, hemorrhaged all over me, I just kept talking to him and didn't allow either of us to get excited. . . . So I thought I would call you. I've been thinking about you, but I haven't diagnosed my thinking. I'm sorry to have missed the appointment. . . . Could I come see you?"

"Now?"

"Yes."

"Of course not. No. What do you want?"

"Dr. Feucht tells me there's nothing wrong—I'm exaggerating. He says new residents always exaggerate, dramatize. Maybe that's all it is . . . maybe it's nothing real. . . . I can't come see you then?"

". . . in love with you, eh? Don't be coy!"

"Dr. Culloch, please—"

"A long nocturnal conversation—special considerations—is this what they taught you in Baltimore, Jenny? The John F. Kennedy Clinic, did they teach you such things there?"

"He missed his appointment and sounded very excited over the phone . . . I don't know how he got my number, there must be so many *Hamiltons* in the city. . . ."

"He isn't seriously disturbed; he's pleading for your special attention, your love. . . . You'll learn to recognize these symptoms and not to be flattered by them."

"I'm sorry, Dr. Culloch, but I—"

"Being professional is the acquisition of a single skill: not to let them flatter you into thinking you're—what? Eh? *God*, eh?—Or V*enus*?"

"But . . . but Dr. Zimmerman . . . Saul. . . . Why did you bring that here? Why . . . What are you going to do with that?"

"Don't be frightened!"

"Saul—"

"The last three or four days I've been awake straight through, by my own choice. I don't want to be a zombie, I want more control. . . . Don't be so alarmed, I just brought it to show you: it's rather handsome, isn't it? I'm not going to hurt you. I wouldn't hurt *you*. From where you sit, it probably looks like a toy gun, maybe; it's amazing how life-like the toy guns are, and how toy-like the real ones are . . . makes your head spin. There's a difference in price though."

"Is that a real gun?"

". . . insulting . . . castrating. . . . No, you're very nice, the first time I saw you out in the hall I thought *She's nice, any nut would have a chance with her* . . . remind me of a cousin of mine, haven't seen for years, slight little girl with freckles, pale skin. . . . It's an insult, to ask a person whether he's carrying a toy gun, don't you know that? Don't insult me. Under the circumstances I must strike you as strange enough, but not so strange that I can't give you professional advice . . . don't insult them when they're armed. . . . I'm just joking. I'm really just joking. . . . The only women at County General are the nurses. I don't think they like me."

". . . You'd better give that to me, you know. To me. You'd better . . ."

"Certainly not. Why should I give it to you?"

"I think it would be a good idea if . . . if you gave it to me."

"Why? It's my own discovery. It's my secret. I want to share it with you in a way, but I don't intend to give it to you."

"But you can't be serious! . . . Why did you bring it here, wrapped up like that—what is that, a towel?—why did you bring it here, if you don't really want to give it to me? You—you really want to give it to me—don't you? Wouldn't that be better?—You've put me in such a terrible position—I'm sure I should report you—it—you've made me an accessory to—"

"To what? I have a permit for it."

"A permit? You have . . . ?"

". . . walked into the police station down the block from the hospital, bought a permit, went to a gun store, bought the gun. . . . They're expensive but I didn't buy much ammunition. . . . You know I'm just fooling around with this, don't you? . . . just fooling around. I certainly don't intend to use it, on myself or anyone."

"That's right. That's right. . . . Obviously, you brought it here this afternoon to give to me, didn't you? . . . to give to me?"

"It's the smallest size. They have enormous ones . . . with longer barrels so that you can take better aim . . . something so small, so the man told me, has a poor aim, the bullet is likely to veer off in any direction. I don't know anything about guns. Not even rifles. I'm from Winnetka. I didn't have a father interested in hunting. It's amazing, all the things I don't know . . . don't have experience of. Now it's too late."

"Saul, why don't you let me keep the gun for you? Please?"

"I do have a permit for it. . . . However, not for carrying it on my person; I don't have a permit to carry a concealed weapon. So maybe I'd better give it to you after all. . . . But can I have it back when I'm well?"

"You're not sick."

"Yes, but when I'm well can I have it back? . . . I can pawn it at the same place I bought it; the man might remember me."

"Yes, of course you can have it back . . . I'll keep it in my desk drawer here . . . I can lock it, this desk is assigned to me for the year . . . no one can open it except me . . . I promise . . . I promise that . . ."

". . . only afraid that if I surrender it I'll lose this feeling I have most of the time . . . it helps me get through the night shift especially. . . . With one part of my mind I realize that it's absurd, that the whole thing is absurd . . . I did my stint in psychiatrics too, and I must say I hated it . . . really hated it . . . my supervisor was a bastard, and that wasn't just my private opinion either. I realize it's absurd that I'm talking to you because you don't know anything more than I do, maybe less, you're sitting there terrified and the only advantage I have over you is that I'm not terrified . . . but if I give *it* up I might lapse into being terrified . . . and. . . . I've always been so healthy, that's the goddam irony. I *am* healthy. Kids dropped out of school, blew their minds entirely, wound up in the expensive asylums along the lake, but not me, not *me*, and my father would go crazy himself if he knew I was having therapy three times a week with *you*. . . . He could do so much more for me! . . . I can hear his voice saying those words, his whining voice. . . . The one thing I'm ashamed of and must apologize for is frightening you, Dr. Hamilton."

". . . I'm not frightened. . . ."

". . . Feucht is away for a conference, Hawaii, he says it's ordinary nerves and exaggeration, I know he's right . . . but where does he get the strength from? . . . Aikley, they said he killed himself, did you hear that? . . . no, you didn't know him . . . what it is, is, something to circle around, a fixed place . . . a thought . . . the thinking of it, the possibility of *it* . . . what is it, transcendence? . . . At the same time I'm an adolescent, obnoxious bastard, to come over here and frighten a pretty young woman like you."

". . . aren't you going to give me the gun? . . . to put in the desk drawer?"

". . . maybe I only want revenge, maybe it's simplistic revenge against the usual people . . . the usual innocent people: my father, my mother. Sometimes I think that if it were possible for me to wipe out my own father, my personal father, I might get to something more primary . . . but . . . uh . . . it's difficult to talk about these things, I really don't know how to talk about them. I don't have the vocabulary. . . . must tell you, a kid in emergency hallucinating . . . shrieking and laughing and really blown . . . *very happy* . . . hadn't a good vein left in him. . . . All I want is to wipe out a few memories and start again from zero but the memories accumulate faster than I can even notice them, faster faster faster . . . all the time. But how do you wipe the memories away without blowing away the brain?"

". . . This is the drawer, see? . . . and I have the key for it, here. Here."

"Okay."

"Thank you. Thank you."

". . . sorry to be so . . ."

"Thank you very much, Saul, thank you . . . now, you see? . . . Dr. Zimmerman? . . . you see, I'm locking it up, it's your property and I can even, I can even give you a receipt for it . . . yes, I'll be happy to . . . I'll . . ."

"Are you all right? . . . not going to faint?"

"I—"

"Are you going to faint? Jesus!"

"No, I'm all right—I'm all right—"

"You sure?"

"I've never fainted in my life."

". . . sorry to be disturbing you again . . . you weren't asleep, were you? . . . answered the phone on the first ring, you weren't asleep, were you?"

"No. What do you want, Saul?"

". . . just to apologize, I feel I've made such a fool of myself . . . and it isn't fair to involve you . . . you're younger than I am, aren't you? . . . you have lots of other patients assigned to you, God, I hope they're not as troublesome as I . . . because you know, don't you, Jenny, *you know* . . . I'm really harmless; I'm just temporarily troubled about something. It isn't uncommon."

"I understand. I'm not angry, I'm not frightened . . . well, I admit that I was a little frightened at the hospital today . . . I shouldn't have been so easily upset . . . but the gun itself, seeing it, the gun shocked me . . . it was so real."

"Yes! It was so *real*. So that struck you too?"

"Oh yes it struck me . . . it struck me too."

"Where do you live, Jenny? The operator doesn't give out that kind of information, she says . . . you're not listed in the new directory, are you, you're new to the city just like me. . . . Could I come over or is it too late?"

"It's too late, it's very late, Saul."

"What time is it?"

". . . very late. Please. Why don't you visit me at the hospital tomorrow, wouldn't that be soon enough?"

"I realize I'm disturbing you but I had the sense . . . the sensation . . . that you aren't married . . . ? I mean, there's no husband there with you, is there?"

"I'll see you tomorrow. I'll squeeze you in somehow . . . somehow . . . or . . . or, please Saul, please, we could talk in the first-floor cafeteria, at the back, I'll wait for you there at noon . . . we can talk there . . . please."

"Look: you demanded I give you the gun. And I did. I obeyed you. *Good boy* you probably thought, *good boy, look how he obeys.* Now you lose interest in me. . . . What do you care what I've been going through?"

"I care very much. . . ."

". . . I noticed a fly crawling out of some guy's nostril over here, some very old black guy in a coma for five days . . . filling up with maggots, he was, wasn't even dead, they're jammed in here and so stinking sick . . . and the pathologist making jokes about it . . . I wondered if *he* was the one I had wanted to kill and got very upset, to think I'd lost the gun. . . ."

". . . *What?*"

"What?"

"What about that man?"

". . . cardiac seizure, he wasn't that old . . . fifty-five, sixty . . . it's hard to tell, they're so wrecked when they come in. . . . We're busy over here. . . . What kind of a tone did you take with me? . . . You sound *annoyed.*"

"What about that man?—I don't believe—"

"What, are you annoyed that I woke you up? Hey look: we're in this together. I trusted you, didn't I, and you promised me, didn't you, and there's a professional bond between us . . . I'm not just another patient off the streets, off the campus, there's a professional bond between us, so don't take that tone with me. I order people around too: all the time, in fact. I order women around all the time. And they obey me. You bet they obey me! So don't you take that annoyed tone with me."

"Saul, I'm not annoyed—but I think you must be—must be imagining—must be exaggerating—"

". . . the purpose of this call was, I think it was . . . uh . . . to apologize for frightening you earlier today. And to ask you to keep it private, all right? The business about the gun. I mean, don't include it on your report, will you, you needn't tell him everything. . . . Don't be annoyed with me, please, I think I'll be through it soon . . . out the other side, soon . . . I'll be rotated to obstetrics in seventeen days which should be better news . . . unless some freaky things happen there too . . . it's a different clientele here, you know, from what I was accustomed to. . . . Hey look: don't be annoyed with me, you're my friend, don't be annoyed that I almost caused you to faint today."

"I didn't faint . . . I didn't come near to fainting."

". . . well, if . . ."

"I've never fainted in my life."

"You *what*?—Oh, you romantic girl! You *baby*!"

". . . What? I don't understand. Did I do something wrong, Dr. Culloch?"

"Wrong? Wrong? *Everything you have done is wrong.* Oh, it would be comic if not so alarming, that you came to us knowing so little—so meagerly trained—Had you only textbook theory, you could have handled that problem more professionally! And with the background you have, before the Baltimore clinic you were where? Nome, Alaska?—an adventuresome young woman, not a lily, a wilting fawning creature—and a year at that girls' detention home or farm or whatever in Illinois—*didn't you learn anything*? To be so manipulated by a cunning paranoid schizophrenic—to have him laughing up his sleeve at you—"

"But—"

"But! Yes, *but*. But but but.—You did exactly the wrong thing in taking that gun away from him. *Don't you know anything*?"

". . . I did the wrong thing, to take it away . . . ?"

"Absolutely. Now, you explain to *me* why it was wrong."

"It was wrong?"

". . . why it was idiotic, imbecilic."

". . . but. . . . It was wrong because . . it must have been wrong because . . . because . . . I affirmed his suicidal tendencies? Is that it, Dr. Culloch? . . . I affirmed his suicidal tendencies . . . I took him seriously . . . therefore . . ."

"Go on."

". . . therefore . . . I indicated that he didn't have rational control and responsibility for his own actions . . . yes, I see . . . I think I see now . . . it was a mistake because I showed him that in fact I didn't trust him: I took him at his word, that he would commit suicide."

"Not only that, my dear, let's have some fun with you . . . eh? Under cover of being the Virgin Mary and mothering him out of your own godliness, you in fact used it as a cover, the entire session, to act out your own willfulness and envy of men. . . . Eh? What do you say? Ah, blushing, blushing! . . . And well you might blush, eh? . . . So you turn him loose, the pathetic little bastard, a castrated young man turned loose . . . and you have the gun, eh? . . . locked up safely, eh? . . . so you gloat about it and can't wait to rush in here to let me know the latest details, eh? Fortunate for you that Max Culloch has been around a long time . . . a very very long time . . . and knows these little scenarios backwards and forwards."

"Dr. Culloch—are you joking?"

"Joking? I?"

"Sometimes you—you tease us so—"

"If you silly little geese giggle, can I help it? I have a certain reputation for my wit, I do admit it, and a reputation—wholly unearned, I tell you in all modesty—as—what?—eh?—being rather young for my age, eh?—is that what they gossip about?—but you won't gossip with them, Jenny, will you? Of this year's crop you are *very* much the outstanding resident; I tell you that frankly. . . . Only because you struck me originally as being so superior can I forgive you for this asinine blunder: affirming a paranoid schizophrenic in his suicidal delusions."

"I did wrong . . . I did wrong, then, in taking the gun from him?"

"Don't squeak at me in that little-mouse voice, you're a woman of passion and needn't make eyes at me and look through your hair . . . and don't sit like that, as if you're ashamed of your body, why be ashamed? . . . you're attractive, you know it, your physical being is most attractive and *it* senses that power whether you do or not, Dr. Hamilton . . . right? I'm decades older than you, my dear, I'm seventy-three years old and I know so much, so very much, that it's sometimes laughable even to deal with ordinary people. . . . It's become a burden to me, my own reputation, a genius, my own fame is a burden to me because it obliges me to take so seriously and so politely the opinions of my ignorant colleagues . . . when I'd like simply to pull switches, shut them up, get things done as they must be done. At least you young people don't argue with me: you know better. . . . So. Let us review this fascinating lesson, Jenny. What did you do wrong?"

"I did wrong to take the gun from him and to affirm his suicidal inclinations. And . . . and he had a permit for the gun, too . . . at least to own a gun. . . . It wasn't illegal, his owning the gun. . . . And so I was exerting power over him. . . ."

"Gross maternal power, yes. The prettier and smaller you girls are, the more demonic! . . . Your secret wish right this moment, Jenny, is—is what? eh? You'd like to slap old Dr. Culloch, wouldn't you?"

"Not at all—"

"Someday we'll let you; why be so restrained? . . . But at the moment, I think it wisest for you to undo the harm you've done to that poor boy. You'd better telephone him and ask him to come over and take the gun back."

". . . ask him to take it back?"

". . . or is he your lover, and you would rather not call *him*?"

"He isn't my lover!"

"... who is, then? Or have you many?"

"I haven't any lovers! I have my work. ..."

"Yet you're attracted to him, aren't you? I can literally smell it— I can smell it—the bizarre forms that love-play can take—"

"I'm not attracted to him, I feel sorry for him—I—I'm not attracted to him. I have my work . . . I work very hard . . . I don't have time for . . ."

"*I* am your work."

"... Yes."

"Yes what?"

"Yes, that's so."

"Everything is processed through me. Everything in this department. ... Do you dream about me?"

"Yes, of course."

"And what form do I take?"

"What form? . . . The form . . . the form you have now."

"No younger?"

"I . . . I don't know. ... Dr. Culloch, this is so upsetting to me, it's so confusing and embarrassing. . . . I never know when you're joking and when you're serious."

"I am always joking and always serious. You may quote me."

". . . I've become so mixed up during this conversation, I can't remember what . . . what we were talking about. ..."

". . . not that I'm the Max Culloch of even eight years ago. . . . Yeh, pot-bellied, going bald, with this scratchy scraggly beard . . . but . . . *but*. You understand, eh? Many a young rival has faded out of the dreamwork entirely when old Max appears. It's nature. . . . The one thing I don't like, Jenny, is the possibility of your arranging this entire scenario with the aim of manipulating Max. . . . I wouldn't like that at all. *Did you?*"

"Did I . . . ?"

"Play with the boy, take the gun, rush into my office this morning just to tantalize me with your power? . . . force me to discipline you? . . . No, I rather doubt it; you're cunning, but not *that* cunning.

No. I'm inclined to think it was a simple error, one of inexperience rather than basic ignorance, and that it shouldn't be held against you. It's only nature, that you would like to manipulate me. But you haven't a clue, my child, as to the means."

". . . I . . . I . . . Yes, that's right. You're right."

"Of course I'm right."

". . . nothing was intentional, nothing at all. When I saw the gun I followed my instincts . . . my intuition . . . I forgot to analyze the situation in terms of its consequences . . . when I saw the gun I thought No, *I don't want him to die, no, I like him, I don't want—* So I acted without thinking."

"And did you faint in his arms, my dear?"

"Of course not."

"Love-play on both sides. Totally unconscious, totally charming. Do you see it now, rationally?"

"I . . . I didn't see it at the time, but now . . . now . . . you're probably right."

"Probably?"

"You're right."

"And so?"

". . . and . . . ?"

"And so what will you do next?"

"I . . . I will telephone him and admit my error."

"And?"

". . . tell him I misjudged him . . . that he can pick the gun up any time he wants it. . . . I'll tell him that my supervisor has . . ."

"No, no. No sloughing off of authority!"

". . . tell him . . . tell him that I trust him . . . and . . . it was an emotional error on my side . . . inexperience . . . fear. . . . I trust him and . . . and I know he'll be safe with the gun. . . ."

"Go on, go on! You'll have to speak to him more convincingly than that. And smile—yes, a little—yes, not too much—try to avoid that bright manic grin, Jenny, it looks grotesque on a woman with your small facial features. . . . The boy is an idealist like everyone,

and like everyone he must learn . . . as I learned and you will, eh?
. . . or will you? . . . he's an idealist and stupid that way but not so
stupid that he wouldn't be able to see through that ghastly smile of
yours. I have the impression, Jenny, that you don't believe me: that
you're resisting me. Are you trying to antagonize me?"

"No, of course not! I'm . . . I'm just very nervous. I didn't sleep
at all last night. I'm very nervous and . . ."

"Chatter, chatter! . . . So you've given your young friend his gun
back . . . you've made things right between you again . . . yeh, fine,
fine. Now what?"

"Now . . . ?"

"Now what do you say? Will you say anything further?"

". . . I will say that . . . that he'll be rotated out of the service he's
in, and he'll be eventually out of the hospital . . . maybe he'll have
a private practice in the area . . . his hometown is north of here,
along the lake . . . and . . . and . . . and he'll escape, he'll forget.
. . . I can't remember what I was saying."

"What a goose! . . . At any rate, what do you think *he* will say?
When you give him his masculinity back?"

"He'll say. . . ."

"Think hard!"

"He'll say . . . probably . . . He'll probably say *Thank you*."

"*Thank you?*"

". . . *Thank you*."

*T*he Goddess

"No, *please,*" her husband said sharply.

The black porter had gone to the television set in the hotel room and was about to switch it on.

"Thank you, but it isn't necessary," Claudia said.

"No, it isn't necessary," Alfred said.

Claudia went to one of the windows to avoid the awkward gesture of her husband's tipping the porter—a very dark, peevish man in his late twenties, who had forced himself to smile at them several times, down in the lobby and in the hotel corridor and as he set the suitcases down on the rug, a measured, taut smile. He had not exactly looked at them. Surreptitiously, he had sniffed a few times as if he had a cold and was trying to hide it; he had even wiped his nose on the cuff of his uniform when he thought no one could notice. The uniform was pale blue, with rows of silver buttons and an ornate *S P* on the collar, embroidered in fine silkish silver-blue.

Behind her Claudia heard her husband's murmured *Here* and another quick murmur that was unintelligible.

When they were alone Alfred said, "Is this the same room—? I asked for 1720 but this doesn't look familiar. They've done something to it, rearranged the furniture . . . the beds were over here, weren't they? The television set is much larger than before. . . ."

"If it doesn't look familiar," Claudia said, "it's because they haven't kept the original decorator's scheme. The beds should have bolsters, not pillows, and the television cabinet and the dresser haven't any style at all, they're just functional. But I like the room, I like being back here. I think it is the same room, I remember looking out here, over this way, and seeing that tower. . . . Isn't that it, doesn't it light up at night? I'm sure this is the same room."

"It doesn't matter," Alfred said.

"No, certainly it doesn't matter," Claudia said quickly. She knew that when her husband traveled—mainly to London, Madrid, Amsterdam, and Munich, since the pharmaceutical company he worked for had subsidiary plants in those cities—he always stayed in the same hotel, the Hilton, and always in the same room. He had his secretary book the rooms months in advance. "But it's nice to ask for something you've already been pleased with, since . . ."

"You do like it well enough, don't you?" he asked. His manner was eager and almost apprehensive, as if he were still courting her; but she knew enough not to presume upon it, since it could shade at once into annoyance. They had been married twenty-three years and Claudia had, since the first several months of their marriage, caught on to this quirk in his personality. She always replied *Yes, very much.*

Strangely, it was always true.

". . . but the view has certainly changed," Alfred said. "My God!

Look at the size of that building over there . . . it's obviously new,
very new, it doesn't even look as if it's occupied. I can't remember
what used to be in its place, can you?"

"No," Claudia said. "I don't remember."

"We were here a week, and had some wonderful breakfasts up in
the room . . . I remember looking out in that direction, but . . . It's
all very striking, isn't it?"

"Yes, it's very striking."

The flight from Chicago had been delayed ninety minutes, so by
the time the plane had landed and they had been driven to the
hotel, it was late in the afternoon and the sun slanted across the
view before them, illuminating it in the dizzying drop—light reflected in the windows of other high-rise buildings, orangish, russet,
yellow, a galaxy of constant blinks and flutterings. There was the
illusion, for some reason, of movement, motion. The dark-tinted
plate-glass strips in the other building reflected the Sherwood Plaza,
but in a multilayered, jagged, unsequential way, as if someone had
shaken both buildings, and outlines, the spaces between outlines,
were not yet settled. Patterns swayed and did not come to rest.
Alfred commented on the architectural beauty of that new building,
and of others in the area, though he had heard that such expanses
of glass were a poor investment in a climate like this, where temperatures could drop abruptly as soon as the sun set. In the winter, a
pane of glass that was unwisely long could crack: one temperature
at the top, another at the bottom. But Claudia agreed that it was
beautiful.

While he checked their luggage and went into the bathroom,
Claudia continued to stare out the window. The view was part of
it; part of the expensive room. She had not traveled with her husband for nearly a year, since business trips bored her, and her diffi-
culty at pretending an interest in her husband's associates and their
wives annoyed both her and Alfred. She remembered now the feeling of exultation, of unreasonable freedom, that she had always had
when looking out the window of a hotel room. But this view was

especially fascinating. Shadows, sharp-edged sliding rays of light . . . panels of light that were vertical, crisscrossed with horizontal panels . . . cubistic structures piled gracefully atop one another, some of the upper stories thicker than the lower, unless that was an optical illusion. She did not really care for modern art of any kind, and certainly not contemporary art, but the sheer spectacle of these buildings and the sunset seemed to her as beautiful as any artwork she had ever seen. But it was dizzying, disturbing. A few lights came on —the street lights along the Avenue—and the view was changed at once, subtly but irrevocably. Photographs could be taken minute by minute, second by second, to record these changes, especially at this time of day. It was haunting to her, those cubistic blocks of precast concrete and glass, some opaque, some with the illusion of transparency. Rows and rows of windows, squares, rectangles, ovals of glass, strips of glass that seemed, from this distance, impractical because they were so narrow—hardly more than a foot across—and a vertical, staggered, block-pattern of glass bricks . . . some of them illuminated from within, because they were on the darker side of the building, some glaring with light from the sunset, those in the middle paler, fainter, undefined. One building was obviously an office building; Claudia could see fluorescent tubing, lit for the night, and there were no balconies, not even the absurdly narrow balconies of the apartment building across the street from the hotel. The colors kept changing as she stared: red, orange, a very pale fiery yellow, fading into white. At their tops the high-rise buildings were still in the daylight; near their bottoms, near the ordinary five- or six-story level of the older buildings, dusk had already begun.

When her husband came back she asked him whether it was practical, in this climate, to have balconies?—terraces?—since it was cold most of the year. Alfred said that the balconies she meant weren't balconies in any functional sense of the word but yes, she was fundamentally correct, they weren't practical, nor were swimming pools either. But it was a matter of money: if you can afford it, you can afford it.

Out on the Avenue, they discovered a number of changes. In the three years since Claudia and Alfred had been here, a number of the art galleries and antique shops had evidently closed, and in their places were cheaper stores, though a few of the better stores remained. Claudia saw the small gallery where she had discovered a lithograph of a London bridge by Telford, which she had argued Alfred into buying, though the name of the gallery now seemed unfamiliar—*The Gilberti*. Alfred was pleased. "While I'm at their office you can shop here. Remember? . . . How you argued, how you impressed me, knowing so much! And you turned out to be absolutely right. You were absolutely right."

Next to that gallery was an enormous antique shop, a clearing-house for estates; an auction was to be held at the end of the month, unfortunately too late for Claudia. She stood for a while, staring in the wide window, past the grillwork that protected it from the street, her eye moving slowly from item to item: an engraving that showed the evolutionary development of plants, finely worked, busy, evidently from the late nineteenth century, evidently English; a dining room set, including even a crazily ornate silver service that was slightly tarnished, from, she believed, Victorian England; some amateurish portraits, of men and women singly, and of entire families, in the costumes of eighteenth-century France. . . . "Do you see anything that looks interesting to you?" Alfred asked sympathetically.

"It's too dark," Claudia said.

As they walked along the Avenue, however, there were fewer good stores; every fourth or fifth shop seemed to be selling "adult" books or showing "around-the-clock adult films," and these shops were open. *X-Rated Continuous 24-Hr. Live Entertainment! Guaranteed Uninhibited Live Entertainment!* In place of a boutique Claudia remembered from three years ago there was a sleazy Unisex Drygoods store, also open, and amplified music blared out onto the street, mixing with overloud music from a hi-fi equipment store nearby. Irritated, Claudia paused to stare into the shop while Alfred walked along without her. Racks of cheap Levi's and jump-suits and flimsy, brightly dyed shirts. Everything looked cluttered, shoved together. On one of the walls was a blown-up photograph of Uncle Sam making an obscene gesture, smiling a chummy obscene smile, with rows of garish stars and stripes surrounding him like a crown. There weren't many customers inside, only a few long-haired boys and girls pawing through the clothes; one of them wore a sheepskin coat and even an outlandish tall fur hat, though it was early September.

Alfred said sharply, "Come on, honey, you don't intend to go in there, do you? Come on. It smells around here."

They crossed the street to an art gallery that featured North American art; its show window was lit, but the Eskimo sculpture and line drawings did not look authentic but like reproductions, soapstone seals and ducks and caribou that were too smooth. Alfred admired them. But when Claudia did not reply he sensed that something was wrong, something was disappointing, so he shrugged his shoulders and said, "Of course I don't know anything about these things . . . they could be manufactured, for all I know."

Wedged in between the hi-fi stores and the cheap clothing stores, the "adult books" and the *Continuous Exhibitions!* and an Army-Navy Surplus outlet and pizza parlors, taverns, donut shops, and all-night diners, were a few fairly good stores, but Claudia saw that it was hopeless; this end of the Avenue had deteriorated. She peered in the dusty window of a gallery and saw only a heap of things, the leftovers of a sale or an auction, tarnished candelabra with marble bases the size of concrete blocks, Wedgwood china vases, an earthenware jar with Oriental figures on its sides, German figurines—boy-shepherds, girl-shepherds, old men with pink, grinning cheeks and curly gray locks—unwound brocade, a lace tablecloth, a curious Oriental statuette with garish red and yellow clots of color that arrested her attention. While Alfred checked his watch, Claudia stared at the statuette. It turned slowly into the figure of a woman, but she was standing with her legs apart, pot-bellied, naked, her breasts long and pointed, her savage fat-cheeked face fixed in a grin, her many arms outspread, and around her neck what looked like a necklace of skulls.

Claudia felt her face flush, felt the surface of her skin react at once to this ugly thing—a rush of quick angry blood.

"No, we won't be able to get a cab along here," Alfred was saying nervously. "We'll have to walk for a few blocks. . . . You still want to go to . . . ?"

"Yes, of course," Claudia said. "Why don't we walk?"

"It's too far to walk."

"We walked last time."

"No, let me get a cab."

On the street were young boys and girls, many of them quite well-dressed, as if down here on dates, curious and explorative and noisy with laughter, and some of them very badly dressed—barefoot and filthy; and there were solitary men of all ages. Alfred made such an awkward effort not to brush against one of them—a youngish man in a pea-green blazer—that Claudia supposed, knowing Alfred's feelings on the subject, the man must be a homosexual. How Alfred loathed them . . . ! There were a very few tourists like Claudia and Alfred on the street, hesitant, well-dressed couples who had evidently wandered down from the hotel area a few blocks to the north.

Her hand held out, a girl with a blemished face approached Claudia. ". . . change?"

Before they could move away she was joined by a wispy-haired boy in a canvas jacket who elbowed her aside, shoving his opened hand toward Alfred. ". . . mister, y'got some change? Hey, I'm talking to you. . . . Hey, whereya going so fast? Hey! You two, whoya turning ya goddam fucking backs on like that, huh?" He was shouting after them. "I got a twenty-thousand-dollar training behind me! My I.Q. is in the upper one percentile! You can't just walk away from me—*you'll regret it!*"

But he did not follow them. When Claudia dared to look back, she saw that he was spitting on the windshield of a car parked on the street, muttering at it. He seemed very angry, as if he had confused the car with Claudia and Alfred. A small group of people had gathered to watch him, including the girl.

They hailed a cab and rode to *The Roqueira*, a Portuguese restaurant about a mile away, in a neighborhood that did not seem to have changed very much. There was a squad car parked conspicuously near an intersection, but otherwise it was as they remembered it.

When they returned to their hotel room, shortly aften ten, Claudia knew immediately that something was wrong.

The room was altered. The curtains inside the heavy brocade drapes did not look right. No, it was the shade on the floor lamp . . . it seemed to her tilted in a way she had not noticed earlier. Entering the room hours before, she would certainly have noticed that. . . . But she could not be certain now, because Alfred had switched on the overhead light, which was fly-specked and far too bright, its light raw, ugly, exaggerated; and this in itself altered the appearance of the room. In the dresser mirror, framed by imitation French Provincial white-and-flecked-gold, she saw her own surprised face.

"I think—I think—Someone was in here while—"

But her husband had already discovered the theft: his briefcase was gone.

There was no need for Claudia to be so frightened, since her husband was here. He was angry, incredulous. He kept checking the suitcases—the large tan one they shared, the two smaller ones that matched, exactly alike down to their *French Line* stickers—but evidently nothing else was missing. He asked Claudia to look through her things again. And once again. "Are you sure? Are you? —You're not really looking!" But she felt too surprised, dazed, to be able to concentrate on the unfamiliar things spread out on the bed. Nothing looked familiar. Her husband's voice was not familiar, though she had certainly heard it before, and even some of the words: *the bastard, the black bastard, how obvious of him, they're all alike—* He walked heavily to the closet, into the bathroom,

slammed things around, while Claudia forced herself to sit out of
the way, out of his pathway, wondering if she should bring her head
down between her knees. She knew there was nothing to be afraid
of. She had not been frightened of the boy on the street and had
forgotten about him during dinner . . . she had forgotten all about
him. . . . If she brought her head down between her knees, as one
of her teachers had instructed her decades ago, to prevent her from
fainting at a class picnic, if she did that her husband would notice
her and be very angry.

"This is room 1720! Hello! Look, this is Mr. Buell in room 1720
and I want to report a—I want to report a theft— The porter who
brought our things up when we checked in—I can identify him if
you— He came back to the room while we were gone and— What?
Why should I come to see the manager! I know exactly what took
place and I want that briefcase back in ten minutes or I'm calling
the police—"

He hung up.

He was trembling.

He began to shout at Claudia that it had not been his idea to
come to this particular city: he had wanted to go to the Thousand
Islands, to his lodge there, his dead grandfather's lodge, and—
Then he asked her, more reasonably, if she was certain that nothing
more had been taken?—had she really examined her things carefully?

"Yes," Claudia said.

They waited.

Several minutes passed. Just as Alfred was about to telephone the
desk again, the phone rang. He snatched up the receiver. He was
standing, unable to sit still, pacing around—a broad-chested man,
somewhat overweight but curiously narrower in the waist, and especially in the hips, than he was in his torso—his white shirt opened
now, the sleeves pushed up, the jade cuff links tossed absentmindedly onto one of the beds. Claudia watched him anxiously. She
knew that whatever was in the briefcase would have no value to
anyone except her husband; but she knew it had inestimable value

to him, since this vacation was meant to coincide with a visit to a tax lawyer's office—a specialist of some kind, recommended by their tax lawyer at home. Quieter now, her husband was explaining to someone at the other end that the briefcase contained Xeroxed forms, several hundreds of them, material that had no resale value, just duplicates of tax returns and receipts and— "What do you mean, you don't know anything about it?" he asked. "What? What do you mean? . . . Prove it? Prove what? I know exactly what happened and who— *What?* You expect me to believe that? You expect me to believe that someone has a duplicate key—someone unconnected with this hotel—" He listened. "Give me an outside line," he said. "I'll call the police."

He got the line but didn't know the number; he looked around, confused, and Claudia sprang to her feet to hand him the telephone directory.

He paged through it so clumsily that it fell to the floor, between his knees. He hung up. He told Claudia he was going downstairs to talk to the manager, face to face, and if he saw that porter in the lobby—

"Do you think we really had it?—when we checked in?" Claudia asked. "Maybe it got lost at the airport—or—"

"What? Of course I had the briefcase. There were four pieces of luggage, four, I counted them a half-dozen times, I checked them all the way in and up in this room," Alfred said, "so please don't for Christ's sake confuse me."

"But it might—it might have gotten stolen somewhere else—"

"*He* took it," Alfred said. "That black bastard, that frozen-faced son of a bitch! I'm going to get the police over to this place and get that briefcase back. The manager tried to tell me someone must have had the key to the room duplicated, and came back here to— A guest at the hotel, he said, and no one connected with the hotel— can you imagine that? Can you imagine? *Expecting me to believe that!*"

He slammed the door behind him.

Claudia checked the closet again. She looked into the bathroom but the whiteness of the porcelain and the hair-thin cracks in it made her dizzy. She straightened the bedspreads, moved mechanically to hang things up, not so alarmed now that she was alone. It seemed to her suddenly that her husband would probably come back with the briefcase. There had probably been a mistake of some kind. . . . She realized that the ugly overhead light was still on, so she switched it off. The room looked better with a single lamp burning.

In a few minutes there was a muffled, perfunctory knock at the door and her husband came in, with another man to whom he was speaking loudly. *So obvious! So obvious a theft!* The manager switched the overhead light on again. He was a tall, thick-bodied man in his fifties, with a mottled complexion; he did no more than glance at Claudia, gray-eyed, panting, and muttered a greeting. He searched the room, slowly, absurdly, crouching over, peering under the furniture while they watched him . . . when he opened the door to the bathroom Alfred lost his patience and said, "Look! I want that briefcase back! The porter is still on duty, I caught sight of him downstairs— You people are responsible— *It isn't in the bathroom, we've already looked!*"

The manager muttered something about it being late—"already shift-break"—but Alfred interrupted and said he wanted the police, he wanted a police detective sent over. The manager scratched his chin. His gray-black hair had fallen loose when he stooped over, and now damp-looking quills of hair hung separate from one another. Flush-faced, apologetic, he said, "One of the problems is . . . you don't want to . . . Don't want to make any . . . If there are accusations made, and . . . And the police come . . . Morale among the staff is, it has been, an incident took place on Sunday that . . ." He mumbled something about a false fire alarm set off by a cleaning lady who had been accused of, who had been called into his office and accused of stealing something, it might not be necessary to accuse anyone of anything. It might be the case, he said vaguely, that the missing item would show up in the morning.

"Show up? Where? How?"

"It might have been misplaced in the taxi you came in and the cabbie will discover it," the manager said slowly.

"I had that briefcase when we checked in," Alfred said. He had to walk with the manager toward the door, gesturing at him, almost ready—Claudia saw with embarrassment—to seize the man's arm to stop him from leaving. "*It was stolen by one of your porters.*"

"Can you prove that?" the manager said quickly.

"Can I prove it? Prove what?"

"Can you prove it was stolen by the boy?"

"—he knew exactly when we checked in, he knew exactly when we went out to dinner—"

"Can you prove anything was stolen at all?"

Alfred followed the man out into the corridor, shouting. He followed him down to the elevators. He called back to Claudia that he was going down to the lobby and she should close the door and chain it because the place was unsafe—she should pack their suitcases, get everything ready, because they were checking out—and—

Claudia heard the manager's voice, asking her husband to speak more quietly.

She closed the door and double-locked it.

For dinner she had eaten cod cakes and a very spicy chicken dish, and the wine the waiter had recommended was far too sweet, and something about the restaurant had displeased her: an indefinable odor, musty, shadowy, associated in her imagination with sewage. But she had said nothing to Alfred, who enjoyed the meal very much, who had become boisterous and gallant . . . taking her hand, caressing the fingers roughly, asking her if it wasn't exactly the same, even the menu hadn't changed, and wasn't this exactly the same table they had been seated at three years ago? She had agreed. Strangely, she had enjoyed the dinner well enough, and only at the end did something puzzle her: the memory of the boy shouting in the street, something about $15,000, an ugly Oriental idol, the stench of pizza and greasy French fries and uncollected garbage out along the Avenue. Now that she was alone in the hotel room it came back to her in a sickening rush. She reeled with nausea. That food, that disgusting wine, the way the fado singer, a slim-thighed young man, had rolled his eyes and leaned over their table. . . .

She went into the bathroom to vomit.

Gasping, choking, she closed her eyes and gave herself up to it. . . . Then she could not believe it, she was hearing the telephone ring. Short abrupt rings . . . three, four, five. . . . Sht went back to the room, unsteady, and picked up the receiver, to hear Alfred's anxious angry voice. He was asking her why she'd taken so long to answer the phone, then he was explaining to her that he and the manager and the porter were going to wait for a detective, that he had personally contacted the Police Department, and a detective was on his way over. He would call the room when things were straightened out. He wanted everything packed, though, since he had already checked out—and—

Someone must have interrupted him because he said, "What do you mean I won't get a room! What do you mean all the hotels are filled up! —Good-by, Claudia, I'll call you in a short while!"

When she put the receiver back on the hook there was a ring almost at once, but when she lifted it and said hello there was no sound at all. She felt dizzy. "Hello? Alfred? Hello?" She hung up. Suddenly exhausted, she believed she would not be equal to it: but she didn't know what "it" was. . . . Her mouth tasted of acid, of vomit. She went to the bathroom and ran the cold water, rinsed out her mouth, brushed her teeth vigorously, desperately. It was late now; it must have been after midnight. She had awakened quite early that morning, excited about the trip, a little apprehensive— they did not often travel together, she and her husband, and were not really alone together very much. Alone with her, Alfred tended to talk cheerfully and loudly, to squeeze her hand as if reassuring her, and she found his manner in public places forced and embarrassing, a suitor's manner. *Do you like it here? Is it too drafty from the air vent? Is this all right with you?* Sometimes he seemed not to know, as if not seeing or tasting or listening, what was going on at all, and had to keep checking with her to see if she was pleased with it . . . since he had the general suspicion, as others, husbands of her friends, had also, that something was not quite satisfying, not quite first-rate, though they themselves didn't know what it might be.

The bathroom fixtures were ridiculously ostentatious: brass faucets, hinges, clawlike shapes, a mirror flecked with gold. Some of the flecks had been picked off by previous clients. The bathtub was huge but Claudia saw a rust-ringed drain and a few stray hairs in it. She jerked the shower curtain closed; it was made of a heavy white material, more porous than ordinary plastic, and along its edges were shiny gold tassels. . . . She located an aerosol can of *Klear-Aire* beneath the sink and sprayed the bathroom to disguise the odor of her having been sick.

Then she went out to wait. She packed the suitcases; she sat in the armchair by the bed that was to have been her own and leafed nervously through a glossy little pamphlet called *What's On in Town*. The clock nearby made a wheezing whirring noise. Five to one. The clock was part of a mechanism of some kind, *Magic Fingers*, which would evidently massage you if you put a quarter in it and lay on the bed. The whirring, clicking sound annoyed Claudia, so she pulled out the plug. . . . She was beginning to wonder what was wrong downstairs. Alfred had been gone quite a while. Leafing through the pamphlet, she tried not to think of irrational possibilities—his having been hurt somehow by the porter, led outside or into the basement and—she concentrated on finding another hotel for them, at least the listing of another possible hotel; she should probably make the call herself, from this room. The hotels were listed on a dozen pages, with various asterisks to designate their prices. *Very expensive. Expensive. Expensive-to-moderate. Moderate-to-.* . . . A full-page ad showed a handsome building with a penthouse restaurant, but it was too far away, back out toward the airport . . . another caught her eye, *a charming Continental-style.* . . . She turned the pages. She found herself scanning a large glossy advertisement for a hotel within walking distance of excellent shops and boutiques, then realized this was the Sherwood Plaza.

She tossed the booklet onto the bed.

It was difficult to sit still now. She was becoming quite nervous. But if she telephoned the desk to ask for her husband she would have to talk to the clerk, and he would know what was going on, certainly the entire hotel staff knew about it and were laughing about it—the black porter most of all—she had sensed, hours before, the sly amused arrogance in that man—the way he had sniffed, deliberately, making a disgusting noise with his nose, wiping his nose on the edge of his sleeve— Then, when Alfred did come to the phone, he would be alarmed at her paging him and then, a half-minute later, annoyed that she had disturbed him. But now it was nearly one-thirty and it seemed obvious to Claudia that they could not check into another hotel. And that the police were not coming.

She turned on the television set. It took a while for the picture to come into focus, so she turned the dial, slowly, then more rapidly, impatiently. Around and around, seventeen stations, most of them blank fizzing zigzag lines . . . a movie, the actors dressed in outdated costumes, the women with ugly dark lipstick . . . another late movie, a Western . . . on another channel an advertisement for something in an aerosol can. She turned the dial around once more, so rapidly that the set wobbled. She switched it off.

Damn it.

She went to the window and peered down into the street. An unusual amount of traffic for this time of night—cars, several taxis, a police squad car that continued slowly past the hotel, even some-one on a bicycle, swerving as if he were drunk. Across the way, darkened buildings, a high-rise building with some lights showing, some areas blacked out; the red Seagram sign some distance away.

There was a knock at the door.

She hurried to it, thinking it was Alfred . . . then she hesitated for some reason, not opening it, leaning toward it. Another knock. "Who is it?" she called out. Her voice sounded shrill. "Who's there?"

Whoever it was did not answer.

After a long wait Claudia opened the door, but could see no one in the hall. She had begun to tremble. Yet she was angry, thinking of how unfair it was—how unfair!—people like Alfred and herself paid for so much, paid for hotel rooms and dinners and taxicabs and airlines, they were good customers, responsible and faithful, and yet —and yet— She even undid the chain lock to look out into the corridor. No one. All the way down to the red Exit sign, just an expanse of not-quite-clean blue carpet and, in the other direction, to the elevators—nothing. It must have been the black porter or a friend of his. He must have walked away, not bothering to hurry; he would have taken the service stairs down.

When she turned back to the room it seemed to her so very familiar—and shabby, depressing. Her eyes flooded with hot, angry tears.

The phone rang. It was Alfred: he told her in a tired voice that he was still waiting for the detective. Was she all right?—had she been able to relax?—to watch television, to read? He was sitting in the lobby, he said, so that he could see everyone who came through the revolving doors; he was afraid the hotel management would send the detective away if . . . Well, the manager had gone home. The night clerk was acting as manager now. It was fairly lively out in the street—some drunks—but the detective was late and he was beginning to wonder if perhaps they shouldn't stay at the Sherwood for the night after all. Claudia agreed. Strangely, she did not feel any relief when he said this; she felt jumpy, irritated. Something was wrong and Alfred did not know what it was.

Yes, yes . . . yes, we'll stay the night.

He told her in an undertone that the black porter had deliberately come over to where he was sitting . . . yes, had deliberately emptied ashtrays nearby . . . Alfred had glanced up at him, furious, and the man had faced him coolly, looking right at him. *The nigger bastard.* Of course the porter had denied everything when the manager questioned him, Alfred said, faltering . . . of course he had denied it. He had even asked Alfred directly if Alfred were *accusing him of a felony.*

Claudia's eyes brimmed with tears.

While he spoke she scratched at the back of her neck nervously, then at her scalp. It was difficult for her to pay attention to his words. Outside, a siren sounded . . . for a moment she thought it might be the police, then she realized how absurd that was. The police were not coming. The police did not care about them. Probably Alfred's request for a detective had been laughed at . . . not even scribbled down on a memo, but just laughed at, secretly. In the mirror Claudia saw her own small, slender frame, the blond-tipped hair and the blond, smooth, perfect complexion, as innocent now as it had been twenty years before. Her lipstick had been eaten off. There was a dull shine on her nose; she looked slightly disheveled, off balance, standing there with her weight on one foot. How exhausted she was, how long this day had been! She had put on this dress of lightweight beige wool so many hours ago . . . and the pearls . . . and . . . "Maybe you should come upstairs," Claudia said. "Maybe we should just go to bed. And in the morning . . . in the morning maybe the briefcase will be found. . . ." But this was impossible, he said; the detective was on his way. "You go to bed, honey," he said. "Please. Why don't you go to bed." But, Claudia pointed out irritably, wouldn't the detective want to see the room, to search it?—of course he would. Of course. "So I can't go to bed, can I," she said. Alfred caught the tone of her voice; he said at once, "Look, this isn't my idea of a holiday, Claudia. This isn't my idea of a way to spend the night. Why don't you lie down and try to sleep and . . . you could get partly undressed, at least . . . when the police come you can wait in the bathroom. . . ." Claudia was scratching nervously at her head. She told her husband that it was out of the question—how could she sleep? "For all I know they plan on doing something to you," she said, "the porter and whoever is his accomplice. . . . What if they hurt you? What if something happens?" Alfred told her, annoyed, that nothing was going to happen. "I'm right in the lobby," he said. "I can see the revolving doors and everyone who passes by outside. . . . I'm perfectly safe. But you: *you keep that chain-lock in place.*"

He went on to complain about the way the neighborhood had deteriorated, and how disappointed he was—how everything was falling to pieces—he could see prostitutes hanging around the curb, even chatting with the doorman, and when he went to the lawyer's office in the morning he'd probably collapse with exhaustion and misery. *And all those letters from the IRS!* He had not made copies of the letters but, unwisely, had carried only the originals. What a mess it was, what a hellish mess. . . .

Claudia heard the remark about the prostitutes. She had noticed women out on the street . . . especially when they returned from dinner, after ten, she had noticed women strolling along, unescorted. Of course! She had not realized they were prostitutes. And yet, now, it seemed to her incredible that she had not realized. She had seen a few of them earlier on the Avenue as well, especially in that last block they had walked along . . . some of them hardly more than girls, but a few her own age, perhaps even older, in shoes with heels too high to be in fashion . . . but attractively dressed, with nicely styled hairdos. *The bitches.* Thinking of them made her impatient with Alfred, who was urging her, vaguely, to go to bed again . . . he was certain nothing would happen to him. . . . And in the morning they would check out of this dump. ". . . they're going to charge you for the night," Claudia said suddenly. Alfred was silent. Then he said angrily that they were not going to charge him for the night. They were not. They could arrest him, take him to court!—but he certainly was not going to pay for the hotel room. Claudia did not contradict him, but she knew very well that they would pay. How could they not pay?

After a while they hung up and she was left, trembling, in this ugly hotel room with the foam-rubber pillows and the lipstick stains on the bedspread—what pretentious bedspreads, fake-gold threads woven through a helter-skelter pattern of greens and blues and iridescent purple!—and the television cabinet and dresser that didn't fit in, weren't even cheap imitation French Provincial, only junky formica-topped pieces out of a department store basement. How unfair it was, how unjust! Her mind skidded backward onto similar moments of rage, back years, many years, to her girlhood and her childhood—how good she had been, and how pretty!—if only she hadn't been so pretty, perhaps she wouldn't have been so very good!—and her husband would not have discovered her, courted her, married her, brought her to live in that neo-Gothic mansion his family had built nearly a hundred years ago on Long Island. . . . Her mind seemed to shiver; for an instant she believed herself in their bedroom at home, alone, staring into the empty room and waiting for something to happen.

The moment passed. She felt calmer. She got her purse, took out a tube of lipstick, dabbed some lipstick on her mouth . . . checked to see if she had the key to the room, yes, on a big oval piece of blue plastic . . . then she opened the door cautiously in case anyone was watching the room. The corridor was empty.

It was now nearly two-thirty.

Damn it. Damn them all. Damn all of them.

She closed the door and locked it. Excited, she walked quickly along the hall, past other closed doors, pausing at times to listen—was someone else still awake?—was that a real voice, or a television program? She went to the far end of the corridor and looked out into the night, at a new arrangement of lights, a new skyline. The Seagram sign was not visible from here, but a high radio tower was lit up, all reds. Down on the street a group of men passed, too far away for her to make them out. Were they young?—white or black? Were they drunk? Were they drugged? Who were they?

She opened the heavy fireproof door to the staircase.

On the landing she saw something that disgusted her—a pile of trays and plates, with food stuck to them, coffee cups, glasses, silverware, crumpled lipstick-smeared napkins. She stared, her heart pounding. What wouldn't she give to pick up those trays and throw them down the stairs!—to throw them into someone's face! On an impulse she went down to the landing . . . but did nothing. She went down to the sixteenth floor. The corridor was exactly like that on the seventeenth floor: the same mealy blue carpet, the same brass fixtures. Martini glasses and crumpled cellophane wrappers had been set outside one of the doors. . . . She went down to the fifteenth floor. The same corridor. She strolled along it and, on an impulse, took out her tube of lipstick and opened it. The corridor was absolutely empty. A few voices, some laughter from one of the rooms . . . but she was safe, it was deserted.

She was about to smear the wallpaper with her lipstick but, at the last instant, hesitated. Her heart was pounding so hard that her entire body ached.

She put the lipstick away; she hurried down to the elevators and pressed the Up button. An enormous earthenware crock, filled with sand, had been placed between the two elevators; an ashtray, it was dirty with cigarette butts and ashes. Claudia pushed against it, idly, with her knee. What if someone were to tip that over and spill all that sand and debris onto the rug . . . ? But the urn was very heavy. It would not budge and something in its very inertness, the futile pressure of her delicate knee against its weight, made her want to sob with the injustice of it: the acne-faced girl holding out her hand like that, so insolent, so freely dirty and lost, and the drug-crazed young man spitting on the windshield of a stranger's car. . . .

When the elevator stopped, there was a uniformed porter inside, black, but not the one who had stolen her husband's briefcase. They rode up to Claudia's floor in silence, but very much aware of each other: the man stockier than the other, though about the same age, obviously a friend, obviously ready to smirk at Claudia's discomfort. *He knew who she was.* Probably they had all laughed about it, including the manager . . . probably they had opened the briefcase and looked through the papers, all those documents, all those records of her husband's financial life, the inner, truly sacred core of that man's existence—his very soul itself—and had laughed at that also, and thrown everything away.

When she spoke, just before getting off at the seventeenth floor, her voice came out with a raspy crudeness that surprised her: ". . . if you people want a reward, all right, I'll pay you . . . not him . . . *I will* . . . but only fifty dollars, no more than fifty dollars. . . ."

The elevator door closed upon the porter's startled face.

She was back in the room only a few minutes when Alfred knocked on the door, muttering *It's me, please open up*. He sounded so spiritless that she was surprised to see someone with him—a young patrolman. The man must have been in his mid-twenties, with a natural red tint to his cheeks and a Celtic ingenuous smile. He wore rimless glasses and carried a notepad and a pen. Claudia glanced at the heavy gunbelt and holster and was surprised to see, there, a pistol with a large wooden handle.

Alfred sank into a chair, sighing. The policeman inspected the room, at about the same pace the manager had inspected it, even crouching to peer beneath the writing desk as the manager had done, though it was obvious there was nothing there; even kneeling in order to look under the bed. Claudia experienced a moment of panic—suppose the briefcase had been returned while she was gone? —suppose the policeman would find it? Fortunately he rose, went to the closet and to the bathroom, humming under his breath. Nothing. Nothing. Alfred was rubbing his face with both hands, exhausted. It was not like him to show such weariness in front of anyone else, especially in front of another man; Claudia judged him not quite himself. His skin was drained and muddy, and his eyes, usually alert, darting from place to place, were bloodshot. He looked at least a decade older than his fifty-three years.

"They'll pay for this," Claudia whispered to him.

"Eh?"

He hadn't heard her but she did not bother to repeat it, since it wasn't true anyway.

The young policeman asked them a few questions, but Alfred cut him short rudely, saying he had given all the pertinent information downstairs and now, since it was after three-thirty, he and his wife would like to go to bed. "Of course we're very grateful," he said sarcastically, "that the station sent you over . . . and that you got here so quickly."

"The detectives are all busy," the policeman said.

He had made out a form with two carbon copies, one of which he gave to Alfred.

After he left they went to bed, and Alfred did not toss about and complain as much as Claudia had feared; he fell asleep quickly, as if sinking into a state of total blank inertness, so that he breathed shallowly and rapidly, high in his chest. Claudia lay awake. Her mind raced. She heard brakes and sirens out on the street . . . the murmur of a conversation in the corridor . . . the sound of glass breaking in the distance. The fresh-air vent in their room went off, then on again, then off . . . she imagined she could smell smoke . . . and she almost would have rejoiced at the possibility of a fire. How just that would be, if the hotel burned to the ground! . . . but innocent people like Alfred and she and the other guests would suffer, as they always suffered, while the others would escape. That was always the case. Since those people had nothing to lose they were free, and could escape. . . . The fan went on again and she found herself thinking of the black porter, the one who had stolen the briefcase, and of the other porter as well . . . chunky-faced, thick-lipped, with blunt heavy-lidded features . . . handsome, were they? . . . or ugly? . . . or perhaps it did not matter, perhaps no standards of beauty applied to them? . . . In the morning she would press a few bills' reward into that bastard's hand, if the briefcase showed up. No doubt it would show up. *Found in the alley, Mr. Buell. Found in a trash can, Mr. Buell. . . . Is it yours?*

A strange excitement came over her, a churning sensation; she could not sleep and did not want to sleep. *Mr. Buell, Mr. Buell.* . . . *Thank you, Mr. Buell.* He tipped and they thanked. He tipped with the natural grudging restraint of a well-to-do man whose family had been wealthy. They thanked him, a chorus. A lifetime of *Thank you, thank you!* and little smirks no one saw, except wives.

Claudia slipped out of bed and went to stand at the window. She was warm, agitated. Yet she was not unhappy. Her husband slept in the other bed and knew nothing of her, of this, of the faint beginning of dawn . . . as he had known nothing of the two or three men she had loved, experimentally, in her thirties, men who had turned out only to be other forms of Alfred himself, other husbands. That had been unfortunate, but she did not regret it. He loved her and knew nothing of her. She was entirely innocent, entirely safe—if she had prowled the corridors of the Sherwood Plaza and defaced the walls, if she had wrecked the plumbing in one of the restrooms, if she cared, someday, to drop a lighted match into a trash bin, she would be utterly safe. No one knew her at all. The street-people, the hotel workers, the prostitutes: all were criminals, and so obvious in their criminality, so easily detected. But she was really invisible.

Down on the street, a police paddy wagon . . . a group of three, four figures herded into it . . . men, were they, or men and women both? Hippies? Who were they? It was too far away for her to make them out; she could see only the gross movements, the event itself. She wondered at their lives—jumbled together in the back of a paddy wagon, now being driven off together. The thought of them excited her.

Light came now from the other direction, slowly transforming the buildings. It seemed to her even more beautiful than the sunset of the night before.

*H*oneybit

Honeybit at Home

She was standing in the doorway of her mother's bedroom, listening.

She heard it—the hoarse labored breathing. The inhalation . . . the pause . . . the exhalation. Honeybit stood there in the doorway, listening, but did not look into the room, though her mother had left the door wide open.

Again, again. Slow and labored and rasping. It was horrible to hear, the irregular breathing, the way it lunged into earshot and then died away. A few seconds of silence. No breath. No breathing. And then a catch in the throat, a gurgling sound—then the gasping for air again, the inhalation. Honeybit stood there in her pale blue quilted bathrobe with the soiled cuffs and the velvet ribbon she never bothered to tie into a bow, listening. She had not yet brushed her hair but it lay fairly straight down past her shoulders, pale brown honey-colored hair she washed every evening and had washed the night before. It smelled like lemon, like soap. It smelled very nice.

Her mother's bedroom stank.

There were so many smells, it was useless to sort them out. Perfume mixed in with the odor of unwashed stockings, the heavy stuporous smell of cigarette smoke mixed with something sharply sweet, indescribable. Honeybit lifted her eyes against her will and looked into the room, but she was safe from having to see her mother because the bed was off to the right, out of sight. Instead Honeybit noticed her own pale blue reflection, across the way, in the mirrored door of her mother's closet. The door was ajar just a little, an inch or so, and Honeybit's image was subtly slanted. She looked even thinner than she was. She looked frightened. To bring the image to life, Honeybit raised one hand to her hair, quickly . . . brushed it back behind her ear and lifted her chin . . . and the girl in the mirror did the same.

Honeybit, you will be late for school.

But she could not move from the doorway. She stood there, listening. When her alarm clock had gone off that morning at 7:45, she had groped for it and knocked it off her bedside table, and the plastic front of the clock had fallen off again, but this time it cracked in two and Honeybit thought that might bring bad luck. She knew it would bring bad luck. Trying to fit the broken pieces together, she noticed her hands trembling and then she allowed herself to listen and to hear the noise from down the hall. She realized she had been fully aware of it for some time. She had been aware of it all night, in her sleep.

The hoarse breathing. The irregular breathing. The catch in the throat. The noise that sounded like a choked-off laugh. And again. Again.

And yet again.

Honeybit, it is getting late. . . .

The girl in the mirrored door lifted her chin, as if to reveal her face. It was petal-soft, petal-pretty. It would be even prettier when she put lipstick on. Honeybit was never confident that her skin would stay nice, it had been blemished a little in eighth and ninth grades, so now she smiled uneasily at herself . . . her glance sidelong, as if inquiring whether that sweet-faced girl was really Honeybit Mason. *Is that you, Honeybit?*

Many years ago they had called her Betty. She could remember her father calling her that. Her mother had changed it to Betsy for some reason of her own, and one of her grandmothers had called her Betsy-Honey all the time; then it got changed to Bittsy in grade school, because she was so small for her age; then it came to be Honeybittsy, and now it was just Honeybit and nearly everyone called her that, even most of her teachers, and Honeybit thought of herself only by that name: *Honeybit.* It was really her. Sometimes she whispered it to herself, and sometimes she sat in school dreamy and distracted, not thinking of her mother in this house or her father out in Seattle or of anything real, not even of her problems with one boy or another, but drawing her hand slowly along her arm, feeling the light, soft, but resilient hairs, saying to herself *Honeybit, Honeybit, this is you.* . . . Her father had never called her that name. He had said he hated it. Her mother told her he hated *her,* he hated both of them, but Honeybit suspected her mother of lying . . . and anyway when her mother drank too much you couldn't believe anything she said. At those times it was best just to agree, to say *Yes, yes, Mother,* and pretend.

Honeybit could pretend anything.

She was still trembling from that first instant of hearing her mother's breath so loud from the room next door, but she could pretend she was not trembling. She could pretend that nothing was wrong. The alarm had rung at the usual time, and she had gotten dressed quietly and gone to school, as usual, not hurrying, in no hurry because why should she be in a hurry, it was just an ordinary Thursday morning. . . . She could pretend that. She could pretend anything.

But she stood motionless in the doorway, looking across at the

girl in the mirror who was slanted from her, a little distorted. The
girl in the mirror could probably see her mother's bed. In fact she
seemed to be staring at it. The bed was king-sized, though only one
person slept in it now, and the sheets and blankets had to be king-
sized too, which meant they were expensive, and the heavy afghan
bedspread was expensive too, though stained and marred with a
half-dozen cigarette burns. It was usually on the floor, slid down at
the foot of the bed; her mother only bothered to make up the bed
once or twice a week, and sometimes not at all. The girl in the mirror blandly faced the thickset body there in the bed . . . one leg
maybe sticking out . . . one arm flung back against the satin head-
board, like last time . . . the skin of the face sagging, dead white, old
lipstick from the day before outlandishly bright against the skin. . . .
The mouth must have been open. Gasping for air. It must have
been dried out inside, from a night of this hoarse choking struggle.
The face and body must have been covered with droplets of sweat,
everything sweating, straining, throbbing with desperate life. . . .

Honeybit whispered, "Mother . . . ?"

But no reply. Her image across the way seemed to be gazing indifferently at the body on the bed, and the crimson-shaded lamp on
the night table—the lamp had been burning all night—and the
things on the table, like last time, probably the same things—the
empty bottle of bourbon, the toothbrush glass, the ashtray heaped
with butts and ashes, the bottle of sleeping capsules—empty this
time?—or half empty? But Honeybit could not see around the
corner and she did not know. She was not going to look.

Last time, she had looked.

Honeybit at School

She left home at the usual time and walked to school, but not
along the usual route because she didn't want to run into a boy who
sometimes waited for her in his car, parked out of sight of the front
windows of her house; but she arrived at the usual time, walking in
the front entrance with some girls she knew, all of them dressed

alike—short skirts, sweaters, colored tights—and all of them long-haired and coltish and eager. Honeybit had to pretend a little, in order to be excited over a rumor that the morning lampoon would be about a boy they knew. She walked with the girls to the B-wing on the first floor, where the sophomore homerooms were located, and had time to open her locker and study her face in the mirror she had taped inside the door.

Honeybit, smile!

Back in September it had been a fad for two or three weeks for people to say *Now smile!* when someone looked sad. It had started upstairs in the senior corridor and spread throughout the school, then died out suddenly because everyone get sick of it and some of the teachers had started saying it in their classes. But Honeybit thought it wasn't a bad idea; she whispered it to herself sometimes. *. . . Now smile!*

The warning bell was ringing; it was 8:40. Honeybit approached a group of students talking outside the homeroom, just to stand on the outside and seem to listen. A boy asked her how Jamie Brodie was. Honeybit laughed coolly and said, "Go ask him yourself." The boy asked her if she'd heard about how the insides of the piano up in the Senior Lounge had been torn out and the vending machines jammed, yesterday afternoon it had happened, and the principal was pretending to be mad as hell but was really happy, now the room could be locked up; and Honeybit pretended not to know about this, raising her delicate eyebrows and staring at the boy. Then the penalty bell rang and everyone crowded through the door.

Homeroom lasted ten minutes. The teacher, Mrs. Stanley, read off announcements but Honeybit couldn't pay attention. When the PA announcements came on she flinched, the volume was too high as usual, and everyone giggled when the principal cleared his throat and it sounded like thunder. He talked solemnly about the vandalism in the Senior Lounge, speaking as if someone had died. Honeybit felt tears in her eyes. Then the Morning Lampoon came on—some seniors from Drama Club—but it didn't seem to be making fun of that sophomore boy at all; Honeybit thought vaguely that it was about a senior girl whose last name she didn't even know. She didn't know people in the Steering Club-General Assembly clique at all and had to ask the girl behind her who it was.

First period was just across the hall, Life Studies. Honeybit sat with her notebook open, trying to concentrate on what Miss Jaeger was explaining. They were all writing journals, "Nature Notebooks," and Miss Jaeger was explaining patiently how the notebooks were to be kept. Miss Jaeger was a plain woman in her late twenties, with a strong, earnest face; Honeybit couldn't figure out why the other students disliked her; *she* thought Miss Jaeger was very nice. Today she stared and stared at her, almost going into a trance, and was only brought back when a boy at the rear of the room asked a question meant to be challenging—but it just sounded stupid and the class groaned. "See me after class, Bob," Miss Jaeger said, trying to smile and not show how angry she was.

Second period was Society and History, up on the second floor, and Honeybit tried to keep with a group of girls, because at this end of the corridor Jamie sometimes waited for her on his way to class. There he was, waiting. So she had to talk to him. He was a senior, one of the first-string football players; he was nice-looking except for his nose, which was too small for his face, flattened down as if someone had shoved a hand against it. Honeybit said she couldn't get together with him all day, she was busy and had the beginnings of a sore throat, and Jamie said he had to go to work right from school—unloading newspaper bales from a truck—and that he'd waited for her that morning, where the hell was she? Finally Honeybit just laughed and backed away into class and left him there, staring at her.

In Society and History they were divided up into caucus groups, six or seven desks dragged around in a circle. That day they were supposed to discuss race prejudice, but the kids in Honeybit's group kept joking around and the teacher, who was new that year, got very angry and told them to move their desks apart and just sit there for the rest of the period. He himself sat at his desk and must have been grading papers, red-faced and hurt. Honeybit and the others felt sorry. Then a new wave of laughter began and Honeybit heard herself giggling, thrilled with the danger. Mr. Spicer looked right at her for some reason and said, "What makes *you* so hysterical, Miss Mason?"—and that set everyone off again, calling Honeybit *Miss Mason!*—and Honeybit just giggled until tears streamed down her cheeks.

Third period was gym, way downstairs. Honeybit risked getting hurt in the jam through the doorway, eager to get on the stairs before Jamie showed up; she moved so fast and so cleverly that she was the first girl in the locker room. It was Thursday, swimming day. Honeybit hated swimming class because of her hair, but she had used the excuse of cramps the week before and could not use it again for three weeks, because Miss Bidelman kept exact records of such details in her grade book. So she selected a tank suit from the bin—one of the yellow ones, the smallest size—but something about the suit or maybe the smell of the locker room or the foot-sized puddles of water on the floor made her dizzy. She had the strange idea that she might faint in the pool and be dragged out and taken to the hospital in that ugly yellow tank suit and everyone would gape at her . . . and there would be a photo in the school newspaper with some mocking caption.

She went into Miss Bidelman's cubicle of an office and explained that she had a headache and a sore throat. Miss Bidelman smiled and said sarcastically that this had been *exactly* her excuse last week. "Can't you think up anything new?" Honeybit protested that last time had been *cramps* and Miss Bidelman denied it; then Honeybit got her to look it up in the grade book—and there it was, *cramps.* So Miss Bidelman said ironically, "Okay. Dismissed." That led to a ten-minute lecture out by the pool, addressed to the fifteen or so girls who were sitting out the swimming class on bleachers, about flimsy excuses and outright lies and how Miss Bidelman did not really care at all whether anyone took advantage of this $90,000 swimming pool, but the taxpayers might care. Only five girls were swimming that day and they had to stand around, waiting, staring down at their pale bony toes. Honeybit felt bad about all this and couldn't mistake how nasty Miss Bidelman's glance was when it swept onto her.

So she was already nervous going into French class, which was a split-lunch class: half the period in the classroom, then down to the cafeteria, then back again. First half, there was a quiz and Honeybit could remember nothing, almost started to cry because she could not remember how to conjugate *être* and she really knew, she knew exactly, and Madame Tyler would be disappointed because all this was review material. . . . Thank God when the bell rang for lunch, and Honeybit hurried downstairs to get in line and was perfectly content to wait at the back of the line, but Jamie motioned for her to come up with him—he had senior privileges, which meant he got out of class a minute earlier than the others.

They sat alone at the far end of a senior table, almost behind the raised platform where a four-piece band was playing—one of the musicians was a boy in a wheelchair who had had some disease that left his legs emaciated, and he played trumpet very well, though so loudly that Honeybit sometimes had to put her hands over her ears. Halfway during lunch she made up her mind that she would meet Jamie after all—it would give her something to think about. Maybe she wouldn't be so strange and nervous.

So she made arrangements with him and returned to French class, where she watched the clock for the rest of the period. Madame Tyler must have had a cold, she kept sniffing, and this made Honeybit remember the breathing that morning . . . inhale, exhale, . . . inhale, exhale . . . so it took all her concentration to stare at the clock and not get nervous. But finally the clock hand made the last wonderful jump—and the bell rang.

Fifth period was Honeybit's study hall, in the big study room adjacent to the library. On Thursdays study was proctored by one of the vocational arts teachers, who kidded around with boys he knew from his own classes and was very nice, not too strict unless everyone got out of hand and the librarians complained; so it was easy for Honeybit to get excused ten minutes after the hour. Mr. Singer gave her the yellow pass without even bothering to ask her what she wanted it for. She went right to the girls' lavatory, where she gazed at her reflection in the mirror and fixed her lipstick. There were cigarette butts on the floor and in some of the sinks and the tile was chipped and smeared with lipstick, but the bathroom was really very nice and Honeybit always felt safe in it.

Then she went downstairs and past the auditorium, where she could hear the orchestra practicing, and all the way to the back of the school where there was a strange hall in Wing A, almost like a tunnel. There were folding chairs and other things stored in it, and at the far end there was an emergency exit door leading right out into the parking lot, but like all the extra doors this one was chained shut. Honeybit walked by the hall and saw him back there, waving at her; she glanced up and down the main hall, saw only a vague figure far away—the main corridor was so long you could hardly see to the end of it. Whoever it was, maybe one of the secretaries, didn't notice Honeybit when she stepped into the narrow passageway and Jamie took hold of her and drew her back, behind the chairs.

But with Jamie she couldn't keep her mind focused; it kept slipping from him, slipping and skidding worse than ever right back to that doorway, to that loud hoarse breathing. *Oh no. Oh no.* Honeybit even made a sharp surprised sound, saying, "Jamie—" but he paid no attention, and afterward she was relieved that he hadn't heard. . . . When her mother had done it the first time, Honeybit had told her boy friend everything, crying like crazy, acting hysterical, and the boy had comforted her saying *Poor Honeybit, poor Honeybit.* But it must have embarrassed him, because only a week later he dropped her. And Honeybit herself didn't really blame him, it was all so ugly and shameful, and put her in a strange role: "You saved your mother's life," they told her at the hospital. "You saved your *own mother's life*," the boy had said slowly, staring at Honeybit as if he didn't even recognize her.

So she didn't bring up the subject to Jamie.

Honeybit's last class was Communication Arts; when she came into the room she was happy to see the folding screen and the movie projector were there, which meant a film, and this would give her something to concentrate on. But Mr. Hemick spent fifteen minutes introducing it and underneath his droning voice Honeybit began to hear someone's coarse breathing . . . she looked around but saw no one asleep, not even Butch behind her who sometimes slept because this was the last period of the day. . . . Honeybit shifted her position in her seat nervously. She crossed and uncrossed her legs. She opened her compact surreptitiously, behind Ginny Brand's shoulders, and saw Honeybit looking the same as usual, inside the oval mirror, powdered lightly. . . . The blue eye shadow on her left eyelid looked darker than the eye shadow on the other eyelid, so she rubbed at it with her thumb; then the right eyelid looked too dark, so she had to fix that up. Then Mr. Hemick was ready with the film.

It was called "The Lake District" and lasted until 3:30, when the bell rang.

When Honeybit rose from her seat she was stiff-legged and felt a rush of moisture between her legs—*oh Christ*—but walked out of class and down to her locker with the others, talking absent-mindedly, knowing there was something she had to find out: they were supposed to write a theme on the film, and she hadn't exactly paid attention to Mr. Hemick's instructions. But when she asked where the movie had been filmed, was that Northern Michigan, they just laughed at her, so she pretended it was a joke. At her locker she tried to figure out which books to take home. French—always French—there was always homework in French. . . . She felt how chafed her thighs were, and again that seeping of moisture, and suddenly she was thinking of how her mother had yelled for her to come down to the basement one day, and down there, by the washing machine, her mother had stood with something in her hand that she was shaking—underpants of Honeybit's— She had screamed and screamed at Honeybit, something about how she intended to mail this to Honeybit's bastard of a father and ask him what he thought of his precious daughter whom he never forgot on Christmas or her birthday, the son of a bitch, and he could show it to his wife to get her opinion—Honeybit was stunned, she just stood there paralyzed. It was the worst time of her life. She didn't even know how she finally got upstairs and out of the house, running away from that voice of her mother's—

Now it was going on to four o'clock.

Four hours plus six until noon plus how many hours before that? —three or four. If her mother had fallen asleep at, say three o'clock. That would be thirteen or fourteen hours now.

She peered at herself in the mirror taped to her locker door and decided that her eyelids looked all right. *Honeybit, smile.*

Honeybit at Trish's

"How's Jamie?" Trish asked.

"All right."

"How's school?"

"The same. Do you miss it?"

"Like hell," Trish laughed.

But she looked defiant and sullen whenever Honeybit talked about school, unless Honeybit complained. So Honeybit complained a little, saying she was worried about her grades; she wanted to do well for Miss Jaeger, but hadn't even started her journal yet . . . some of the other kids had leaves and insects and butterflies pressed into their books; one boy even knew how to chloroform and clean out and stuff animals and was going to have some mice and birds and . . . and *she*, Honeybit, she didn't have anything and was worried sick. . . .

Trish took her up on this. "Is something wrong at home?"

"At home? No."

"How's your mother, the same?"

"The same."

"Is she still mad about Jamie?"

Honeybit giggled.

She had described the scene by the washing machine to Trish, and now the two of them began to giggle. They were sitting on the divan, the pullout bed, with their cans of Tab on it, and somehow Trish's can tipped over. This made them laugh all the more.

"Oh shit!" Trish cried.

She was a year older than Honeybit and had a full, pretty face and long blond hair that was curly at the ends. She and Honeybit had known each other since fifth grade. But this was the tenth time at least that Honeybit had seen her in the same pair of blue jeans, which were too tight for her now and couldn't even be fastened at the waist . . . Honeybit was embarrassed to look at the girl's protruding stomach but didn't dare hint that Trish should wear something else. Trish had always dressed well at school, because she had an older sister just her size, and she'd been able to go sometimes for twenty-five consecutive days without wearing the same exact combination of clothes twice; but since her marriage she lay around most of the time in a pair of blue jeans, and from the looks of her hair she only washed it once or twice a week.

"Is Eddie coming home right after work?" Honeybit asked.

"He's going over to his mother's first," Trish said. She yawned. She patted her stomach and twisted her mouth ironically. "Your mother and my mother-in-law," she said. Honeybit waited for her to continue, but evidently she had nothing more to say.

"Does he still eat supper over there sometimes?" Honeybit asked.

"I don't know. He says he doesn't, but *I* don't know, he's hungry enough to eat two suppers anyway. Let her feed him: I don't give a damn." Trish had reached over to the half-sized refrigerator to get herself another Tab, and now she yanked at the pull-top and managed to spill more of the soft drink, this time on her lap. She giggled. "You know what? I decided I hate this place."

"You hate it? Why? I thought you liked it."

"I did. But I hate it now."

Trish and her husband rented a small apartment on the third floor of a house in a residential neighborhood zoned for one-family houses; the apartment was really an attic. It was insulated, though, and a little too warm. Honeybit always felt drowsy here. She tried to concentrate on Trish, who was explaining her reasons for hating this place and the people who lived downstairs; she stared at Trish's flushed face, at her baby-doll sweater and bulging blue jeans, and her feet in big plush pink bedroom slippers. . . . For some reason she was getting nervous again. She didn't like to drink out of a can: it tasted strange. Her mother said it was vulgar—only pigs drank like that, and sometimes men drinking beer guzzled it out of the can like that, but not girls. It did taste strange this way. For a moment Honeybit wondered if it might be poison, to drink it this way. She felt a little nauseated.

Trish was the only one she had told about how nasty her mother had been—after the convalescence, after the tears and the kisses and the mother-daughter outings to the movies—the first time she'd gotten drunk again her mother told Honeybit how she had woken up there, in the hospital, and for the longest time couldn't figure out what the hell was going on, except she felt lousy, and then it dawned on her . . . it dawned on her what had happened. *You*, her mother had said. *You.*

Honeybit tried to concentrate on Trish's complaints but she felt something coiling up inside her . . . like giggling . . . she remembered Mr. Spicer saying, *What makes you so hysterical, Miss Mason?* . . . and thought in a panic that she must not get hysterical now, she must not. But she could not keep still. It would be either laughing or crying, so somehow she shifted it to crying. Trish paused, staring at her. Honeybit was saying, "I don't know why you hate it here . . . I . . . I don't think you should hate it. . . . You shouldn't hate it, Trish, this place is wonderful, it's, it's wonderful. . . . It's the most wonderful place in the world. . . ."

Trish just looked at her as if she were crazy.

"Here? *This?*"

"You shouldn't hate it, Trish," Honeybit sobbed. "You shouldn't. You shouldn't hate anything."

Assault

. . . genesis as a spark in a quivering field of energy. Centralized and then concentrated in the shadowy lower regions of a living brain, a human brain; but, sparklike, flashed down the sinewy spinal column to the creature's loins, where it could not maintain its abstraction any longer.

. . . negative correlation between I.Q. and control of sexual instinct a probability.

. . . in the most general genetic concept, the genome is the potentiality for doing something, but whatever will be done depends upon adequate surroundings existing. . . . A positive correlation between vulnerability of stimulus (female) and potency of response (male) an additional probability.

She knew it was dangerous to come here. *She knew it was dan-*

gerous. She knew it was a risk and her body began to betray her; pinpricks of sweat made her flesh itch. She stared down angrily at the gauzy-sleeved dress she had snatched out of a closet to wear, not thinking of how hot the day would probably get: she was back home now, not safe up north, but back in mid-Tennessee on an August day.

The real-estate agent kept talking. She disliked him so, she'd temporarily forgotten his name. And she had to walk with her arms held carefully out from her sides, to prevent the underarms of her dress from getting damp. Sargent, his name was. She knew most of his conversation was just noise, but she had to extract a few important facts from it. Yet even these facts were not very important compared to her realization that it might be a mistake to be here at all. *A mistake. She knew better. What time was it . . . ? It couldn't be much later than eight-thirty, but already it was dark.*

It was four-ten. When Mr. Sargent turned to struggle with the door at the rear of the house, she had time to glance at her watch. A disappointing time: 4:10 P.M. Almost as bad as 4:10 A.M. It meant that the afternoon was nearly over, the day was sinking to a rehearsed close, and her mind could run crazy with all she had to do. Mr. Sargent glanced back at her nervously. ". . . thought somebody took care of this mess, Miss Pecora, I swear our office got a work sheet on it . . . the thing is, we thought it might be better not to tell you, some kids must have gotten in the garden and smashed things up, some greenhouse windows and, uh, it looks like some flowerpots and things. . . ."

She walked past him. Her eye swept around the backyard, noting that it was as large as she'd remembered, and then paused to take in the details: all the windows of the old greenhouse broken in, the frames edged with jagged glass like icicles; a few bushel baskets of topsoil tipped over; flowerpots smashed on the walk—obviously damage that had been done some time ago. Small weeds were growing in the spilled topsoil. Everything looked quiet, cunning, at rest.

"I know the office got a work sheet on this," Mr. Sargent said.

His voice was both perplexed and angry. He wiped at the back of his neck.

"It isn't important," Charlotte said.

"Well, uh, you know how kids are getting to be . . . there's a gang of little black kids, I mean *little* kids, raising hell right at this moment . . . in that housing development on the north side. . . . Maybe you noticed it when you came in on the expressway . . . ?"

"No," Charlotte said. She walked slowly out into the garden, startled at how overgrown everything was. It was slovenly, it looked a little crazy. Evidently her father had stopped working in it some time ago. She saw certain familiar trees—an apple tree with a low, gnarled limb like a human arm, a sweet-cherry tree at the very back, now partly dead, with filmy clouds of insect nests in its branches— but the willow tree had grown unrecognizable, enormous, drooping, unpruned. The climbing roses sprawled everywhere, even across the walk. Charlotte and Mr. Sargent had to walk cautiously. With nowhere to climb, the bushes crawled like people slumped over, without spines; Charlotte noticed all this and wondered. The change in her father must have set in long ago.

". . . shortage of people willing to do garden work . . . " Mr. Sargent was complaining abstractedly. ". . . and there's a new problem, I didn't write you about or did your father's lawyer tell you?—this school bond issue that the Board of Education won, well, it's going to make taxes soar even higher. You see how deep this lot is? This is a hefty piece of property, Miss Pecora. Your father paid—pays—he paid thirteen hundred dollars on this and when you consider the condition of the house, well, it's a handsome old house but not in first-rate condition, is it?—well, you have to take all this into account and see how hard it will be to find the right buyer. This bond that went through, Miss Pecora, is a tragedy. It's like throwing good money down a rat hole. I hate to complain or possibly sound racist, but . . . but you're from this part of the world yourself and you know what I'm talking about when I say you have to draw lines and call things by their right name. . . ."

Charlotte stopped listening to him. She stood in the center of the garden, looking around. It was very hot. She didn't know if she liked or feared the mess here, the crowding, the nudging. She saw a patch of sweetpeas gone wild: fragile-bodied, with small stubborn blossoms. When she closed her eyes and drew in her breath she could smell the compost and sun, an intoxicating mixture of odors like the skins of tangerines and the sheen of silk . . . purple silk . . . strange, sun-dazzled, sunspotted odors. Dots of color danced on the insides of her eyelids; she half-recognized all this.

A remark from Mr. Sargent made her turn. She stared at him and saw a beefy, sweating man in a stylish blue-striped sportscoat. He was complaining and apologizing about the heat. "Must be ninety-eight or one hundred degrees, just your bad luck, I mean, to come down here for a nice visit right now, in a heat wave. . . . Not everybody is like your father, with his . . ." He hesitated. "Well, I mean, his indifference to things, to comfort and that sort of thing. I didn't know him, of course, but I read somewhere that he didn't notice if it was hot or cold . . . said he didn't have time to notice the temperature. I admire that. Of course he was a genius and not like the rest of us, but . . ."

"Yes, that's true," Charlotte said flatly.

"We respected his privacy out here," Mr. Sargent said. "In fact, that's how come it wasn't discovered for so long that he was missing . . . he left right after the cleaning lady came, they figured, so it was two weeks again before she came back. It's so—"

"I know about it," Charlotte said.

"Well, it's a confusing thing," Mr. Sargent said solemnly. He frowned. Then, after a long pause, he began again in a voice somewhat heartier, as if he had latched onto a familiar speech, "You know, Miss Pecora, one of the things that still fascinates me after thirty-two years in this business is all the people I meet, the different kinds of people. . . . The world is so crammed with surprises! There's a brilliant man like your father on the one hand, a scientist, a famous man with a contribution to make, and on the other hand huge masses of people who simply cannot raise a hand to help themselves. There's a lot of cruel talk about slum landlords, but let me tell you . . . well . . ." As if checked by something in Charlotte's expression, he hesitated. Then he said, "The black races are very ancient, evidently. It's an interesting fact in its own right. On television the other night there was a program about their history, how they had what you might call civilizations a long time ago . . . a long long time ago . . . in Africa, of course . . ."

Charlotte saw with a small smile that he could not figure her out, he did not *know* her. It gave her satisfaction also to note the half-moons of perspiration under the man's arms. He did not know *her*.

". . . from the back the house doesn't look so good, but I have always admired that kind of architecture," Mr. Sargent said. Charlotte murmured an agreement. "People can call it an eyesore, I mean this general kind of thing," he said hastily, "these turn-of-the-century houses, but I admire them in their own way. I even like all the lightning rods; it reminds me of my childhood, when all the houses had them. It's too bad the windows are so narrow, and it would cost a lot to knock them out and widen them . . . because nowadays people want more light, a young married woman would just hate narrow windows. It's a problem. You can point out solid facts of architecture and even hand-carved paneling and so forth, but these young girls just walk in the kitchen and see what's what, and you're sunk. Most of the houses we sell, let me tell you confidentially, aren't built to last more than twenty years, but the kids grab them up. It's hell to get a thirty-year mortgage on some of them, because the FHA is as intelligent as you or me on this score, and in an area under racial stress or change . . . well, you can bank on it, that area is *not* going to stay the same and property values are going downhill fast. This stretch of land out here, going out from Knoxville to Dunbar, it's still pretty good, but you maybe noticed out on Highway Sixteen all the subdivisions going up? Your father's property here is fortunate not to be on the highway, if you want to keep this a single-family dwelling. But it will be difficult to sell. I would estimate, just offhand, Miss Pecora, I would estimate maybe putting it on the market at fifteen thousand and keep it very flexible, you know, and see what happens. . . ."

"I don't care how much you get for it," Charlotte said. "Ten thousand is fine with me. Eight thousand. It isn't important."

Mr. Sargent seemed surprised. "Well, that's a good realistic attitude. . . . That's fine. Are you going back to Chicago right away, or do you want to make some suggestions for us?—I mean about what you might want done, fixed up, for instance the garden back here should be cleaned up, and it would be difficult, frankly, to interest a young married couple in a house with a kitchen like that. . . . If you could maybe just come in to the office sometime soon and go over a list with me. . . . Then there's your father's books and things, the ones he didn't burn, thrown down the stairs into the cellar . . . and you might authorize us to repair the plumbing in the bathroom and fix up the wiring a little. . . . Or are you in a hurry to get back to Chicago?"

"No," Charlotte said. She saw him glancing at her nervously. He could not figure her out. And it was a puzzle to her, a mystery to her as well: she had meant to say *yes*. But as she stared at the rear of the house she felt the challenge of danger, of risk, even the possibility of doing something terrible. Her father was a strange man, or had been, she had the right to be strange as well. It was dangerous for her to come here, after fifteen years, yet she had come. For fifteen years she had avoided this part of the country and had even once refused to take part in an Industrial Psychologists' Conference in Chattanooga, but now she was here, in 98° weather, bitter and bitterly smiling, enduring an endless conversation with a stranger. Since her early twenties Charlotte had traveled everywhere, though not into the South, not back into Tennessee. Not back. But she was here now. . . . *she was standing just behind the*

white line; a sign said "Do Not Stand In Front Of White Line."
She asked the bus driver to stop and he did, without bothering to
pull off the highway. He seemed annoyed. He said to her, "Watch
out when you cross this highway, kid, or they'll have to scrape you
off with a shovel." She had laughed but it wasn't a joke, and she
had managed to step down and walk away and she did not need to
cross the highway anyway, because her house was down the road on
this side. The bus had stopped at the intersection of Highway 16
and Indian Creek Road, and she had gotten off and walked back
Indian Creek Road. It was already dark. Her watch must have
stopped.

"No. I want to stay here a while after all," Charlotte said. "A
week or two, maybe. I don't know. I'll see."

"Here? You're going to stay here?"

His gaze dropped to her shoes and rose swiftly, as if he had been
startled into seeing her for the first time, as he might have seen her
in some public place in which the two of them were anonymous.
Charlotte looked away. "I don't mind the mess. I can live anywhere," she said.

"I thought you were working in Chicago. . . ."

"Yes, I was. But the job is over. It was a short-term position and
I don't plan to begin working again immediately. I don't need
money," she said, speaking rapidly, embarrassed. None of this was
true, exactly. She had been working on an encyclopedia yearbook
and her part of the project was completed, but she had intended to
sign on for another year. And she did need money; she lived ex-
pensively in Chicago, in an apartment she could not quite afford.
But now she could not take any of that life seriously.

"If you think you'll be all right, out here alone, I suppose it . . .
it would be a nice vacation," Mr. Sargent said. His expression
showed how he doubted all this. "It's quiet and private here, after
Chicago. It's . . . But do you think you'll be all right? Alone out
here?"

"I'm sure no one will bother me," Charlotte said. She managed a dim, sarcastic smile. "I'm sure *he* won't show up. After all, he's been missing now for so many weeks. . . . It's obvious that he's dead. He won't bother me."

Mr. Sargent stared at her. In spite of her surface calm, she felt uneasy; she knew she had spoken in an unwomanly manner. She knew Mr. Sargent would tell everyone what she had said. Self-consciously, she touched her face . . . ran her forefinger gently, very gently, along the shallow scar that stretched from her ear down to her jaw, three and a half enormous inches. This man could not see it or even guess at it, since it was invisible except to the touch. And no one except Charlotte ever touched it.

> . . . reproduction alone is the law of life: exact reproduction. Any invariance is the result of accident that must be considered error. There may be an exogenetic medium for the transmission of culture, but it is flimsy and unreliable and in itself accidental, and since the duplication of the mechanism of life is the evident function of animate nature, it is not an exaggeration to say that evolution itself is the heterogeneous result of many errors, quite undirected and irrelevant perturbations in what might otherwise be a perfect mechanism. A human being is an inefficient process of animate nature, a means by which certain life-elements are replicated; a far less efficient process than bacteria, for instance.

A harsh, reedy voice. A cynical voice. Or was it cynical?—was it perhaps desperate? Charlotte leafed through her father's book, turning pages that smelled of the damp dirt floor of the cellar. She had started to clean the house and had gone immediately down into the cellar, down the wooden stairs and into the old, familiar darkness that she had forgotten . . . but it came back to her swiftly, along with an unaccountable childhood fear of the dark. Panicked, she heard herself thinking *What if he's down here?—hiding? What if he's down here, dead?*

But of course the police had searched the house. All this had taken place weeks ago. The house was empty and safe.

One mid-summer day she had read of her father, really her ex-father, in a newspaper picked up idly by accident in some public place. She had picked up a discarded paper and leafed through it and come upon a minor headline: G. PECORA, NOTED BIOLOGIST, MISSING FOR SECOND WEEK. After the first instant of shock, she had forced herself to read the story slowly. She had not known he was missing at all. She had had no direct news of him for years, and if she sometimes came across the unusual name "Pecora" she felt untouched, uninvolved. The story reported that Pecora, last seen by a woman who cleaned his house, had evidently packed one or two small suitcases and disappeared. Contradictory reports about his health and "mental equilibrium" were given by ex-colleagues of his at the Bedford Institute in Knoxville; he had been Director of the Institute until his retirement a few years before, and occasionally went back to use the laboratories or the library. A man named Rice, whom Charlotte had never heard of before, told police that in his opinion Pecora was "as vital and responsible as ever," but the new Director said: "He had changed drastically since his retirement. I made every effort to get to know him, but he avoided me. It was a pity, since he had made some brilliant contributions to his field and to science in general. . . ." The article concluded with a statement by the Chief of Police, who said that the investigation was still continuing and that his office would welcome any information concerning Mr. Pecora. "It's a crazy case but not so unusual," the Chief of Police said.

Oh why didn't he die, why wasn't it ordinary and normal? Why couldn't anything about him be normal? Charlotte had torn the story out of the newspaper and she had waited, waited, feeling herself cunning and safe. A few weeks later a letter came for her from a Knoxville attorney; he explained that he had received a letter from Pecora, fifteen days after Pecora was reported "missing," and the letter had indicated that the old house and its possessions were to be given to Charlotte.

The Knoxville lawyer had had a difficult time tracing her. Since her mother had divorced Pecora so many years ago, and married a Chicago high-school teacher, there had been no communication between them.

The strange thing was, Charlotte's mother had predicted all this: after the bitterness following Charlotte's "accident," at the age of fourteen, she had said that Pecora would go crazy someday and she only wanted to get out before it happened. *He won't last,* Charlotte's mother had said viciously, though Pecora had always seemed to Charlotte stable and permanent, like geometry. And close-mouthed also, in spite of his sarcasm. Charlotte herself had refused to hate him. No, she was neutral. Neutral. Not afraid. A means by which certain life-elements are replicated, and that is all. Not efficient but not hateful. Neutral. If she thought of him by accident, she thought of an older man with a narrow, evasive stare, a man often observed *walking away.* He had often walked away from her mother, when they had argued. It was an effective conclusion to any argument: walking away, deliberately and politely closing a door. As an adult, Charlotte had sometimes found herself staring at strangers on the street, especially in foreign cities, watching the figure of a man walking away, through a crowd of pedestrians, just turning a corner. Men walked away. Turned corners. Even elderly men: dignified old men with white hair, high-lifted heads. They grew old, they grew whiter. They too walked away.

"Mr. Pecora, he was a very unusual, quiet man," the cleaning woman had told Charlotte; she lived in Dunbar but she was obviously from the hills. "He only wanted them three rooms cleaned. He told me not to fuss about the rest of the house, so I didn't. He said he didn't have a lot of money to throw around. . . . So I took the bus out every Thursday morning, for the last three years. He wasn't

what you would call, you know, a talkative man . . . he had a kind
of sign language for when he opened the door to let me in . . . just
kind of nodded and pointed for me to start with a certain room,
which was always the same room: the kitchen. I got used to it. He
would go out back in the garden sometimes while I cleaned, but
sometimes he stayed at his desk working. He didn't seem to notice
me. . . . You don't look like him much. You maybe take after your
mother . . . ?"

"No," Charlotte said. "Neither. Did he work in the garden?—I
mean, did he hoe or pull weeds?"

The woman shook her head. "Somebody else must have started
that garden, not him. He didn't seem to notice it. I thought it was
a shame, how them nice rosebushes went wild like that, but I never
said anything to him. He was a very hard-working man and always
seemed to be in a hurry, like something might happen to him before
he got his work done. Of course," the woman said, shifting her
shoulders uncomfortably, "he was a genius and didn't have time for
conversation."

"He didn't seem unhappy?"

"Unhappy? I don't know."

"He didn't seem troubled?"

"I don't know. His face wouldn't show much difference anyway,
would it? . . . You do look like him a little, maybe, around the
eyes. I can see it now."

"So he didn't talk to you?" Charlotte said coldly.

"Me? To me?" the woman laughed. "But why would he talk to
me, or anybody?"

Around the old house, alone, surprised at the quiet and the inertia, Charlotte tried to imagine his voice. Lifting suddenly, in
annoyance. Had he been annoyed that night when she had
stumbled from the lane sobbing . . . ? Oh yes, annoyed. And afterward outraged. She tried to recall his voice, but wasn't sure of it.
It got mixed up with the voice of the half-destroyed books, the
burned papers, the scorched notebooks. . . . *an inefficient process of*

animate nature . . . only advantage after millions of years of evolution seems to be increased autonomy with respect to environment, but the complicated structures required reduce efficiency. . . .

She felt the burden of complication: a structure too refined to be efficient.

He must have wanted his books and papers destroyed, so she piled them into an old wire-mesh container and burned them. Last year's leaves and various bits of unburnable debris gave to the fire a sharp, pungent odor: again she thought of fruit, of the skins of oranges and tangerines. The smoke made her eyes sting. She backed away from the fire and happened to glance at the rear of the yard, to the partly collapsed wooden fence, where someone seemed to be standing, watching her. But when she looked again her vision had cleared and she saw that there was no one there.

"He's dead by now. He won't come back," she thought.

She knew it was dangerous, it might be a mistake. But it was necessary: someone seemed to be calling her by name, transfixing her in spite of the panic that was beginning in her body. "How was I to know? Why do you blame me?" her mother had screamed. But he had walked away. His face had darkened with disgust, with rage. Somewhere inside the rage was his love for her, for Charlotte, *the daughter of*. But there was no time for it, it got crowded out, pushed impatiently aside. "How did I know the highway would be so busy?" Charlotte's mother had asked, pleading with him. "All those drivers?—a race at the fairgrounds? We never bothered with the local newspapers so how was I to know? How can you blame me?" So many questions! It did no good, he walked away. After all, he had a weak stomach, a chronic digestive ailment, never satisfactorily diagnosed. And he had his work to do. He had the thinking of certain thoughts to do.

Charlotte regretted setting the fire, because it burned late into the night. The trash at the bottom of the container began to burn as well; it must have been garbage of some kind. She tried to sleep, smelling the mysterious nameless smoke, thinking of how her father's meticulous words were reduced to ashes just like the ashes of old dried branches and leaves. . . . But if he were dead he would not mind. But if he were not dead he would mind.

He had loved her, in his anger. Because of him the newspapers had not printed the "news"—no rape headlines, not even headlines of assault, that ambiguous term. *Charlotte Pecora, 14-year-old daughter of. Indian Creek Road. Race: Caucasian. Assailant: Negro.* "I don't hate Negroes," Charlotte thought, lying awake in the dark. "I hate them all." But no, she didn't hate anyone; she was a neutral agency through which nothing could be stimulated to act.

She slept. The fire must have burned itself out, because by morning the odor of smoke had vanished.

She knew it was dangerous, walking here alone. She had only a half-mile to walk. But it was dark for eight-thirty; her watch must have stopped. She raised it to her ear and heard its small confident ticks. The watch was a birthday present from her parents, picked out by her mother, but she could not trust it. Only a half-mile from the highway to her house. . . . Why was it so dark? The air was balmy as summer and yet it was no longer summer.

In short abrupt disconnected sentences she put it together: began to arrange it, before it even started.

Traffic was heavy on the highway behind her. It was mid-October and tranquil, except for the traffic. There had been a race of some kind at the fairgrounds that afternoon, and now traffic spilled out in all directions, leading out of town. Charlotte noted the tranquillity beneath the noise. *Beneath the noise, tranquillity.* Years later she was going to remember it. Sharp hot pangs in her, inside her, up inside her; if you could just get beyond the noise to the tranquillity of October! If you could get beyond her father's shouts to the love he claimed for her! But love had to be noisy. She was the daughter of, *the daughter of.* He had written a number of books and "he" was Director of the Bedford Institute in Knoxville. Years later, trying to sleep in his abandoned, musty, ugly old house, she would call all this back to mind and try to make a dream out of it instead of a nightmare. *The daughter of* stepped down from the bus and the bus driver's unfunny joke and hurried down Indian Creek Road, toward home.

"Watch out when you cross this highway, kid, or they'll have to scrape you off with a shovel," the bus driver had said, but it wasn't a joke, though she had tried to laugh. That was something you could do: laugh, as if responding to a joke. And then walk quickly away. But it troubled her that it was so dark and that she was alone. . . .

From the age of fourteen onward she was to remember the way she half-glanced over her shoulder, back to the busy highway. Why? Why had she paused? No need for it, no reason. But she had seemed to sense something, the wind so suddenly and painfully fragrant, smelling of marshlands near the river . . . something feathery, whispering, like a breath. *Charlotte?* Yet it was not her name because she had no name, not at that moment. She paused, she breathed in the evening air, she prepared herself for an experience she would never comprehend.

Traffic flowed past on the highway, except for one car. A single car turned off onto Indian Creek Road. *The headlights turned sharply, suddenly.* And in that instant she seemed to realize that it was too late to hide, to run, even to walk quickly and resolutely along the edge of the road. She paused, staring. She could not have been more transfixed had she called the car to her, summoning it onto this dark side road, away from the illuminated highway.

So she stood, transfixed. The blades of grass about her bare legs were still, silent, oddly cold. And a little sharp. As if something had already passed into her, more powerful than any mere blow, she stood waiting for the car to pull up alongside her. It happened only a hundred yards from the lane that led to her parents' home . . . had she turned her head she could have read *Pecora* on the mailbox, in its perfect gleaming black letters, professionally lettered according to Dr. Pecora's specifications. But she did not turn her head.

Her body shrank, in an impersonal animal terror, but her mind was stubborn, fixed in concentration: her face blank and hypnotized, lips slightly parted, eyes gone blind with the glare of the headlights. *Why . . . ? Who is . . . ? Did someone call . . . ?*

The car was braked to a stop. A door was thrown open and Charlotte felt "Charlotte" pass from her, she felt herself pass over into the noise, the excitement, the insect-swirling pathways of light. Not a person, not a girl, not even a body rigid with terror: but noise, shouts, blows. Noise. Light. Disembodied shouts. Someone's arm was gripping her, a forearm jammed up beneath her chin. She was being dragged somewhere. She fell, was dragged along, her bare knee scraped against the gravel; still she did not scream because her assailant was like a force that demolished all sound, all words. Words would fade into air, into ashes light as air.

Only one boy had jumped out of the car. The others remained in the car and she heard them shouting, punctuating their shouts with *Carlie! Carlie!*—as if warning him, terrified for him—but it was already too late, she had somehow fallen and he had slammed her head viciously down against the ground so that her jaw seemed to crumple, there was a hot explosion of blood, and it was too late. She smelled the whiskey on his breath. His shirt must have been stained with vomit, hours'-old vomit. It was too late. Too late. Another boy ran to grab him, they scuffled, but her soul had already contracted to the size of a pin, going inward to zero, to an iris-sized thing. She was neutral.

Carlie, damn you!

Afterward, the police had questioned her. She had replied woodenly, staring at the floor. At any floor. No, she didn't know who her assailant was. No. She did admit his race: black. But she didn't know him and had not seen his face and had not heard his name, she did not know him, she did not know him. And he had not known her: she had been faceless to him. Oh, it was fists and knees mainly, a memory of flesh weighted and urgent, grunting and stinking of whiskey and vomit and urgency, but mainly fists, a knee brought up hard into her chest and stomach, not loving, not love. Not hate either, because it was too fast. No emotions were possible at such speed.

Years later she woke, out of a dream that involved her body but left her mind coldly separate. She woke, she sat up. The old nausea was back. And the sharp sour night-dry taste in her mouth, like acid. Where was she, what had happened . . . ? She forced herself to wake up and see how she was safe, alone and safe, in her father's old house, alone. Nothing could happen to her because you could not be damaged twice like that. It happened to each person only once.

After a few days she drove to Knoxville, with the idea of looking for him. She knew it was probably hopeless, yet it was possible that he was not dead; he might have gravitated to some wrecked, devastated part of the city, to sit with other old men, blanked-out, speechless, each alone with the noise of voices in his head. She drove slowly along the streets and noted without agitation the number of bums— not only men but women as well, aged and sexless, seeming inert even when they stood on the sidewalks to stare out at passing cars. What anger in their blank faces! Charlotte did not dare pull up alongside them; she drove slowly by, staring.

One old man, in filthy clothes, stood in the gutter and stared back at her. His face was a wreck, yet he eyed her with dignity. Pecora? No, not Pecora. Not her father.

She found herself driving along a residential street: too ordinary a street. So she turned back. And then she found herself downtown, fighting traffic and pedestrians, all of this bustling and ordinary, too ordinary. Where was he...? It was assumed by the police and by the authorities that he was dead by now, probably a suicide, though they had never told Charlotte this obvious truth; she believed it, accepted it, yet she halfway expected to see her father lurching toward the car as he waited for a traffic light to change from red to green. She had been surprised in the past.

It was another hot day. A week of heat. Energy flows from a

higher plane to a lower plane, she knew, and this would account for
the running down of the universe. Eventually it must run down.
She knew this, she had read it in one of her father's books, before
burning it. Life moved from a concentration to a dissipation: tension must be reduced. The genetic structure is programmed in this
way. Unless her father had been mistaken. . . . *It is not just a matter*
of summoning with the eyes, the flicker of response in a brain to
tendrils of air, marsh-grass hazy as smoke, fireflies by the hidden
river and in the infinite darkness of the deep back yard. . . .

She gave up and drove back out of town on the expressway. Driving faster, with her windows open, she felt cooler, saner; she was
really a sane young woman and had been so for decades. Many
years ago her mother had taken her away from this part of the world,
away from "Pecora" and the old trouble, the old house, the quarrels.
Her mother had moved with her across a number of rivers, safe in
the North. She belonged there, really. As soon as she arranged for
the house to be sold, she would return to Chicago and take up her
life where she had abandoned it. . . . She would begin it again, her
"life." But in the meantime something drew her back, back along
the highway to the turnoff at the dirt road, and back the dirt road
to that house. Smirking, she thought: *I hate them all.* But this was
an outlaw thought, one that flashed to her between moments of
lucidity. Sanely she thought: *I don't hate anyone.*

She got through the rest of the day and, at ten o'clock, turned
off the lights and lay on the sofa in her father's study, to wait. She
was alert, cautious. Outside, the crickets kept up a steady raucous
sound, a multitude of sounds, interspersed with stray chirps and
cries—birds, insects? She raised herself on one elbow to stare at the
window, but she could not see anything. The shrubs outside the
window were too close to the house, too thick. Everything was
night. Hardly had the sun set but it was night: black.

So she lay back to wait. In the morning she would leave, but
tonight she would summon him back. She dreaded him, loathed
him, did not even know him—he was faceless to her—they were all

faceless to her—but she did not hate him, not really. Why hate, why so much shouting? She had acquiesced when the arm jammed itself across her, she had given in to the blows, the tearing of cloth, the sudden swift tearing of her skin—how could she resist? An animal panic had made her body go cold. She could only lie there, waiting.

. . . Yet she must have slept, because she woke suddenly and believed that someone was present in the room with her. It was not exactly a new sensation: she had had uncomfortable dreams like this in the past, even when she had shared a room with another girl in a college dormitory. She would wake, disturbed, sometimes sexually disturbed, and feel with amazement and loathing the sensation fade from her as soon as her conscious mind came into power. In a second, a half-second, it would become remote, inaccessible. It would fade so rapidly that she need not even feel disgust.

She sat up, alert. Her heart pounded. Yet she could see that there was no one in this room with her—she was alone. "Are you here? Are you hiding?" she whispered. How strange, if he did return and she could not recognize him! All she had to go by were a series of images, blurred memories, and the out-of-date photograph of him in the newspaper. She snapped on a light: nothing. Only the room with its nicked desk, its straight-back chair, its old-fashioned wallpaper and filmy, stray, lifeless cobwebs.

Faceless, he could walk anywhere. Faceless and not white, not black. O love, it was fists and knees mainly, and another fist of flesh that entered her blundering, painful, without personality. Charlotte brushed her hair out of her eyes as if brushing cobwebs away. She had not bothered to undress, since the house was so dirty; so now she got up, stood swaying above the broken-backed old sofa, inhaling dust and a sharp knife-like odor of night, sheer night. In such a confusion she could not distinguish between the smells of earth and air and vegetation. And her own body, its sudden helpless sweating: all odors were confused.

She knew "G. Pecora" was dead by now, maybe drowned; maybe

beaten to death; maybe slept-out into death, having swallowed all
of his sacred capsules—he had always had insomnia and had taken
barbiturates, years before they become generally popular in America. He had tried to destroy his books and papers as if swallowing
all his own language, his special language, so it was death, serious
death. But: a noise somewhere in the house challenged this theory.

"Father? Is it. . . ?"

Charlotte heard her voice raised, shrill and daughterly. It was an
embarrassing voice, *hers*. Pecora's attorney had written her and had
included with his letter a photostat of her father's letter, *not a letter
addressed to her*, but it had mentioned her name and had indicated
that she was *the daughter of*. "The house and its possessions" were
given over to Charlotte for her use or for sale, according to her
wishes. Receiving this information, in her Chicago apartment on
an ordinary wind-swept Saturday morning, Charlotte had thought
immediately that it must be a trick of some kind. The old man
must want her back, must want her to return to the house for reasons of his own. If she did return maybe he would show up, maybe
it was all part of a plan. . . . But though she had had this premoni-
tion she had almost immediately forgotten it. Now she remembered.

"Is someone there? Is . . . ? Father, is it you?"

The night was loud with crickets. She listened, concentrated,
tried to sort out the multiplicity of sounds, which were confused
with the pumping of her overworked heart. Her heart was too small
an organ to be supporting so much sound. . . . She waited, listening.
No more sound. It had seemed to her to be in the house, somewhere
above her. But she must have dreamed it. A rustling of leaves, or
limbs, or the languid night-loving wings of owls, large half-seen
birds of darkness. . . . She walked through to the kitchen, but she did
not turn on the light. She could see fairly well in this room. The
refrigerator gave off a ghastly phantomlike glow, dead white; the
linoleum was still shiny in spots, which reflected light sullenly.
A cleaning woman had come every Thursday morning to clean

three shabby rooms and evidently she had applied floor polish to the linoleum of this room, so that it might glow in certain patches at this time. Charlotte stared at the floor and then raised her eyes to the window.

Outside, a jumble of shapes. All dark. But some were darker than others, some bushes and shrubs were darker than the rest, tangled together, breathing together, leaf pressed into leaf, vines and thorns and blown blossoms face to face, mouth to mouth. . . . Even in daylight, the light of noon, even armed with a shears and a pair of stiff protective gloves, who could make his way through such a tangle? Charlotte approached the window and stared out into the back yard, pressing her palms against the window sill in order to steady herself. Without the support of the window she would sway, trembling, sickened and embarrassed at her shrill heart-beat. *She knew it was dangerous.* . . . A man, the real estate agent whose name she could not recall, she was too nervous to recall, a man, a well-intentioned kindly man, had expressed surprise when she told him she intended to spend a few days here, in this wreck of a house, a woman alone: *Here? You're going to stay here?* But she was stubborn, she was pleased to be so stubborn. She possessed secrets he would never discover. Now it was late at night and she was too confused to remember even the day it might become in a few hours, but she imagined a secret unfolding itself, mixed up with the rustle of leaves outside and the rustle of grass, high grass, as if someone were walking through it.

She went to the screen door and opened it cautiously. The back yard was so wild, its shapes so dark, that she could see nothing. Only the sky was illuminated, but darkly; opaquely. The sky was overcast and the moon nowhere in sight. Charlotte drew in a long slow breath, meant to quell panic, but the breath itself turned cold, perverse, the breath of wing-beats of owls and bats and other night-loving birds. She knew she should cry out, "Is someone there? I know you're there!"—and indicate her anger, her presence. She should turn on all the lights and frighten him away. She should pretend to be telephoning the police, dialing the unconnected phone. But she could not speak, could not draw back from the door. She began to sense the presence of another person, another personality, and something in her gravitated toward it, a tangle of dark earth-loving roots, the easeful silence of vegetation, the dis-connected sounds of crickets that were all the same sound at differing intervals. Her blood surged darkly, warmly. She stepped out onto the rickety back porch and waited.

Charlotte . . . ?

But it was not her name, no one called her. She waited, perfectly still, to see what would happen. If daylight came she might be able to distinguish between the overgrown climbing roses and the tangled sweetpeas and the drooping bug-eaten leaves of the willow trees and a human shape, human presence, that might be somewhere out there, waiting as she was waiting, in perfect stillness. But it was too dark now. And she felt herself going neutral, unresisting. To speak, to call out a name or a warning or an angry threat—to plead for help —to scream for help—She could not speak. It was somehow wrong.

For perhaps twenty minutes she stood there, waiting. She did not move. Her breath was shallow, almost imperceptible. She seemed to be descending, sinking, into the languid earth-damp life of the wild garden itself, to lie down somehow with the most formless of all vegetative life—rotted leaves, compost, organic matter of a sweet, foul, tart personality. A night-bird called out; she did not really hear it. She breathed lightly, shallowly, in a rhythm gentle as the breathing of the night, a perfect silence within the stray self-contained noises of the dark.

It passed. A span of time passed. And she seemed then released to herself, suddenly drenched with perspiration or aware of it, at last, aware of her chill panicked body. She came to herself, she awoke. Yet her body seemed to her detached, not very important. It smelled of clamminess, an odor without sex, neutral and defiant as the odor of the wild vegetation. Waking to consciousness, she seemed to recall that she had heard someone or something in the garden—she had heard the sounds of another presence, withdrawing from her. But it was gone now: minutes must have passed since it had vanished.

Father . . . ?

She shivered and returned to the house, to the darkened kitchen. As if still in a trance she saw her hand, a pale shape in the darkness, reach out to touch the refrigerator—and how smooth it felt to her smooth, frightened fingers! It was as if she had come a great distance just to touch it. "He wasn't out there. He didn't come back," she said.

Yet she was unable to sleep. At dawn she went out into the garden and saw, near the back, in a dense but partly dried-out patch of weeds, what might have been footprints—yes, the weeds had been partly trampled down, in fact it looked almost as if someone had lain there—maybe lying there for hours, waiting?—watching for her? She felt dizzy, staring at the trampled grass. There was a vague path that led to the collapsed fence and she followed it, conscious of being alone now, safely alone. She knew she should feel something: terror or anger. It would be normal to feel something. But she was still so neutral, so pure . . . it seemed to her a neutrality beyond anything she had known in the past, almost a newness, centered somehow in her eyes; so that her eyes stung a little with the morning light, as if they were new, newly opened. She climbed over the broken fence and felt a dull scraping of wire on her left leg, not sharp enough to cut the skin. The wire was rusted. She stepped down into a patch of weeds and saw something nearby—a pink comb, a plastic comb. And a few inches away a crumpled tissue. She picked both up, staring. What were these things, what did they mean? Why were they here? The tissue was smeared with lipstick. . . .

It had not been her father, then. Not her father. Instead, strangers had trespassed into the garden, the old Pecora garden; they had come here to make love, not knowing about Charlotte. They had been strangers. They had not known about her and had not cared.

And she had stared out at them, invisible to them, she had been
present at their love-making. . . . It was a world of strangers.

Charlotte let the tissue fall disdainfully. The comb was dirty,
with black hairs stuck in its soiled teeth. Bought at a five-and-ten-
cent store, bought by a young neighborhood girl . . . perhaps a black
girl . . . It was made of cheap plastic. Last night someone had lost it
out here, in the weeds. A girl had crept in this place with her lover,
trusting him, or perhaps not quite trusting him: fearing him,
anxious, desiring, fainting, clutching at him and begging *no don't
hurt*—Charlotte did not want to think about it, not about who they
were or what had happened. The act between them might have
been drawn out by the night itself, some heavy odor or quivering
pressure in the air, a need for tension to be reduced. But it did not
matter. The event had taken place: only the event mattered.

He hadn't come back.

She had stared out into the darkness, invisible, and she had stared
out at the invisible lovers, a presence they must have sensed just as
she had sensed them. So she had not imagined it after all. She was
sane and had not imagined anything. . . . She looked again at the
comb and felt suddenly a pang of certainty, of tenderness. She recalled the instant of someone's plunging into her, flesh like a fist,
flesh like metal, and it seemed to her not much different from the
act of love that had probably taken place out here the night before.
Something flowed through all these lovers in their contortions, shaping their bodies and their straining faces, leaving them helpless and
pure. It flowed through them and through her, leaving her pure.
Dreamily she recalled the instant of her pain and it seemed to her
now an empty pain, the memory of another person. . . . So her
mother had endured pain: all her mothers, her ancestors. They had
endured it and transformed it. . . . *Love, what did it matter?* Pain
or spasms of pleasure or neutrality itself, the pure, untrammeled
passage of consciousness through her body, what did these matter?
. . . there was no one to differentiate them except Charlotte. And if
she refused, they were all one. If she refused to remember the pain,

if she chose instead to transform it into something else, who could overcome her? Love, hate, pleasure, pain: they were identical, descending into the firmest, most stubborn layer of life, a vegetative neutrality, and then rearing up again into human life, innocent even in consciousness.

So her father had not returned. And he would not return. Instead, strangers had crept in here. Charlotte had been present at their loving.

She dropped the comb and forgot it. Early morning, just past seven. The sounds of birds overhead: everything flowed through her, leveling itself as it flowed, a single event. She could drown in this, it was so perfect. Individuals did not matter, did not exist: only the event mattered. Nothing could reduce it, nothing could force any interpretation upon it.

When she washed that morning, preparing to leave, she noticed red half-moons on her palms, four neat imprints on each palm. She must have been clenching her fists the night before, pressing her fingernails into her flesh, as if to call something to her, someone, some presence, some power, some image greater than herself. . . . At the time she had felt no pain. Now it did not matter. Now she would forget; she was restless to leave this place, to return to her own life. She washed herself methodically, though it was awkward, since there were no towels or washcloths left behind. He had either packed them or thrown them away. Or perhaps he had not even owned such things, in the end.

*T*he Wheel

The steering wheel—

Everything broke, came loose, the left side of my car exploded inward from the impact of the other car—I was thrown forward against the steering wheel—my head struck the windshield—

Distantly there was another crash, another explosion. Another car must have smashed into us. But I could not feel it: I was gone.

What place was this?

I did not wake up, because I seemed already to be awake. My eyes were open. A film or a slight mist covered the eyeballs. . . . I blinked helplessly. It was a strange room, no room I knew. When I tried to sit up, something stung me in both arms, the inside of the forearm where the skin is so soft. Bandages, adhesive tape, pinpricks, tubes.

I sat up cautiously. Now I could see that I was attached to two tubes—I could see by the faint light from the window and by another, crosswise light that slanted under the door. The apparatus was attached to a bottle at my bedside. A faint gurgling noise. . . . All along I must have been hearing it, not knowing what it was.

Moment by moment the room defined itself: a hospital room, with an empty bed several yards to the left of mine, by the window. The bed was made; the blanket pulled up neatly, the sheet turned down, the immense pillows propped up, very white, ghastly white. In addition to the small bubbling sound of the fluid dripping into my veins there was another deeper sound that underlay everything: a ventilator fan in a metal cabinet just beneath the window. A steady, unhurried hum, an almost imperceptible whirring of tiny wheels and cogs that I must have heard in my sleep also . . . that might have muffled the awful gasps of my breathing . . . and formed a link between each breath, in that patch of raw silence during which the next breath is contemplated and the tremendous strength required to perform it is summoned up. Now I heard everything plainly. There were even slight irregularities in the noise of the fan. And somewhere outside the room was another noise, gentle at first and then increasing—not from the hospital corridor, but from outside, from the night—a deeper, less patient sound of engines sailing across the sky. The roar increased until it began to accelerate my heartbeat; it must have been a jet plane, flying low. Then it began to fade, though it was slow, very slow, in fading. Finally I was left alone with the faint gurgling of the fluids and the noise of the fan.

What place was this, and why was I here?—a question rose helplessly in me, not my question. But it shaped itself to me in my throat; I nearly spoke out loud. *What place was this? Why was I here?* I lay back against the oversized pillows, the newly laundered, fresh-smelling pillowcases and sheets close about me, my gaze moving swiftly and anxiously over the shadowy objects of the room. The bed beside mine—thank God it was empty—and a single chair, and a television set on a platform in the corner of the room, propped up there at a precarious angle as if it were about to topple down on the viewer. Close beside my bed was a table on wheels, and on it a large pitcher of water and two glasses, one filled to the brim, untouched, and the other turned upside down on a paper napkin.

I tested my legs, drawing up my knees cautiously. My leg muscles felt distant, as if unused. There was a cramp in one of my toes, or the memory of a cramp. I could not be certain: were these my legs? or had my legs been amputated? The blanket rose slowly before me, the bedsheets rustled, impulsively I kicked the blanket off— it didn't quite clear my feet but fell sideways across the bed. I saw now that my legs were bare, that I was wearing a white cotton gown, softened by many launderings in harsh soap. My legs were so white . . . the dark hairs twisted and curly, springing out of flesh that seemed too white to have contained them. . . . My thighs seemed very thin, the fatty tissue wasted and only the hard, flat, stubborn bluish muscles remaining. But I swung them around, tried to touch the floor with my toes . . . at once the stabbing sensation came again in my arms, but I picked off the adhesive and bandages and tore out the tubes. Droplets of blood welled out. I wiped them away on the bedsheet. When the bleeding wouldn't stop, I put the bandages back, pressed them in place, wound the adhesive around like a tourniquet.

I slid off the bed and for a moment the floor seemed to slant. The tile was cold. The floor righted itself; I walked cautiously around the foot of the bed; an attack of dizziness made me reach out—I grabbed hold of a shoulder-high metal table on wheels that was placed at the foot of the bed. It made a surprised, creaking noise. . . . When the dizziness passed, I was able to hear new sounds. A voice out in the corridor, almost out of earshot . . . a rattling sound of a cart being pushed on an elevator. . . . Suddenly I remembered the way I had been brought in, past a large horseshoe-shaped counter or desk near the elevators, the nurses' station. Though it was late at night now, nurses would be on duty there. No one could escape in that direction.

In the lavatory I turned on the light, which flickered. The tiles in here were cold. In the mirror a hand sprang up to touch my hand, its palm and outstretched fingers covering the image of my face, *look at his face!* and I stood for a while with my hand against that hand, fingers touching fingers. At that moment a woman's voice close outside my door exclaimed softly: "No, no, it's Room 530!" I shut my eyes, weak with apprehension. But a man replied in a deep voice I seemed to recognize: it must have been one of the orderlies assigned to this floor. His voice was familiar though I couldn't remember having heard it before. The two voices met, mingled, drifted away down the corridor. . . .

I was safe.

There were some clothes on hangers in the closet. I pawed at them, anxious to see what they were. Trousers folded neatly over a hanger, a shirt made of a lightweight material, my favorite shirt, I remembered it. . . . A small grip on the floor of the closet and in it some underwear, some socks, shoes. . . . I dressed quickly. The bleeding had stopped and would not get on my shirt sleeves. Bending over to put on my shoes, I felt dizzy for a moment, lurched forward, caught myself . . . then I was all right, I was not going to faint. *He's awake. His eyelids are blinking.* I went to the door and pressed my face against the crack, suddenly desperate, like a man sucking at air, gasping, choking for fresh air. But I knew enough not to turn the knob at once, but to go slowly, very slowly. It took ten or fifteen seconds just to get the knob fully turned. Then, pulling back gently, I opened the door about an inch.

Outside was the corridor—the wall opposite my room a dim beige color that looked like shadow, permanent seamless shadow. Behind me there was no light. So I opened the door wider, safe from seeing my shadow appear on that wall. Nothing appeared there. I was safe.

I stepped out into the corridor.

My gaze swept far down to the left, as if sucked into a tunnel. For an instant I thought I might be drawn down it, helplessly, and then I would never escape from this place. . . . But I looked in the other direction, where there was an Exit sign in red, and a stairway. The elevators were by the nurses' station but the emergency stairs were at this end. I walked quickly past the closed doors of the other rooms, the other patients, and at the moment I got to the door, by coincidence there was a faint sound of bells, a mysterious tinkling sound I had been hearing in my sleep. But nothing happened: it had nothing to do with me.

I began to descend the stairs, hanging onto the railing with both hands, not trusting my strength. It had betrayed me in the past. It did not belong to me. There was something in me, coursing through me, a big fist-sized thing pumping me, down, down from the fifth floor, down the well-lit stairway with the railings of simulated pine. Careful on the stairs! The railing seemed smooth but somehow a splinter poked itself up, stung the palm of my hand, and a woman stood above me with a hypodermic needle raised as if for me to see and whispered, *Lie still, lie still!* I was in the basement now. The lighting was softer here, as if no one was expected to come this way. I went out into the corridor and looked in both directions but saw no one. The Out-Patient Clinic was closed for the night. In the hallway some machines hummed—automatic vending machines that sold sandwiches and candy and coffee. No one was around. I was alone. My heart began to urge me to hurry, hurry!

I walked to the doors leading out.

Six heavy glass doors. *Push.* Just beyond them in the foyer was a brightly lit counter with the word *Emergency* painted on it. The floor dipped downward from the outside of the building; it was made for sliding, for wheeling. They had brought me in this way. I knew this place, I had seen it through my closed eyelids. They had wheeled me in here though I had not broken any laws. Now I was leaving; it was only a matter of crossing a few yards of rubber-matted floor, a matter only of walking without faltering. I went out. A nurse on duty at the Emergency counter, a girl with pale, freckled skin, stared at me. She was holding a crossword puzzle book the size of a comic book. She stared at me, pityingly. Someone cried, *Open the door!—don't let it swing shut!* The needle was withdrawn and the spot where it had entered my skin was strangely cold. It dried quickly. But I walked through the glare of lights and pushed the outer door open, and now I was outside, out of the hospital, walking up a rubber-matted ramp. It was raining a little. An ambulance was parked nearby under the awning, but I walked in the other direction down the driveway to the street.

Everything changed suddenly—lights were glimmering, blinking on and off, cars were passing, lights turned to specks, tiny dots, then expanded again to soaring drawn-out rays, and out of all this I saw the car wheels moving, revolving, white-wall tires turning round and round, a hypnotic motion. I stared. I stood in the rain, staring. Then I saw a few pedestrians hurrying by. A middle-aged man in a raincoat, walking fast, with his head ducked. He glanced at me and then through me. I felt weak, suddenly confused. I didn't know which direction to walk in. Another man passed quickly; he held his suitcoat closed about him, shivering. Some distance away were a man and a woman walking together, but not as quickly as the others—they didn't seem to notice the rain. They were arguing. As they approached, I could see that the man's face was creased, worried. The woman walked with her eyes lowered, her face sullen; from time to time the man nudged her accidently, then excused himself, and she turned away from him, exasperated. He seemed to be explaining something to her. She listened, half-listened . . . I stared at the two of them, fascinated. I could not move. The man's face was turned toward me and I could see it clearly, but he didn't notice me . . . the woman, however, saw me and her gaze somehow held . . . I felt the strange, powerful focusing of her attention. . . . How lovely she was, in spite of her peevish expression! And how blind was the man who walked beside her, his hand on her wrist, while she stared so openly at me!

"The thing is—you don't see—I do love you, but—but—it isn't the right time now—if we could wait—"

The man was trying to explain, explain, using words, but who can listen? They approached me. The woman was going to brush against me because there wasn't room enough on the sidewalk for three of us. She and I were both aware of this. I saw her face soften, the lips now fixed in a tentative smile, while the man beside her saw nothing, blindly, he couldn't even see the reason for her smile, the slow dawning love in her that was not for him, not for *him*. What can I say about her face? How can I speak of her? *Now, don't move!*—they cautioned me. But my desire for that woman drew me forward. Her face was both human and inhuman: pale and glowering like a moon, a creature knowing herself beautiful—beyond beauty—How I hated the man beside her, how I loathed him!—and how violent my love for her, a hunger, a thirst that made my throat contract with misery—I forgot everything but her. I forgot everything. Was it raining, was it night or day, did I live, did I die, was I bleeding to death internally, or was I being pumped full of expensive fresh blood, were the machines of the emergency room humming to save me or murmuring, chuckling, with the knowledge that I was already lost?— *Don't move!*

But I could not help myself. As the woman brushed near me I stepped toward her; she touched me, I touched her; and the violence of that touch ran through me like fire exploding everywhere in my veins. My eyes went blind. My throat dissolved: only the pain remained. I went into nothing, I felt the thoughts that had held me together scatter, popping away in all directions like sparks. I dissolved, I went into nothing, I lost even the words that had held me whole—

I was born.